My De_____

INSPIRED
BY A TRUE STORY

by

Jill Wallace

Thank you for
coming! Lovely
to see you!

Love, Jill

WAR SERENADE

by Jill Wallace

Print ISBN: 978-0-9997768-0-3

Ebook ISBN: 978-0-9997768-1-0

First edition

Cover by Sky Diary Productions

Published by Tsotsi Publications

www.jillwallace.com

CONTENTS

Every once in a great while, you make eye contact with someone you have never seen before, and it's as if you see into the other's soul. The connection between you is so deep and so strong, you blindly accept with all that is true, although it's beyond all logic and reason, that the person before you is as necessary to your existence as the very air you breathe.

You are everything my Dad could have wished for me.

EPILOGUE, PART I

THE SHOEBOX

Durban, South Africa
1960

The girl was more excited than she'd ever been in her life. She'd never waited so long for anything. She finally understood why her dad said, "Anticipation is the greatest part of life."

It had been three hundred and sixty-five days, two hours and eleven minutes since she'd found the shoebox when the garage stuff was moved around, so her dad could lay out the train set he gave her for her eighth birthday.

She'd been a whole lot more excited about the shoebox than the train set, which was similar to the model planes and antique cars of past years. She suspected her father had wished for a boy, but he adored her, and as long as he was happy, she was perfectly content. He was her hero, you see, and she'd never disappoint him.

The shoebox.

When she'd accidently bumped into the old bookshelf during the train set-up session, soft crocheted blankets tumbled on top of her head, bringing down the box.

She'd held the well-sealed rectangle in her hands and immediately felt its ounces of weight become pounds, with all the secrets within.

It was covered in brown paper, double-tied with string, and everywhere the string entwined, a dark red blob of sealing wax pulsed. Not molded in a crest or a coat of arms like in the days of spies and kings, but hasty, hot-melting wax, creating urgent blobs the color of congealed blood, throbbing with danger.

For a magical instant, she saw an outline of shimmering yellow around the box, like a halo. Blood and sunshine. She shivered and smiled at the same time.

"Daddy, can I open this box?" Her words were breathy.

"Ask your mother." He wasn't paying attention to her at all. He was too busy with the train set.

Inside, when the girl asked innocent permission, holding the box, her mother's face was tinged with crimson. The girl knew trouble was coming.

"That box is only to be opened when you are old enough. Do you hear?" The girl was taken aback by her mother's seldom-used harsh delivery.

"Why is it so secret, Mommy?" the girl asked logically.

"It belongs to your uncle and aunt. We are keeping it for them until it's safe."

"Safe from what, Mommy?"

"From authorit— from people who could make it difficult for them," her mother said, her accent thicker than usual.

"But when I am old enough, I can open it?" the girl asked, holding her breath.

"When you're old enough, you can tell their story, but only

then. Do you understand me?" The girl nodded, understanding completely that nothing would change her mom's mind.

But from that day forth, she wondered how old "old enough" could be. She figured that if she didn't ask, she could make her own decision as to when that time had come.

Now she was nine.

Since she was much older and wiser, to celebrate her birthday, she decided she would open the box. Her gift to herself. And her first decision.

Though it was they who encouraged her independent spirit, she doubted her parents would approve of her first undertaking.

It was all she could think of during the weeks before her big day of turning nine.

At last. She pretended to be really excited by the gleaming plastic blow-up globe she unwrapped that morning. It was her father's wish that she have a keen sense of the world outside the little dot of Durban on which they lived. In truth, Charlie the rabbit, who was revealed in a cage in the back yard, would have been enough to set her nine-year-old-world on fire, but she held back for the ultimate pleasure her birthday could bring. The gift she'd promised herself.

Her mother's head bobbed around her bedroom door. "You be good. I'm going to tennis with Aunty Wendy. Take off your school uniform. Do your homework. Maid's in her room if you need her. When I come home, I'm going to make you the best dinner ever in the history of the world, with Christmas crackers in November and chocolate cake! Then you can play with Charlie." Her mother's words rolled with the rich, musical lilt she loved so well.

The girl smiled at her mom, not because she loved her, though she did, but because she couldn't wait for her mother's car to pull out of the garage so she could get in.

She felt like a criminal as she snuck into the garage. To calm her nerves, she sang, "Happy birthday to me ... "

She pulled a small table in place and, balancing preciously, managed to access the box her father had strategically placed out of her reach after her mother's reaction. She swore she could feel her hand get hotter and hotter as it got closer to the shoebox. Her fingers found the box, and joy filled her.

"Happy birthday to me ... "

Balancing on her perch, she carefully brought down the box and stood silently just holding the secret cardboard vault. She sat down on the concrete floor and traced the string slowly with her finger, from one smooth, blood-red blob to the next. *Once the seals are broken, there is no going back.*

She didn't know how long she sat there, but when she knew it was time, she picked up the small knife and sliced through the string. The twine sprang back.

She sat looking at the delicious keeper of secrets in her lap. Her fingers tingled. *Open the bloody box.* Instinctively, her hands covered her mouth to stop more bad words coming out.

She gave in, eased off the string and, denied too long, quickly ripped off the brown paper.

She tried to justify her actions. "If I'm to tell their story, I need to understand their secrets," she thought with solid logic and felt even better about her first decision as a nine-year-old.

As she gingerly lifted the lid, she smelled flowers and earth and paper. But not just any paper, papyrus perhaps, from the ancient Egyptians in her history book, such was the richness of it all.

She gently laid down the lid and began the ultimate treasure hunt ...

I SEE YOU

"Every once in a great while, you make eye contact with someone you have never seen before, and it's as if you see into the other's soul. The connection between you is so deep and so strong, you blindly accept with all that is true, although it's beyond all logic and reason, that the person before you is as necessary to your existence as the very air you breathe."

— *Dad, 1960*

Pietermaritzburg, South Africa
27 July 1943

Her city of Pietermaritzburg was but a speck on the horizon as they bumped along toward the prisoner of war camp in the rugged two-seater jeep.

Iris shivered as she thought of tales of unspeakable horrors that caused the locals to give the square mile of flatlands a wide berth. They feared being haunted by the Boer War atrocities against the women and children who died in the concentration camp thirty-five years ago, before the Geneva Convention. At least now it was referred to as a "Prisoner of War" camp, which had less hideous connotations.

Iris swore the roads had not been tended since and thanked the lord that she sported a well-padded behind. But just this once. She didn't want him to get carried away and add an inch or two for further comfort. She thought of Lena, her beloved Zulu surrogate mother, whose voluptuous ebony folds had given Iris comfort all her life, and though she wouldn't change her for the world, she certainly didn't want to inherit Lena's large bum by osmosis.

She thought of Lena and her determination to teach Four-feet, the gardener next door, how to read. The *Sunday Times* was Lena's curriculum. She'd insisted he attend her school of one while she cleaned the kitchen. She'd patiently enunciate each word in preparation for Fourfeet's lesson, and when she didn't understand, she'd quiz Iris or her mother for explanation and pronunciation. Frankly, it kept them all on their toes and up to date on war news. Iris admired Lena's inquisitive mind. What better way to learn yourself than to teach another? This morning the lesson read: "Palermo Falls! Allied Invasion of Sicily Inspires Coup d'etat Against Mussolini. RAF Bombs Kiel: Heaviest RAF Raid of War." It was a hell of a mouthful for a Zulu who only learned English when she was twenty-five, and then just by paying attention.

When Iris reported for duty at the hospital that morning, she was mentally redesigning the dull volunteer uniform she wore—a dab of color here, a simple dart there—when she was cornered by a cheerless nurse who brought no softness to her hard profession.

"Doctor De Kleyn needs help at the POW camp today."

"Can you ask somebody else?"

"You're a volunteer, girly. You'll do what you're told." She snorted. Iris was fascinated by the nurse's thin nostrils flaring. "A *real* nurse should go, if you ask me," nurse grumbled.

Iris jumped at the chance, her eyes never leaving the nurse's nose. "Good idea. You go."

"He asked for you. Specifically." The nostrils were now flapping faster than a Venus flytrap.

"Can't *they* come *here?*" How hard could it be to bring them over, for gosh sakes? Who was in charge of logistics? And while she was making her suggestions, perhaps she'd also mention the simple little changes that would give their uniforms a little va-va-va-voom!

The disgusted look the nurse shot Iris required no verbal response. She whipped around, throwing words over her shoulder: "To nurse's station so I can educate you. *Someone* has to."

Hmm. *This is your penance. Suck it up, Iris! Go to the bloody prisoner of war camp. Oh God, imagine if Gregg was in one of those?* Then she relaxed. Knowing her brother, no matter where he was, he would be making them all laugh, planning game nights and tennis matches. She fathomed the war regardless of Lena's headlines. Still, it felt so very far away.

Two hours later, she was in the jeep bound for the camp. Iris stood up, locking her hands around the bar on the dashboard. The doctor beside her was pleasant and easy on the eye, but she'd sworn off men. Since, well … she didn't want to see Julian today. Ever again, really.

She lifted her face to the early sun and felt its gentle morning rays warming her wind-brushed cheeks. If she was any smarter, she would have worn a hat to stop her blooming freckles from multiplying, which they were apt to do. She smelled wet grass and the dark, dank tang of thick, seldom trodden foliage. Every now and then she inhaled the pungent whiff of animal droppings. Not unpleasant, just African.

A long, curly, copper tendril slapped wildly at her cheek.

How she hated her hair! She'd painstakingly tamed and pinned the thick waves that hung to her waist to conform to the shoulder-length bob that was so fashionable in the grainy, black and white photographs from abroad.

The *Sunday Times'* women's section was her weekly and only reliable source of fashion information now that the smaller towns were off the fashion grid for runway shows. The pictures confirmed London's elite were, luckily for Iris, exempt from the ravages of war. They continued to push fashion boundaries, and Iris lapped it up like milk to a rescued kitten. She pored over the cut, flow, patterns and nuances of hem length until her pencil came alive with her own whimsical designs. Grainy pictures transformed magically into a vivid color palette in her mind, then under her sharp pencil, taffeta, chiffon and silk were ruched, gathered and twisted, evolving into her unique and stunning creations.

She smiled as she thought of Lena and her friend Sofie's disappointment when she began designing clothes for herself. Though she still made them each a dress every month with money she saved, she wore the most daring creations herself.

She caught the doctor smiling back as if her flash of teeth had been for his benefit. Men! They were by far the vainer sex.

"This bloody hair!" she complained as another thick tendril covered her eyes for a second, but the feeling of fast wheels, wind and freedom outweighed the need to tame her wild tresses for the sake of fashion. Well, just for a moment.

Too soon, the jeep pulled up outside the brick building on her left, the hub for the army staff managing the camp, Iris surmised.

The smell on the opposite side of the road was overwhelming. She felt her face pucker in disgust as mud and feces fought for first place in her delicate nostrils. Two high fences were separated by a walkway, where a pair of soldiers holding dogs on tight leashes patrolled in opposite directions.

She looked from left to right and was jarred by the contrast. Neat, solid, brick normalcy on the left and make-do depravity on the right.

A four-foot coil of razor wire at the base and peak, both sides of each fence, made sure anybody trying to climb over would be cut to pieces after their first three-story hurdle. However, if they escaped that, dismemberment, courtesy of the Dobermans on the walkway, was a dead certainty. And if, by some miracle, they escaped those jaws, the second lethal fence would ensure they bled out before they landed outside the perimeter.

She shivered in the warmth. Her cursed imagination! She always had to take a vague thought to completion, like a design dreamed up, penciled, patterned, cut, sewn and debuted.

And what if they had protective clothing? That was absurd! The few men she saw inside the camp were in rags, *and* it was the middle of winter. Poor buggers must be freezing.

So, hypothetically, what if they made it out, then wanted to trek the fifty-odd miles to the port in Durban where they could miraculously stow away on a warship for four thousand nautical miles, back to Italy?

Thick foliage between Pietermaritzburg and Durban hid seven deadly South African snakes, killer bees, hungry lions, protective leopards, lethal spiders, charging rhino, angry elephant, crocodiles in excess of twenty feet, and Africa's biggest killer, the hippopotamus. They all had a stake in the land between, and humans were the enemy. No! Armor couldn't save the poor buggers. She sighed. So this giant, hellish cage Julian, the-man-in-charge, had constructed for them, might not be so bad after all.

She sniffed. Surely this stink hole, filled with khaki tents surrounded by moats—for the rain, she supposed—was in violation of the newly set Geneva standards? Perhaps there were so few captives, they could make do until the onslaught arrived and more modern latrines could be installed. Maybe the wind was just blowing the wrong way.

Oh, hell, what did she know about such things? Her stomach clenched, and she purposely looked at the "normal" side. Hmm. Pity one could never un-see human depravity.

She swallowed hard. *I'll be strong for you, Gregg. Please God, don't let my brother be in one of these inhumane waste pits.* She saw Greg's right eyebrow rise as it did when he was either amused or annoyed with his only sibling. Conjuring up his face was becoming harder, but here he was now, clear as the day he'd left them, and her heart calmed. But not for long. She remembered Lena's lesson: "RAF Bombs Kiel: Heaviest RAF Raid of War." Her brother and the likes of these prisoners were trying to kill each other, and her brother's side was winning. Thank God. The war was closer, all of a sudden.

As the jeep's engine cut off, she busied herself rearranging untamed hair and straightening her dull blue uniform.

A commotion beyond the razor fence erupted. A gaggle of ragged men emerged from the hundred or so tents. No wonder Venus-Flytrap-Nose thought Iris dumb as a shoe for wanting to bring the mountain to Mohammed. There were literally hundreds of them surging en masse toward her.

Her heart pounded a million miles a minute, and she was about to run away as fast as her legs could carry her, when she realized the charging masses weren't even looking her way. She felt ever so slightly disappointed. See? She knew the volunteer's uniform was dull, dull, dull!

She blushed deeply as she saw their deplorable state of neglect, and she was abysmally ashamed of how vain she was, to imagine these deprived ragamuffins would cause a stampede to get a better look at her!

She followed the men's eyes upward. A shoeless prisoner climbed up the inside wire fence. His feet were bleeding. Not surprising. The deathly-sharp barbs wound around the thick wire and poked out at different angles, like haphazard one-inch nails.

The guy was by no means surefooted, so she guessed this was not a daily occurrence.

The tattered prisoners shouted from the ground. Iris imagined it was some sort of Italian encouragement as the man climbed higher. He seemed oblivious to the goings-on below.

A beefy guard shouted: "Get down now, man. You want us to shoot you?"

Several guards pointed guns at the prisoner, but the guy on the wire was either stupid, brave, blindly determined, or didn't give a damn. Something important drove him ever upward.

As he reached the top, she wondered why the guards didn't stop warning and start shooting, and she covered her ears in anticipation of the blasts.

She found she'd inched unwittingly nearer the perimeter and was close enough to see the face of the climber. There were lines on his cheeks where, in happier times, there might have been dimples.

His angular face changed from detachment to tenderness, and the ragged chorus of onlookers cried out.

She was aware the doctor was next to her when he shouted the interpretation in her ear: "Get the bird!" She was too absorbed to be impressed by his linguistic skills.

Then she saw it. A fat pigeon was caught in the barbed wire at the top of the high fence. By the scant frames of the malnourished prisoners, a plump pigeon over a hot fire would not go amiss. But a look of tenderness? The man *must* be starving!

A city girl through and through, Iris refused to think of the sweet little lamb or the cow with kind eyes, as she enjoyed the sumptuous dinner before her. "It's just meat" often became her mealtime mantra. She refused to think about the living creatures sacrificed for her palate's pleasure. Who, then, was she to judge this starving man bringing down a portly pigeon to roast over a fire?

The crowd roared with delicious anticipation.

She was amazed by the prisoner's gentleness as he reached for the bird while he clung to the wire for dear life with his other hand. Blood oozed from new lacerations as he manipulated the pigeon slowly through the razor edges, his own hand taking the pain, while gentle fingers encased the bird protectively.

Goodness! No wasted drop. They *were* hungry. She couldn't watch the poor bird's imminent demise, yet she couldn't look away.

He manipulated the pigeon from its lethal trap and held it above the fence while his other hand still gripped the wire, stopping him from falling three stories to a razor-sharp death.

She winced at the taste of blood and realized she'd bitten the inside of her cheek.

The man still held the bird firmly in one big hand. What a showman.

"Get it over with!" she wanted to shout. She'd learned to nip torture in the bud the hard way. *Don't be dramatic, Iris.* She heard her mother's voice but managed to ignore it as the fascinated guards lowered their guns, and the gleeful crowd was quiet. All eyes were raised up to the man on the wire.

He held up his hand as high as he dared without losing his balance.

"A sacrifice?" wondered Iris.

His tapered fingers opened. The pigeon froze. The prisoners were still and silent.

The bird took flight. Wobbly at first, likely overcome by its unexpected freedom, but mercifully, it caught the wind and soared away.

Free.

And then she understood: He freed the pigeon because he couldn't free himself.

Wild, angry "Boos" broke the silence. That was Italian she understood.

The man's face remained expressionless. He simply started his downward climb, and as he dropped his chin for a good look at where to secure his next footing ...

He found her eyes instead. His bleeding, bare foot remained suspended in midair.

And the world stopped, as did her heart, suspended in her chest. Then the blooming thing somersaulted. A great, big, double Boswell & Wilkie Circus high-wire dismount kind of somersault. Breathing wasn't important as his eyes penetrated her hidden, most private core, and seeing into his deepest self, she felt at once immediate recognition and the ache of long separation. Then joyous relief at the reunion, unfathomable understanding, and above all, deep, satisfying, all-consuming emotion she didn't understand. It pierced her heart like a long pin into a well-stuffed cushion.

"Get down now, or we shoot." Guns were cocked again, but the sound was far away, in another world. Another time.

From far away, she heard Dr. De Kleyn's insistent voice: "Let's go where it's safe. It's dangerous out here."

She blinked, breaking the connection and jolting her senses. She inhaled her first breath in what seemed like two days.

Before she turned away, Iris tried to find the bird savior's eyes again, but he was close to the barbed wire, so his concentration was on the careful placement of his naked foot. She felt empty. The doctor's last words echoed in her head, and the most profound thought hit her like a hammer: "Dangerous? I've never felt safer than I did just then," but she followed his white coat into the brick building.

She had jelly legs, a new, awfully odd sensitivity, but as they were ushered into Julian's office, she lost all sensations other than distaste.

The bird savior had made her forget how much she was dreading this ordeal.

Julian bounced on the balls of his feet, and his thin smile was as wide as she'd ever seen it as he led them to the mess hall. He was gloved as usual, and the bunched hand held his whip, which tapped against his leg. A kind of out-of-sync metronome. "So effens skeef," came into Iris's mind unbidden. She rarely spoke Afrikaans because she was English through and through, and that mattered when the Boers and the English were still smarting over their vicious war. But sometimes the Boers' Afrikaans language truly captured a situation as no other could. Julian was indeed "a little bit off-center."

"I didn't dare hope you'd come, though I requested you." His cloying presence was the perfect antidote for her still fast-beating heart.

Iris feigned indifference. "Here to do a job, Julian. Trust you're doing well?" A rhetorical question. She didn't care how he was.

Doctor De Kleyn had no time for small talk with the acting head of this dismally run camp. "Get the prisoners in so we can get this over and done with, Colonel." The disdain that tainted the undeserved title was clear to Iris and lost on Julian.

As she worked, Iris was acutely aware of Julian's eyes on her, no doubt waiting with bated breath for her reaction to his new lofty title. She refused to curtsy to his ego. She busied herself for the onslaught of the growing line of prisoners by placing the heap of cotton balls in a sterilized bowl, filling the malaria pill dispenser and prepping the vicious-looking needles for the penicillin shots.

The single line of ragged men wove in and out of the hall, through the doors and down the long passage.

The first emaciated prisoner was in front of her. She went to give him his malaria pill, and he put his hands behind his back and stuck out his tongue. The stench of his open mouth made her recoil in horror. Doc was quick to intervene. "This is not a communion wafer, my friend. Put out your hand." Julian appeared like a demonic genie, his whip raised ominously. The man's tongue disappeared like a lizard who'd missed a fly.

Iris was startled by the naked fear she saw on the prisoner's face as Julian's whip was raised. She shivered. *Shame on you, Iris, for dreaming up the whip!*

The line kept coming, and a pattern was established: hands out for their malaria pill; turn sideways to have a couple of inches of upper arm cleaned by Iris; turn sideways to Doc for the penicillin shot. She was grateful for their dirt-encrusted bodies, because the mud trapped their odor underneath. When she caught the odd whiff of dank flesh the alcohol couldn't mask, it made her stomach clench.

After a couple of dozen administrations, she turned her head away from the masses, waved her hand in front of her nose and whispered to the doctor, "Noxious!"

"No showers. They have to wait for the rain to bathe."

"Oh my gosh, I didn't think past the smell. I feel so bad now. Who could do this to human beings? Or animals, for that matter?"

For an answer, de Kleyn jutted his jaw at the hovering Colonel Julian.

How would Gregg handle stinking to high heaven like this?

She vowed not to show these likely once-proud men that

their stench was beyond endurance. It was quite a feat, but she did it. For Gregg. Just in case.

And still they streamed in. Though very few spoke English, they seemed not enemies at all, just skinny, neglected men in rags, many without anything on their dirty feet. Like pigs in manure. *Don't be unkind, Iris.*

Now and then she caught a glimpse of the vital men they might have been before the war. A flirty wink. A kind smile. A wicked grin. She knew the interest in their eyes wasn't for her particularly, but rather *any* change was a welcome break in their mundane, pitiful existence.

As she cleaned spots on muddied deltoids and revealed sun-bronzed skin, she wondered if this was how her brother looked. Dirty and disheveled. Just a face in a long line. *Oh, Gregg.*

Thoughts of him overshadowed the sympathy she felt toward these neglected men. The likes of them were aiming guns, bombs, and heaven only knew what else at her brother. Trying to kill him, but please God, not succeeding. Last she heard, Gregg was flying his Spitfire over Italy. Life was fraught with ironies, she'd discovered.

Her ludicrous thoughts of Gregg in a POW camp making up games and arranging tennis matches now shamed her. These neglected men in front of her were the realities of war. *Oh, please, God. Protect him from this horror.*

He'd left them brokenhearted on the platform the day he went off to war. She, Mom, Lena, Sofie and Buffer feared they would never see him again. Not even Buffer's doggie kisses could make her feel better.

Recently, her department store, the fanciest in all of southern Africa, made volunteering for the war effort compulsory for all staff. They were paid for two days out of their work week to offer their services where needed. But Iris knew she had to over-achieve in order to pay her dues to keep her brother safe.

She doubled her hospital duty, working dozens of hours without pay in her own time. She had the time since she'd sworn off ... well, since Julian.

But sure as hell, she hadn't anticipated cleaning off the grimy arms of Gregg's enemy so they wouldn't die in her own country. Not from malaria or diseases cured by penicillin, at least. Malnutrition under Julian's neglect was another matter.

How ironic, too, that she assisted in protecting her country's enemies from the very disease that had so cruelly taken her father. Life was full of disparity between what actually happens and what, by all accounts, should.

Too often she dreamed Gregg was faceless. Her own screams, and faithful Buffer's wet nose nudging her, mercifully woke her and she'd force his familiar face into perspective, or if all else failed, looked at the photo next to her bed. She shivered. It had been a long month since his last letter.

She felt herself applying unnecessary pressure to the man's arm as she prepped for his injection. She apologized softly to the prisoner. She was grateful he seemed oblivious.

And then *he* was in front of her.

The pigeon savior.

Her legs buckled again. What the hell? Since when had she become the fainting sort?

His eyes were dark blue, and his hair was jet black, but there was nothing dark about his spirit. She felt at once warm and safe and hot and flustered as his eyes captured hers again. Close up this time. She was transfixed.

They opened their mouths at the same time. To speak? No. They were more like flowers opening to receive the sun or rain or some necessary sustenance to survive. She breathed him in through her nose and still open mouth, inhaling him, consuming him. She saw tiny little scars around his mouth, and she longed to kiss them softly, to take away their cause, if not the scars themselves, because they saved him from being just too good-looking.

"Keep the line moving, Iris." The command made her jump.

How close had they been standing? How close had their open mouths come to being connected by magnetic force, or whatever the hell it was that pulled them together?

The doctor's voice brought her back from wherever the mystifying swim in those dark blue pools had taken her, and she placed the malaria pill in his hand.

They both jumped as her two fingers touched the inside of his palm. A current. An actual electricity sparked between them. Their eyes were locked when he smiled. Afterward, when she could think, she realized she was right about the dimples.

Guilt surged through her, and she busied herself with applying alcohol to cotton balls.

He was the enemy. *Gregg's* enemy.

She could feel his eyes burning into her skin, a warm, delicious burn like sunshine after a violent storm.

As she rubbed his bicep with alcohol, she tried to calm her breathing by thinking of ... who was she kidding? She couldn't focus on anything but the color of his skin. Namib sand. Smooth and fine like that sandy coast where precious diamonds were found. *Don't look up, Iris! Where's it going to get you? Eyes DOWN.*

Her mind dictated, but her heart ignored. She raised her eyes slowly, fearful the connection would be different this time, but his eyes waited and, if anything, the magic intensified to hot and all-consuming.

Her bliss was short-lived, as Doc pulled her savior's shoulder around so he could jab in the needle, followed by a gentle push to move him along.

Iris felt a deep sense of loss as soon as her savior was gone. Emptiness had replaced the languid, warm place he'd taken her with just the depth of his eyes and the sight of his skin.

"Her" savior? Emptiness? She had touched him clinically once. *Don't be ridiculous, Iris.* Her mother again!

But those eyes. Interesting. Magnetic. Looking into her very soul.

The Savior dominated her mind throughout the afternoon as Julian hovered in her peripheral vision. As she and the doctor were leaving, Julian called to her.

She heard her voice, clipped with irritation. "Julian, I can't chat. We have to get the balance of the medicine to the lab for refrigeration." She thought that sounded impressive, though she made it up on the spot.

"Iris. Give me another chance. I can make you happy."

"Please, Julian. We've talked this to death." Then she felt bad. She didn't want to be unkind. Iris turned toward him. "There are many girls who would love your attention. I just don't have time for a relationship right now. Go well." She hated being false, but she suspected his vindictiveness ran deep, and she wanted no part of it.

And why on earth had she suggested the gloves and the bloody whip? She'd created a monster. She shook her head hard to free her mind of the guilt and resolved not to think about it again. She turned and left the room in a hurry, feeling Julian's eyes drilling into her arched back.

The prisoners must have been in their tents, because none were to be seen, and there was a guard with a gun posted ominously outside every fourth V-shaped canvas.

She wished she'd seen him again. Rags, bare feet, and all. He'd somehow cleaned the blood off his hands and feet before he'd come to the makeshift clinic. She remembered, too, that his arm was just a wee bit dusty and not encrusted with mud. He hadn't even smelt like the others. She was pathetically touched by the effort he'd made when running water was not a benefit they enjoyed.

As the jeep careened back to town, she pushed hard on the outside of her thick cotton uniform and felt the sharp angles of the folded paper inside her pocket. A tangible reminder of the adventure that lay ahead. Her delicious secret. Her salvation. Her future.

But today she needed more. Her hand found its way into her pocket, and she clenched the piece of paper. It wasn't the original. She'd gone through four replicas since she got the letter two weeks ago. Desperate clutching had blurred the content.

His blue eyes were all she could think of. The balled paper felt prickly in her hand as she squeezed tighter. Ridiculous! Why was she fantasizing about the impossible when a dream come true literally lay in the palm of her hand?

Out of the blue, she began humming a tune. She didn't know the words, just the title and the tune. How odd.

"O Sole Mio," she sang softly, well-disguised by the jeep's noise. As she la-la-la'd the rest of the tune, she was infused with calm, and she loosened her grip on her paper talisman.

2

THE GIRLY HOTS

Pietermaritzburg, South Africa
  28 July 1943—next day

Lena and Sofie sat on the steps of the *stoep,* the South Africanism for back porch, leading from kitchen to backyard of the one-story brick home owned by the Fuller Family. These slate steps were their morning meeting place after the most essential housework was done.

This slightly elevated vantage point was perfect from which to observe the comings and goings. The women enjoyed the smell of the lush, wild banana and mango trees within easy reach, were they so inclined.

Many debates had ensued on these steps, and this day was no exception. "Ibhubesi has a spring in her step today," said the robust Lena.

"Ibhubesi," the Zulu word for lioness, was their name for the vibrant youngest of the Fuller household, whom both had known for nearly all of the girl's twenty years.

Others knew her as Iris.

"I am telling you, Lena. Every day she is more like a cheetah with her long legs and her spotted face." Sofie was in her own world as usual.

"A cheetah? Eikona, Sofie. You have forgotten the wild animals from the hills. A cheetah may be agile and solitary, but it's timid and shy and it doesn't roar. Does *that* sound like our Ibhubesi?" Her large body wobbled with mirth and exposed a dark gap where recently a front tooth had gleamed. Ibhubesi had paid the dentist to extract the offender with her own money. The healing herbs Lena would have used were not to be found in town where buildings and roads replaced nature.

Sofie was determined to be contrary. "A leopard then, still spotted, eating its prey in a tree, like our girl who spends her life suspended above the ground, drawing dresses."

Lena was adamant. "Why do we not agree? For nineteen years and more, we see her legs grow longer, her eyes get more catlike, and her red mane get wilder."

"But a lioness with a mane?" Sofie won the argument with that. Sort of.

"Perhaps a Big Cat with the spots of a leopard and the legs of a springbok, her favorite prey," Lena sniffed. Compromise was the only way the two women remained friends.

Sofie's face and demeanor softened. "But she is our Ibhubesi in fearlessness, I will grant you that, you old cow." She giggled to lighten her insult.

But Lena had other things on her mind. "And I am telling you, Sofie, since yesterday she carries the fire down there. She has the girly hots."

"How can you see this heat through her clothes?" Sofie was confused.

"A mother knows her child, even if she was birthed by another. And Sofie, our girl became a woman yesterday. I know this."

Sofie spun to face her friend, shocked out of her quarrel-some mood. "No! A woman?"

"Eikona. Not *that* kind of woman. Not yet. Just one who has found what she wants." Sofie relaxed. She thought she'd missed something mammoth.

"Today Ibhubesi looks like me when I see Philemon from the petrol station," Lena said.

"Those girly hots are clear on your face when you see him. Does Philemon know he makes your isibunu full of juice?"

"Are you crazy, Sofie? I am a married woman." Lena looked at her friend with disdain.

"Married to a usually impotent man in the hills who smokes the dagga and does nothing." Sofie's filter had long ago collapsed.

"Married is married, but it doesn't prevent the girly hots. I look at him. I feel tingles. Juice flows. I am happy. It is Philemon who is responsible for my pleasure when my husband is *not* impotent."

Sofie snorted. "Well! Praise the ancestors for the girly hots then!"

"I wish *you* a Philemon from the petrol station, Sofie. Then perhaps the carrot you have lodged up your bum would fall out, and you would not be so bad tempered."

"Carrots have good nutrition," Sofie said, straight-faced.

Lena started to giggle, then she laughed until her whole body wobbled and Sofie joined in. As they laughed together, Lena put out a big arm and squashed the thin Sofie to her in a bear hug. All was right in their world. For a minute.

The women came to town from their separate kraals, beyond the Pietermaritzburg hills, a score of years before. Their daily grind in the kraals as young, married women was to toil and chat together with the other wives, making sure food was gathered and prepared, chickens, cows and goats fed, and young girls properly guided to womanhood.

Perhaps the developments down the hill would not have held the same attractions had their husbands remained virile and fighting-fit, rather than lazy and dulled by the wild weed that inflated memories of their own importance.

Once great warriors, claiming their corner of the South African continent, in the recent peace they became puffed-up and useless, filling their days by outdoing each other with tales of great battles, their heroism growing monumentally with each retelling.

At night they barked orders at their wives and drank too much Kefir beer. They could seldom fulfill their own urges in the darkened huts, let alone those of their ripe women.

True, there were no surprises and life was mostly peaceful, but "Town" below the kraal grew with settlers and industry. The air was filled with strange languages, odd music, moving machines, interesting smells, new noises and bright colors of every hue. A longing to be immersed in the madness tugged at these unfulfilled women, like hungry puppies yearning for ripe teats.

"Town" was where they could work for a little money (they'd never bartered with coins before) and live in the servants' quarters attached to white men's homes and relish life in the thick of all the change.

The young Lena and Sofie came from two different kraals, though they arrived in town on the same day, drawn by the same lust for life. But, on arrival, they found themselves lost and overwhelmed in the new chaos.

Recognizing the bewilderment in the other, they immediately linked hands and set off together, knocking on doors, in search of any white families needing "a girl."

It was pure luck that the Fuller family was socially on the

way up and needed help with their redheaded newborn and five-year-old boy with the lightest of spirits and the darkest of hair; at the same time, the van Niekerks next door lost their last maid to a leopard attack on her way up the hill to her kraal.

The ladies were snapped up and had been neighbors and friends ever since.

Usually the outside of the servants' quarters looked as handsome as the large manicured brick homes they were attached to, but inside they were nothing more than rough-plastered caves with no amenities.

But not for long. Lena and Sofie soon had cozy nests, courtesy of their new families' castoffs. It was all they needed to rekindle their pride and allow them to experiment with their newfound individualism.

But, like all the other Zulus who gave up their traditional life for servitude to the white man in the colonies, they quickly learned their place. They were servants.

As heady as Town was, all Zulus were pulled home to their roots in the hills on occasion. An invented relative's funeral was the perfect remedy for homesickness. It began with loud keening and high-pitched wailing traditionally used for Zulu ceremonies. The ear-piercing, mournful sounds, along with the threat that if forbidden to go, their ancestors might retaliate, were enough to convince the most hardened Christian employer to allow their servants time off.

They labored most of the day up the steep hills to their kraals, excited to see old friends. They spent the next two days satisfying their homesickness and their husbands, then with wings on their heels, they came back to the action and the lessons in humility.

Their visit sustained them for some time. A powerful reminder of where they no longer wanted to be.

Town had its own problems, and the white man took some

getting used to with his vanity and his need for social prowess. The saving grace was that the Town Zulus still had their language, their keen sense of humor and each other.

No white folks were remotely interested in understanding or talking Zulu, so their native tongue allowed them to openly criticize and make fun of the world around them. Their employers were none the wiser. In fact, such was their white self-importance, they simply presumed, because the Zulus beamed through their gibberish-sounding exchanges with each other, that their servants were always jolly.

Their delicious comedy buffered them from feeling downtrodden; it was their outlet for pent-up anger and their bonus for putting up with the whites they served.

Zulus were keen observers, and Lena and Sofie were no exception.

Ibhubesi's mother, well, her birth mother, had no patience or softness toward the girl child. Lena understood then why, as she grew, the child sought her own company, her older brother's or that of Lena and Sofie's, rather than her mother's. But when her father came home, he was the child's focus, and she, her father's delight.

Lena was always there when real mother gallivanted off to tennis or teas or galas with other upper-class white women. She watched Ibhubesi living mostly in her own world, perfectly happy with paper and pencil, drawing everything her eyes fell upon.

Brother held his little sister's heart very gently in the palm of his hand. He was every bit his father's son. Like the sun, he emitted warmth, and people and animals alike basked in his healing rays.

The Zulu friends often reminisced about the huge event in Ibhubesi's life that had so enormously affected their own. All because of the mister's thoughtfulness, the ladies became celebrities amongst their peers.

Sofie loved her mister. On this remarkable evening, Ibhubesi's seventh birthday, he'd struggled out of his driving machine with a big box that the ladies helped him carry inside.

The child was overcome when she saw her father's beaming face and the big box. She tore at the paper like a hungry hunter ripping open the belly of a fat rabbit.

The ecstasy that came from her little voice box was a special something the ladies would always remember. Little white arms hugged her father so tight, they caused water to spout from the elder's eyes. They were baffled by the cause of the unbridled excitement: the heavy black machine, with a little wheel and a sharp needle, didn't look worthy. Ibhubesi's cry, "A sewing machine!" shed no light on its prowess at all.

But in the months that followed, they learned what magic the "Whirr Whirr" had in store for them.

Lena and Sofie became the black fashion icons of Pietermaritzburg courtesy of that crazy little black buzzing machine. Their status had taken some trial and error as the child experimented with her adult toy: Their hems came undone while strutting their stuff; sleeves were at odd angles; and wrongly positioned darts cut their breasts in half; but their garments were brand-new and tailor-made. No make-do castoffs for these ladies. They wore the finest of fabrics. Well, certainly in the first few Whirr Whirr years.

The three spent hours in Lena's modest quarters, the youngster on a box to reach their strong naked shoulders, draping them in exotic cloth that felt cool and opulent against their ebony skin. They felt like queens in the making.

Like statues they stood, thoughts of dazzling their peers was their end goal, as Ibhubesi pinned and pricked, tilting her copper head the same way as the fabric she'd just draped, likely imagining the finished creation. The ladies' status improved at the same remarkable pace as did Ibhubesi's expertise.

It was true the men in her house adored Ibhubesi, but to Lena's eye, the more she enthralled them, the colder the birth-mother became toward her girl child.

And then, out of the bluest skies, the darkest raincloud gathered without warning and beat down mercilessly on the Fuller household.

Lena and Sofie couldn't laugh for months, so broken were their hearts when the mister died. He had thrashed and sweated in his bed, delirious with fever, as the misses wrung her hands in the bedroom doorway. Lena wiped his sweating face and shoulders with cloths soaked in vinegar-water to take down his fever, while Ibhubesi held her father's hand and said softly, "It's all right, Daddy. I am here. I will never leave you. It's going to be all right."

But it wasn't all right.

The fever took him early one morning, and Miesies' wail brought Lena charging in to find Ibhubesi curled in a fetal position, next to her dead father, her head and her knees touching his cold body, soundlessly weeping and still holding his hand.

Brother held mother's head against his shoulder as she wept, and at that moment he was the older, the stronger and she, the younger, the weaker.

Once the mister's soulless body had been removed, and Lena aired and freshened the dark space, Miesies announced that she was not to be disturbed and disappeared into the room where she had last seen her husband.

And didn't come out.

Ibhubesi was lost. She wouldn't go outside. She wouldn't be tempted to lie like a leopard, above the ground, on what they called "the hammock" that she so loved. She wouldn't go to school. She wouldn't eat. She wouldn't stop wandering around aimlessly. She wouldn't even draw and, worst of all, the Whirr Whirr was silent.

Friends came by with food and concern, but either Lena or Brother made excuses as to why the Miesies and the child could not visit with them that day.

People stopped coming.

Lena and Sofie's eagle eyes followed their lost nine-year-old cub as she wandered around, sad and confused. Though she hardly noticed them, the ladies stepped in. They took turns holding her tight and stroking her wild, un-brushed hair. Often tears streamed silently down her white cheeks. So many days indoors had rendered all her leopard spots, which the mother called "freckles," nearly invisible.

The ladies had to be cruel to be kind and bathed her, albeit kicking and screaming, plaited her hair neatly, even cooked her favorite meals, which went mostly untouched. They weren't sure they were helping at all. It was not *their* comfort she needed. Not *their* love she longed for.

And still their girl-child's mother hid from the world.

Their concern over Ibhubesi's emotional survival was genuine, but they confessed after a month of nothing to show off that the lack of new outfits also affected their deep sorrow.

Their little redhead resembled a prairie dog going deep into the bush looking for a place to die, except it was her spirit that wanted to die, not her body.

No amount of cajoling could convince Ibhubesi to use the two ladies as her models anymore. The child's keen sense of humor disappeared, too. Lena strutted to the opposite side of the kitchen with her "front business" leading the way, then turned her buxom frame ever so slowly and pushed her bum out on the way back. But the performance produced no upward movement of the little mouth.

To console themselves, Lena and Sofie made some tea and

added six heaped spoons of sugar (because Miesies wasn't there to scold them) and reminisced about happier times just a few short months before: An excited Ibhubesi had pulled them by the hands to watch skinny white girls from Durban walk the same way Lena just demonstrated, up and down a wooden plank at the town hall. The ladies weren't allowed inside—it was, of course, whites only—but their budding lioness presented a strong case that these ladies were her guardians.

The only nonwhite faces in the cavernous hall, the ladies got dirty looks from the women packing the space for this rarest of fashion events, but they didn't care. If filthy glances paid the price to be on sacred white ground, they paid happily. Looks couldn't kill, and stories they would later share with their Zulu friends would be worth every disapproving scowl.

As long-legged, hungry-looking ladies walked awkwardly hither and thither in various garments, the child squiggled in her drawing book and, within a week, Lena and Sofie were sporting variations of the dresses they'd seen that very day.

But the inventive fashions had proved too much for their usually envious peers, who made fun of their fussy ruffles and encouraged them to join the traveling circus.

They sighed. Even those ruffles would be better now than this new dress-starvation.

For two months, which seemed like two years, Miesies hid from life in her dark room. Twice a day Lena quietly slipped into the blackness with her tray laden with tempting newly dried rusks and steaming rooibos tea, with just a hint of milk, covered by a crocheted doily to keep off the flies. Three hours later she'd take out the tray, untouched but for a nibble and a sip.

Lena made Miesies' bed with her in it, and when Lena couldn't stand the odor in the room anymore, she opened the windows while Miesies, lying face down, beat her hand on the bed like a spoiled child having a silent tantrum, until the room was restored to its black cocoon.

Lena found Ibhubesi lying curled up outside her mother's room, a stray cat left out in the cold, waiting on the off chance it would be let in and stroked, before it was tossed out again. Wondering how long she'd been there, the Zulu tried to pick her up, but young heels dug in, and her resistance was so strong, the child magically became too heavy to lift, her young face determined and angry. So, Lena left her there, checking on her every twenty minutes.

Only Brother could coax her away from the doorway when he came home from school. He'd shout, "Where's my Sunshine?" and for just an instant, the child's eyes lit up.

The fourth time Lena found her curled up—the lonely cat lying outside the bedroom door—her heart broke, and she crept up stealthily and scooped up the child before she could resist. Little hands beat at Lena as Ibhubesi screamed bloody murder, but the Zulu held her tight, rocking her and making the baby sounds that brought her quiet. Tears ran down both ebony and ivory cheeks until all the child's resistance ebbed, and she sobbed, hardly able to draw breath.

Lena's tears reflected her inadequacy as a surrogate mother. She couldn't heal the child, nor did she have the audacity to interrupt the mother's grief, even if she knew that would ease the anguish and fear and sadness of this abandoned soul.

Though Brother visited the darkened chamber briefly morning and night, not even he had the guts to tell his mother what she needed to hear.

But he alone could make Ibhubesi smile during that dark time. He eventually made her laugh again and invented clever games to make her brush her teeth, eat and go to school.

Buffer was Brother's idea. He'd asked around the black locations on the outskirts of town. It was an obvious place to find a stray dog. Sure enough, an emaciated Alsatian had delivered three puppies that freezing winter morning but was too weak to survive their births. Only the puppy who had instinctively found his way underneath his mother's body to pull at unyielding teats was shielded from the icy sleet and spared.

Lena and Sofie well remembered the day Brother presented Buffer to the child. That little helpless puppy made Ibhubesi come alive again. She nursed it, like Sofie showed her, with a baby's bottle, teasing the little closed-eyed puppy with the pretend nipple. With every ounce of fresh warm milk he suckled hungrily, Buffer and Ibhubesi both grew stronger.

They saved each other.

The two women marveled at how the puppy realized their prophecy of this child becoming Ibhubesi, the lioness. The little runt gave back the courage that loss had stripped away.

Three long months after the mother went into hibernation, Ibhubesi tucked Buffer under her arm and, not bothering to knock, marched into the dark master bedroom.

"Get up, Mom. Get out of bed and meet Buffer."

Nothing.

"Buffer was alone. He was so sad. He needed a mom."

Not a twitch from the outline in the bed, Lena noticed from the open doorway.

"I am alone and sad, too. "Still nothing.

"I need a mom." Child and dog were still as can be. Waiting. Refusing to move.

"Will you be my mom again?"

An eternity passed. Finally, the mother lifted her head.

It was enough. The nine-year-old with the tousled red hair held the puppy tighter still, kissed the top of his head and then left the room, deliberately leaving the door wide open.

Much to Lena and Sofia's great surprise, Miesies appeared in the kitchen within the hour, groomed and dressed, and as if she hadn't missed a beat, resumed her position as bossy mistress of her home.

Buffer became the first puppy-model in Pietermaritzburg, but he hated every minute of being paraded in colorful outfits. It was not dignified for a boy dog, so Ibhubesi reverted to her more experienced and willing models. Lena and Sofie were enormously relieved. The Whirr Whirr was back in business.

If Buffer brought back Ibhubesi's spirit, then Brother (who became a tall, handsome man) continued to make her shine like the brightest star in the heavens.

But, just two summers ago, the word "war" rounded lips on white faces. Since then, young, white men, all dressed the same, kept disappearing in flying machines or *steamelas* (as trains were called in Zulu).

When The Brother came home, wearing that war outfit, they knew hearts would be broken again. Their seventeen-year-old Ibhubesi's mournful wail when she saw him was heard all the way from the servants' quarters. The sound hurt their hearts and damaged their souls.

Miesies' screams were louder but not nearly as heartbreaking. It was understandable the women were distraught at the thought of losing the only man of the house. He was the umbilical cord connecting the cub with her mother, long before they were both damaged by loss. But the glory of war was stronger than the needs of his family. Even the adoration of his little sister couldn't keep Brother uninvolved in what they called "bigger issues."

The day he left was a black day as Lena, Miesies and Ibhubesi sat sobbing together on a "whites only" wooden bench on the platform, long after the train puffed over the horizon.

Buffer paced back and forth in front of the bench protectively, stopping only to jump up, paws on either side of his mistress, and shower her with sloppy kisses. In spite of herself,

Ibhubesi smiled, perhaps only because she wanted to give him the comfort he was giving her.

When they returned home, Sofie was waiting to help the heartbroken women, and it was then that both ladies witnessed their cub become a lioness.

The grief-stricken birth mother ran toward her room to hide from the world. But Ibhubesi was prepared and ran ahead, blocking the master bedroom doorway with splayed arms and legs so her mother couldn't cross the threshold.

She shouted: "Mother, stop! Don't you dare hide away from this pain we share. Not again." Her anger was like a rumbling mountain before it shed big boulders.

Miesies stopped dead and hung her head in shame. As the tears came, Ibhubesi wrapped her arms around her mother, and they wept together, as they should have, eight years before.

The old Zulu saying came to mind: "However long the night, the dawn will break." Ibhubesi's surrogate mothers beamed at each other and wiped tears from their own eyes, because they knew then that they'd played a part in bringing their mutual child to strong maturity, as good Zulu mothers are wont to do.

3

BOOTS

Pietermaritzburg
   28 July 1943 — morning

Pietro lay on his lumpy cot, which one of his tent mates, Antonio, had filled with hay. He felt a pang of guilt that he hadn't appreciated *any* of the deeds done for him by either Antonio or Enzo since he'd met these men, months earlier. He wasn't used to people doing anything for him or him being expected to do anything for anyone else. All this interaction wouldn't last long. Nothing survived in hell. He knew.

But then his heart sped up as thoughts inevitably turned to the redhead who'd jolted his existence yesterday. *Dio mio.* His body and mind reacted in ways he'd long forgotten.

Mia Cara Rossa. In her he saw hope. He'd felt it yesterday when he saw her, windswept and intense. It was indeed more than hope. She'd given him back a desire for life rather than a mere existence. He saw in her eyes a recognition he didn't understand, and when her fingers barely connected with his palm, he was almost electrocuted by her touch. He knew he could never live without that touch again. He couldn't make sense of it, but this intense physical and mental need for her, seemed ... well, necessary, thereby eliminating the need for comprehension. The yearning was beyond logic. It felt almost spiritual. Sort of like being Catholic. As if she was a deep part of his soul, which, like it or not, believe it or not, he couldn't let go. But what use was it? He was a prisoner of war. She? An English-woman on the other side ...

Yet the first thing he'd done after he saw her was restore his basest dignity: the need to cover his bare feet.

He couldn't go back yet to the depths that drove him to throw away his precious boots. He wouldn't remember before he had to.

Right now his hand touched the "new" pair of boots neatly placed next to his cot. His hand wiggled inside, finding the bunched-up newspaper the wiry Enzo had found caught in the barbed wire. He'd picked it off the fence and converted the over-sized fourteen boots to an acceptable size eleven.

These men seemed kind. A human attribute he hadn't seen for a long while. But when you were fighting for water and food and to simply stand up so you wouldn't be trampled to death, there was no time for kindness. *God only knows what we will be fighting for here.*

His mind turned back as far as he dared ...

Indian Ocean
  11 February to 5 March 1943

Bella had brought him back from the dead. He'd never been thankful to a woman before—grateful, yes—but he thanked

Bella each time his body moved in the direction he intended. He knew if you didn't move, you were trampled to death. And why didn't he welcome that finality? He couldn't quite remember.

Because of Bella, he was able to use his bony elbows to fight for room in the bowels of the *New Amsterdam* and managed to sit down on the uneven ship's hull. Before the war, this great passenger liner had cruised the Mediterranean Sea, serving the rich and the famous. Pietro had sat at one of the lounge tables with a duke and duchess, sipping champagne, when the ship docked in Venice for the day. Two years ago? What did it matter! The once white luxurious leather was brown now, cracked and tired as he was, as he marched past with the rest of the prisoners, down, down to the dark hold, where dull lights were strung up intermittently.

At first there was just the stench of mildew, barnacles and rodents. Within a few hours, body odor and oil added to the bouquet. Desperate bladders were emptied in corners, and soon the bowels of that once gorgeous ship were like everything else: a crowded, stinking hell.

He glanced down at what was left of his uniform. Two buttons held it closed, but his boots, though scuffed and pockmarked, were dust-free. As he leaned forward to polish the hard leather with his hand, a skinny older man sat almost on top of him, then bent back, as if limbering up his spine, and lurched forward, vomiting up his meager breakfast, turning Pietro's boot into a sickly Picasso.

"No! Please, not my fucking boots!" There was, of course, no reply, and Pietro used the guy's pants leg to remove the vomit. "Skinny" was too sick to care.

Pietro closed his eyes in an attempt to remove himself from the claustrophobic hell, but memories came flooding in. No, No, not that. He didn't want to remember the good times. Where would that get him? Only to a place he could never go back to.

And once he accepted that, he could give in to the nothingness again. It was the most viable alternative.

From the hospital where Bella had helped put him together again like that silly English rhyme about the broken egg, Humpty something or other, he was entirely unprepared for the Helwan Prisoner of War camp, about thirty miles from his hospital, still in North Africa. The camp held about 10,000 prisoners divided into cages of a thousand each. Pietro was sure the count was grossly underestimated. In each cage was one tap. They queued night and day for drinking water. By the time you got there and lapped up all you could to satisfy the aching, desert-induced thirst, you went straight to the back of the line because you knew by the time you got back to the tap, you'd be thirsty as hell again.

There were eleven men to one bell tent, and you slept on the hard ground with only the men on either side of you for warmth in the freezing desert nights. You were so cramped, when one turned, you all had to. If you didn't turn, you were either too sick or too dead to do so.

He tried to engage people in conversation, but most had been in a long time already, and they were nothing but husks. Their interaction, their social skills, their desire, their expectations and their humanity had been left long ago at the single, razor-edged gate that kept them in, like animals in a pen. No! Not animals. At least beasts served a purpose.

The horror mounted when men around him fell almost every day as they were jostled along to get meager rations or blessed water during the burning hot days. He tried to reach out to the fallen to help them up, but the masses drove him unwillingly forward. When he saw the downed man again, rigor mortis had set in, and still he couldn't bend down to close the lifeless, staring eyes because a thousand frantic feet forced him ahead toward their own base needs.

Early on, Pietro tried to sing, to cheer, to entertain, and dull eyes were momentarily sparked by his audacity. But just for the briefest of moments. Then they placed hands over ears and turned their backs on this small pleasure. He felt hurt. He thought he could make a difference, but this massive cage was the end of the road. Hell. To drum up memories to make you feel something was to torture yourself all over again. What use did you have for feeling anything when all hope was gone? Within a month—or was it a year?—he'd stopped trying. He let his voice go with his spirit and his hope.

And here he was in yet another overcrowded hell-hole. The incessant roar of engines was different, but the stench of human depravity was the same. Seeing his boots puked upon severed the last gossamer thread of his optimism when he was corralled out of the camp and brought on board. You see? Hope did you no fucking good.

Five sailors entered the hold. One, with a Cockney accent, clapped his hands as if gathering inattentive children for story time, an English sort of thing. "Come along. Let's all go up. It's time we showed your landlocked brothers and those peering up from their submarines that there are enough of you on board to avoid shooting at us and destroying our ship."

Another seaman shouted: "It's about time *you* bastards protected *us!*" Around him, listless faces looked blankly at the seaman.

"One miserable audience," Pietro mused but quickly quelled the thought. Any reference to his past life would only make him feel. And he was done with that "feeling" shit. No one moved from their newly fought-for positions.

Skinny pointed upward and croaked to Pietro, "He wants us

to go on deck," and Pietro was mildly impressed that the man spoke English, too. Skinny was clearly new to this prisoner thing. "Let's GO, Nazi lovers. Playtime!"

Many flights of stairs they climbed. Pietro, in the third tier of climbers, felt joy resonate down to where he was, as the first lot of his cohorts reached the sunlight. Pietro felt a brief moment of fear. The sun. A cure for body and spirit, unless you'd been in the Sudanese desert. Alone, thirsty and broken.

Once on deck, the prisoners were pushed toward the sides of the ship to line up along the perimeter, in plain sight of any other ships, reconnaissance boats, planes or sneaky submarines.

He and his motley crew of 400 or more prisoners were carefully watched and chastised if they leaned too far over the rail. A clear voice from the ship's bullhorn repeated this message constantly: "HOLD YOUR FIRE. *The New Amsterdam* is filled with ITALIAN PRISONERS and will be sailing down the African coast. HOLD YOUR FIRE."

Thereafter, the exercise was repeated five times a day with smaller groups from the hold. Pietro had heard a broadcast by Churchill on the radio of the British transport truck on the way to the port. It went something like: "*The losses we suffer at sea are very heavy, and U-boats hamper us and delay our operations,*" He and his fellow Italians were being used as armor to protect the vessel and its Colonial crew. The bastards didn't miss a trick.

Pietro got to smell the sea air and feel a softer warmth on his face, one that made him forget the harsh desert sun for a time. But as he deeply inhaled salt-tinged air, he wouldn't allow himself to enjoy the sensation.

God only knew where they were heading. There were no landmarks even from the deck. It was all sea from one horizon to the other. Pietro had been counting. Three grueling hell weeks passed when suddenly, the loud engines that never ceased to hurt Pietro's delicate eardrums were quiet. Blissful, frightening silence. What new horrors awaited them?

The human spirit is ever hopeful, Pietro mused, as detached, he watched the wild jubilation around him once the merriment filtered down from the upper decks. The skinny hurler sat next to him again, and Pietro was immensely relieved to see that he'd turned from green to white. Pietro buffed his boots and gave Skinny a dirty look, just in case.

With sour breath, Skinny leaned in to be heard: "They say we are in Durban, South Africa. Nothing could be worse than this hell on water."

Yes, indeed. Most of these blokes were POW virgins. They cared. They were still in the honeymoon phase of hell.

All the prisoners allocated to the Natal area camps were corralled toward the gangplank. Pietro, in the midst of the horde, looked at the crashing, angry ocean to one side and the greenest hills he'd ever seen on the other, and he imagined they were on an exotic island. What the hell was a Durban, anyway? Then he heard the dreaded words, "We are on the lower east coast, close to the southern tip of Africa, the largest continent in the world. You are five thousand, three hundred and thirty-four miles from Italy. To ensure you stay put, we're moving you a further fifty-three-point-two miles inland."

Pietro was unprepared for the panic that attacked him. *How in God's name will I ever get home from here?* The fear worsened. His body began to tremble, and his teeth felt like they would shatter against each other.

He wasn't expecting any sympathy or, God forbid, any help.

But Skinny and a stocky, square man helped him up from his quivering state on the ground and out of harm's way from the hordes of marching boots, going God knew where.

"You'll be trampled to death, friend." How could Skinny be so kind? It wouldn't last long, and Pietro knew better than to have expectations. The square one said nothing but smiled innocently and, without ado, hoisted Pietro's limp frame over his broad shoulders and carried him along with the rest.

What the hell? He didn't know whether to bless them or curse them. Death might well be a better alternative than being ripped from Mother Italy and carted away, too far away to ever return. He realized just knowing Italy was close was the only thing keeping him sane in Helwan.

When Pietro opened his eyes, he was sitting upright, bumping along on a dirt road in what smelled like the inside of a cattle truck. He was propped up between Skinny and Square-man, both smiling at him from either side. How could they be so damn glad to see him?

Fear invaded his every pore as he realized each mile took him farther from his motherland. "How long have we been driving?"

Skinny put out his grimy hand. "Enzo." Pietro shook it absently.

Grinning, the square man did the same. "Antonio."

"For fuck's sake, how long?" Pietro barked.

"About two hours." Skinny Enzo was annoyed. Pietro didn't care. Friends were the last thing he needed, and soon all this pally-pally stuff would come to an abrupt end. He'd *been* these two, eager-to-please clowns.

"There are a hundred different colors of green," Antonio said dreamily. *Colors? What was the use of talking to these morons? How the hell was he going to get home?* He dropped his pounding head in his hands.

In a flash, square Antonio's big arm was around Pietro, patting his back as if burping a baby. Pietro moved away from the man as far as the limited space would allow. "Leave me alone. All of you. Just leave me the fuck alone."

Enzo switched out with two men opposite, patted the empty spot next to him, and thank God, Antonio went away, too.

The rest of the trip was a blur. Afterward, Pietro remembered vaguely that once they jumped off the cattle trucks, they'd walked for what felt like from Rome to Florence in a sloppy column, because there were too few guards to keep them orderly. Men darted out of line to pull at branches, mostly to use as walking sticks, but Skinny ... Enzo, was it? Enzo whittled away at a branch with a knife likely stolen off the ship. Why were Enzo and the square one still close by? How could he embrace oblivion if they pestered him?

And then the square one started to sing. "O Sole Mio." Of all things!

Quick to show solidarity, the men around them joined in. Then those behind. Soon the loudest and most out-of-key rendition of "O Sole Mio" rose from the ragged line. Pietro held his head down, his forearms over his ears, trying in vain to block out the only song that ever brought him peace. He couldn't find any peace so far from home. And he'd certainly never sing again.

Pietro couldn't believe his eyes.

They'd been surrounded by lush, exotic greenery for miles and miles, but when they rounded a hillock, the contrast was astounding. There were hundreds and hundreds of acres of barren soil, with only one structure. It was open on all sides with a corrugated iron roof.

The entire perimeter was enclosed with thick, tightly knit wire that climbed probably thirty-five feet high, beginning and ending in spiked barbed wire. A duplicate "wire wall" ran parallel to it, about eight feet away. Pietro had seen enough POW perimeters to know that the path between fences would be constantly patrolled by soldiers with guns and dogs.

Inside the lethal fences, they were corralled toward the only structure, which turned out to be an old chicken coop where massive pots had been filled with what they called "pap," some kind of maize meal, and stew. Smart, uniformed men handed out spoons and iron plates, onto which large helpings were ladled from each pot. They hadn't seen this much food in years.

A few wooden picnic-type tables with benches attached were soon occupied. Pietro squeezed in, balancing on the end of a long bench. He used two spoons like a knife and fork. Perhaps because his culture and decorum were self-taught, this mannerly habit was more important to him than to those who were well bred, now shoveling plentiful food into eager mouths with their hands.

The guards, who had been fairly amiable on their long journey, seemed to stand straighter and lose their casual manner. Then Pietro saw why.

A tall, thin-lipped man swooped into the coop, wearing the castle and two stars that Pietro supposed was the English equivalent of a commandant's rank. They called him "Colonel." A leather whip tapped at his leg, no doubt with the intention of looking suitably foreboding. It worked. He wove his way through the men, in and out, tap, tap, tap. Pietro immediately christened the colonel "Tap Tap."

His voice was low and soft, which made it all the more menacing: "First, if you don't speak English, learn. Second, and even more important, there will be absolutely no singing in this camp. I intend to make your life as unpleasant as I can. Don't test me. I may just show you what I'm made of. Then you pussies will voluntarily choose the wild, hungry, man-eating animals beyond these fences."

Without warning, Tap Tap jumped onto Pietro's picnic table. His unaided leap landed him on the edge of Pietro's plate, tipping stew all over the colonel's shiny boot. A fine Italian crafted boot, Pietro, the shoe man, assessed. *My captor wears Italian boots. How ironic.* Pietro jumped back to avoid the oozing stew soiling what was left of his uniform.

Tap Tap kicked the plate toward Pietro in a fury. "My new boots. Christ. Bloody filthy now." The congealed stew landed on Pietro's trousers and also, he realized in horror, onto his own pair of newly buffed boots.

Pietro felt fury burn in his chest as he watched a carrot slide slowly down his right boot and felt lukewarm liquid penetrate the worn leather. He looked up at the son of a bitch and immediately felt the excruciating flick of the whip on the tip of each ear, so deft and quick, he might have imagined it, if it wasn't for the sting.

"You need to know your place, you piece of Eye-Tie shit."

Pietro felt immense hatred as he looked to the man with the whip towering above him.

"Lick it," Tap Tap said in a menacing tone. Pietro's eyes on Tap Tap were unwavering. He didn't move an eyelash.

"I said lick my boots, Fuck Face."

Pietro didn't move until the swift whip grazed his temple. It stung like a bitch. Pietro dropped to the bench.

"Lick it!"

Quick as a cobra, the whip struck the back of Pietro's head, and as he reflexively moved forward, Tap Tap used the whip as a vice grip on the back of his head, forcing Pietro down toward the stew-sodden, brand-new Italian boot. Closer, closer. The pressure was amplified by Pietro's resistance as he watched a long green bean become the size of a green mamba.

He was helpless. The tip of his nose touched the cold stew, and it wobbled like gelatin.

"Lick it. Eat it all. Pretend it's macaroni. That should make you happy. LICK IT or SUFFOCATE in it."

The whip's vice grip was relentless. Pietro had nowhere to go. He held his breath and closed his eyes as his tongue pushed the stew off the Italian boot and onto the picnic table. As long as he lived, which he hoped wouldn't be too much longer under these circumstances, he'd never again eat fucking stew. Or carrots. Or green beans.

The only contribution Pietro had made to his new society was christening "Tap Tap," which had stuck. Fortunately, they'd not seen the evil colonel since the no-singing, boot-licking episode at lunch.

Sergeant Rogers was their chief most of the time, and he seemed a decent sort. He treated the men respectfully, as did most of the guards. Tap Tap's chief guard, a beefy mountain of a man with a glum disposition, was dubbed "Burbero," Italian for "surly." They surmised that this one's brawn, coupled with Tap Tap's evil intent, made a lethal combination.

A bullhorn blared, and Pietro recognized the clipped voice immediately. "Gather and strip, you pieces of macaroni shit." Guards corralled the men away from their newly erected tents toward an open area from whence Tap Tap's voice had hissed.

Burbero was on the bullhorn: "Time for a pleasant wash. Strip. All of you! Guards!" Uniforms surged to ensure the order was carried out. "Bundle your clothes and put them in this bin for fumigation, but not your boots, they'll shrink!" Burbero's voice boomed, but his heavy Afrikaans accent was a challenge. Pietro, who'd developed an ear for languages, understood. Others did not. He pulled off his once-precious boots, hesitated just a moment, then threw them into the bin along with his clothes. Those who were copying Pietro did the same.

Pietro shouted to them: "No! No! Not yours! Just mine. They're forever ruined, but not *yours!*" But it was too late, and for a long time, Pietro felt responsible every time he saw a barefooted fellow prisoner.

Naked and humiliated, Pietro and the others were jostled into line. A dozen guards held a humongous fire hose and blasted the men, first en masse and then in groups of ten, to rid them of months and months of accumulated dirt. Pietro saw Enzo blasted to the ground by the water's force. More men bit the dust. Men stood shivering in lines as guards doused each one thoroughly with DDT powder until they looked like precooked, uncensored gingerbread men.

Pietro and his stripped cohorts spent hours wandering around, the modest among them hunkering down to cover their privates, waiting for their clothes to come back from wherever they went. At last the bullhorn blared: "They're fumigated. Get them." Burbero pointed in the direction of a huge pile, which looked like a mountain of rags. Pietro groaned. Heaven forbid he would have to wear someone else's clothing. When he was at his poorest, even if he could only afford one shirt, it was always clean, ironed and every button was double sewn. Hell, even in the hideous Helwan they'd been issued non-denominational uniforms on arrival. Not here!

The men converged on the pile, a naked scrum of bodies and flying clothes. It wasn't long until Pietro amazed himself and dove into the thick of it. When in Rome ... Ha! He emerged with his lower half clad, then went back in and came out with a huge shirt with one less button than his last.

He knew at that minute vanity had forsaken him once and for all. No! He'd lost the last vestige of pride earlier that day, when he was too busy licking the slop off a shiny, new pair of Italian boots to preserve his own.

May 1943
  Pietermaritzburg

Pietro overheard the guards discussing the latest war news. It paid to have English as his secret weapon, because unlike when Enzo came close, they continued talking around Pietro.

Rogers said, "We're whipping the Jerries and their motley crew. Allies took Tunisia last week, and just today I read that German and Italian troops surrendered in North Africa."

"Blerry war's nearly over, man. Watch mooi," said the surly guard in his Afrikaans-tinged accent.

Pietro felt his heart lurch for a second, and then Rogers, unquestionably the more educated of the two, replied, "There's a lot more that needs to happen to win the war than just capturing more POWs in a piece of Africa nobody wants anyway." Damn it. The man was right.

Tents covered one quarter of the once-barren acres. They'd been instructed to dig around the perimeter of each four-man canvas tent, and when the torrential rains came, they knew why. Even with the mini-moats, water still seeped in. Everything was always damp. Mud was in every orifice. In spite of the daily deluge, there was no running water. The buckets they left out became their source for drinking and bathing. There was no sewage system, and no matter how far from the tents they went when nature called, the downpour washed a good bit of it back toward their living quarters. Conditions were worse than a pig's sty.

Enzo and Antonio marveled daily at their luck that there were just three of them in a four-man tent. It was only a fucking tent. True, there were less of them and they could smell the air and see the sky, but they were still a million miles from home.

The two did all they could to befriend him, but Pietro made sure his shell remained impenetrable. He was relieved that nobody recognized him but not surprised—he was a different man, for sure. He'd learned to be invisible in Helwan. Anonymity had its merits.

Pietro felt Enzo's eyes on him more than usual and knew it was coming but was unprepared for the venom-spiked delivery.

"Why are you so detached? We are all in this together, pretty boy. What makes you think you're better than the rest of us? In the same tent and yet you may as well be dead. You don't participate. You never laugh. You never become involved. It's as if you think you are something special. What did you do, Pietro, before this godawful war?"

"Nothing important. Nothing worthwhile. I've nothing to offer." Pietro was defensive.

"A smile. Conversation. Anything would be better than what you offer us now," spat Enzo. "Rue the day that Antonio saved you from being trampled to death."

Antonio, whose heart was bigger than his big, square frame, tried his best not to get involved, but since he couldn't walk away and into the deluge, he turned his back.

Enzo was older than most in the camp, but his energy was enough to drive the full supply of electricity to Africa. The decoration in their tent was, thanks to Enzo the Whittler, first a map of Italy and second, an intricate carving of The Virgin Mary.

Enzo had Italians lined up outside the tent once word got out that the Holy Mother resided within. Enzo added a dash of superpower by whispering to one of those seeking sanctuary that this carving was blessed by The Pope himself, and he simply couldn't part with it, but he'd be happy to make another, and another. Pietro reluctantly admired his enterprising spirit. Enzo's price for a piece of his art or to some, a piece of quiet for the soul: an extra slice of bread for the always-hungry Antonio, a bucket of water, his knife sharpened, or a whittle-worthy tree branch.

Meanwhile, Pietro found peace in the chicken coop. It was here where the older men, or the infirm, or those literally bored to death, went to die. Quietly. They stayed under the shade of the picnic tables until mealtimes, when they pushed their lethargic bodies against the walls and away from the hungry men. Sustenance would only delay their agony.

After their first day of abundance, the camp's food helpings drastically diminished on some days, and on others, there was none to be had. There were no set meal times. Men waited for the bullhorn announcement that came at odd times of the day or night and sometimes not at all. Predictability made for comfort, and comfort was not Tap Tap's style, of that Pietro was sure.

Like the wretched men Pietro hung around with, he didn't care about food. A dead spirit didn't need much fuel. Besides, the stench of feces overcame any gnawing hunger.

But Italians are an enterprising sort, and it wasn't long before one of them spearheaded the digging of the most impressive long-drop in the southern hemisphere, and the floating feces became one less issue to plague their endless, uncertain days.

Their biggest problem besides boredom was the menacing Tap Tap who always seemed to magically appear. Pietro heard whispers of beatings by that cursed whip on men's bare soles. Camp rumor had it that the evil one would catch boot-clad prisoners en route to request medical attention for one of their own, or to beg for more food for the camp. He'd order them into his large private office, sit them down in an easy chair, then make them take off their "loud" boots, place their feet on an ottoman, stuff confused mouths with old rags, and whip the soles of raised feet. Men limped back barefoot, without medical care or more food for hungry bellies. But there were no scars and no drops of blood and nothing to prove what had been done to them.

Though no one publicly witnessed his blatant cruelty in those early days, there was never a doubt Tap Tap was more than capable and culpable.

They continued existing in appalling, muddy squalor. The worst of it all was the curse of boredom. When a mind has nothing to stimulate it, the wires fuse together, looking for a spark, and burn out, Pietro thought as he watched two men carted away in straitjackets. Tap Tap was notably present to watch the writhing, frightened men removed from the camp. Each of these episodes was punctuated with Tap Tap on the bullhorn: "You bastards are so lucky the Geneva Convention exists. If it were up to me, you would all be in padded cells. Sane or not." He punctuated by spitting over his shoulder.

After many months in the camp that felt like years, only one structure had been built under Tap Tap's rule: an eight-by-eight box, two stories high, made of solid brick but for the steel door and the steel drawer, which could be unlocked at meal times to transfer meager rations. Air holes the size of half crowns dotted the top of the structure, providing the only light and air source. The Hell Hole. It was Tap Tap's pride and joy, and he was dying to find an excuse to use it.

There wasn't a mean bone in Antonio's big body. Antonio told Enzo that he had worked for Marconi as a radio technician, and Enzo encouraged him to make something to keep his trained hands busy. But Antonio was too agitated to apply himself to anything. His right eye began to twitch, and he constantly muttered, "Go home. Go home. Go home."

A week later, the camp was awakened by a shot fired, followed by blinding perimeter lights and ballistic, barking dogs. Men poured from their tents to see Antonio halfway up the first fence, clinging on for dear life. Antonio's legs were in bloody tatters from the barbs, and his big face was streaked with tears as he cried: "Let me go or shoot me, just don't take me back to the mud. Shoot me. Shoot me so my spirit can go back to Italy. I beg you." Of course, none of the guards understood his lament as he hung on relentlessly.

There was no escape. The guards sat down on a mound nearby and simply watched and waited for Antonio to fall off.

Tap Tap appeared, and the Italians were ordered back to their tents. For the first time since Pietro left Bella at the hospital, he felt—well, *something* as he watched the kind Antonio, broken with hopelessness. Later in the chicken coop and away from curious eyes, Pietro wept for them both. The unusual taste of his tears awoke something in him he'd thought he'd lost forever.

An hour later, the bullhorn: "COME ON, MACARONIS. COME SEE WHAT HAPPENS TO THOSE WHO DEFY ME. COME YE, COME YE."

They all shot out of their tents and converged on the place of activity.

Antonio must have lost his grip and landed in the barbed wire at the bottom of the fence. Bleeding, he was being dragged into the wire enclosure that housed Tap Tap's solitary torture chamber as the evil one's tinny voice boomed through the bullhorn: "The Hell Hole's first victim. May this be an example for you bastards to understand you're at my mercy. We'll leave him in there for two weeks, bubbling in his own stew."

Hoisted by the elbows, between Burbero and another beefy Englishman, the delirious Antonio sang tunelessly: *"O sole mio sta nfronte a te! 'O sole, 'o sole mio, sta nfronte a te, sta nfronte a te!"*

But another sun that's brighter still, it's my own sun that's upon your face!"

———————

That night, Pietro set up his command post on a rise outside the Hell Hole's perimeter, about fifteen yards away from the structure, close enough for Antonio to hear he was not alone. Pietro hadn't spoken so much in over a year and was surprised by how very much he had to say.

He thought of his old friend Stef. He was the only one who knew Pietro's heart. What had become of Stef once Pietro was whisked away to war?

During the blackest part of the night if Pietro fell asleep, he awoke with a start, fearful that Antonio might have thought himself alone. When food was delivered to The Hole, Pietro begged the guards to let him push the offerings through the built-in, steel delivery tray. "Be my guest," said one guard sarcastically and stepped back. Pietro offered in English, "Mine nose eeze deaf!" which seemed to amuse the guards, who happily allowed Pietro the food-delivery honors from then on. During the half a minute that he and Antonio breathed the same air, he knew the gentle man could hear him close up: "Antonio. Remember how clever your hands are. You are Italian. Nothing can break you. If you need to bend, I will be here to help straighten you. But don't break, Antonio. I need you. I am never far away."

During his vigil, he left his grassy post only to get his food. At night, he was so still, nobody realized he was there, and if they did, they didn't care. His loud whispers were camouflaged by the night sounds of the African bush: primates mating or hunting; hyenas laughing; frogs and crickets. Pietro figured that as long as he could hear the muffled mewling coming from within the structure, Antonio could hear Pietro. He hoped the poor man might take comfort from his prattle.

During the day, Pietro snuck from his post to ask Sergeant Rogers about the animal sounds, and Rogers was happy to oblige, giving an animated explanation of their wild neighbors, complete with the sounds each made.

One night, he heard something unusual inside the camp and strained to see.

Tap Tap pulled a man kicking and flailing away from the tents. When they got closer, he saw the man's mouth tightly compacted with a rag. Tap Tap dragged his thrashing victim to the farthest point of the camp. A knife glinted as Tap Tap ripped apart the man's shirt, then slashed a surface wound from right nipple to left hip, just enough to tantalize sensitive snouts searching for the easy prey of the wounded.

Tap Tap handcuffed the man to the camp's perimeter fence, splaying resistant arms out, as an invitation to predators. Then Tap Tap moved to a mound thirty yards away, lay down and waited to watch his macabre tableau. Fortunately, he was a hundred yards from Pietro and too absorbed in his own sick game to imagine anyone else out in the dark of night.

Pietro thought he was done for, when after ten minutes of silence, Antonio started shouting, "Where are you, Angel? Why do you not speak to me anymore? Hast thou forsaken me?" And great, hiccupping sobs emitted from The Hole. Pietro felt his heart would break, but he dared not speak or move until Tap Tap had his perverted fun.

The fresh blood drew the carnivorous hunters closer. Yellow eyes glinted through the bush. A roar so loud and so powerful it sounded multi-dimensional literally lifted Pietro's butt off his turf about a foot and confirmed that a "big cat," as Sergeant Rogers described a lion, was closely watching. Tap Tap's captive let out a muffled, mucus-sodden cry through the rag. Without the buffer, his scream would have been heard in Durban. Not even the lethal wire barriers that separated the man from the lion could quell the fear of being watched by Africa's largest man-eating beast.

Pietro heard the hysterical laughter of a pack of hyenas, then a distant whistling was a sure sign one of the guards and his dogs would soon make an appearance.

The sole purpose of all this security was to keep the "bad guys inside." Had he found an iota of amusement, Pietro would have laughed at the irony of having the worst of humanity, in the form of Tap Tap, free to wander about *inside* and commit his atrocities. But Pietro lay dead still and watched helplessly as the evil one moved quickly to the shivering man, expertly unlocked handcuffs and pushed him toward the tents, letting him go when he was far enough away not to be seen from the perimeter. The terrified prisoner ran like hell, as Tap Tap sauntered in the opposite direction toward the approaching guard on the other side of the fence.

Tap Tap pocketed the handcuffs. "You see anything untoward tonight, Corporal?"

The man holding the dogs gawked with fear, his cigarette dropped from open lips, and limp hands dropped the leashes. The dogs immediately went into attack mode and charged at Tap Tap behind the fence.

"Sarie! Marais! Down!" The Dobermans obeyed. "Sorry, suh! No, suh!" the sweating corporal managed, saluting.

"Any predators with undue appetites tonight?"

"I heard a big cat, Colonel. But those bastards have plenty to eat outside there," he pointed haphazardly into the darkness, "unlike the bastards inside." The corporal's shoulders shook with nervous laughter, but Tap Tap had already disappeared into the darkness.

Pietro continued his vigil, day and night, chatting away for Antonio to hear. Never a confessional or a soul search, rather a monologue targeted to his one-man audience. He talked of what he believed Antonio would find important, although sometimes he got carried away by his unique observations, which he simply had to share.

Within the barbed wire corral of the Hell Hole, unscarred by the daily churning of earth by hundreds of feet, nature had a shot at going about her phenomenal business. He shared with Antonio the miracles he observed as they unfolded each day: prairie flowers opening and closing with the sun; bees finding untapped flowers of all colors that popped up in the Hell Hole's enclosure; butterflies of a thousand hues. Nature tried desperately to repair what man destroyed.

By the third night, the animal noises became a symphony of interesting keys and harmonies to Pietro's musical ear, and his most incredible discovery was a tiny little critter with the biggest, most crappy ideals. The bug's tenacity reminded Pietro of his young self.

The little black beetle was a quarter the size of Pietro's pinky nail, and he captured what looked like a piece of feces. He was a busy little guy and worked relentlessly to get the sloppy turd into a ball. It took hours. Pietro was entirely mesmerized by the little guy's determination as the ball grew ten times its size. Seemingly, his little woman was by his side, egging him on. When the ball was the size that satisfied them, she scuttled away on a mission, and he turned around and pushed the ball with his powerful hind legs. No obstacle deterred him, even if he had to try three or four times. The ball went over stones and divots, dips and tufts. There was nothing that was too much for him to overcome, such was his commitment to the end result.

At times the beetle stopped dead, taking his hind legs off his big ball. His shell-like head tilted upward and beady eyes went heavenward, as if studying the night sky. He seemed to alter his course according to whatever it was he saw in the heavens.* Finally, he reached his mate, who impatiently tapped all six legs for him to get on with it. She buried herself into the earth, pushing it up with her back to soften it, Pietro guessed. Then together, they buried the ball under the softened earth and disappeared.

Pietro later learned that the ball became the love nest on which their eggs were laid, and the parents and the larvae dined on the dung until the family was ready to rescue more dung and procreate. What an important part of nature the little guy was! The more dung beetles, the fewer flies. Nature was indeed a wonder.

Damn it! He was just finding things to tell Antonio; he wasn't going soft.

Ten more days passed before the lights came on in the middle of the night. Pietro leapt up and clung to the fence. The wait was finally over. Others soon joined him around the chain link. Burbero arrived and ceremoniously unlocked the enclosure and sauntered toward the steel door. Tap Tap appeared and leaned on the gate casually as if he was watching a street performer but didn't want to get too close in case he'd feel obliged to throw a tip into the worn hat.

Burbero unlocked, then pulled open the door. He took a giant step back, gagging.

Nothing happened. Men barely breathed as they watched the open steel door. Still nothing. Calling for another, Burbero tied a handkerchief around his mouth and entered.

The two came back out, dragging between them a drooling, feces-encrusted, quivering specimen that was once Antonio.

The POWs peeled off the fence and away, refusing to watch Antonio's debasement.

The guards dropped Antonio as soon as they were out of the brick building, and after locking it, they walked quickly away, stopping only at the entrance to salute Tap Tap.

Tap Tap had not moved an inch. "Yes, he is quite *done.*" The sadist's eyes were ice-cold blue in the glaring light, and his smile was satisfied. He turned his back and began walking away, but Pietro's loud shout stopped him.

"You fucking *macellaio!*" Pietro's loud exclamation of hate shocked him as much as everyone else close by.

Butcher.

Julian's eyes found Pietro's and he shouted, "What are you saying, Macaroni?"

Enzo pushed his way around Pietro protectively. "This one no English, sir. He say you are good cock, how you say, cook. You are top chef." He ended with the universal thumbs up.

It was enough to get the egomaniac to move away, but Pietro's face was distorted by hatred as he ran after the colonel's retreating back. Enzo caught up with Pietro, grabbed and hung on to his arm with his body almost to the ground, like a spoiled, insistent child.

"That's a battle you will lose. Antonio needs you," Enzo said very softly. It was enough. Pietro rushed to the heap that was once a man and hauled the big frame upward. By slinging his limp arm around his shoulders, Pietro was able to support Antonio all the way to their tent.

"Ma n'atu sole cchiù bello, oi ne' ... "

Pietro called for Enzo's help to get the big man into his cot, then tucked him in like one would a small child. In the days to come, Pietro seldom left the tent other than to fetch Antonio meals or empty his pee bucket. Men stopped in to pay their respects, but the broken man stared blankly ahead, rocking, rocking.

Pietro caught Enzo gazing at him. "What?" Pietro barked.

"Sing to him, like you did the night of his release," Enzo urged. Pietro hadn't realized he'd been singing at all. "Try it. I think it may help,"

Only when Enzo was safely gone from the tent did Pietro sing "O Sole Mio" to Antonio. Miraculously, the rocking stopped, though there was no other sign of cognizance.

---

28 July 1943—morning

When his hard-on woke him, Pietro's index finger was pointing in midair, connecting the dots that sprinkled her nose. Surprise that he had juice left in the tired stick was secondary to the absolute awe and fascination Mia Cara Rossa provoked.

Was it just yesterday he'd first seen this remarkable creature with her animated face and dark red hair? Perhaps it was because he'd thought of her so much in the last hours that she felt so vividly familiar. No! She'd felt that way the minute he'd set eyes on her.

Weak was he with tenderness, yet his body pulsed. Ridiculous, these meanderings. He was a prisoner of war, for God's sake, and she on the right side of a barbed wire fence!

Ah, the angle of her cheekbones! Her hair a million shades of sunset and long, he surmised, because long tendrils snuck over her shoulder, belying her short style. Her eyes, green, not usually a color that burned, but they did, all the way to his soul.

Enough!

He put his hand to the floor and felt for the "post-Iris" acquired boots—but immediately let them drop, remembering where the giant boots came from. How had he stooped so low?

It was true that before his mission to keep Antonio sane, Pietro went to the coop daily to die, but there must have been a hint of life burning within, because he was interested in the men he saw there. Well bred, they were likely once vital to Italy's infrastructure as councilmen or influential leaders, and when Mussolini involved Italy in Germany's war, they were given high military rank and sent off to lead fighting troops. Then they were captured and stripped of their long-held status. As prisoners, they were wrecked and hopeless, some into their fifties, with no hope of enduring anything but Tap Tap's macabre rule until the day they died. So they did their best to bring the inevitable forward. They stopped eating. In the nooks and crannies of the chicken coop, they slept all day in an effort to evoke memories of happier times. They were never missed, because they mostly shared the same tents, and day and night they were either wandering aimlessly in the mud or sleeping anywhere but in the confines of their tents.

And so it was that back to the chicken coop Pietro went, right after seeing his Red, not to find the oblivion of death but to troll for an available pair of boots. His plan was to ask one of the older prisoners if he could inherit his pair when the time came the elder no longer needed them. Until his "encounter" with her, he'd been perfectly resigned to his bare feet. Now he was obsessed with restoring his dignity from the bottom up.

Where the hell did this hope come from? Aha! The dung beetle!

An unusually tall Italian lay on his side, under a bench. The boots were way too big for Pietro, so he intended just to check on the elder and move on to a man his own size. As he leaned down to gently shake the man, he stood on the corner of the elder's open shirt. The man rolled over, mouth and eyes wide open. Pietro swore and jumped back, then felt desperately bad. He prayed in Latin, so the message would be quickly delivered, and gently closed papery lids over glassy eyes. He felt regret that he had not been able to do this for fallen men in the past.

He was about to move on when his eyes caught the huge boots. Pietro glanced this way and that, guilty as hell. Was he, Pietro Saltamachio, about to steal a dead man's boots? What had he become? He shook his head, disgusted with himself, until ... until her freckled face flitted across his mind. He lost not a second more. Back in their tent, Enzo stuffed the boots with the newspaper he'd found.

Had he or Enzo read the headline on the windswept *Pietermaritzburg Gazette,* their mission to get Pietro into fitting boots would have been severely marred. It read: *Mussolini Arrested! Italian Fascist Government Falls; Marshal Pietro Badoglio Takes Over —Negotiates with Allies.* Sometimes, ignorance is bliss.

Pietro glanced down and angled his boots to catch the moonlight. Clean as a whistle. Thank God the bulge in the blanket had gone down, but with that thought came a vision of his Rossa, and there it was again. Strangely, contrary to the evidence below, his stimulation was not just sexual but cerebral. He wanted to *know* her. Imagine that!

He *would* see her again. He didn't know how it would happen, only that it would, if he wanted it badly enough. And by God he did!

And then it came to him.

He pulled the newspaper from one of his boots and

smoothed it out on his cot. He slipped over to the snoring Antonio. A safety pin kept the white bandage in place around the big man's head. Yesterday Pietro had returned with their meals and found Antonio outside gazing into the wilderness. Antonio gave a primal scream, and in his attempt to escape the chasm between him and home, he banged his head on the ground, over and over, until Pietro took him gently by the shoulders and sang to him. Pietro took him to Doc, now permanently on premises courtesy of someone higher up and clearly more humane than Tap Tap, to get bandaged up, but there was naught any medical training could do about Antonio's homesickness and despair.

Pietro gently reached for the safety pin on the snoring, heaving head, slowly unhooking it, then pulling it free.

Utilizing pegs used for washing, Pietro hung the newspaper up between the open tent flap. The midnight sky's light shone on the print, and he went to work with the pin.

Her exquisite face popped into his head, and he grinned. Just like the amazing little dung beetle, he'd found a way.

---

* In 2013, a study was published revealing that South African dung beetles can navigate when only the Milky Way or clusters of bright stars are visible. They are the only insect known to orient itself by the galaxy. The remarkable beetle can roll a ball ten times its weight, making it one of the strongest animals for its size on earth.

ROSES

Pietermaritzburg
 4 November 1942

> *Somewhere in Italy.*
> *OPEN ONLY ON YOUR BIRTHDAY and NO earlier, Iris!*

Iris had received the letter a week ago. She'd torn open the envelope and read the opening line. It took every ounce of restraint not to gobble up the rest, but she managed, only because this letter would be her only gift.

> *My Beloved Sunshine,*
> *Happy, happy birthday. May all your dreams come true. Thinking of you every day. but especially today. Close your eyes, and you'll hear me sing to you. "Happy Birthday to you..."*

Iris closed her eyes. But she heard nothing.

I bet this finds you lying in the hammock strung between the fruit trees in the farthest corner of the yard. I know Buffer's nestling his nose between you and the twine. He's nine now, isn't he? Sixty-three dog years, and every bit the wise old man. Even when you were both pups, he was the mature one, and frankly, he was the only reason I could leave you in good conscience. Having a decent bloke in charge of my baby sister was essential.

Iris smiled and gently laid the precious letter on her chest. She manipulated Buffer's flexible ear as she squinted into the sun peeping between the untrimmed leaves of the peach and apricot trees above the weed-infused lawn. She swore she saw the fuzzy yellow, green and orange fruit laboring to maturity, as the colors became more vivid with each swing. Hmm, she loved the idea of that color combination. She grabbed her always-nearby sketch pad, and her pencil flicked and angled. In no time at all she'd designed a dress with a no-nonsense bodice and a flounce in the skirt that could stop an aircraft propeller. She imagined her handsome brother in the captain's seat of the plane and picked up the letter, holding it to her nose.

She sniffed. Nothing. She inhaled. Her eyes filled with tears. "Nothing, Buffer. I can't hear him, and I can't bloody smell him." The dog's big brown eyes seemed to apologize for the tears that poured down his mistress's cheeks.

She was a child born of the Scorpio constellation, and her mother always said she had a sting in her tail. The only sting she had was when her mother forgot her birthday! Without Gregg and her dad, today was just a day. She wasn't expecting gifts. Times were too hard for that. Her mother usually remembered sometime in mid-November but made no effort to apologize or, heaven forbid, make it up to her. Lena and Sofie had good excuses. Birthdays weren't a Zulu thing. But her birth mother?

Amazing that even though her brother, on another continent, in the midst of a world war, managed to make her day, when those closest to her didn't give a damn. She could actually taste her own bitterness.

The shrill sound of the daily air raid siren never ceased to surprise her and made girl and dog jump in unison. Was the siren designed to remind South Africans that there was a world war raging? So far and yet so near. Even saying goodbye to the local boys and men who left from airstrips, ports and stations was surreal. Their imminent danger was vague. There was no way to experience the shattered state of North Africa, the U.K. and Europe from thousands of miles away. Only fuzzy, reproduced photographs in the *Pietermaritzburg Gazette,* well after the incidents occurred, kept them in touch with the war. And the wireless of course. Her mother swooned every time she heard Winston Churchill's voice. They heard about lost, maimed or dead brothers and sons and fathers and lovers, but like unwed pregnancy, you didn't believe it could ever happen to you. Then, like a knife in her chest, she thought for the first time about losing her brother, her best friend. *Life without you would be so very lonely, Gregg. Please don't let yourself be taken from me.*

Iris reckoned it was this dread of earth-shattering change and loss that gave South Africans a "carpe diem" attitude, as they damned the consequences. Women became more promiscuous, men more vulnerable.

Where once, only written invitations entitled one to socialize with one's equal in status, now private homes opened their doors to all and sundry: privates and colonels, volunteers and surgeons, hat makers and hat wearers. As long as they were white, rank and financial status mattered not at all. At least for the night. Loud music, wild revelry, enthusiastic dancing, copious cigarettes and too much local brew made from sugar cane were the order of the night and well into the wee hours of the next day. By God, they would make life fun if it killed them!

Iris touched the letter and, exercising great restraint, managed to resist picking it up. It was like popping a last, precious, delicious block of chocolate in your cheek and keeping your tongue in check, so the creamy delight could trickle down slowly, giving your taste buds bursts of delectable, indulgent satisfaction.

But then resistance shattered, and you just had to bite the bloody thing!

I hope you're going to have some fun tonight, my sunshine. Go meet a deserving man and dance the night away. But just don't get too carried away. I'm still your overprotective brother, no matter how many miles separate us!

On this, her nineteenth birthday, Iris was still a virgin. Not because she was opposed to the looseness of the times, nor was it her Catholic upbringing, but because of her lack of interest in the men she met.

She had two incredible role models in her late father and her brother, and frankly, no boy or man in Pietermaritzburg had ever come close to winning her admiration. She welcomed spinsterhood but would go there experimenting, *after* she'd found a special man worthy of her maidenhead. She'd yet to meet one titillating enough to bed her before he bored her.

Buffer licked her hand and, at the same time, Iris smelled an overripe peach fermenting, which jolted her from her reverie. The smell of decay triggered her other senses as the mildewed corner of the sagging roof dominated her vision. As she looked at her once greatly envied childhood home, she felt abysmal sadness. How tainted by time and neglect it had become.

The Fuller household hit hard times two years ago, seven

years after the malaria virus attacked her father in a bank, no less, not even a jungle. The abundant insurance policy he believed would take care of his family forever diminished much sooner than expected. As the cost of living increased, the lives of luxury they were born into became a memory.

It was fortunate that Iris's Catholic school and Gregg's snob-bish college educations were accomplished before they ran out of money. Her mother would have been shamed into oblivion had her children been forced to attend common public schools. In spite of her bravery when their money ran out, her mother heaved a sigh of relief when the Great Depression was so wide-spread, it even included the southernmost part of the great African continent. Everyone had to tighten their proverbial belts, not just the poor Fuller widow.

Lena worked mostly for her wardrobe these days. If it weren't for Iris's job at Ross & Co., the fabulous department store, new dresses for the entire family would have been in short supply. As the only sales clerk on the haberdashery counter, she had inside information as to what fabric was going on sale when. So she had a few days to design a dress for whomever the material suited best among the four of them. These days, the remnant pile was the only alternative, but Iris found that being frugal fueled her creativity. The finest and brightest materials made any garment attractive, but it took real talent to make cotton interesting.

She found her eyes drawn to the bloody steel handle bars that had once led down to inviting, aquamarine water. Fuller pool parties were the hottest invitation in Maritzburg.

She tasted the grit of wet soil and clotted compost in the back of her throat as she relived the shovels patting down the last of the dirt that covered up their richest indulgence. The pool was gone. Albert, their garden "boy" who was at least fifty years old, and his three cohorts stood, spades in hand, exhausted and grinning, proud of their mammoth task.

Iris, her mother, Gregg, Lena, Sofie and Buffer stood at the pool's graveside with hanging heads. Iris thought somebody should break into: "Yea, though I walk through the valley of the shadow of death ... " but instead, her mother declared with excitement, "What a perfect place for a rose garden! Oh, look! Those steel handle bars are ideal for climbing roses."

Iris lifted the letter off her chest. As always, she and Gregg were on the same wavelength.

I wonder if Mom's been able to cover the bars with roses yet. Blood from a stone and all that! I still dream about diving into our pool and hitting dirt.

First awed by their mother's resilience, they were stupefied with her follow-through. Roses of every size, color and fragrance adorned the kidney-shaped area. All except the steel bars. Nothing worked!

She read some more.

I know you pay Mom half your meager salary, and I wish I could send more of mine, but a man has needs: cigarettes, booze and money to woo a girl ... if I ever find one in this godforsaken place. North Africa only has sand and ...

Black ink obliterated the location that must have been too close to a strategic position.

Mussolini knows how to fight a war. When we fly "reccies" (reconnaissance missions to the non-RAF: your education for the day) over the Eye-Tie bases, we see a dozen women in each. Word

*has it they are courtesans, paid to pleasure the boys. I think I might
be fighting for the wrong side!*

That made Iris laugh out loud. There was no more loyal man
than her brother. Loyal to his family. Loyal to his country.
Change sides indeed! The Fullers were British and proud of it.
One of her mother's parents was a Boer, but no one spoke of
that. Perhaps because of what the English would call "a smear,"
her mother spoke the King's English better than a duchess.

Gregg was right about how quickly her salary disappeared.
But other than materials and essentials, every spare penny went
into the sewing machine's secret drawer to bolster her lifelong
dream of joining a fashion house, somewhere, anywhere, who
would welcome her into their creative fold.

She picked up her precious letter.

*I hope you're getting to see a film now and then. We get a picture
night we can catch when we're not flying. Inevitably, the bloody film
burns out right near the end and we're left hanging. Please go to the
Alhambra so you can tell me how the bloody thing ends!*

The Alhambra theater. She swore she could smell fresh
popcorn and melting butter. She splurged a precious sixpence
every month to escape with Fred and Ginger or gorgeous
Veronica Lake or Marlene. She saw the films once for the
costumes and a hard-earned second time for the story. The
Alhambra inspired her to include Hollywood in her fashion-
house fantasies.

Now, where was she? Ah, roses! A design for her mother,
perhaps. Iris sat up quickly, almost capsizing Buffer, and
grabbed her lineless sketchbook. She pulled out the pencil that
held her fast-fashioned chignon on the top of her head, and as

her damned unruly hair fell heavily down her back, she skill-fully sketched a special-occasion, floor-length dress.

With a dexterous twist of her sharp instrument, she fash-ioned a gathering on the left hip, an illusion that the flimsy folds were "caught" while waltzing too close to a thorny rose bush, causing the random ruche, but as if to hide nature's thorns, fresh, perfect rosebuds adorned the lower hip. She thrived on throwing a touch of surprise and a little danger into her designs. She hoped, when she found the guts to send off her designs, the recipients would recognize her dally with the unexpected.

Sunshine, I hope you're doing something solid with your talent. Don't let grass grow under your feet. Life is too short. I see it every day. Do what you love. Though I hated to leave you, I had to follow my heart and fight overseas as opposed to staying at home, pen-pushing, safe and close to you but, God forbid, a million miles from the action. As selfish as that might have been, it was what was best for my soul. So it must be with you. No regrets, Iris. Rather regret what you did, than what you didn't do. I think somebody else said that more succinctly, but the message is the same. Do it, and bugger the consequences. Somehow, life works out as it should.

Could she really get serious about an adventure in fashion? But she'd have to leave her mother, and Iris was all she had left. Iris sniffed dismissively. For what that was worth. Oh, well, Gregg would likely be home by then, and she wouldn't be missed.

The thought of leaving Lena and Sofie tugged at her heart. And Buffer? Oh my, she couldn't even go there in her mind. She hugged her adored friend, who opened his eyes warily.

"It's all right, my Buffer. Truth is, only Lena, Sofie, mother and I are enamored with my designs, so you will have me for life, have no fear."

Her mother wafted outside in her wide-brimmed gardening hat and gloves. She could have been on her way to the Durban July, South Africa's premier horse-racing event. Iris had inherited her mother's sense of style, if nothing else.

"What's your brother say?"

"Oh, just chit-chatting, you know, like he does. He doesn't talk about himself. He seems to love to reminisce. I suppose it brings him closer to home," said Iris.

She saw her mother roughly wipe her eyes with the crook of her arm. Iris observed her mother like a kid watching a monkey at the zoo: fascinating from a distance, but you didn't want to get too close to the cage in case the monkey attacked.

The elder turned her attention to the blooming roses and immersed herself in the scent and perfection of each delicate bloom. Then, out of nowhere, the lethal pair of scissors appeared, and she mercilessly cut the heaviest of the stems with razor precision, like a leopard's sharp incisors cutting into the throat of its prey.

Iris touched her throat. She knew only too well how those poor roses felt. *Snip!* Mind you, her mother had kissed her on the cheek for no reason a few days ago. Iris nearly fainted! But then she remembered she was the only one left in the house. One had to make do.

Snip, snip!

"The Hartenadys are having a party on Saturday night. Fred's always had a crush on you. Come with me! We'll swoop in, fashionably late. I'll wear the teal number you made me."

"I'm not in the mood, Mom. Buffer and I will lie in the hammock for a bit, then I want to finish Lena's dress."

"You spoil that girl, you know."

"She spoils me."

"And Buffer is not husband material."

Here we go again. "I am not looking for a husband, Mom. I

want a career. Besides, men bore me. Buffer's a lot more scintillating than any of them."

Snip!

"You need to give them more than two weeks before you cast them aside. Fred's become a partner in his law firm. Junior partner, granted, but he's on the right trajectory. And handsome. And taken with you."

"Buffer is strong, handsome, dependable, adorable, faithful. What more could a girl want?" If a dog could smile, he just did. Iris scratched his chest.

The poor drooping rose petals were getting the brunt of her mother's frustration.

Pluck, pluck, pluck.

"You're a woman, Iris. Women don't have careers. They have husbands for financial security and love if you're very lucky. You'd better nab a husband now, while he'll overlook your wildness. Your looks will fade, my girl, and those gorgeous legs will be laced with spider veins some day. Then who in the world will deal with your wanton spirit?"

"A blind man might work, Mom. One who enjoys lively conversation and can't see my freckles. Speaking of which, a girl at work said washing your face in baby's wee will take freckles away. Do we know any babies? Honestly, I could think of nothing worse than a baby. OK, I can. Being tied to one man for eternity."

"Your independent thinking is unbecoming, child."

Iris tugged at the big furry ear as she looked up at the endless blue sky dotted with all sorts of interesting dress designs she might consider whipping up when heavenly blue material went on sale again. Hmm, she could almost feel the gathered chiffon.

She kicked at the ground to speed up the hammock's momentum, and the forward swing brought the house within spitting distance. Nicks and stains, chips and mold got closer and closer, like when she had a fever and a bad dream kept repeating.

Her mother's facade was crumbling. No wonder she wanted to marry off her only remaining asset. Or was she a liability? Iris guessed according to her mother, considering all this, any guy would do, as long as his pockets were well-lined.

She couldn't go that far to please her mother.

The thought crossed her mind that as a parent, it seemed you inevitably disappointed your offspring. And they you. Another reason *not* to have a child.

She had a vision of her parents together. How they'd adored each other.

Iris had an epiphany. The loss of her mother's husband must have been far worse than the loss of their father. Her mother must have been deathly afraid and desperately lonely and acutely aware that she would soon become average. "Average." The kiss of death in their colonial society, where status was everything. Could her steel-edged mother really be so deep? Here was a woman Iris hadn't thought to get to know. Could she be interesting? Layered? Onion-like? What a concept!

"OK, I'll go. What do you think I should wear?" Iris asked.

Her mother stopping plucking, looked up and smiled at her only daughter. Iris put the letter to her nose again and this time, smelled her brother's Brylcream, and she smiled back at her mother. All was right in the world.

From Home: 8th November, 1942.

Hi Big Brother,

As usual, loved your letter. Even took your advice and went out to meet a man. Mom was my date at the Hartenadys' party. I heard

*our mother laugh. It was a husky, joyous sound. She's surprising me
these days. Even called me "Jinx." Imagine! The first time she's ever
called me by Daddy's pet name. I've missed the endearment as much
as Daddy himself.*

*Oh, I digress. Well, it started off as the typical end-of-days party.
The shades of laughter, the lyrical (well, mostly!) piano, a
harmonica playing off-key and enthusiastic singing in varying keys
and degrees of talent. Boring!*

*There were a plethora of pilots, soldiers and sailors in dress
uniform, civilian men in suits and ties swirling around us, lighting
cigarettes and delivering fresh drinks long before our glasses were
empty. Of course, Mom was trying to get me off with Fred. He's film-
star good-looking with the personality of a flea. A dead flea. Live fleas
have the gumption to jump. He would be quickly squashed in our
steel-toe'd household.*

*I'd revamped an old favorite into a daring yellow art-deco
number (Sorry! I forgot you're a boy and would have no interest!).
Anyway, it hung to the floor. I knew it worked when mother
whispered: "Women are gasping at your daring, but secretly they
think you're wonderfully chic."*

*Well, I didn't stay in favor for long! A blond whipper-snapper
sauntered up and asked me what color I use to dye my hair. Dye? If I
was of the mind to dye my hair, it would be bloody platinum, not
bloody red!*

*I saw red, Brother, and you know how that goes! I furled my
yellow dress up from the hip as I said "My color's in a bottle?" I was
determined to prove a point as the silk moved up my leg, past my
knee, to my thigh. "I was born red all over, you mutt. I'll show you!"*

*Reluctantly, I admit, it was probably best for my reputation that
mother turned and yelled my name before I entirely exposed myself.
What gall of the girl! Presuming a woman dyes her hair is equal
only to asking a large-girthed girl when her baby is due!*

The usual long lecture ensued about curbing my red temper and how our mother brought me up, she didn't drag me up, as my embarrassing show had indicated. All this with a smile on her lips as a venomous whisper hissed in my burning ear.

My bloody hair. Bane of my life. But then there're the bloody freckles. You remember taking me to hospital after you found me using Dad's sandpaper on my nose? That didn't work, nor have any of the other outrageous "cures." Your telling me that I was like an Afghan in a lineup of black and yellow Labradors gave me hope that my uniqueness held some merit. Thank you for that. And for so much else.

Gregg, do you remember your old friend Robbie? He called me "a curious creature. Ravishing, rare, and quite, quite delicious." You socked him in the jaw and said, "Never talk about my sister like a piece of meat." I ran away and never told you I'd overheard, but Robbie's butcher-like comments often became my mantra. With Robbie's positive perspective of what I thought of as my ugly self, your encouragement and a whole lot of Pan-Cake (that's the new makeup in case news of this life-changing asset hasn't made it to war bunkers and aircraft hangers yet), I've finally accepted my carrot top and my freckles. Hell, I even defended my redness at the party. (Giggle) I've concluded I'm not interested in impressing anybody anymore. (Please consider my yellow-dress escapade an act of providing vital information only!)

Oh, again, I digress. So this striking man in uniform elbowed his way into our circle, his hand in his pocket, cool as a cucumber. A new face in town. Julian Kaiser has gaunt sexy features, a wide (but disappointingly thin) mouth. He's tall, older and intriguing, with eyes that are almost spooky they are such a light blue. Of course we teased him about being a "zed" away from being a Nazi. (Kaizer—in case my reference is too obscure—or Brother, you're losing your edge —tee hee.) He says he will be running the new POW camp in Maritzburg. Italians are being relocated from overflowing North African camps to our fair city. What a cheek! Enemies on our doorstep! The price we have to pay for being a British colony, I suppose.

All for now, dear Gregg. I love your letters. Can't wait for the next. I will report on my date with Julian to the Howick Falls in a couple of weeks. I bet you can't wait for the next installment! Blame our mother for not having another boy. You got a sister, and since you're my best friend (not counting Buffer), I need to share these tidbits with you. I give you complete permission to skip that which becomes too much for your masculine sensibilities. (tee hee)

Don't woo any girls who aren't Allies! You might become your mother's second favorite!

I love you,

Your Sunshine. xx

Lena was polishing the scuffed kitchen floor. Her scholar stood at the kitchen counter, staring at the headline. "Read it slowly. Remember to look at the word two letters at a time, then put them all together," she said officiously, not looking up.

"Pow camps in North Africa overpopulated. Select South African cities may become home to Italian pows in the new year." He made it through quite impressively. Lena smiled proudly. Fourfeet was excelling at The School of Lena.

------

8 December, 1942.

Hi Again Brother,

Loved your letter, as always. Sounds like you're headed to Italy. Try at all costs not to damage Venice. I dream about walking over the small bridges, water everywhere. Sigh, some day, if this war is ever over! Congratulations on becoming a "Pilot before Pontius." That's my brother! Heralded as an experienced flyer!

Guess what? I found an old book by Kahlil Gibran in the bookshelf while looking for a dress pattern. *The Prophet*. It must have been Dad's. So like him to be so introspective. Gregg, not only did the book make me feel close to him, reading it was a revelation. It addresses life's every eventuality, un-complicates each, then offers a solution or a balm. Amazing. You must read it. I'll keep it for you.

So, my confidant (tee hee), here's my report on my date with Julian, the one an "s," the spooky eyes and the cool-as-a-cucumber demeanor.

Our Howick Falls, cascading 300 feet over the lip of the cliff, never ceases to thrill me. It's so beautiful and dangerous. One of your favorite places—I thought of you as always—and it's perfect for a picnic.

Julian came prepared. Blanket, basket and brew. All the ingredients for a romantic dalliance. It didn't start well because when I asked him if he'd read *The Prophet*, he said he wasn't one for economics! And it didn't get better as the day wore on.

He was a different man to the devil-may-care, confident, cocky lieutenant-on-the-way-up I'd met weeks before.

WARNING! Here comes the girly stuff, so feel free to skip a few paragraphs.

I tried desperately to make conversation, to no avail, then figured I should let him kiss me so I could get that out of the way, and if it was less than expected, we could call it quits. No need to waste time. I have letters to write and dresses to design. I leaned in, but that didn't work. I thought I'd lost my allure.

So I reverted back to conversation. "What's the real reason you aren't fighting with the rest of our brave men overseas?" He said nothing but struggled with something in his trouser pocket and finally extracted his left hand and let it flop on the blanket.

Oh, Gregg. Nothing could have prepared me for the bright red, mangled mess flapping on the blanket like a newly caught fish. It was a scarlet-colored blob of meat with a few fingers attached. Not all, mind you.

I realized his cool-as-a-cucumber, hand-in-the-pocket persona was just a means to hide The Thing. I wondered if people saw it when we danced at the party, but the tiny dance floor was crowded, and a blue haze of smoke blurred most things. And by the deep, tight, crisscrossed lines of scar tissue, he'd had a long time to learn how to hide It.

Actually, I thought of how you always found a way to make me feel better and I tried, I really did. I made myself touch the thing, so he would think it didn't bother me. I gently picked up the red, mutilated hand from the blanket and held it in mine, so I could cover it up. I closed my eyes to stop from either throwing up or screaming bloody murder and running like the wind.

I asked what happened. His body crumpled as if his strings had been abandoned by the puppeteer. Eyes averted, he tried to pull his hand away, but I held on for dear life, if only to prove I could.

"Who did this to you?" I asked gently. It was as if floodgates opened.

"I was five. My mother secretly bought me a secondhand violin. A welcome escape from my always drunk, abusive father. I had to hide it from him lest my mother be blamed for spoiling me. I couldn't play it, but just one string at a time transported me away. He came home drunker than usual and earlier than expected. Mad as hell. He began hammering my mother. With his fist. I jumped onto his back. Tried to stop him. He flung me off, into the wall. But it worked. He stopped beating my mother. I ran to my room and was hiding my violin when he threw open the door. He was beyond furious when he saw it. He pulled the violin from under me. Imprisoning my hand on the wooden table. He used his other hand to bash my own with my prized instrument. Over and over.

"He screamed, 'Which of your mother's lovers gave this to you?'

The violin broke my skin. It cut deeper and deeper with each blow. I felt shards of old wood driven into my hand. 'Who? Tell me?' A splintering crash to match each question until my violin shattered into a million pieces. So did my hand. But not enough for him. He used the bow to zigzag deep into my tendons. Eventually we both passed out. For different reasons.

"My mother was too ashamed to take me to hospital. She bound my hand and prayed.

"When I could afford it, I went to see about surgery. It was fifteen years too late. Nothing they could do."

Oh, Gregg. Can you imagine? I felt abysmally sorry for him. What kind of person would I be if I showed my repulsion? I was still holding the meaty mess with both my hands. I was careful to only look into his pale blue eyes when I lifted the thing to my lips and managed to softly kiss my own hand. I hoped he had no feeling so he didn't notice I'd missed the actual target, and I came up with the first thing that came to my head: "You should be immensely proud of this hand."

So! With me fighting revulsion with the raw T-bone steak in my hand, the guy moves in for a kiss. I have kissed quite a few frogs, but this was of toad stature. Could be the circumstance added to my nausea. And I couldn't pull away; he'd think it was his hand!

Gregg, may I say it was the most unselfish thing I've ever done. I gave it a long minute. I was counting. Boy, did I want to run and run and run, but then I saw his meaty hand and all my Catholic guilt came back in droves.

Dad and you must have been whispering in my ear to form the words in my head, because I surprised myself by saying, "I know you have bravely lived with this for twenty-something years. Not that I noticed when I met you. Your hand was skillfully hidden. Truth is, that very hand saved your mother. Such a courageous act for a little boy. We must find a way to hide it, so that you need only share your moving story with those you choose to. My goal is to make your brave hand an asset, not a liability."

I was suddenly inspired. "I work at the haberdashery counter at Ross & Co. Style is my forte. I know how to camouflage bumps and imperfections. How about I get you two soft kid gloves, one smaller than the other, in black, the magical color that tricks the eyes, and you wear them all year round. No one will know about your hand. The distinction will give you an air of mystery."

Shame, Gregg. He seemed so very grateful and vulnerable. At that moment I wished he knew how to kiss. He's easy on the eye in a sexy, cold, dangerous kind of way and with gloves, I may never have had to see The Thing again.

I was on a roll. "Perhaps we could find something to hold in that, ahem, bigger hand, which would give it a function. I know that would make you feel better. You should feel proud, you're really quite a hero," I said, meaning it.

What's a girl to do? I certainly couldn't run screaming. It would devastate the man since I'm the only one with whom he's shared his story. Your sister, a martyr! I bet you never dreamed you'd see the day.

I miss you so.

Your Sunshine xx

Radio broadcast, May 19, 1943

Her mother had the radio on full blast and appeared to be swooning, as usual, at the sound of Winston Churchill's voice reporting to the British House of Commons:

"The sense of victory was in the air. The whole of North Africa was cleared of the enemy. A quarter of a million prisoners were cooped in our cages. Everyone was very proud and delighted. There is no doubt that people like winning very much."

Pietermaritzburg
   28 July 1943 — late afternoon

The radio in the living room blared: "Supreme Allied Commander and U.S. Army General Dwight D. Eisenhower urged the Italian people to withdraw from the Axis powers in the wake of the overthrow of Mussolini."

A crackle, then Churchill's distinctive voice: "You can have peace immediately, and peace under the honorable conditions which our governments have already offered you. We are coming to you as liberators. As you have already seen in Sicily, our occupation will be mild and beneficent. The ancient liberties and traditions of your country will be restored."

Was her mother going deaf? So young? Iris thought of yelling to ask her mother to turn the radio down, but she'd be scolded for her "unladylike" tone. Oh, what the hell. If cherub-faced Winston did it for her on full blast, that was fine too.

Iris was in a generous mood. It was her lucky week! Yesterday she saw the Bird Savior for the first time—or was it the hundredth time? In her dreams, perhaps? It felt so strange; he was new to her and old to her at the same time. Silly. She was likely just enchanted by the thought of a man she couldn't have. Strangely, that hadn't come into her thoughts before this moment, and it didn't have a place there. Where he was and where she was, what he was and what she was, had no bearing whatsoever on what she felt and what she felt from him. He felt like a piece of a jigsaw puzzle that connected perfectly: where she indented, he filled, and vice versa until together, they were a whole picture. *Ridiculous!*

Well, yesterday was a day she'd always remember because of him and the way she'd felt, but she'd better start mourning the fact that she'd never see the Bird Savor again. He was the bloody enemy and guess who, of all people, was guarding him to ensure he'd never escape?

She shivered and pulled the blanket around her shoulders, tucked Buffer in reluctantly, used her leg to give the hammock some swing, and turned to the letter in her hand—the *other* reason this was her lucky week.

15th May, 1943. (Black ink), Italy.

Hi Sunshine,

No wonder you dream of Venice. You're right! I flew over the other day and it's otherworldly in its magnificence.

I think of you too. Every single day. Getting post here is hit and miss. I only just got your last letter and the one written ages ago, I got just last week! Two letters from you in less than a fortnight? What a gift for a bloke. Your letters bring me home. Thank you.

I laughed till I contracted a hernia reading about your "Girls' card night"! Only you could have the balls (excuse me, been in the RAF too long!) to consider bringing together our pretentious mata and Lena to make up the essential three for cards! Who knew Philemon from the petrol station had such phenomenal appeal? That our mother opened up and described the essential ingredients for the perfect kiss (oh no, I don't want a visual of that, please!), let alone danced around the kitchen with you and Lena, was hard to imagine, but when I was able, I laughed myself into a coma. You two waking up, heads on Lena's cushiony stomach, was an image I'll take to my grave. Thanks to you, I'll go there laughing my ass off. (Isn't that so

American?) It was Cane Spirits, I realize, that made it such a wild night, but it was your balls (excuse me again) which got this party started in the first place. Well done, Sis!

Oh, good riddance to old meat-hand! It's about time! Your guilt had you hanging on for too many months. Disfigurement or not, the guy has some really odd tendencies and a chip the size of Italy on his shoulder. And Buffer didn't like him. That right there is enough reason to be rid of him. Listen to me, you did your time and then some. You found a way to camouflage his problem in the most distinguished manner, and I hope he wears it well after all the penance you paid.

She thought back to the day of her "release," as she now thought of it.

"Why can't you go to church on Easter Sunday, like the nice Catholic child I raised?" her mother clucked disapprovingly.

She'd decided that her date was not worthy of her last pair of silk stockings and replied absently in her mother's direction. "Now, Mom, you sound like Julian. He's dogmatic and narrow-minded. Thinks he's better than anyone else. Please don't you, the mother I've come to admire, remind me of the worst in him."

Iris smelled the hot cross buns toasting in the oven and her mouth watered. The aroma of sweet spices and raisins made her imagine the cross of icing, melting on the top of the bun. Oh goodness, she would slice one open and slather it with thick butter before she left. That was another indication that she had no interest in Julian. She'd never lost her appetite.

Iris disappeared into her cupboard and slipped on her newest creation. She turned dramatically to show it off, but the doorway was empty.

She turned to Buffer with arms spread in presentation. "Well? How do I look?"

She swore he grinned his approval. He never let her down.

An hour later, strolling through the city center holding Julian's "good" hand, her pantsuit turned heads. It was terribly daring for Maritzburg, and she felt daggers from the women as keenly as she did the ogles from the men, but Iris was comfortable in her non-conformity. Coco-inspired, Iris-embellished, the pantsuit was perfect for a day in the warm April sun. Wide striped legs were nipped in at the waist by a broad band of stripes going in the opposite direction. Vertical stripes continued up from her waist, giving the illusion of a fitted top, ending in a sweetheart neck and tied in a halter. The naughty twist that was her trademark? Her back was completely bare.

There was hustle and bustle as never before in her sleepy town. The Military Hospital of Oribi had been recently enlarged to a twelve-hundred bed hospital and convalescent depot for two thousand more. These imperial wounded troops hailed from various theaters of war all over Europe and North Africa.

Smells of spiced hot cross buns were everywhere in town, and boerewors, the South African invented sausage, was braaiing somewhere in the open air. She could taste the coriander of her succulent favorite food and vowed to ask Lena to stoke a braai for supper tonight. Meat was abundant in Pietermaritzburg because of the perfect farming conditions.

Julian's arm looped possessively over Iris's shoulders and stiffened every time a guy passed by. In the new order of things, that was quite often. Julian glared at a perfectly nice-looking chap whose smile she may have unwittingly returned. It was just a friendly gesture, for gosh sakes. Julian's overreaction spawned her fiery self, and she deliberately made eye contact with every good-looking passerby, rewarding their hungry looks with her best smile.

Iris could feel the heat of his hand through the thin kid glove on her shoulder. Thank the Lord, after the glove fitting, she'd never seen the mangled thing again. And she quite liked the soft leather texture on her skin, though it took some serious diversion to forget what lay beneath. Mind you, she didn't allow any under-clothing exploration, because his kiss had yet to really stir her girly hots. Perhaps one day she would find her Philemon from the petrol station.

Julian carried the lean whip in the larger gloved hand. It was a shrewd move, because his constant tapping of the switch took all the attention. It certainly gave him an air of authority, just as Iris had proposed. He was, she mused ironically, one of her most put-together creations. His self-confidence had soared with the new look. He was a far cry from the insecure broken man who'd sought her approval. Had he not been so cocky, she might have been thrilled for him.

In fact, that needy man had never reappeared, which made her wonder if he'd ever really been there at all. What did it matter? Today was the day. She just had to time it right.

Julian whined, "Here we are in the male hub of Africa. Seems every other Johnny is recovering. Almost always a wound worthy of the Victorian Cross. Then there are the all-powerful healers. All looking at my girl." Iris ignored him. She pulled him toward the large temple, where an eight-meter pit of red-hot embers had been constructed for the annual event to honor the Goddess Daupadi, who would "cool the coals and make them feel like flowers" for her devotees. The smell of Marsala curry tickled her nose, and she inhaled the heady richness.

She noticed that very few local whites stopped to watch the ceremony; most gave the spectacle a wide berth to avoid … what? Being contaminated by brown skin and petals?

"Why must we watch bloody body snatchers?" Julian complained.

Iris remembered hearing that term was used during the Boer War to describe volunteer Indian stretcher bearers. "That's appalling!" She pulled her hand away. "I think your 'S' in Keiser is really a 'Z' after all. You're a bigot, Julian. I despise bigots. South Africa is a melting pot of colors and cultures. That's what we're founded on. Get used to it or move to China!"

He stood in front of her to block her view so he was all she could see. "You still don't know when I am joking, Iris." He tried to take her arm, but she pulled away. He stroked the hand he managed to hang on to. "Spending time with you is my only true pleasure. You know how much I need you."

She chose to ignore the comment but to get under his skin another way. "By the way, as well as my own volunteer work, I start volunteering at the Oribi hospital two days a week for the store's war efforts." Her Scorpio sting was making up for lost time. In the last month, he'd frequently brought out that nasty little zinger in her tail.

"No way! I forbid it!" Julian spat between clenched teeth.

"*You forbid it?* Who the hell do you think you are? You have no right to tell me what I can and can't do. If you can't live with that, move on. If you can, for now, let's watch the fire walking!" She tried to pivot back to watch the ancient ceremony, but he caught her arm.

Julian's face was white with fury. His eyes were as cold as the snow-capped Drakensburg mountain peaks in late July. His jaw was so tightly clenched, it was surprising she could hear him spit out his next words: "Never. Ever. Ever talk to me that way again."

She was speechless as a thin bolt of fear chased from her brain down her spine and made her shiver. She knew she'd just witnessed the *real* Julian.

As quickly as the avalanche of his rage appeared, so it evaporated. Iris was still facing him, agog. He took her hand and twirled her around so she was in front of him facing forward. He crossed his arms possessively over her shoulders, so close behind her she could feel his manhood throbbing against the small of her back.

The revelation was white-hot and terrifying. Anger turned him on.

She tried to jut her pelvis forward, so she didn't feel him hard against her. Enough! She pivoted in his arms to face him and couldn't hide her loathing when he mistook her movement for more intimate contact, thrusting his pelvis further into her. She tried to step away, but he held her fast, and her repulsion at the feel of him was the impetus she needed.

"Julian, we have exhausted our possibilities. You are handsome and sexy, but we have nothing in common. I'm going to find my own way home right now. I wish you well."

He held her tighter. She dared not look at him. She tried to pull away. His vice grip tightened enough to make her reflexively cry out: "You're hurting me."

"You OK, lady?" A private wanted to know as he tapped Julian on the shoulder. Julian's fury transferred to the gallant soldier, and he reached for the whip he held vertically between his thighs so he could hold Iris with both arms. His grip on her slackened. Just enough.

She ducked and rushed away, pushing her legs to their limits in her high heels. She needed as much distance between her and Julian as possible to feel safe again. She heard the commotion behind her. No doubt Julian was using the whip on the innocent soldier. Her frightened, fast-beating heart slowed in direct proportion to the distance between her and her ex-boyfriend.

Soon after the household knew of the relationship's demise, Mrs. Fuller told her wayward child that she was looking forward to an avalanche of visitations from "new" men, preferably doctors and surgeons from all the colonies who staffed the new hospital, who might be blind to Iris's liberal ways, strong enough to climb over her daughter's solid wall of resistance, and prove to be excellent marriage material.

Iris sighed. *There are none so deaf as those who will not hear.*

Now Iris shivered as Julian's face intruded on her thoughts, and she quickly went back to the comfort and safety of her brother's familiar hand.

Good riddance, Sunshine. Think nothing more of it.

You are D-O-N-E.

Give Lena and Sofie a big hug for me. I miss those great big smiles and their bigger hearts. I always thank God that you have others close by who love you. I'm just a thought away.

And don't worry, there's no keeping a good flyer down!

Love always, little sissy. G.

How she adored his letters. He knew her so well and knew just what to say to make her feel better. She could tell him anything. Wait! She certainly couldn't tell her fiercely patriotic brother that she had felt at one with a prisoner of war. An Italian, no less! She closed her eyes and breathed deeply, trying to quell her uneasiness, and as if it was her pacifier, she found Buffer's ear and twirled it.

"Klein Miesies!"

Instantly on attack, Buffer, likely embarrassed that he'd been caught unawares, barked ferociously at Fourfeet from next door.

"Down, Buffer. It's all right." The barking eased to a low growl. "You scared us to death, Fourfeet. Everything all right?" The young Zulu held out a grubby rolled-up page of newspaper.

"It's for you, Klein Miesies."

"What in the world?" Her hand didn't move. "Where the hell did you get that thing?"

"Solomon works in hospital at pow camp." He pronounced it like a boxing blow. "He cleans floors. Man comes in with sore head and ... " he ran out of English words but twirled his finger around the circumference of his head.

"Bandage?" It was like playing charades. Iris was enjoying herself.

Fourfeet nodded. "When doctor looked at Bandage Man, another pow man gave paper to Solomon and say soft, 'Important. Take to young lady in town. Hair like sunset.' " Solomon gave to Sponon. Sponon to me."

Iris swore a gnat buzzed right into her open mouth. She coughed.

"How do you know it's for me?"

Fourfeet looked at Iris like she might be a little slow. He tried again. "Klein Miesies, you are only 'sunset head' in town." He proffered the grubby newspaper again, and she snatched it from him.

"What a gift you are. Thank you, Fourfeet."

"Gift, Klein Miesies?"

"Like a present. People see you and feel happy. Today you made me feel like it's Christmas. Thank you." Fourfeet's grin was as bright as the star on top of the Christmas tree.

Iris tried everything. It was just one page, front and back with articles about the Battle of the Bismarck Sea, a few local obituaries—no one she knew, thank goodness—an advert for her very own Ross & Co., news of a bomb landing in a London shelter, killing 173, and a big to-do about Hitler and Mussolini coming together in Salzburg.

She looked for everything. There were no letters underlined like spies used to do. No deliberate mud stains on words. Nothing.

She leaned back in the hammock, re-covered herself and Buffer with the crocheted blanket, and picked up the newspaper as she absently sought Buffer's ear.

Then she saw them.

Deliberate pin pricks underlined words. She sat bolt upright, but the secret letters disappeared. Down again, she held the newspaper into the dying winter sunlight and pulled her pencil and sketch pad close, jotting down each underlined word or letter.

My eyes sees you for first time, yet my heart knows you long time. I am your enemy but I long to see you. My name P-I-E-T-R-O.

He spelled out his name using the Ross & Co. advert. How could he know? Simple. His heart knew hers, as hers knew his.

5

CURSED MEMORIES

28 July 1943

Pietro didn't want to leave Antonio, so instead he wore a trench inside the tent's dirt floor. What if that newspaper fell into Tap Tap's hands? Surely he wasn't smart enough to see Pietro's pin code? He had no doubt that if it got into the right hands, his Rossa would know exactly how to read it. But then, what would she do with it? How would she feel? Had he imagined it all? NO!

Back and forth. Back and forth.

He forced himself to think of other things ...

Pietermaritzburg
23 June 1943

There was a huge commotion outside the tent. So huge that Pietro left his vigil of Antonio to check it out. A bedraggled bunch of about a hundred newly captured prisoners was being herded through the main gate.

Thirty-eight of them carried musical instruments.

The sight of the instruments stirred up yet another raw emotion in Pietro, and he rushed to find Sergeant Rogers. "Per favore. If Tap Tap see," Pietro pointed to the instruments, "he destruction!" Letting his enemies know he spoke good English was not in Pietro's best interests.

Mercifully, Rogers called together a small posse, who joined Pietro in digging a three-foot-deep, twenty-foot-long trench under a protected portion of the chicken coop's overhang. The instruments were carefully laid inside and covered with anything they could find to protect them: potato sacks, a dead man's clothes, anything to cover saxophones, guitars, cellos and violins. They carefully patted dirt over the trench and camouflaged their hiding place by placing the picnic benches strategically over newly churned soil.

In the midst of the flurry, Pietro blinked, as he thought he saw a familiar face. He shook his head and looked again. *Dio mio.* It was Stef. "*Stefano!*" He shouted.

The familiar face turned. Stef's war-hardened face split in a bony smile. "My God, Pietro! Not since Teatra Alla Scala. Word was that you were dead in Abyssinia. Girls were mourning all over Italy." The two hugged.

"Only the good die young. Where do you boys come from?" Pietro asked.

"Eritrea. The whole orchestra was captured while performing."

"Ah, Stef ... I can hardly believe ... what news of Venice?"

"Germans have taken occupation. You remember Professor Carulli? He hanged himself rather than hand over the list of Jews living in Venice. They were smuggled out and likely spared."

"We knew him as a good man. What of Arbit? Brilliant baritone! Mirella?" Pietro asked.

"I don't know of Arbit, but Mirella was devastated. Contemplated slitting her wrists on hearing of your demise." Pietro couldn't even smile. It meant nothing. But Stef was not to know that he had died inside. "But don't kid yourself. As soon as that Danish tenor Melchior made his jovial appearance, your vivid face, undeniable charm and rich voice dimmed into oblivion."

His friend's beloved, familiar face erased the years of deprivation and disappointment, and just for the briefest moment, Pietro touched his old self, the bon vivant of Venice, and for a millisecond he felt carefree. But the feeling was gone as quickly as it had come.

"You look like shit. Where are your shiny shoes? Where *are* your boots?" Stef's mouth was agape in disbelief. He knew the power of the boot as far as his old friend was concerned.

"Boots and music. Music and boots. They were destroyed at the same time."

Stef was confused.

"An evil butcher rules the camp. He banned music. We live in disconnected squalor. There is just one man I give a shit about, and his three marbles are scrambled."

Pietro hated that his friend's face showed sympathy. And then Pietro remembered that Stef was the only one who'd ever really known him, so it was allowed. Fear surged through him suddenly. "Don't tell them who I am, Stef. Promise me. I have no desire to do anything but exist. I don't want them thinking I will change things for them."

"Good God. You look like something an alley cat vomited up, and still you have the ego of a ... words escape me. You think you're the musical Jesus whose disciples will wither and die without your voice to lead them to heaven?"

Pietro looked deep into his old friend's eyes, and he heard

the deadness of his voice for the first time and was distantly surprised by it. "Understand, old friend, I no longer have a voice to save even myself. I don't give a fuck what happens to me or you or anyone else. I no longer need you to remind me of how little I actually matter. Find someone else to bring down to size. I can't go down any lower."

Pietro walked away from his only friend, his feet dragging in the dirt. Lifting them up was just too much effort.

Pietro headed straight for the chicken coop and lay down in a fetal position as far as he could from the buried instruments. But to no avail. Damn, you Stef! Memories flooded in...

La Fenice Opera House, Venice, Italy
  1938

In the midst of his dramatic aria, Pietro Saltamachio smelled money. And he loved it.

His "poor artiste's lament" had lasted too many years: "I don't need to get paid for doing what I love. I refuse to be a prostitute of commerce!" Bah! There was nothing noble or enlightening about being hungry or rejected.

He'd paid his dues. It had taken training his instrument day and night, night and day for fifteen years, taking advantage of every possible spotlight, and understanding with absolute clarity that, without his voice, he was invisible. All of this had brought Pietro Saltamachio to this most celebrated stage in all of Italy.

This memorable night he shared the marquee, the bill, the stage and the honor with Canio, the tormented character he played. No. No. He never *played* a character. He *was* Canio. Until the curtain fell.

Pagliacci. A chance to revisit the light and the dark, the comedy and the tragedy of life. Pietro had tasted life's contradictions and ironies. He understood Canio's torture.

As his rich tenor boomed out an agonizing aria, Pietro dramatically slathered white clown makeup on Canio's face ... or was it his own? Nonetheless, a perfect parallel—the tormented Canio pretending to be a carefree clown.

For an instant, the smell of opulence was replaced by sickly perfume and vomit. Drunk-vomit or "Oh-merde-I'm-pregnant!" vomit. Usually a combination.

The smell is of money, class and appreciation, Pietro, not puke, fear and disappointment. Dio mio. Breathe in. Smell peppermint and leather, dark chocolate and fine rice powder dusted on imperfect noses.

Together, he and Canio pushed long, vibrating notes from the very pit of Pietro's stomach, through open lungs, up to the waiting throat, where Canio and Pietro as one delivered perfection through quivering vocal cords.

The delicate shaded lights to the left and right of every box seat in the famed opera house were dimmed demurely to focus attention away from the opulence and splendor of the theater and toward the stage spotlight.

But then it struck him: The solid gold leaf winking at him was not for his audience's benefit, but for the artiste's. All for him. The act of dimming the luxurious surroundings to focus full attention onto the performer promised the elegant audience—who'd paid more for one ticket than Pietro had earned in three years—that the person on that stage was worthy of their undivided attention.

He knew in this most important moment of his life, he had to be better than he had ever been. He had to push every boundary. Great wasn't good enough. Spectacular was the least he must be to keep him performing on this caliber stage for a lifetime.

He pulled back his controlled vocal instrument and felt the audience collectively jolt, because the rich velvet had been snatched away.

Trying something new and reckless in this great forum? Not just ballsy, but quite, quite mad. He found himself savoring their surprise for as long as he dared before he let his timber and richness flow back, ever so slowly, like a deep, rich, lazy river of Swiss chocolate. Thick, slow and unstoppable, he gathered them up from the brink, one, another, a full row, the middle section, the whole auditorium. They clung tightly to him, invading his every pore, as together they swayed and gently changed direction. Easy and languid. Then without warning, up, up, up to full volume, beyond what was expected, and up yet up another rung and another. Yes ... yes ... yes ... and they climaxed over the hill. Together. A delicious, satisfying union.

"La Commedia e finita!" The comedy is finished.

The orchestra was silent.

Canio lingered.

When the applause was not forthcoming, Pietro opened his eyes. Canio was gone. Pietro stood alone, waiting. Naked and vulnerable.

Not a sound.

Don't let me show how afraid I am. Think of something, anything.

He usually loved the clarity of the moments after his final note when he slipped from character into himself, before the applause began and the house lights went up. He must be a fairly decent Catholic, since God always allowed him to savor these sublime seconds in slow motion so he could witness the minutiae of the results of his performance: young, delicate tongues wetting red lips, silk fans cooling puffy, powdered, middle-aged faces. He'd come to expect the men's stoic reaction; macho was what macho was.

How long did that thought take? And still no hint of a response? Now, he was just damn terrified. He had never run off a stage before, but it seemed this was something he should consider. *But not yet. Just wait a second more before you turn and run like hell.*

Silence.

Dio mio. Dio mio.

He needed to blink. He must look like a bug-eyed baboon. Served him right for taking them beyond the brink on impulse. And then he had the audacity to take them further, much further, to a place he'd never dared go alone, let alone leading a whole auditorium. Nay, not just an auditorium, the crème de la crème of society, whom he schlepped along for the ride! *What have I done in this most prestigious opera house in all of Europe?*

Blink or run? He closed his eyes instead.

He wasn't worthy of this magnificent stage.

Can't run; my legs won't move. Tried them. Our Father who art in heaven, I will never take this gift you have given me—my voice—for granted again, if only …

A load roar. He opened his eyes.

En masse, the audience stood and they were clapping, nay, *beating* their hands together. Gloriously, responsively impolite. The thunderous applause was louder than he had ever heard for anyone. Ever.

A standing ovation? *Dio mio.* Relief had never been so sharp and all-consuming. Was their clapping really that loud, or was his heart beating in his ears because it had burst out of his chest?

"Bravo, bravo!" reverberated through the distinguished theater.

Thank you, Jesus!

His body collapsed at the waist. He bowed, deeply.

Still bowing, he lifted his head ever so slightly, and looked at the shoes lined up in the front row. The men's shoes were top-quality leather, measured, manipulated, massaged and hand-made to perfection, then shined for reflection. Reflection not just of the shoes, but of the man himself.

Perhaps now he could have good shoes. Not just clean shoes. Perhaps expensive shoes.

Applause was still going. They were still standing. Here In La Fenice Opera House. *Praise be!* His grateful grin was so big he didn't care that he was not a single shade of nonchalant. He stood upright and his smile burst as the surreal became real, and he reveled in this actual moment he became a star. The audience smiled back and clapped louder still. He heard shrill whistles. His genteel audience's finesse was gone, such was their moment of unbridled pleasure.

As he bowed again deeply, his chest expanded, bursting with a new surge of joy as he realized he would never again be invisible.

The after-party was a heady mixture of glitter and gush, smoke, expensive perfume, strong liquor, laughter and lipstick. And he basked in it all.

He breathed in the thrilling headiness—opening his mouth to absorb every nuance to taste, to savor and recall forever. His future was ...

"What you always wanted, Pietro." His old friend, Stefano, was at his side, grinning.

Pietro slapped the little guy so hard with the joy of seeing his trusted face that Stefano nearly tipped over his drink. "Scusi, Stef." Pietro laughed, "Can you believe it? You playing lead violin right there in that famous orchestra pit and me, the other thing?" Stef shook his head in amazement, and Pietro's head mirrored the movement, as old friends tend to do. Their blissful reverie was interrupted by a tall, striking blonde in what seemed to be a gold dress painted straight onto her naked body.

"Come with me, blue eyes." Her voice was husky, and sex oozed from every pore as she grabbed Pietro's arm. "Someone wants to meet you."

Understandably, her wish was his command.

Halfway through the crowd, Pietro turned to Stefano and with the shrug of his shoulders intoned: "I don't care where she's taking me." The heady intoxication continued as Pietro recognized famous faces from business and the arts, even foreign heads of state and a sheik, as he was led through the smoky room. He was amazed that no matter what the loftiness of their social or political status, people seemed to stop talking as he passed. A passage was created. It felt like the Red Sea parting. He assumed the golden girl was the cause. She was quite stunning and ...

No. No.

It couldn't be.

Mussolini? He chastised himself silently: *No. Don't be foolish, Pietro. How quickly your head inflated. Our Venetian impersonators get better all the time.* He scrutinized the large bald head in front of him, looking for flaws in the disguise. But no. It really looked like ... *Santa Maria!* It *was* Il Duce!

Italy's revered leader attended *his* performance? *Dio mio!*

Pietro shook his head to clear it, but the powerful man was still there, just ten paces away. Amazing that his weak legs were still moving forward, following the blonde.

And then there stood Pietro in front of Mussolini himself. Tall, shoulders the size of an army tank, bald as a coot and unsmiling.

Pietro's gut did a flip-flop. Unsmiling? What was wrong? The audience really seemed to like him, but the stern, disapproving dark orbs that held his own told a different story.

It was as if pure fright had glued Pietro's eyes open. He wanted to look away but couldn't. And then ...

The bald statue's face erupted in a smile as big and refreshing as Lake Garda.

"Pietro Saltamachio. I thank you. Italy thanks you. God thanks you for your tenor, which makes angels tune their harps."

Pietro heard nothing, but he saw cheeks puff as smiling lips moved over teeth, and he knew he was in good favor. *Grazie a Dio!* The larger-than-life leader put out his hand.

Pietro took his first breath since he'd laid eyes on Il Duce, and grasped the pig paw in his own, no doubt sweaty, hand. They shook.

"A brilliant performance, young man. Your career in Italy, nay, Europe and the world, awaits. You are the proof that Italy is superior. Your operatic supremacy will make them wonder what other surprises we Italians have up our sleeves."

They were still shaking hands, looking each other in the eyes when, without further ado, Mussolini turned on his heel, the golden girl tucked her hand into the proffered "V" of the leader's inner elbow, and they regally left the room, followed by a beefed-up entourage.

Pietro stood rooted to the spot for a good few minutes, savoring his every heightened sense and inhaling the swirling power Il Duce left in his wake.

When it finally wafted away, he opened his eyes and turned to face the hordes of elegant onlookers. Every eye in the room was upon him. One group, then another, began to applaud. Then, as one, the hall erupted in short staccato claps as hands joined in unison. They began to chant. "Pietro. Pietro. Pietro."

He smiled wanly to show appreciation, but his body was

overwhelmed by a new and frightening experience. He shook from head to toe. He had seen it and its debilitating results countless times in the wings, but he couldn't relate. He was born to entertain. His body and mind propelled him on stage, any stage. The feeling of euphoria was like a drug to him, stimulating and powerful.

Stage fright. Secretly he doubted that this thing existed and thought the cause was more a lack of preparation than fear. How wrong he'd been.

He resorted to the only thing that calmed him. A balm to his soul, "O Sole Mio" had magical powers: It soothed. It comforted. It healed.

Through the din, they'd never hear. Hopefully they'd never suspect his great fear.

"Che bella cosa na jurnata 'e sole, n'aria serena doppo na tempesta! Pe' ll'aria fresca para già na festa ... "

The time-honored song lulled him until Stef's familiar smile emerged from the sea of faces, and Pietro was reassured and his confidence returned.

Stef was his safe place. His only home.

Venice, Italy
Late 1940

Pietro chose his mask carefully: black leather with an elaborate swirl of gold and crystals over one eye, tied behind his head with a silk ribbon. The half-mask was favored by upper-class Italians at carnivals, and he'd earned the right to wear it.

Since his debut at the La Fenice Opera House, his immediate embrace by Venice's crème de la crème was a blissful blur for him. He'd adjusted as if he was born into their sphere of opulence. The oppressive, slummy dressing rooms with the aroma of desperation were only in his nightmares now, enabling him to wake and forget.

He and Stef never talked about those days. They were best suppressed.

Pietro paused on the night-shaded cobbled street, hoisted his foot on to a small retaining wall and polished his already gleaming, expensive, handmade shoe with great precision.

There were two things his mother had taught him.

One was to be a good Catholic. She took him to mass every Sunday, no matter how late her sordid profession kept her busy on Saturday night. It was the only time he spent alone with his mother. He learned all the hymns and found a penchant for Latin, but the most sacred thing about church was the two hours he had his mother's attention, and he saw what she might have been. She wore the same simple dress, perhaps her only one, every Sunday. During mass, all he did was gaze at her, as if she were brand new. Without her thick makeup, she was the epitome of innocence and beauty. Though she spoke only of what he should learn from the day's sermon, the time with her was as sacred as the holy communion. He was sad, though, that unlike the other little boys his age with their doting mothers, there was no physical bond with his own, no hand-holding or hugging or head-patting. But she must have liked him enough to have him come along. So, that was a good thing.

The other thing she taught him was that shiny shoes were the mark of a real man. "A man can get away with anything," she promised her son, "as long as he's charming and his shoes look cared for."

Through the years, he wore hand-me-downs that never quite fit properly, but he could always wiggle his toes, and starting from the age of three, Pietro made sure they were shiny as new coins. That was in great part because every couple of nights, his mother drunkenly waggled her finger in front of his nose, warning: "One scrap of dirt on those hard-earned shoes, Pietro, and even I may doubt you are The Great Caruso's son." He was sure his heart had never thumped harder the first time he heard her declaration about his heritage, and brushed his kid's size fours till his arm felt it would fall off.

Pietro concentrated on his charm. Testing it out on the dressing-room ladies was the ultimate challenge. They'd heard everything, so he was always forced to come up with a fresh approach, until he learned that being himself was the most winning way of all.

Pietro was always ripe for the stories the ladies of the dressing room fed him.

"He was still handsome at the end of his career when he met your mama in Naples."

"Aah, The Great Caruso. What a loss to the world."

"What's 'a loss'?" he asked.

"He died. August 2nd, 1921. A day every Italian will remember."

"He's dead?" Pietro was mortified. Should he and his mother not have gone to church to pay their respects?

"Many mourned."

"Did Mama cry?" Pietro asked, wide-eyed.

"Bawled her eyes out," someone said sarcastically, but the tone was lost on him.

"Tell me about The Great Caruso and Mama."

"She was barely sixteen and a great beauty."

"Do you know when he was poor, early in his singing career, he failed to pay a claque in Naples and he was booed off the stage?"

"What's a claque?" the boy asked.

"People who get paid to applaud."

"I want them to clap because they want to clap for me, not because they are paid!"

"Bravo, my boy, bravo."

"And later everybody clapped for him and he didn't have to pay?"

"Oh, yes, he was Italy's darling. He sold a million or more records. They called him 'The Man with the Orchid-Lined Voice.' But he swore never to sing in Naples again and would return only for the local spaghetti."

"And Mama smelled like spaghetti and meatballs?"

The women stopped what they were doing to laugh at his innocence.

"She smelled like spring," said Stef's mother. She was always so very kind.

"It was only after she 'met' him she smelled like garlic and meat." The bawdiest of the women moved her fist this way and that along her jaw line. Pietro couldn't work out why she was pushing her cheek out with her tongue at the same time.

All but Stef's quiet mother laughed at this strange behavior.

Pietro got to find out more about his mother in her absence than she ever shared with her only son. The youngster would pump the ladies for stories about her night after night, while she was on the stage doing what, apparently, all mothers did.

"And then what, tell me, tell me."

"We've told you the story a hundred times."

"A hundred and one then, please, please."

"Your mother was lithe and alluring." It was Stef's mother again.

"And he loved her very much." The thin blonde thrust her hips back and forth, and he thought she was practicing for her stage performance.

"Well, he surely loved what she did *to* him," the brunette

muttered, not lifting her head from the difficult task of rouging her nipples.

Most of the women chortled, but not Stef's petite mother. She knelt down and wrapped her arms around him. "The real truth, Pietro, is that The Great Caruso only had eyes for your beautiful mother."

"Then why did he leave us?" Pietro scowled. It was the only way he knew to mask the water squirting from his eyes.

"Because many women needed the love of The Great Caruso." Stef's mom said softly.

"But we were alone, Mama and me."

"And then *we* found you," whispered Stef's mom, who was the only one left in the conversation. "And you're well on your way to singing just like him. You are doing him proud."

His vocation started when one of the ladies missed the opening bars of her number, the compare plopped a hat on his head and a cane in his hand, carried him to the wings, then pushed him on stage where the spotlight found him.

He'd been singing to his father's records since he could talk; the famous man's voice was everywhere! On the gramophone in the dressing room, on the radio. He knew all the words, so it wasn't a stretch for him, and besides, he was just doing what he was born to do. One had responsibilities as the son of the "The Man with the Orchid-Lined Voice." He even taught himself how to imitate the cadence of his father's voice. After all, it was his plight.

He became a regular, and his stage training began in earnest amid the thick smoke of the music hall. When he was old enough to understand, he realized that his nearly nightly appearances had less to do with the velvet of his young voice and more do with the antics of the "dancers" before they got to the dressing room. They were either too drunk, too pregnant or too beaten up to make the stage. And so it was that though he knew that the spotlight was his by default, he believed it was The Great Caruso that kept him there because he earned it.

Young Pietro chose only to think about the man wearing the shiniest shoes in the hall, watching Pietro proudly from the dark pit that was "the audience." If he closed his eyes after his song, during the strong applause (which surprised everybody, because the randy audience had not paid to admire a young twerp sing his heart out), he swore he could hear The Great Caruso say, "Well done, my son." That the voice came from heaven instead made it even more compelling. As he grew older and more aware of the limited possibilities for his future, the only thought that consoled him was that he'd inherited the genes of the greatest tenor who ever lived.

But when he was around ten he heard his mother, a few sheets to the wind on cheap sherry, confessing to her best friend of two weeks, that when Caruso left town and she'd found out she was pregnant, she'd had an abortion.

Hidden behind the rack of feathers and sequins, tasseled nipple caps and grubby bras, Pietro felt the tender fiber of his being shatter, starting in his chest, up through his vocal cords to his throat, his tongue, his brain. He felt as if he would pass out. The motivation for his pathetic existence and the only hope for his dismal future had been that his operatic genes would hold him in good stead.

His mother wouldn't shut up: "Well, back to his shrew of a wife he went, and though it was tempting to bring a Little Caruso to term, what was the use? A nondescript but kind enough John, who was satisfied by my hands and my mouth while I recovered from the abortion, paid for a month's worth of accommodation when I'd nowhere to go. Of course, the John expected to get paid in full once I was ripe and ready after two weeks, and so, *voila!* There came Pietro!" she'd exclaimed sarcastically.

Stefano bumped blindly into Pietro, pushing acrid thoughts of his youth mercifully out of his head. They were on their way to Pietro's impromptu carnival, and by God, he would enjoy every minute! Stef stumbled again on the cobblestones, landing on his posterior. Poor little guy couldn't see a thing through the costume of The Plague Doctor.

Pietro hauled Stef up. "Your outfit becomes you. You look taller!"

A hollow curse pulsed though the long beak as he righted himself. It was a macabre costume choice, but Stef's would be the most popular at the carnival.

A little dog came trotting toward them, tail wagging so profusely, it broke into Stef's limited vision. The soft-hearted dog-lover couldn't resist. Off came the hideous headpiece, and he knelt to pick up the mangy mutt, hugging her tightly as she licked his nose.

"This is your kind of woman, Stef. Hairy and obliging. You should hold on to her."

"You know, old friend, you've become a *testa di cazzo!* I liked you much better when you knew your *merda* stank. Bring back my modest friend with a dream and well-kept shoes," Stef complained.

Pietro laughed, "You call me the head of a penis and still I love you! Ah, maybe you're right. But it feels good to be on top, and I don't intend to fall easily from grace. Ever. And I always want you along, my old friend. You, your violin and your hairy woman of the moment. And leave my shoes alone."

The dog lay blissfully in Stef's arms, and Pietro leaned in to scratch the tatty ears. "You are kind and true. You humble me." Pietro's voice was choked with sincerity.

"Somebody must. It might as well be me," grumbled Stef.

It had been Stef who was there to save Pietro when he found him crumpled underneath the hat stand, still hidden by haphazardly thrown costumes and soiled underwear.

"I am not Caruso's son. I have no gift. I am nobody, Stef." Tears poured down smooth ten-year-old cheeks. Stef's own eyes misted. He'd never seen such heartbreak, and in a dressing room full of desperate women, he'd seen a whole lot.

Stef knew that what he said next would affect Pietro's life forever. It was a tremendous responsibility, but as his friend, Stef was Pietro's only salvation. Stef's own mother was performing, and nobody else cared enough about him to say the pivotal words that would keep him on course.

Stef stood up, knocking over the hat stand, but none of the wearers gave the colored costumes or the boys the courtesy of so much as a look.

The slight boy put hands on his hips in typical scold-style, and in his gruffest voice, he said: "Pietro Saltamachio. Listen to me. For seven years you have been entertaining lustful men who only came to see tits and derrieres. And yet, you, Pietro, made them sit up and listen. The opera you learn like Einstein learns mathematics. You use your voice to delight these men, many of whom are wealthy and some even well-bred. You've made them stand up in unison and cheer for you. Does that not tell you that you have a gift? Does that not confirm that one day kings and heads of state will shake your hand or kiss you on both cheeks after each performance?"

Pietro had stopped crying, and his eyes focused. Stef lost no time. Ducking through the manager's legs, he whispered to the *compare*.

When the sexy music stopped, from the dressing room the boys heard, "And now lady and gentlemen"—the compare fancied himself a comedian—"for your great pleasure and by popular demand, our very own Pietro Saltamachio, Crown Prince of Opera."

There was a decent show of applause. Stef pulled Pietro up by the arm. "Do it, Pietro. Go and do your best and see for yourself that you don't need Caruso to be great. You have been great without him since before you were born."

Pietro shook his head.

The comedian was getting restless. His jokes were getting worse.

Stef picked up his precious violin. "Come. Don't let me make a fool of myself on my own. Pietro, if you do this, you can do anything. Prove to me. Prove to your mother. Prove to dead Caruso that you don't need his pompous seed. Do it the only way you have ever done it. *Your way.* Let's go!"

He hauled Pietro to the stage by his shirt, pushed him in front of the microphone and began playing "O Sole Mio" on his violin. Pietro was so conditioned by years of performing and the feeling of being important and special on this stage, that for a minute he forgot he didn't have the genes to support his talent.

And he sang his heart out.

As the dirty old men and lustful younger ones stood in unison to applaud his talent, Stef whispered to Pietro, "You see, my friend? Fuck Caruso. You've never needed him. You are important all on your own."

They put their masks back on, and Pietro, followed by the Plague Doctor and his newly acquired girlfriend, wove through the unusually dry, cobbled stone streets toward St. Mark's Square. *Cazzo!* Was that a Blackshirt in his peripheral vision? Pietro pulled Stef by his cape behind the nearest building.

"Blackshirt" was the nickname for Fasci di Combattimento, usually ex-soldiers whose job it was to bring in line those who opposed Mussolini. These thugs maintained an iron rule and always found innovative ways to debase and publicly humiliate those who did not conform.

Gratefully undetected, Pietro and Stef continued quickly and silently over small bridges with lapping dark waters, past wet concrete buildings emitting the odor of slow, wet decay. Pietro inhaled the odor deeply, like expensive opium. Venice. Pietro and Stef's home of choice, where they could pretend that success had been easy.

As a boy, Stef spent much of the time with his maternal grandmother, but when the elder was sick, then too old, Stef came to play with him in the pungent, dingy dressing room. Young spirits, kindred by their mothers' dark professions.

They spent their youth swatting the chips off each other's shoulders. Pietro had no idea what he would do without Stef. Stef was the parachute holding fast to Pietro's free-falling recklessness, reeling him in as needed, and stopping him from plummeting with heady abandon to his own destruction.

They reached Piazza San Marco, and Pietro was struck again by its formidable beauty. The impressive, centuries-old square with its hundreds of arches was awash with cobblestones and adorned in marble. The intricately chiseled St. Mark's Basilica and the tall clock tower, about a hundred feet away from the gently lapping Grand Canal, completed two corners of the square. This was the spot where every civil and religious ceremony took place, and it was here the Venice Carnival was held for centuries before it was banned by Mussolini.

And what a terrible shame that was.

Without the substantial revenue the wild carnival generated, thanks to droves from all over Europe who came to revel in her colorful freedoms, there was little to pay for Venice's inevitable, disastrous water erosion, which pulled constantly at her centuries-old buildings and her many bridges.

All the residents of the many islands resented their government's detachment and ached over Venice's neglect. Pietro, with his newfound celebrity, thought it was his job to rectify the situation in his and Stef's adopted home.

The friends walked briskly toward the northern arches, scattering the constant parade of pecking pigeons in their wake. Pietro smelled pasta and fresh tomato with basil and garlic and his mouth watered, but he was distracted by the mercifully dry streets in the square.

"You see this, Stef? God has condoned the carnival with the low tide."

"It's called the moon, Pietro. The moon controls the tides. God controls the moon. Your loftiness does not reach all the way up to heaven."

Pietro jabbed him in the ribs. "Yet, Stef. Yet. That's coming. I'll keep going straight up. Watch!" He was really only half-joking as he put his fingers to his lips for a shrill whistle.

As if by magic, the Piazzo came to life.

Colorful, costumed, masked and painted men and women oozed out of every crevice. In the fading light, acrobats back-flipped, bearded ladies preened, accordion players swayed, tightrope walkers secured their cords of choice between fragile looking T-bars, ballerinas twirled, belly dancers jingled, mimes mimicked and musicians of every style and instrument warmed up.

And by that very same magic, townspeople—barristers, thieves, men in uniform, prostitutes, housewives, tourists and businessmen—amassed around the perimeter of the square to enjoy the enchantment they had been so long denied.

Some of them wore costumes, and most wore masks. Dozens of people looked like Stef's Plague Doctor, but no other carried a limp, happy dog in his arms. Pietro's grin couldn't be contained. "It's back, Stef. The carnival's back! Let's see if we can keep it here."

Pietro didn't have long to marvel at the cacophony of a million carnival sounds. The rambunctious noise brought the Blackshirts running toward the square from every direction.

"Merda. Too soon, too soon," Pietro shouted.

The ominous presence of the Blackshirts brought the gaiety to an abrupt halt.

Though seconds before, they'd been rooted and rapt, the now-guilty audience skulked into thin air. In the square itself, animation was suspended as performers dared not move for a second, but when they did, it was in a flurry of fear. Bedlam followed in a scrum of vibrant color tainted with black.

Quick to find a dark, hidden nook between buildings from which to view the onslaught, the friends witnessed the Blackshirts beat the artists they could catch with their batons. Instruments, treasured for generations, were used as shields from the merciless blows.

Pietro was mortified by the mayhem. *"Porca miseria,* my idea. Now people will suffer."

Stef sounded like he was justifying Pietro's project: "They're here because they want to be, performing and free, even for moments, though there are consequences—"

Pietro interrupted Stef: "We all knew there would be consequences. But I'd hoped the risk would be worth a good few minutes of artistic collaboration. I fear we only made a minute or two. Was it enough, for those who experienced its magic, to fight for the carnival back forever? *Cazzo.* God knows what those bastard Blackshirts will do to the ones they captured. I heard they stripped down and tied a "troublemaker" to a tree, forced pints of castor oil down the victim's throat, and made him eat a live toad. They humiliated him until enough time had passed for the inevitable shit-storm. They laughed their *culos* off when the man debased himself in front of the hordes. Shocking!"

To Pietro's dismay, Stef's angry words tumbled out: "You didn't let me finish. The truth is, you sold them on the idea and reduced their fear of the consequences. Did you even tell *them* the toad story? You put them up to it. I believe this new arrogance of yours has taken you over the edge ... " Pietro put a firm hand over Stef's mouth, and though his dog-full arms rendered him defenseless, his eyes shouted a thousand insults until he realized why he was being silenced.

A tall, muscled Blackshirt stood on an abandoned organ, using it as a podium. His voice boomed: "This act of defiance will be dealt with in the most severe fashion. Each one of you will suffer public humiliation of the worst kind." Pietro could smell oppressive fear in the air. "Or do yourselves a favor. Expose the ringleader who started it all," the voice boomed.

One by one the performers went up to the closest Blackshirt, hands in the air. Giving themselves up for their art. Stef took one look at Pietro and knew what he was thinking. "Yes. Show me your heart is still in the right place."

Pietro considered his angry friend's words and was amazed how, even as a grown man, Stef's disappointment in him was worse than the most painful beating a Blackshirt could muster.

Pietro walked into the square singing "O Sole Mio" on the top of his velvet voice. All heads turned toward him. Mask off, he strode toward the spokesman of the Blackshirts, still balancing on the organ.

"Let them all go, and I will tell you who organized this treasonous event," Pietro shouted, though he would have been heard had he whispered.

A few of the Blackshirts abandoned the artists they'd collected and moved toward Pietro, smiling, slapping him on the back.

"You're the tenor."

"I saw you last Tuesday."

"You gave my sister a hot flush in the nether region."

Great laughter. An ally, they were sure.

The Blackshirt leader spoke up, grinning: "Hey! You're one of Il Duce's favorite opera singers. We'll take you at your word and let them all go in lieu of the one responsible. Who, pray tell, is this traitor?"

Pietro locked eyes with each of the artists and then back to the leader. "I organized our carnival for the good of the City of Venice. To show you how harmless it is and how it attracts tourists like bees to a honey pot. We need their money to rejuvenate our Venice."

The Blackshirts were shocked and appalled. "You?"

"Yes. I am a loyal Italian and an artiste, like all of these talented people before you. We love what we do, and we want to share it. For some of us, there is no forum without the carnival. We meant no disrespect. Quite the contrary." He bowed respectfully. "We Italians are famous for our esteemed Il Duce, our delicious food, our powerful history, our exquisite art and culture, but I ask you, gentlemen, what greater Italian attribute is there than the ability to entertain? To make people laugh or dance or sing or cry because they have been moved by a performance?" Pietro used his operatic skills to milk the silence for a long moment: "Perchance we will change Il Duce's mind about our carnival?"

The colorful crowd couldn't contain themselves. A burst of applause. The Blackshirts made no move but glared at them so ominously, they all froze, and not even a passing seagull had the gall to squawk.

All looked to the leader, still balancing on his musical pedestal, his face puckered like he'd bitten a sour apple. He jumped off and grabbed Pietro's arm.

"Pietro Saltamachio, come with us. We will take you to Il Duce. He will determine what's to be done with you."

As he was being jostled, he shouted, "Yes! Please! He will listen to me." He turned to his eager audience and shouted: "Viva la Carnival!" The crowd roared, and as Pietro smiled confidently, he had no idea why Stef's face was so glum. Even his mangy girlfriend had a solemn look! He looked forward to being hailed as "The Artiste Who Saved Venice." He was excited to meet Il Duce again. *Da uomo a uomo.* Man to man.

6

WHAT IF?

Pietermaritzburg
  29 July 1943

"Fourfeet, how do I send message back to pow man?" Iris asked.

"Solomon, Klein Miesies, only Solomon."

"What if I write something, can you get it to Solomon for me?"

"It very scary there, Klein Miesies. Solomon says bad colonel always looking." Fourfeet turned his head quickly, eyes wide in demonstration. "We must be sneaky."

"Good idea. But how, Fourfeet? I am an awful spy."

"Solomon takes out all pow-rubbish, Klein Miesies. He is only black man there. Pow people do everything but can't collect rubbish and take it out of camp, because in and out and in and out of gate, pow people can run away. So Solomon puts rubbish on donkey and takes it out of camp when guards open."

"So that means Solomon starts off outside the camp and goes inside?" Iris asked, and Fourfeet nodded. "What if my message is written on the inside of Solomon's upper arm? Then when Solomon finds a man called Pietro, he can read it when Solomon pretends he's reaching for something." She demonstrated, and Fourfeet nodded enthusiastically.

"Lena teach me to read only. Maybe Solomon knows someone who write."

"Fourfeet, I can write. Do you think Solomon would come here tonight? I will ask Lena to make him supper for his efforts."

Fourfeet's grin was stunning. "Zulus come run from faaaaaaaaar away kraals to eat Lena's supper, Klein Miesies." Iris was amused. She knew that any adjective or adverb that had many vowels described length of time or distance or intensity in the Zulu language.

"What's your favorite food, Fourfeet?"

"Cottage Pie, Miesies, much cheese on top of squashed potato."

"So it will be, Fourfeet." She smiled as he hurried to his mission. Even if she had to go into town and buy the minced meat, carrots and peas to simmer under the mash, Iris would make sure Lena made Fourfeet's Cottage Pie just the way he liked it.

The words came to her as if angels whispered in her ears as she watched Fourfeet sprint away in search of Solomon to extend the invitation to supper. She thought of the letter and the copy of another she'd sent to Gregg a few days before, and panic seized her ...

25th July, 1943.

Dear Sweet Gregg,

It's me! Your only sister! Thank you for your wonderful letter. You bring so much joy into my world. What would I do without you? You just keep safe, so I never have to find out!

So, mother hasn't called me "Jinx" again. If I could, I would have another card night to loosen her up, but once bitten and all that. I think she would rather eat glass than remember seeing sunrise from the kitchen floor, her head cushioned by Lena's stomach!

Creepy Julian appeared out of nowhere at my counter at the store the other day. The usual "I miss you's" were strewn about by him (imagine!) and he "accused" me of not going to parties. When that failed to elicit a response, he asked if I was meeting lots of men in the name of "healing." Oh my. That set me off. I told him hospitals were not places to look for lovers and besides, I don't see any joys of healing, I see buckets of pee, vomit and shit. (Oh, mother would have died hearing my lack of finesse! It was liberating!)

Speaking of my illustrious duties, quite a few of the doctors thought I should transfer to the terminal wing to "hold the hands of the dying." How cheerful can your volunteering hours actually be? When the hospital administrator approached me with the "fabulous opportunity" I told him, "No thank you, sir. Feces, urine and vomit are my moral limit." I could see he was stupefied and he likely deduced only a complete moron would prefer handling human waste over being an angel of mercy. Even though it might lend itself to doing something worthwhile, wouldn't that be entirely against Karma's grain—since when did one actually ENJOY penance?

Your familiar, messy handwriting brings me delicious anticipation as it slides out of the post box. I feel you close then and remember all the times you've protected me and made me smile. Hell, even from afar you inspire me.

To that point, immediately after your last letter, I unearthed Grandma's Boer War chest, covertly covered with a Union Jack (no doubt Dad's handiwork) and stuffed with my drawings from the year dot. I wish I could have shown you all the dresses and pants and suits and costumes I've designed over the years. Hmm. On second thought, your enthusiasm would have been less than Buffer's. At least he sniffed them for a few minutes!

The emotions she felt when she browsed through her creations came back to her in droves. It was like looking at someone else's work, and she was able to study each design objectively.

There was lots of juvenile stuff, of course, but she thought she might tweak some pieces if they held merit. There were somber, dark creations after Greg left and she realized that the way she felt was reflected by her color choices, embellishments or subtleties, or lack of them.

There were loads of sexy designs, the best of which looked ultra-conservative until the second sketch showed the garment in motion, and a split emerged going almost too far north up the leg or too far south down between the cleavage, though she always saved her styles from downright indecency, if only by a few threads. Subtlety was an art, and coupled with unexpected risqué, it became haute couture.

I painstakingly copied the best of the drawings, improving where needed, then signed my name with a flourish. I felt like a true artiste! I was having so much fun, I played "Let Me Call You Sweetheart" on the gramophone you gave me, and I was dancing with Buffer, when mother's head shot around the door. I felt like I was having a hot, illicit affair.

"What are you doing, child?" our mother asked, with disdain only she can muster.

"Just looking at some old drawings." Oh, boy, Gregg, I felt I'd been caught with my pants down.

"You need to lose your fussy and find a boyfriend, Iris!"

Buffer and I sighed with relief as we watched her stiff back retreat down the passage, the inevitable roses in hand, and then she threw the zinger, "And one who can kiss this time, so you can marry him, and stop dancing with your bloody dog!"

It's a circus here. I bet war-torn Italy, bombs, the threat of capture and hair-raising reconnaissance flights must pale in comparison to all the domestic excitement you're missing.

So, brother mine, I sent off three sets of drawings: one to Maxwell House in New York City, one to Rouf Fashion House in Paris and one to Bonnie Cashin. The last's an interesting one. Born in California, she had a new concept: ready-to-wear garments. The Gazette says she was just wooed by Hollywood to design costumes for the movies.

I considered them long shots, one and all, but as you taught me: You have to aim high; otherwise you waste a dream.

And then guess what? I got an invitation. Yes, an INVITATION to join the most intriguing of them all—Bonnie Cashin. And a CONTRACT. I'll pen a copy and send it in this letter so you can see for yourself that your sister is on the move career-wise and physically, to another continent! I am giddy at the thought! As of this minute, my life has changed forever. I shall never, ever get this chance again and you had better believe, I am clutching on with both hands and hanging on for dear life until I am safely in Hollywood, U.S.A. Can you believe? I will be where movies are made?

I must just figure out what the best time is to start the clock ticking, by sending my reply. By then you might ... no, you must be home to take over my responsibilities. I have a year. As soon as I've thought of how to tell mother and I've got all the funds for my travel commitment, I'll send confirmation to Ms. Cashin. And guess what? I'm about four months away from getting the full quota to pay for my part of the passage, so, come home already!

I need you home so a.) I can stop worrying about you b.) I can stop my foul penance c.) I can leave home without worrying about

Buffer, Lena, Mother and Sofie (in that order). Oh, and better add Fourfeet from next door. He's a delight.

Thanks for listening. BE SAFE. I love you forever,

I. xx

Dear Miss Fuller,

It is my great honor to extend an invitation to join my house of design in Hollywood, California. Your innovative creations fit my visions for haute couture, ready-to-wear and movie costuming for our new Hollywood studios.

My board and I believe you will be an excellent fit. My company will provide you with a one-way ship's passage to New York, U.S.A., from Durban, South Africa. We will hire you for a minimum of two years at a salary of $100.00 per month, and you will report directly to me.

However, we will require that you pay for your own passage from New York to Los Angeles, California. Our reasoning is to prove that you will be as invested in this opportunity as we are in your talent.

Our offer is finite, and we require that we receive your acceptance by July 31, 1944. Upon your acceptance, a ticket for passage to New York will be held by the Durban Harbor Master for one year.

Your failure to activate this ticket will render your contract with Bonnie Cashin null and void. We look forward to your confirmation and are extraordinarily excited to welcome you into our creative fold.

Sincerely yours,

Bonnie Cashin & Team

NB: Since wartime travel adversities have been accounted for in this most generous timeline, no extensions will be granted under any circumstances.

Buffer nudged Iris' hand, ready for some attention, and she was bolted back to the present.

What if Solomon was caught by Julian? What if she endangered Pietro? She rolled his name off her tongue. And tried it again.

How soon could she get the money she needed for her trip across from New York to Los Angeles? She knew she could save what she needed in four months, tops. Pity she'd found the *only* man to give her the girly hots before starting a new adventure.

No telling who you'll meet in America, Iris! Her mother's voice pierced the left side of her brain. Pietro was a prisoner, her country's enemy, surrounded by barbed wire and guards with guns. She needed to concentrate on her future in high fashion.

Secret notes wouldn't be enough to keep her from following her ultimate dream, but it was a delightful pastime. She thought about the intensity in his eyes and her stomach flipped. *Pietro's not my future. Bonnie is.* But her Pietro's face wove into her thoughts and unwillingly turned her body to molten lava.

7

OPEN THE FLOODGATES

27 June 1943

Pietro saw Stef coming through his half-open eyes. By the look his old friend wore, Pietro wished he could wiggle in with the buried instruments and throw sand over his own head.

Stef kicked at him softly. "Why do you hide in the coop like an old man tired of life?"

"It's how I feel," Pietro whispered.

"So, now you feel sorry for yourself?" Stef knew just how to needle him.

"Fuck off. Leave me alone."

"So you are the only one affected by this war?"

"We deal in different ways. Go do what you do and leave me alone!" Pietro begged.

"Have I ever left you alone?" Stef's voice was matter-of-fact.

"Sadly, no. Now do it for once, and fuck off."

"You shame me." Stef's tone emphasized his disappointment.

"Go be 'shamed' by someone else. Lots to choose from."

"Get up and talk to me like a man, not a dog." Stef kicked lightly at his friend's ribs.

"You love dogs," Pietro grumbled.

"I love dogs that sit up. Do it, Pietro, or I walk away, and everything you are to me, everything we have shared, will die."

"You are too fucking late. Everything, everyone is dead to me already. Now, fuck off."

"What about poor, mewling Antonio? He cries for you all the time. Since I arrived in your tent, you have abandoned him. You want that on your conscience, too? Oh, I forgot. The great Pietro Saltamachio has no conscience." Stef's tone was mocking.

Damn it! The bastard knew just how to get to him. Antonio. After the joy of seeing Stef's face wore off, Pietro avoided him, because the last thing he needed was to be sucked into remembering how his hard-earned life had been snatched away. He hadn't been back to their tent since Stef moved in, it was true, but damned if he didn't feel bad about poor Antonio, who relied on him. He'd abandoned him. Trust Stef to point out the obvious and make him feel like shit. He had a gift for it.

"How is he doing?" Pietro realized he was sitting up.

"He just rocks and calls your name as he cries."

"Why do you tell me this?"

"Because you asked, you stupid son of a bitch." Stef aimed to kick him in the ribs again, but instead, sat down.

Straight-faced Pietro said, looking into Stef's eyes: "Don't speak of my saintly mother that way." Stef started snorting, trying to control his mirth, but then he looked at Pietro, who burst into laughter. The two friends rolled in the dirt, howling, giggling, spitting with side-splitting laughter like neither had laughed for three long years.

Once they'd sobered, the floodgates opened, and Pietro laid his heart bare.

Naples

1940

Pietro slapped a wet curl off his forehead and concentrated on his hand of cards. Gray and white smoke swirled from the tip of the cigarette dangling from his mouth. Another queen.

There were a hundred newly trained Italian pilots, just like him, loafing around the hangar, bitching like old women, waiting to be useful.

"I heard on the radio that Mussolini said, 'I only need a few thousand dead so that I can sit at the peace conference as a man who has fought.' I hope to God we don't end up as part of the bald bugger's head count!" Pietro noted glibly, to provoke conversation more than anything.

"If we hadn't got involved in Franco's war and been raped of our men and ammunition, we might be a fighting force," said a new recruit.

"Why doesn't the old fart just languish on his yacht in the Italian Rivera, surrounded by women, and watch the Germans fight their own war?" asked another.

Bored, Pietro threw down his hand and leapt onto the makeshift card table. *"Che cavolo?* Listen, you pussies. How often do you get to go to war? And not just to war in the trenches, freezing your toes and *natiche* off on the fortified Alpine line, or on the low ground, like insects scurrying and hiding. No, gentlemen. We are the elite. We have a vantage point, a bird's-eye view of this war. We are pilots, for the love of God!"

As was usually the case, the shortest, skinniest man in the crowd was the most aggressive. "Easy for you to say, Pietro Salta-machio, darling of the opera. I heard Mussolini himself pushed you into this war when your act of treason should have put you in front of a firing squad."

Pietro concentrated his most intimidating stare on the puny one for a second before he embraced his entire audience. "Act of treason? Bah! Mussolini was just put out I overstepped his authority. And clearly, little runt, you are no artiste. Italy's finest export is its ability to entertain, to delight the senses. What can you do? What is *your* special something, your unique gift you bring to the world, to show your fine Italian-ness?"

Spurred by the flyers, the runt jumped onto the table to face Pietro square-on. He unbuttoned the top half of his flying suit with aggressive force, exposing his comically white, naked torso, all protruding ribs and concave stomach. He even had the gall to beat his chest. Pietro hoped the guy didn't injure himself with his own enthusiasm.

"Are you readying yourself to fight me, Half Pint?"

"Much, much, worse," Half Pint promised.

What have we here? Perhaps three back flips off the table, landing on one hand. That'll be very impressive. An "artiste" after all.

The imp stood proud, chin to the ceiling, and with great flourish, circled his right arm around his torso, as if holding a large ball and rolling it, from side to side, across sternum and back, a few times.

Sacred mackerel, he's preparing for a triple pirouette!

Half Pint pushed his hand under the opposite armpit and pumped like hell until some massively loud, contrived farts emitted. Pietro swore he had never seen such pride on a man's face as the noises became more and more revolting.

Pietro laughed so hard he nearly fell off the table. Clapping his hands heartily, he shouted, "Bravo, bravo, encore!" and the shrimp obliged until the hall was overcome with mirth, and the little guy's sweat had all but dried up. By that time, Pietro was lying flat on the floor, crying with laughter. It didn't take much to entertain these bored, bright young airmen. Not a single one in the room, Pietro would bet, felt any great patriotic desire to be a hero. They were drafted. They had no choice.

This war was a massive interference for him, that was true, but Pietro had long learned to make the best of a bad situation. His sights, like the other men's, were set stoically ahead, except he would not be satisfied with just returning as a trained pilot. He must ... no! *He had to* return to his life of fame, recognition and growing affluence. Nothing less and much, much more.

True, his "act of treason" and public rebuke by his "great admirer" would hurt his future box office for a while, but returning as a war hero would ease the sting of Il Duce's disgrace, and he would, he *could*, sing himself back into favor.

Right now, he had to do something about this tedium. He lifted himself off the concrete floor and walked to the hangar door.

There were random shouts: "Hey, Pietro. We're meant to wait for an update from commandant." He took no notice as he opened the heavy metal door.

The jibes came, but it was the runt's voice that was louder and higher than anyone else's: "Did I intimidate you so with my talent that you're off to commit harakiri? Come back and sing to us, Caruso. You have a small amount of potential. Come back and sing." Pietro grinned, hearing fake, pitiful cries behind him. How ironic that his fellow fliers' nickname for him was "Caruso." As he rounded the four-wing aluminum plane, he glanced at the men stacked like a bunch of overacting circus clowns along the cracked door of the hangar, collective eyes wide. Someone shouted: "You have the balls of Zeus himself!" and he felt the wind on his teeth and knew he was smiling again as he hoisted himself up and into the one-man aircraft.

Up and up he flew, wind in his face, and then he leveled the fragile-looking plane. He turned the bird in ever-decreasing circles, looking down over farm fields and scattered tiled roofs. Everything looked so different from 2,000 feet.

There! She stood on the steps of her casa, and he swore he could see her face turned up to the clouds, alight with joy. She waved her arm so gracefully, and in such a wide arc, she could be dancing "Swan Lake." Two potential ballerinas in one day! He smiled.

Ah! She was still waving. He thought of her navel and the lint he always found there, as if she was stocking up for winter. He tipped his aluminum wing in greeting.

Around again, just to show how much he appreciated her attentions.

Another tipped wing, an exaggerated wave, then he flew back. Miles later, she was but a black dot. He was fleetingly sad he would leave her soon, but he always found it best to depart during the honeymoon phase, before he tired of them and while they still loved him.

Pietro landed the aircraft, aware that the commandant was standing on the tarmac, thunder-faced, hands on hips. Though Pietro was acutely aware of the necessity of foreplay in love, he'd be damned if he would bother with it in war.

As he alighted, the German stomped toward him, a study in fury, but Pietro deliberately deprived his superior of his much-needed outburst as he saluted and asked: "How many days, Commandant?"

The old soldier spat between clenched teeth. "Fifteen. Starting *now*."

Two military policemen appeared and hauled him away. After being thrown to the concrete floor of the tiny jail, Pietro looked up and winked at his hostile escorts. "She was worth every minute of the next fifteen days." The door banged shut.

Gondar Air Force Camp, Abyssinia
   8 January 1942

Pietro scanned a piece in the *Roma* about U.S. President Roosevelt declaring that it was the will of the American people to make certain the world would never suffer again. "Good luck with that," he thought as he folded the newspaper and threw it down. He reached for a pomegranate among the array of fruit on the uneven table, shaded by a huge, camouflage canopy.

Gondar was in the area known as the Italian East Africa, the largest part of Abyssinia, with immense plateaus covered with rich pasturage.

He cracked the hard shell of the fruit open on his knee, exposing a plethora of ripe red and pink shades, which looked not altogether dissimilar to the sweet delicacies of a ripe vulva his eyes and tongue had recently explored. Hmmm. Valentina's? Violetta's? Or was it the wing-tip girl's? He couldn't quite remember.

Pietro pondered why Mussolini had turned to the man he had first considered "a silly little monkey" and asked for Hitler's help to secure this peculiar piece of the world. And then, why did their bald, pompous leader choose to support Hitler or anybody, for that matter, in this cruel war? War was for fighters. Not lovers. Or Italians.

Pink pomegranate juice ran slowly down his hand, pulling his eyes away from the peculiar scenery and back to the luscious fruit, igniting more titillating memories.

"You, pilot. Report to ops."

Pissed off about being dragged from his fantasy, Pietro looked up slowly.

"Now!"

But he couldn't resist placing his mouth sensuously over the tempting fruit for a few seconds, before the bloody war made him throw nature's sweet miracle over his shoulder, harder than necessary, to follow the commandant's second in charge.

Within half an hour, a group of men held the Ca. 133 Caproni aircraft with all their might against the revving engine. Feeling the engine at its optimum, Pietro, in the captain's seat, gave the thumbs-up, which the mechanic at the back relayed to the ground. He heard the faint shout from the tarmac, and immediately their plane rocketed into the air at a forty-five degree angle.

A mighty cliff loomed directly in front of them, and he turned his bird sharply.

After the thrill of takeoff over the steep range, the stoic commandant in the co-pilot seat visibly relaxed. "Well, at least you can fly."

"It's all you, Commandant. You taught me."

"So, Caruso. What did you do to Il Duce to piss him off enough to send you to war?"

"Ah, Commandant. That is between me and the great one. But I promise you, it was not a woman. Not even my charm can compete with Mussolini's power. I know my limitations."

They shared a chuckle.

"I noted your 'limitations' were endless on the ship over here." The colonel's voice was tinged with envy as he remembered Pietro's ease with the Mussolini-issued courtesans.

"Just trying to take the pressure off you, as the ladies' first choice, Commandant. Always looking to relieve you of your more trying duties."

They had a 180-degree view of the dismal "Corridor of Camels." In the dry season, the arid earth was rock-hard, and the terrain was made three-dimensional only occasionally by a mammoth bald tree, with what appeared to be an upside-down root system, or a deep, wrinkled, multi-layered crevice where water had stood fleetingly before it evaporated again and again over a millennium.

"What's our mission, Commandant? Without the gunners in the back, I'm guessing some secretive reconnaissance?"

"Intelligence says we have a growing British camp to the north. This will help us structure our attack, so the higher you can fly, the better for us to go undetected."

Pietro pulled the joystick up, and his bird began to climb quickly.

A "tzwing" and a jolt, and another and another.

Damned enemy fire. Pietro leveled for a minute, then pulled up the stick, forcing the plane up and out of range. "Fine time not to have our gunner boys on board," Pietro shouted.

The devious enemy plane stayed in Pietro's blind spot, directly behind his tail. He pushed his bird to its maximum of a hundred and forty miles per hour.

Another bullet hit them, and the plane shuddered. The damned commandant was shell-shocked and silent. *What the fuck?* Pietro shouted over the din: "You watch him. See where he is, anticipate which way he's going to turn, or take over the *cazzo* joystick and I'll do it."

Nothing. Pietro took a second to look all the way to his right. Blood oozed from the commandant's gaping mouth, and his eyes stared lifelessly ahead. Pietro saw the hole in the fuselage where the lethal bullet had penetrated just below the window.

"Cazzo. Madonna. Cazzo."

A barrage of bullets hit the plane, and their third flight member, the radio operator, collapsed between the pilot seats, dead.

"Alberto!" he shouted to the last of the crew, hoping his voice could be heard at the back of the aircraft. But there was no time for an answer before another blistering barrage struck, and as

Pietro turned back to quickly assess the damage, he saw the mechanic convulse in a macabre death dance.

Pietro was alone.

"*Dio mio. Madonna. Dio mio.*" In the slow-motion haze from which he strained to emerge, he forced himself to pull his broken bird left to escape another attack from behind.

But it was too late.

Another blaze of bullets hit the aircraft, and as his plane hiccupped with the force of the blows, Pietro caught sight of his aggressor to his right. Their eyes met, and the fleeting moment was suspended by shock as enemies—nay, just young, frightened men—recognized the surprise in each other's eyes.

Pietro turned his head and pushed his plane into a climb as fast as its bullet-infused fuselage would allow, but the ace behind him let go another spate of death-yielding bullets.

Three bullets hit Pietro in the back. Although the impact completely knocked the air out of him, the parachute pack attached to his back diminished the harm to his body. He was alive. Broken ribs, fractured lungs perhaps, "But I am alive!" he shouted to God ... or the devil?

A fire flared in the starboard engine, and Pietro wasted no more time. Adrenaline pumping, he lifted the hatch and jumped as far from his machine as the resistant cross winds allowed.

And not a moment too soon. As he jumped, hand on his ripcord, the mangled machine that held four vital men scant minutes before tumbled and spun past him to its spectacular, fiery demise on the desert sand below.

So mesmerized was he by the spiraling plane, he was late in tugging hard on the ripcord. As he did so, relief was overwhelming.

But short-lived. His parachute was so severely damaged by bullets that as he descended, the holes tore wider and wider, making him fall faster and faster.

With no resistance, he plummeted thousands of feet down ... down ... down.

His body was suddenly jerked ferociously and then slammed into something huge and hard as concrete. He heard a sound like an inner tube of a tire being sliced by a knife. He realized pragmatically that his lung had just collapsed.

His body was broken. He was battling to breathe, but he forced himself to look around. He was dangling from a massive, centuries-old baobab tree, the only vegetation he'd seen from the sky.

He heard a drone above him and pushed his head back to look above him. His enemy was circling to make sure he'd been obliterated.

As he heard the whine of the plane disappear, he mustered all his strength and shouted at the empty sky, "I am still here." He tried to laugh, but it came out a strangled, gurgling mess.

Then he looked down.

For the first time in his life, he saw an obstacle he didn't know how to overcome. Three stories below was a rocky stretch of hard, dry desert. *I'm like Jesus on the cross. Only higher.* It was not a blasphemous thought, rather a comforting one, until he thought: "And look what happened to Jesus."

There was no option. He loosened the parachute belt, and the hard jolt made him scream in agony. Disappointment was fierce as he looked down and saw the belt under his armpits. He'd only dropped about two feet.

He had no strength to free himself. *I am so happy the belt is not restricting the only lung I have left. What a lucky man I am. Lucky. Lucky. Lucky.* Then tears streaked down dirty, smoke-covered cheeks. *Fuck it. No amount of positive thought will help you now. This is the end. But, where's the light?*

He hung in the beating sun, drifting in and out of consciousness, praying for a quick death in Latin whispers. The wheezing emitting from his lung became a distorted, broken melody. Then the chorus repeated over and over again, disrupting his musical sense, and like a fever-induced nightmare, repeated over and over and over again.

He awoke when the sky was dark, shivering from shock and cold. He gasped for breath, opening his mouth so wide, both sun-swollen lips split as if an enemy's switchblade demanded his silence. He knew what he had to do.

Sweating, he forced through the pain and pulled himself up to release the buckle under his arms. Silently, only because there was not enough air in his lungs to produce a noise, Pietro crashed three and a half stories to the ground.

As he lay, still and broken, what was left of the silk parachute delicately descended, landing like a protective whisper over his inert form.

Pietro awoke sweating and panicked in thick blackness. In spite of the excruciating pain in his chest, he reached up to God, to anything. Nothing happened. Nobody appeared.

As his hands dropped in despair, his body screamed, but he made no sound because he couldn't. The parachute billowed gently, and light shone down. Encouraged, desperate, he tugged at the silk, and an endless sky with a million stars came into view.

But a freezing wind forced him to move again, slowly, to cover his head, drawing the curtain on the magnificent silver-streaked sky in favor of the warmth of the silk.

Pietro meandered in and out of consciousness. He thought he saw his mother and swore at her for deserting him and then wept with joy that she had bothered to come and begged her not to leave him. In his mind, he sang parts of all the Catholic hymns he knew in Latin. In his mind, when his mouth opened to sing, there was the sound of a crushed concertina.

Later, when the winds had blown the parachute off his arm and the stars willingly gave their luminosity, he watched ticks crawl over his hand and past his elbow. Finding an open wound, they attached themselves and sucked. He knew they were all over his body, but he couldn't feel them because the pain was so intense.

Stef. Stef? Can you see me? Look! Look! I am their manna from heaven. Their only liquid source in this barren abyss. I am useful, I am useful, I am still useful. Stef, can you tell God I am still useful? Maybe he will listen to you. You are the good one. You are the kind one. You're the only one I know who is a really worthy human being. He might listen to you, Stef, because you're my very best friend.

Each time he felt the blackness come, he was grateful.

The metallic sound of a loading rifle bolt tore open his eyes, which were blinded by the blazing sunlight. He heard an animal noise coming from his own broken lips.

High above him were hazy, white tunics atop camels with the most ludicrous looks on their distorted faces.

"Moya, moya, moya," Pietro begged. One of the troop threw down a leather water-carrier, which Pietro scrambled to reach, breast-stroking spastically with one arm across the sand. Just as he was about to pick it up, the trooper kicked the water bladder farther away, laughing. If Pietro had any water in his body, he would have wept like a newborn.

An ostentatiously dressed man in a turban gazed down from atop a donkey. "I am Muslim priest," he told Pietro, who had a fleeting thought of God being very angry that his last rites were read by a Muslim.

It sounded like the priest chastised the mean-spirited young man, and mercifully he soon had a water bottle in his hand. Water poured over his broken lips and down his parched throat.

Under the direction of the priest, Pietro was none too gently hauled up and his hands tied together. Three of the troupe then pushed him over the rear horn of the camel's saddle. Throughout the ordeal, Pietro's pain was so severe he begged for death, but he couldn't even conjure up oblivion. This Muslim priest had really pissed off his God.

With his chest resting on its rump and his legs astride the camel, the Sudanese tied a rope under his butt and then around the same horn. The camel labored to its feet, pulling on the ropes, and Pietro's pain was so intense, a scream forced its way through his swollen throat. There he dangled until the camel decided to sit down and the troopers untied him.

Once more they tried to secure him on the saddle, but he was too weak to keep his balance and thumped to the ground and, at last, into merciful unconsciousness.

When he awoke, he was propped up under the giant tree from which he'd fallen, a water vessel next to him. The troop, the camels, the priest and the donkey were long gone and could easily have been a figment of his imagination, except for the water bottle. Pietro glanced at his scuffed, dirty boots, and silent sobs forced themselves out of his throat until he thought he would choke to death.

Pietro felt, more than he heard, the rumbling. His body convulsed in pain, causing shock waves in every nerve of his acutely tender body.

Then he saw the truck. A man wearing a white coat jumped out, along with one of the Sudanese troopers. *Grazie Dio. Un dottore.*

The doctor was surprisingly gentle as he assessed Pietro's bashed-up body. He looked into Pietro's eyes. "You must be a bloody tough one," he said in a British accent. "Let's see if we can put you together again, Humpty Dumpty."

The needle moved in slow motion toward his arm, and he was grateful. As if from high in the baobab tree, he watched himself being loaded onto a stretcher, then into merciful blackness.

***

Bright spotlights were on him, and he couldn't sing. There was something over his mouth. His audience waited silently for him to finish his aria. He must get this thing away. He couldn't disappoint them.

"You're hitting your chloroform mask, you clown. Do you want to be awake while I re-break and set your bones?" The doctor spat out his exasperation. "This bastard doesn't know how lucky he is." Pietro watched woozily as the white-coated man pointed to the broken windows and bullet-riddled walls. "You bloody Italians did this to my hospital. Now I have to heal you. Bloody Hippocratic oath's a curse sometimes. Nurse! Tie him down."

Pietro watched a hefty nurse tie his arms to the bedrails, and he felt his legs being restrained. The doctor held the chloroform firmly over his nose and mouth. Pietro managed to get out "Bastardo!" before he succumbed to the chloroform.

He awoke to the intense stare of the homely, square-faced nurse who had tied him down. How many years ago?

"It's been five days since you came in. You were really a mess. Doc had to do some heavy-duty repair work on you." His left arm was in a cast, as was his left leg, and a cage covered his chest. Clearly whatever had happened, Bella, as he sarcastically christened her, was none too happy about it.

Well, as long as he had a voice, he could charm her. No problem. Once she'd fed him the thin broth with a hint of rosemary, he started to sing "La donna e mobile ... " but it came out as a long, sick squawk. She roughly brushed his lips with petroleum jelly, lifted his head and squeezed water from a soggy towel down his parched throat.

Pietro woke only to eat soup or drink water for the next week, all administered by his big Bella. His body could only heal itself with sleep, and he welcomed the oblivion when his mother wasn't making an appearance in his dreams. But, no matter what time of day or night he awoke, the same homely nurse came into focus. She was always there for him, his beautiful Bella.

The doctor bounded in once when he was *compos mentis* for only long enough to declare: "You represent some of my finest work, young man. Don't you forget who put you together. I pumped you so full of antibiotics, you'll likely be immune to their cure for the rest of your life." He was too sleepy to care, but at some point he woke up thinking that it was wisest not to let them know he understood English.

One day he woke up feeling human, clear-headed and interested in the world around him. His body was stiff and sore, casts were still in place, but the cage was off his chest. His first instinct was to test his voice. Softly at first, then louder and louder until a group of nurses gathered around his bed. When he finished, they clapped, whooped, giggled and shouted, "More, more." His smile was as wide as his Bella's behind.

Bella pushed her way past the cuties, and she put her face close to his. "You must rest. Don't think you can wake up and show off."

As she pivoted to exit, her big head held high, he pinched her rump with two of his operational digits. She jumped and slapped his hand. There were screeches of great hilarity from the doorway, which stopped abruptly with a single glare from his Bella. Pietro comically pulled the sheet over his head to hide from what he knew was her meanest gaze.

And so their dance continued.

Pietro looked forward to their banter, though Pietro continued with his no-English charade. Bella's tone and body language were a study in duplicity. She was determined not to let anyone see how much she cared for her ornery patient. Once during a particularly savage dream, he beat his way through the haze of sleep, and through slit eyes, he saw Bella sitting on the bed with a wet cloth, her manly face troubled. As she moved in to gently mop his sweat, Pietro started singing "Oh Sole Mio" very softly, as if still in a dream. Her smile softened ruddy, square features, and her head moved to the tune. Her surprising, gentle brow-mopping continued until he sang the final note, then she rearranged her soft smile into a frown before she left the room.

As the days passed, Pietro specially made a huge fuss of her in front of others. She was the kind of woman who had never had any male attention, and it became his mission to make her feel like a desirable goddess until he went home. He pushed through her English correctness, called her "Mia Bella" and sang only to her, though a constant bevy of nurses and a doctor or two were always watching as soon as his first note emitted. Pinching her ample bum was part of their dance, as was the hell he earned for doing so. It was Bella who challenged him to heal through her strong therapy, and she worked tirelessly, refusing to let him give up, though his body ached and rebelled. She relentlessly pushed him through the pain as she flexed and bent his arms and legs and gave him breathing exercises till he felt his lungs would burst.

During one particularly frustrating day of physiotherapy, he literally threw down the towel: "Voglio andara a casa," and followed with a battery of perhaps romantic-sounding words, which really said, "I am fed up with this shit, and I need to go home to where people understand me, and I can eat real food and flirt with a woman I can sleep with!"

One of the newer doctors overheard the tirade, and he turned to a perplexed Bella, explaining, "He wants to go home. Fat chance in hell."

How could he not have known it was coming? He was as well as he could be after what he'd been through. But he'd always been of the opinion that if you didn't think about the worst that could happen, it probably wouldn't; and if it happened anyway, you found a way to deal with it that no amount of worrying could have improved.

He'd had too many fucking surprises since he'd been cocky enough to assume Il Duce would say yes to his carnival and marvel at Pietro's cleverness for thinking of it before he did. Yes! He should have known there would be an end to this, but he'd hoped the war would be over by the time he got well. Still he refused to consider what lay beyond this hospital and the safety of his guardian angel, Bella.

A few weeks later, as he heard her solid footsteps coming toward him, he burst into song during his pushups to delight her, but when she stood in front of him, her eyes were red-rimmed.

"Today is the day, Pietro. You are leaving us."

On his way to the jeep, under escort, Pietro turned and fled ... but just to the doorway of the hospital, where a nest of nurses stood waving. And there she was.

He put both arms around Bella's hefty frame and hugged her till tears poured down her cheeks and she hugged him back, languid in his arms.

He dipped her down as if they were in the midst of a sexy tango on the dark streets of Argentina.

Then he kissed her with lusty passion and pinched her bum. A slap was exactly what he expected, and she didn't disappoint.

---

28 June 1943

It was midmorning by the time Pietro had finished catching Stef up with most of what had happened to him since last they'd seen each other in Venice.

"And what happened to *you,* old friend?" he asked Stef.

"After that story? Not a lot!" Stef chuckled. "When you left, our orchestra was commissioned into the military ranks, and we played for the troops all over, until we were captured and brought here by what was once a passenger liner."

"I know it well. Come, let's go and see Antonio. But promise me, no word about my past to these men. I don't want to sing ever again, but quietly to Antonio, and only because it seems to help him. Singing makes me feel, and I don't ever want to feel again. It hurts too much."

Back at their tent, the flap was thrown up from the inside, and Enzo's wiry frame blazed out, his cheeks hot with anger, spittle flying from his lips.

"You fucking coward! Have you been hiding from your own voice? You know I've heard you sing to Antonio. Why in God's name don't you sing to all of us?"

Pietro said nothing but stood his ground as Stef skulked away.

"You sing like a songbird. An angel. And I saw you save those instruments. They meant something to you. I see how Stefano looks at you, he hero-worships you. You were *somebody.*"

"We were all 'somebody' once." He turned away from Enzo's hot wrath.

Enzo's bony finger was thrust half an inch from Pietro's face. Man, this guy moved fast. "Listen to me, you selfish son of a bitch. You could have saved all those poor bastards who were carted away in straitjackets. You could have brought Italy here, to all of us. But you stayed silent." He spat in the dirt to show his disgust. "You could have made the last nine months tolerable for us. But you didn't have the balls, did you? You are just too fucking scared to sing and be heard by Tap Tap and to face the consequences. You are a despicable coward. You look after your own skin at the expense of saving everyone else's sanity. Shame on you!"

Pietro nodded ever so slightly. There was nothing to say.

"With our fading memories of home, your singing would have been the very fiber that would have sustained us, but no! Your fear overcame your Italian-ness. I hope you die with this camp's lack of morale on your deplorable conscience. You chicken shit. Go back to the coop and die." He spat again and stalked off.

Pietro wasted no more time and ducked into the tent to see Antonio.

The big man grinned and spoke his first words in two months: "Can you sing anything other than 'O Sole Mio'?"

8

ARMED

30 July 1943

Enzo was like the nagging mother Pietro never had. It was the first time he considered himself "lucky" in the mother department.

"So. You yellow-bellied son of a bitch. You don't even have the balls to catch a pigeon for your hungry friends."

"Pee-ET-row." The strange noise came from outside the tent. When Pietro popped his head out, he had the oddest feeling of deja vu. *Please, not another donkey!* Atop it was a Zulu man. *Thank God! Not a Muslim priest!* The man pronounced his name as badly a second time, and Pietro nodded slightly. He was wary as hell.

"Please. Come close," the nervous Zulu whispered as he jumped off the donkey. Pietro recognized him as the man he gave the newspaper to in the infirmary and felt a glimmer of hope.

The man took off his tired Boer War military jacket, pushed

his shirt sleeve high on his arm and pointed to the sky. Pietro followed his finger upwards. "Look at arm," the Zulu hissed.

And there it was. Written on the lighter inside of the man's upper arm.

"I know you too. My heart understands, my mind does not. I wish it too, but how? Iris."

The Zulu dropped his arm and started to push down his sleeves.

"Please. Again." Pietro felt his heart beating faster than it had in La Fenice opera house.

The Zulu rolled big eyes and pointed heavenwards, eyes following as Pietro read and re-read as long as he could, before the arm dropped again.

"What the hell's going on here?" It was Burbero, Tap-Tap's surly guard. Neither had seen him coming and both men jumped. The mammoth man stood towering over them, intimidating the hell out of them both.

"My fault, sir. I want to know what kind of bird fly here. Man very kind to show me," Pietro explained, still gazing up at the sky.

"Why is your jacket off in the dead of winter?" Burbero had a point.

"My fault again, sir. The bird so quick. I have ask Mr. Zulu many times to point. *Di sudare?* He sweat."

"*Mister* Zulu? What the ... get back on your bloody donkey and on with your rubbish job, Solomon. No more buggering around or giving bird lessons to blerry prisoners, understood?"

Solomon bowed subserviently. "Skies, Baas," he apologized, walking backward and bowing his head as he pulled the donkey's rope.

"Grazi, Solomon. You are very kind, clever man of birds."

"And you, Eye-Tie, leave the blerry Zulu alone. No more donderse bird education!"

Pietro was spared more groveling by a screech of car tires and loud singing coming from the direction of the officer's quarters. The sound was so rare under Tap Tap's rule that it drove the entire contingent, led by Pietro—grateful for the excuse to flee—toward the large brick building to watch the commotion on the other side.

A robust man in a colonel's uniform spilled out of the too-small jeep singing "The White Cliffs of Dover" at the top of his voice, forced between teeth clamping down on a cigar.

Balancing a gramophone, he strode through the heavy doors of the army building, where two officers saluted. Sergeant Rogers followed with suitcases. In seconds, an army truck rolled in with six men balancing an upright piano on the flatbed. The POWs' mouths hung open as they watched the piano being roughly manhandled into the building. Pietro and Stef cringed.

A light-bulb moment. Pietro hit himself on the head, hard, as if to wake up. Here was the answer, right in front of him and singing out of tune. That little black beetle planted the first new seed of determination in his soul since his fall from grace started at the carnival, then spiraled with him as he fell from the burning plane. No doubt, Cara Rossa was his driving force, but the spark the dung beetle ignited, coupled with the burning need to find a way to see his Iris—*his* Iris—again, blazed like a veldt fire in his belly.

He grabbed Enzo's sinewy arm and hauled him to the guards' compound at the front gate.

"Must see new colonel," Pietro stated as a matter of fact.

The guards ignored him. Enzo tried: "He says he must see new colonel."

"We understand, moron. We just don't think there's a necessity."

"Life or dead." Pietro growled, but he could have been invisible.

"He says it's life or death."

They turned their backs, dismissing them both.

"New colonel, *now*. Please?"

Still nothing. Pietro sprang on to the officious gate, barbed wire and all.

He fleetingly thanked the dead man for his shoes, and as he began climbing upward, he heard guns cock. He continued higher, shouting, "NEW COLONEL NOW. NEW COLONEL NOW. LIFE OR DEAD. LIFE OR DEAD!"

At last, a guard ran inside the brick building shouting, "Colonel Cairns! Sir!"

Petro had to admit, this one had a sunnier demeanor.

"What can I do you boys for?" He leaned back on the chair, hands behind his head. The massive Rhodesian teak desk was dwarfed by the man's solid presence and thick cigar smoke filled the room. Aromatic. Rich.

"Pietro wants to save camp." Enzo bowed slightly in his partner's direction.

A smile erupted, lighting up Colonel Cairns' face with boyishness. "Really? Pray tell."

Enzo's face was shrouded in confusion, but Pietro was not here for Enzo to learn the mysterious quirks of the English language. Pietro gave Enzo's ribs a jab.

"Ow! He opera singer. In Italy very famous. He make concert for men. Here." Enzo thumbed in the direction of the enclosure.

Pietro threw open his arms as if embracing all of those within the broad area of his extended limbs. "For everyone," Pietro promised.

Colonel Cairns' eyebrows came together in confusion.

Enzo shone in the spotlight. "Your men. They will like also.

He sings like angel. Men go mad with nothing to do." He twirled his finger around his head to illustrate. "Help us, please."

Enzo was about to continue the rampage when Pietro put an "easy" palm on the other's shoulder. Now was the time to wait. To watch. To gauge their next best move.

And they waited as Colonel Cairns sized them up.

And still they waited.

Then, when Pietro was sure they were on the brink of being kicked out of the Colonel's fancy office, he took a deep breath and sang his heart out.

"O Sole Mio" had never been more poignant, as each word came from his need to find a way to see his Iris.

9

HEEBEE-JEEBIES AND CONFESSIONS

24 August 1943

Iris had wondered if she liked girls.

She didn't know any girls she'd care to share secrets with, let alone her body, but she'd been amused at the thought of how it would push her mother over the edge. Her sting again. She smiled, then looked up to see rain gushing down the hospital window. Rain usually made her feel blue, but today its copious flow pounded the pane in three syllables: Pee-Et-Ro. She imagined that's how he would pronounce it. Pee-Et-Ro. *You're okay, Mom. I'm 100 percent heterosexual.* Pee-Et-Ro. The very pronunciation gave her the girly hots. She felt like a dog shaking itself after a swim. The mini-spasm started at her head and shook all the way to her tail.

She pushed the mop through the ward on automatic. Would he write back? And how would he get the message to her now that Fourfeet had reported Solomon was D-O-N-E with secret messages? Not even Lena's famous cuisine could convince him otherwise. He'd complained that he'd nearly been caught because the excited reader begged to "read" his arm until it turned blue. Apparently "Being caught" was a little more severe *inside* the prisoner-of-war camp!

The hemp strips slopped their way into her reverie, and she remembered why she was with mop in hand. Gregg. Not a word from him for ages. What if something had happened to him? How could she leave her mother alone while she pursued her career on a different continent? She needed him, damn it! Now that was selfish. Her brother had to go AWOL from a world war so she could feel better about leaving home? His letters could have been lost. They were just lucky that hadn't happened yet. Any news from Gregg was a godsend. *God, please look after my big brother.*

When will I hear back from Pietro? However will I see him again? God, he got under my skin. He made me feel like ... "Fuller. Bucket. Full." The nurse's voice loudly penetrated her reverie. She heaved the bucket of fresh urine from where the nurse stood expertly manipulating the empty catheter and carefully carried it to the drain outside.

Her hospital work would never have lasted had it not served many purposes: karma and her brother; excuse for avoiding boring apocalypse parties; means to make time speed up her adventure to America; extra money toward that very cause.

The hospital staff were always doing things together and socializing on their days off, and though the men often invited her, she had no desire to join them. Her creativity had all but dried up, and there wasn't a new outfit she felt the urge to work on. She was in limbo. Biding her time, accruing her train fare for America. But when she knew the time was right, she'd tell her mother. She shivered with dread.

Did the thought of leaving a man she felt she'd known for lifetimes who she had no bloody chance of actually seeing close-up again cause the shiver? Or was it the feeling of being watched that she couldn't shake lately?

Was it just this morning she'd woken up slowly as navy sleep drifted away and yellow wakefulness fluttered gently under her eyelids? It was Sunday and this was the way waking up should be: a slow, colorful progression of awareness. Not her mother shouting "RISE AND SHINE!" from the doorway or teacups deliberately clattering from the kitchen, causing the household to wake up and get busy on Mrs. Fuller's schedule.

As was always the case, her hand had sought out the heaviness on her bed, and she was rewarded by Buffer's quick lick of assurance on the back of her palm. She could smell the bacon sizzling in the kitchen and knew button mushrooms and fresh yellow eggs would follow. Life was as it should be.

And then she remembered. She'd sat bolt upright as Buffer, immediately crouching on all fours, responded to her anxiety and threw his head vigilantly from door to window. She patted him absently, and his legs relaxed, but not his perked-up ears.

Last night, Paul gave her a lift home from the hospital. It was late. She'd gone there straight after work because they had a fresh batch of wounded sailors off a warship. Added to the war wounds, the poor buggers had disembarked with an exotic gastric virus that took no time at all to spread to the other patients in their hospital wing.

How she remained immune to all this disease was beyond her. She ran hither and thither all night, emptying and filling puke buckets. Her brother would laugh till he cried at the very thought. Gregg's baby sister wouldn't *talk* about her *own* body fluids, let alone *clean up* somebody else's. The vision of Gregg's disbelieving face was the only thing that made the awful smell disappear.

Paul was an intern at the hospital, a sweet guy who would've been happy with a kiss on the cheek, but she didn't have the energy or the inclination. "Intern." Her mother would train him to give Iris the girly hots herself, given half the chance! A doctor's salary, once the war ended, would come in very handy in the Fuller household, thank you very much.

She felt a prickle of fear as she remembered: As Paul drove away, she'd felt uneasy. Standing-hair-on-the-back-of-the-neck kind of uneasy. She'd run up the path, and as she fumbled to get the key in the front door, she thought she heard a car starting around the corner, but she couldn't see any car lights. Odd.

She'd never had cause to feel fear, and she longed for her mother's shielding arms. The thought surprised her. She'd refused to yearn for her mother's protection so very long ago.

She and Buffer had bounded out of her bedroom this morning and found her mom in the lounge, having tea in a delicate China cup. Lena was dusting in the same room.

"Well, well, well. If it isn't Florence Nightingale, risen from the dead." Her mother was on form so early in the morning. It was a gift.

"Eich. Ibhubesi is a good gal, Missus. She work hard in hospital. Her clothes stinky." Iris smiled her thanks to Lena for sticking up for her.

Her mother was indignant. "Well, she's not being paid enough to be stinky. She should be smelling like June roses at parties, with her mother." Aha! Therein lay the real cause of her mother's sarcasm.

"Have some fun, child, don't spend your time at the wretched hospital. There are plenty of natives who would welcome being paid to clean up body fluids. I bet *your* people would gladly do that, wouldn't they, Lena?" Lena immersed herself deeper into the bookshelf, trying unsuccessfully to disappear. Boy! Her mother badly needed a card night and a bottle of Cane Spirits to loosen the ramrod lodged up her tight bum.

Iris looked at Lena and made an apologetic face. "I do it for Gregg."

"Gregg? Good God, Iris. In his last letter, Gregg was languishing on the outskirts of Florence in a RAF camp. He's probably enjoying the local beauties and the fine pastas while you mop up God-only-knows what." She sniffed. "That's probably why he hasn't got time to write."

Iris had heard of "the change" when women got to be her mother's age. Just when she thought she knew her mother, she changed!

So much for finding comfort here. She called Buffer, and as soon as they were out of sight, both Iris and Buffer increased their speed, running away from her mother's protests, which, thank the Lord himself, got harder to hear: "Don't go outside in your pajamas, Iris. Good heavens, if the servants or the neighbors see you … " Iris was far enough away to safely finish her mother's sentence as her daughter would have preferred: " … they'll beg you to make them a pair of these fabulous PJs, as the Americans call them, but with wide bottoms that only you, my clever child, would think of." *In my dreams.*

Her dreams. She remembered that Pee-Et-Ro had been in her dreams last night. That soft, sand-colored skin, his deep, velvet-blue eyes. Goodness. What thoughts of him did to her! She sighed. Just dreams, they were. He was a prisoner. And she was going overseas. She'd tell her mother once she'd sent back the letter of confirmation. But as it had done earlier, the thrill of embarking on her Great Adventure was marred by disappointment that she'd never have the chance to know her Pee-Et-Ro. She sighed. C'est la vie. Then she remembered the breakfast her mouth watered for earlier and realized thoughts of her Pietro had quelled her hunger.

Her eyes followed the rest of the stream of feces. Hmm, what color was this exactly? Khaki with a dash of lime green? Then she shook her head and whispered: "If you are languishing in the arms of an attractive woman while I clean up shit, Gregg, I will kill you myself." The thought of his infectious grin brought out her own.

"Nice to see you smile, Iris." Doctor Paul Snyman again. Her mother had spotted them out of the window when he'd dropped her off after a long shift a few months ago. It must have been the newer car and the white coat, both dead giveaways, that propelled Mrs. Fuller out of the front door at the speed of light, with a smile and an invitation to share a cup of tea.

Dr. Snyman easily made himself at home and chatted comfortably to her mother while Iris gave all her attention to Buffer. The doctor followed her mother into the kitchen to carry the tray, and that single courtesy caused endless scolding when the teacups were cold and he was gone at last.

"You could have warned me. The top of the fridge ... "

"I had no intention of bringing him home. *You* invited him in. Don't blame his height or the dirty top of the fridge on me, Mother."

Now here he was again, in her way, grinning at her. Apparently, his sense of smell was as dead as her own.

Iris avoided eye contact, concentrating on wielding her mop. "Busy day again today."

"Yes, they're streaming in. How's your mother? Should I pop in and see her sometime?"

The less the men interested her, the more interested they were. She shot over her shoulder: "Be careful. My mother might think you're marriage material. So unless you fancy an older woman with a child my age, it might not be a good idea."

———

Later that night, she'd hurried into the house like there was an ax murderer after her. She couldn't shake the heebie-jeebies or her heavy heart and found herself knocking on Lena's door long after her mother had turned out her light.

"You all right, Ibhubesi?" asked a sleepy Lena, her turban off. A shock of white and black hair, like a half-good, half-bad halo, circled her shiny forehead.

"I need you, Lena," Iris wailed. The elder moved away from her door to allow her white child and the ever-present dog access to her small, windowless room. Iris seldom went into Lena's room anymore. It was the woman's sanctuary, after all. Unlike her younger years, when she spent hours in there, learning the shapes of Lena and Sofie's bodies and using them as models, she could now make their outfits with her eyes closed. But here she was, in the middle of the night, with her head pillowed in Lena's matronly bosom, crying her eyes out.

"Tell Lena, Ibhubesi. Tell."

And so she spilled all her beans about her new adventure in a foreign land and her guilt about leaving them all.

"It is as it must be, Ibhubesi. You have too much dress-clever to stay in Maritzburg. The world needs my clever girl. Not just Lena and Sofie."

"But will you be lonely, Lena?"

"Of course. But you are of my heart, and to hold you back would be to take away your wings. What mother would wish her butterfly to use only her long, skinny legs? You will always be here." Through Lena's chest, Iris felt the vibration of Lena tapping her own heart.

Lena's kindness was worse than her fury or disappointment, and a fresh torrent of wails emitted, unbidden.

When she'd recovered for a minute, she remembered a verse: " 'For life goes not backward, nor tarries with yesterday. You are the bows from which your children as living arrows are sent forth.' It's from a centuries-old prophet. He was almost as wise as you, Lena."

"Nobody as wise as Lena." Her Zulu mother chuckled as she stroked Iris's hair, rendering her a little girl again.

Out of the corner of her eye, Iris saw Buffer pacing with concern. Lena's pudgy bare foot found his neck in the cramped quarters, and with splayed toes in his fur, she calmed him.

"And Buffer, Lena? How will he cope?"

"Ibhubesi, my child. Dogs are like faithful servants. When their master has gone, to ease their hearts, they find another to give their loyalty. It's what they must do to survive. I will be here to love him also."

"And my mother?"

Lena took a while to answer. "Your mother." She sighed. "For your mother, we must find a husband. Before you go."

Iris stopped sobbing for a minute, then started to giggle, hiccupping between sobs. "A husband? Oh, Lena. You are so funny. Where the hell do we find one of those?"

Lena answered, looking down her broad nose and imitating her mother's voice to a tee. "At petrol station, of course!" The two laughed with the kind of gusto you can't stop and that inevitably turns to tears. But it was worth it.

Iris so badly wanted to tell her about Pietro. But what was there to tell, really? She was lulled into calm by Lena's stroking of her hair. "Pee-Et-Ro. Pee-Et-Ro." His face. His electric touch. His fathomless eyes that mysteriously understood her completely.

SPILLING THE BEANS

29 August 1943

Iris absently doodled in her sketchpad, intending a new design, but it became a gorgeous pair of eyes. His eyes. The Savior's. Her Savior's. Pee-Et-Ro. "You fool." She chastised herself harshly. She certainly wasn't looking for a man, any man, to step in the way of her new career. And a prisoner? It was laughable. Must be the feces exposure making her prematurely senile. Ha! And she thought she was immune.

Immune to love? Perhaps not. *Don't be stupid, Iris.* She could always count on her mother's voice to keep her straight. Sadly.

A career was all she needed. All she'd ever wanted. The letter that she had all but forgotten, because of those fathomless eyes, ignited a new hole in her pocket. She needed to design fashions or elaborate Hollywood costumes. It was her calling.

It was late, but sleep eluded her. She tickled the rough paper with the tip of her lead pencil again, but instead of a bodice, his body emerged. Not Hercules, but strong, though a little too thin.

Who was she kidding? He looked like a ragamuffin with bare feet.

Those mesmerizing blue eyes, a mouth—oh boy, did he have a mouth. It was wide and full and one front tooth overlapped the other, ever so slightly. She licked her lips and squirmed. What? A *mouth* made her squirm? Only daring designs had that effect. She looked down and felt a squeak as she saw his face, *his* face staring out at her. She must have drawn as she thought of him. It was an uncanny likeness. Boy, was he gorgeous.

But she'd known many gorgeous men. It was the way *he looked at her* that gave her the girly hots, not just the way he looked. And it was more, much more. It transcended usual understanding ... *You see? That's what going to un-Catholic ceremonies at Easter will do for you!* Would her mother's scolding voice penetrate her happiness forever, she wondered?

Damn it. She was a logical sort. She knew she'd *never* have the chance to be consumed mentally or devoured physically by him. He was behind a lethal barbed-wire fence, for gosh sakes. He was a prisoner of war. He was the enemy. *The* enemy of her country and its citizens. The *specific* enemy of her brother. The very nationality under Hitler's command that Gregg was risking his own precious life to destroy.

She crumpled the expensive piece of design paper into a ball and threw it against the wall. Buffer watched the misshapen ball bounce once and roll. But based on her mood, the dog would never presume to make it a game. He crawled subserviently toward her, and loving arms circled his neck. "Silly me. You're the only male I will ever need in my life, Buffs."

There was a loud knock on the front door. At this time of night? Her heart sank. Bad news of Gregg? Buffer sprang off the bed and charged to the hall. Iris heard her mother open the door, and a man's voice boomed over Buffer's barks.

She launched herself off her bed, into the hall. Julian! His civilian shirt un-tucked, his face shiny. When he saw her, his face lit up. "Irish!"

Her mother reluctantly moved to the side of the open door, but Iris wasn't moving closer. She confronted him from the doorway while holding on to Buffer's collar. Her faithful dog's growl was low, and his teeth were bared.

"What are you doing here?" Her voice quivered. It could still be bad news. *Oh, God. Gregg. Or had he intercepted Pietro's note, to which she'd signed her name?*

He drunkenly launched himself onto one knee. "Marry me." His grin was wicked.

She stepped back and laughed, hugely relieved. "You're out of your mind. And drunk."

"I'll ask you the shame thing when I'm shober."

"My answer will still be 'no.' I don't want to get involved, Julian. With anyone. I have a career waiting in another country. Now get up, please. You're embarrassing yourself."

He precariously launched himself back on two feet. "Would you marry me if I hadn't been demoted?"

"Demoted?"

"New bashtard. Cairns. Came in above me. I'm jusht a captain now. Night duty moshtly."

"I'm sorry."

"I'll make shure I get my 'Colonel' back. Will that make you happy?" He wobbled.

"Julian, it's your life. You have to do what makes *you* happy."

"*You* make me happy." His smile was lopsided, and he battled to keep his eyes open.

Iris thought it best not to say anything.

"I can't live without you."

"You don't even know me."

"We shared hot kisshes."

"That's not nearly enough."

"I can give you more." His face took on a drunken sexy look that was entirely obscene.

"No, Julian. You can't. Go now. Please." She looked away, dismissing him.

"I've changed. Sho popular now. You would be proud. WOPs call me 'Top Chef.' That'sh me. 'Macellaio.' " He grinned and moved closer, but Buffer would have none of it. The dog hunkered down, ready to spring, purple lips bared over sharp teeth, growling.

"Call off the dogsh. Macellaio inshists!" He giggled at his own his cleverness.

Maybe he should be drunk more often. He has a shard of humor in his cold soul.

Iris moved Buffer with her knee and quickly closed and bolted the door. She leaned against it as Julian continued to beg on the other side.

Her mother completely ignored the crying, wailing and gnashing of teeth outside and looked at Iris. Hurt marred her attractive features, and her eyes brimmed with rare tears. "You're leaving me? You're moving to another country?"

1st September, 1943.

From: You know where—or have YOU forgotten where your home is?

Beloved Brother,

This is getting beyond a joke now! "Where the hell are you" seems so very inadequate! Well, I will pretend that you are still reading my letters and not ignoring them in favor of something or someone more titillating!

So, this is what happened 'tween your mother and me when Julian (of meat-hand fame) dropped to a knee in a drunken stupor outside our front door and asked for my own lily-white hand in marriage. To make him go away, I told Julian I had taken a career overseas.

"And you couldn't tell me about your imminent abandonment?"

"I'm not abandoning you, Mom. I am exploring a phenomenal opportunity."

"And the difference is?"

"You should be happy for me. You should be celebrating instead of chastising. I feel like I'm back to nine years old, gazing at your closed bedroom door. If it wasn't for Gregg ... "

"Oh, don't be so dramatic, Iris. I recall no such thing."

"That's because you weren't there, Mother, you were wallowing in your own self-pity."

"Watch your tone, young lady."

"I'm an adult, Mother. Your scolding will no longer stop me from telling you the truth."

"It's your truth, Iris, and complete, utter balderdash."

"Why do you think I don't want children, Mother? I'll tell you! I'm afraid to disappoint them." I couldn't help myself, Gregg.

"Like I disappointed you?" She batted her eyelashes at me! Like that might elicit pity!

I nodded, and she shouted: "Horseshit!" Yes, she did. She said "Horseshit" without any Cane Spirits! I'm telling you, Brother, inside that hostile prim exterior lurks a wild, wanton, foul-mouthed woman.

Which brings me to my new mission! The only good Julian's visit did us was let us know there was a new man in charge at the POW camp.

Well, into the store the new colonel barraged today. Seriously, this man doesn't just enter anywhere, he makes a formidable impression and leaves a feeling of importance in his wake. He is big and tall and has the personality and charisma to match. The ladies in the store, irrespective of age, were all a-twitter. I hear he's a widower! JACKPOT!

If I can find Mom a husband, I will get a guilt-free sendoff (except Buffer and Lena and you, not necessarily in that order), and you will get your own life when you come home!

I meant to tell you I went to the POW camp to help with inoculations some weeks ago. Gregg, it was so strange to see these men, YOUR enemies, up close. I confess what I saw were just neglected men, mostly in their twenties and thirties. Their spirits seemed to push through their dire circumstances. I had a profound realization. These could have been our allies if Mussolini chose to fight with the British. Ah, things to ponder on a spring day.

I love and miss you. Please write! I can't deal with your silence. If you're in the loving arms of one of our enemy, I'll forgive you. Would you do the same for me?

Wish me luck in my Cupid Quest! Now I must away to put raw onion on my face for fifteen minutes. A "new and sure-fire way" to rid my face of you-know-what. Yes, my eyes will likely lose their color from all the onion-induced weeping and I'll smell like a Greek salad, but it will surely beat baby's wee as a "proven" cure!

Your ever-loving, still-freckle-faced, little sister,

Iris aka Sunshine xx

NEW BEGINNINGS

7 September 1943

Sacks, lights, rolls of remnant fabric, paint and balsa wood were passed via manmade chain, all the way from the Red Cross trucks and into the new mess hall they'd built in the camp.

As the last link in the chain, Pietro deposited the donated goods onto the "stage"—newly crafted wooden tables stacked together well in advance of this exciting delivery. Sitting on the floor to eat their solid three meals a day, courtesy of New Colonel, was but a small price to pay for their much-anticipated entertainment.

Pietro took a moment to look around at the men's faces. He hadn't seen such animation since the Venice carnival. *And my animation is all for you, Mia Rossa.* Thoughts of her made his head spin in a way no other human being had accomplished in his twenty-five years.

Colonel Cairns had proved to be every bit as good as his word. In two months, the camp was transformed. The manpower in the razor-enclosed area was aching to be generated. All it needed was someone to drive it, which the colonel did with aplomb. An ablution block with showers and latrines sprang up courtesy of Italian muscle. Then the mess hall. Some prisoners were bused out to fix roads and design bridges. The Italian work force was in business. There was no more going off to die in the chicken coop corners. The camp oozed with vitality. Its only blemish was Tap Tap, still around and angrier, having been stripped of his lofty, albeit temporary title. The men were on their guard at night, five times a week, when the butcher was on duty. His inconsistency kept them on their toes.

New Colonel miraculously convinced his brass that it was in the interests of the prisoners' mental health that they should be allowed to stage their own operas. That's where the Red Cross and their generous donations came in.

Pietro watched two men hoisting an old, donated mirror off the truck, and a Red Cross employee handed them his morning newspaper to use as insulation against cuts from the jagged edges. Pietro followed the mirror, and as soon as the men positioned it, he grabbed the smudged pages, scanning them for something specific. Aha! Now all he needed was a pin and a Red Cross volunteer who would prove to be a suitably naive postman.

---

8 September 1943

Fourfeet beamed like a ray of sunshine as his feet worked a million miles a minute. It was as if he had St. Vitus's Dance, but Iris knew he was just honoring his given name. The guy must have popped out of the womb dribbling a soccer ball.

"Tell me again, Fourfeet."

"Klein Miesies, Singingman find Solomon on his donkey picking up rubbish in pow camp. He say, 'Solomon, you gave your first newspaper to Fourfeet and you told me he was soccer man, no?'"

Iris nodded and impatiently cocked her head this way and that to hurry him on.

"Today, Solomon find me after work and he say, 'Fourfeet, you are soccer star. Singingman gave you this.' I ask Solomon to read it to me, but he has no time, and Lena is at market, so I come to you."

"Perfect!" Iris smiled at him and scanned the newspaper's grimy pages.

"Here. Here!" It was Fourfeet's turn to be impatient as he pointed to the sports section. Of course, Iris was looking for those precious little dots.

"Aha! 'Soccer's Place in Our War.' Hmmm ... looks like they are saying in England, factories are setting up women's soccer teams ... ah, and soccer helps war recruiters who sign up whole teams together ... and POWs are setting up leagues sponsored by the Red Cross."

"The whole thing, Miesies, read the WHOLE thing." Fourfeet's impatience increased the speed of the man's feet, *if* that was possible.

"Give me just half an hour, then come back and I'll read it to you as many times as you like," Iris promised.

She watched Fourfeet sprint away as if his speed could push time's hand a little faster. Then, her heart beating as fast as the young Zulu's feet, she held that page up to the light. Sure enough, there were the pinpricks she'd hoped to find.

She pieced together the words: "My Iris. May I call you that? Please be patient. I will find a way. You are all I dream of. One day I will call you 'My Love.' " She felt strange stirrings in the bottom of her tummy and raised her face to the sun—or was it to heaven?—to say thank you to whomever might be up there.

QUID PRO QUO

15 September 1943

Colonel's generosity of spirit was impressive, but nothing's for nothing. It was a lesson Pietro had learned in the dingy dressing rooms, and it wasn't long before he found out what he had to pay for all these new privileges.

Pietro hoisted a box of paint and brushes onto the stage as Sergeant Rogers tapped him on the shoulder.

"Sergeant?" Pietro asked, dreading the answer.

"Colonel wants to see you."

It was time.

Inside the office that was stark and clinical when occupied by Tap Tap, Colonel Cairns's version was filled to the brim with mementoes and memorabilia: a pair of signed, tired rugby boots next to an autographed oblong ball; pictures of a self-satisfied team of cricket players; a mounted Scottish tartan with a clan brooch; and, most encouraging, a gold frame boasting an auto-graphed photo of The Great Caruso. It drew Pietro in, and he found his nose inches from the brown and white portrait.

"You look a bit like him," Colonel said blithely.

Pietro did a double take. The only reason that could be was because he was Italian and an opera singer. He had long since stopped kidding himself.

Colonel was distracted as he fiddled with the knob of the radio that stood on his desk.

"Trying to figure out how to deal with you lot now that Italy's surrendered to the Allies."

The news hit Pietro like a brick. *What? Were they now on the same side? Would they be deported back to Italy soon? Oh, God! No! Would he be allowed to freely see his Iris?*

It took all his resolve and his voice training to keep his question on an even keel. "Colonel, what does this mean?"

"It means that you will be paid for any work you do to enhance the camp or the roads and such. Not much, mind—perhaps a shilling a week just to satisfy the Geneva—"

"And we can leave the camp?" Pietro couldn't hold back.

"Not on your Nellie! What do you think this is? Make-believe? No, man—here you will stay, in captivity, till the war ends."

Pietro was surprised that his first feeling was relief that at least he would stay close to Iris till the end of the war.

"But we are on the same side now?" Perhaps then seeing her would no longer be a crime?

"No, son. You are still an Italian POW. You were captured during your German affiliation. You have to pay for that. You will never be 'on our side' as far as the majority here is concerned. Many local boys lost their lives by an Italian hand. We have to keep you guys locked up now as much for your own safety, as for your war crimes against us that got you here."

A lot of loud "whishing and whooshing" ensued on the radio, rendering their conversation done.

Colonel turned down the volume but kept fiddling. "How's

the prep for the opera season going?" The radio shushed, buzzed and beeped. He gave it a good slap, which made no difference to the offending sounds, then looked up at Pietro.

Pietro nodded and smiled. "Good. Very good."

"Do you play the piano?"

"Piano? Si. Si." Pietro was still keeping his English close to his chest, so to speak.

"This blasted thing hasn't worked since I bought it. It deserves nothing but destruction." He slapped the radio so hard, it flew off his desk and onto the floor, shattering.

"Well, good bloody riddance is all I can say. Will you throw the blooming thing in the rubbish on your way out, please?"

Pietro couldn't believe his luck. New Colonel absently handed him a small sack, and Pietro hastened to pick up every single piece of the mutilated radio. Colonel handed him a sheet.

"Learn this. Sergeant Rogers will fetch you when I'm ready."

Pietro held fast to the music sheet. Every step he took was one closer to seeing his Iris.

The sack caused a problem reentering the prison enclosure. Fortunately, the radio was unrecognizable, so he was able to convince the guards that the bag of wires and knobs were from the New Colonel for opera use. He was beyond excited about presenting the radio's thousand parts but knew he had to wait. The gift's presentation shouldn't be diluted by the anticipation of their first camp opera. Antonio was a big part of opening night.

Back in the mess hall, he was unprepared for the beautiful sight that greeted him. Exhausted men draped themselves over rolls of materials, propped their heads upon cotton stuffing or huddled in groups between paint cans and balsa wood. Pietro joined Enzo, Antonio and Stef, who sat with their legs dangling over the edge of their stage, like excited young boys.

One of the first things New Colonel did was to get his "boys"

new underwear, uniforms and gloriously welcome *leather boots!*
South African made, but prisoners couldn't be choosers.

Having jumped up on the stage to join them, Pietro held the
colonel's sheet of music, humming the tune as he read the lyrics.

"What's that?" asked Enzo.

Pietro gestured broadly around the mess hall. "Santa Maria!
My penance, no doubt." But he couldn't contain his mammoth
grin. Whatever he had to pay, Iris was worth it.

13

'LET ME CALL YOU SWEETHEART'

20 September 1943

Pietro held the music sheet in his hand as he was ushered into the officers' mess hall and heard the swoosh of Sergeant Rogers's retreat, followed by a quickly closed door and a lock being turned. From the outside too?

New Colonel's face appeared between the red velvet stage curtains, and he beckoned to Pietro to come up. On stage, only one spotlight highlighted the piano. On a couch behind the piano stool languished a blond woman. Her ample breasts bulged out of a low-cut dress. Attractive to be sure, but Pietro recognized a paid companion when he saw one. She smiled, but he turned quickly to the task before him, sitting on the soft piano stool. *Dio Mio.* He hadn't felt this kind of softness under his backside in years. He smoothed the music sheet on the rack and began his penance. He swore he would do it so well, he would pay in advance for Colonel's favors.

And so began the first of many, many hours of "Let Me Call You Sweetheart."

Apparently it was a way for the Colonel to let this woman of ill repute know that he could call her something other than "paid for."

It would have been a mindless chore for Pietro, singing this repetitive song, over and over again, but for the reflection in that damned shiny piano. It was like a mirror. From the very first note, the two lost no time pawing each other. Bobbing naked breasts popped out of their skimpy restraints, and the colonel used some impressive moves to make the working girl moan like a virgin. Pietro would have been impressed, had he not been thwarted by an unexpected, hugely embarrassing erection. He lost traction on the pedals trying to adjust himself. Nobody noticed. He tried changing keys to the song to see if that would make an impression enough to stop the action. Not at all. So much for flashing his talent. It went quite unnoticed. As soon as he finished the song the sixth time, he turned around, and though the colonel's face was immersed in white voluptuous flesh, he managed to wave a "continue" motion.

And so he began the song again. And again. His damn erection getting bigger each time.

14

'YOURS, MAF'

20th September, 1943

Darling Brother Mine,

Remember me? I'm your sister. Your only sister. Longing for you. Please God you are safe. I would hate all that feces I've mopped to be for naught. Really, really miss you.

So news here is that Lena and I continue on our mission to find Philemon from the petrol station for our mother. I know, I know, we can't visualize our mother with the girly hots because that would just be so hideously wrong but truth is, you can't un-ring a bell, so you may as well exploit it!

You also know, if you're getting my letters, that larger-than-life Colonel Cairns is the target. And so, though Lena wanted me to go to Jurita Bakery to buy the blooming cake, I thought it was important that the giver had gone to the trouble for the colonel, so Lena and I muddled through baking a chocolate cake. You must remember that though our Lena is a cook of note, she refuses to bake anything. She still buys our scones, hot cross buns and breads from Jurita Bakery. Now tell me, Brother, wouldn't you just die for one of those koeksisters, the pair of entwined syrup-soaked fried dough sticks, dripping in sticky sweetness as you bite into the crunchy shells! Oh!

My own mouth waters! Come home and we'll have a dozen each, to celebrate!

So back to the colonel's cake. I think we overdid the bicarbonate of soda. It came out of the oven looking like an anthill, so we squished it into shape and upped the cocoa content to mask the tart taste. It spent the night in Lena's room, then today the bloody thing collapsed on the way to the camp and I had to restructure the thing with my hands. I nearly made the poor driver chunder, and he a doctor to boot. I think his sterile sensibilities were hugely offended since I wiped my hands on his engine rag during and after the reconstruction.

This Colonel Cairns would be so perfect for mother. You should see what he's done with the POW camp. It has buildings and must have a sewerage system, because the stench was gone and all the men inside wore uniforms and boots. I felt an energy there today, so sadly missing the last time, as khaki-clad men bustled purposefully. What a difference a good man makes.

Sadly, the colonel was otherwise engaged, but I left the chocolate anthill there in the fancy container, having placed two fresh roses I brought from the garden on the very top, and thank the lord, it improved the tired look immensely. I also gave the sergeant an envelope with a note, spritzed with Mama's rose perfume, of course, which read:

"Dear Colonel, Welcome to my neck of the woods. I hope it becomes 'home' very quickly, and if there is anything at all I can personally do to help make it feel that way, please don't hesitate to ask. Yours, MAF."

I hope the intrigue will get him before he samples the cake. Otherwise, dear brother, we may be screwed, because not even the sight of the roses will improve the taste! I pray he's allergic to chocolate and won't touch the stuff.

I'll probably write again really soon because it's wonderful— wait—it's necessary to share with you, Brother.

I love you forever.
Your Sunshine xx

What Iris didn't tell Gregg was that contriving a "Philemon" possibility for her mother was only half of her quest today. Her stomach did the second somersault of her life, thinking about her Pietro. It came so naturally to her now—putting the deter-miner before his name.

But he was nowhere to be seen.

She scoured hundreds of faces trying to find his. Somehow, she knew she would feel him before she saw him. But nothing. She heard the wolf-whistles faintly, but they were diminished by the pounding of disappointment in her ears. Reluctantly, she turned her back and walked into the building holding her, ahem, her mother's offering before her.

The most beautiful sound came from somewhere up the passage. The richest, clearest voice she'd ever heard. "Let Me Call You Sweetheart." When the song ended, Iris felt a regret so deep, it was as if she had lost something vital. But thankfully, not a minute later, it began again. She realized she'd stood quite still as she listened, mesmerized. A uniformed man appeared.

"What is that? Who is that?" Iris asked the man looking side-ways at her offering.

"Army business, Miss. May I help you?" Iris handed him the cake tin.

"For Colonel Cairns. Please, will you make sure you put it in his very hands? Oh, and just a minute." She carefully took off the lid, pulled out the roses and the scented note and arranged them all, and popped the lid back on.

"Is that all, Miss?" She only heard that vaguely as the golden voice started the song again and goose pimples covered her arms. Was somebody practicing? He certainly didn't need to. She closed her eyes, letting the sound seep into her every pore. What the hell was wrong with her these days? Her body was doing odd things.

"You all right, Miss?"

"Thank you, Lieutenant?" She smiled and tilted her head in question.

"Sergeant, Miss. Sergeant Rogers." He smiled too.

"You sure you can't tell me who's singing, Sergeant?"

He lost his smile. "Army business, Miss."

"Iris, Sergeant. I'm Iris. And thank you." She so badly wanted to linger, but she'd obviously been dismissed. She walked slowly so she could hear the end of the song. Before she left the building, halfway through another repeat, the song stopped abruptly. She heard a door open, slam, then loping footsteps. She turned, but the footsteps were in a faraway passage she couldn't see. *How incredibly powerful that voice must be. I heard it through closed doors when I have to strain to hear footsteps!*

HOT AND COLD

20 September 1943

Was it the thirteenth time? He shut his eyes tightly to avoid the ever-increasing rubbing and sucking and dry-humping reflected on the shiny fall board of the upright piano. Thank God he played by ear. But not even his closed lids, or the increased volume of the ivory keys, or the upped decibel of the song he sang, could block out the noises from the couch. *Dio mio!* There were body parts that would live with him forever, reflected in that piano! And not in a good way.

Yes, without doubt, his was a surreal attraction to Rossa, his Iris, sacred almost, but his body acted in a most un-saintly way. Just a quick recall of her face, and the problem down yonder got completely out of control. By the umpteenth repeat, feet off the pedals and cross-legged, he could stand it no longer. Midway through the song he jumped up, ridiculously uncomfortable and bulging at every angle. He half-turned with eyes on the ceiling and said very loudly, "Scusie, Colonel." There was an ever-so-brief rest for hands and other body parts as four eyes looked at him, surprised he was in the room at all.

There was no waiting for dismissal. He limped off the stage and ran awkwardly to the door, unlocked the deadbolt, which thankfully worked inside as well as out, and launched himself into the passage, dragging his foot, rendered heavy by the weight of his crotch, down the hall. It was the only way he could walk quickly without his engorged member being strangled.

As he left the building through the back entrance and rounded the corner, such was his obsession with her, he thought he saw Mia Rossa getting into a jeep. But once he shook his head to clear it, the jeep was bouncing away from him down the road. She so overwhelmed his senses that he believed he saw strands of long, red hair blowing in the wind, teasing him. That image almost sent him over the edge, but he managed to drag himself through quickly opened gates and straight to the new ablution block.

Minutes later, "O Sole Mio" heralded the relief of the cold shower. He knew his volume was turned way up, courtesy of sweet release, and he wondered if his Iris could hear him in town, eight miles away.

On the ride back in the open jeep, the oddest thing happened to Iris. She felt him. Her Pietro. He must be close. But when she turned, a blooming wild, red tendril covered her eyes. As she hurriedly tucked it behind her ear, all she saw from this distance was a khaki uniform limping into the camp.

Strangely, it was not the oft-repeated "Let Me Call You Sweetheart" that echoed in Iris's head, but a triumphant "O Sole Mio" which made her smile. Everything would all work out as it should. Just like her brother had always promised.

OPENING NIGHT

19 October 1943

They'd built a mess hall with a stage, but tonight it wasn't a stage at all, but the inside of a Japanese house on a hill in Nagasaki, Japan.

With their limited supplies, they had created a believable other world, complete with a view of the harbor below the house and through the window.

The last time he was this excited to perform was his defining moment a lifetime ago, in La Fenice opera house. Who would ever have known that this coming performance was more important even than that? It was the continuation of his journey toward his final destination. To see Mia Cara Rossa.

Oh, that she could be here to celebrate this milestone. His redhead. He laughed softly. He was distinctly soft in the head. He hadn't seen her for two months, twenty days and three and a half hours. Since his inoculation. But their notes back and forth kept him going. They were scarce both to her and from her, because their challenge was finding a way to send them. He was in a prison camp, after all. But somehow he knew she felt as dizzy as he.

At Enzo's admission booth, the price of entry was either something the patrons had made or an IOU for a chore they were prepared to do for someone else. The army personnel dribbling in on New Colonel's orders ignored Enzo's admission policy.

Inside, prisoners sat on the floor and stood against walls. Colonel Cairns sat in the front row, with the rest of the personnel on the remaining chairs and tables. Antonio, beaming with joy, distributed hand-printed programs weaving the story of *Madam Butterfly*, though most found their way onto the floor, unread, much to the square man's great disappointment.

The orchestra squeaked, tuneless in warm-up.

Each one of the men contributed to this evening in some way. The excitement was palpable from the Italians, tittering and giggling like schoolgirls, but there was a distinct reluctance and resistance from most everyone else except the colonel.

As a show of their indifference, officers and NCOs increased the volume of their bitch sessions: "We have to be here, but we don't have to enjoy this crap."

Peeping through the slightly pulled-back curtain, Pietro saw Tap Tap leaning against the door frame at the back of the hall, no doubt for an easy escape. His arms crossed over his chest. Over his arm, the black whip hung down, splitting his body in half.

As the orchestra struck up the overture, Pietro watched his friend Stef, back in his element. Playing his violin. He loved that little guy. Stef looked up, catching Pietro's eye, and behind their smiles were a thousand memories shared and an unspoken thanks for being together again and sharing their mutual joy of performance. This was *their* world. The overture continued and Pietro's beady eye, still peeping through the curtain gap, saw distinct surprise on many faces.

He let the curtain fall behind him as he watched the actors take their marks and turned to pat the leading "lady's" shoulder. The man was quivering so severely with stage fright, his teeth were chattering. "*In bocca al lupo*, friend. You will be a sensation. They have no expectations, so you will be a hundred percent better than they imagined. You can't lose." Pietro had deliberately used the Italian expression of good luck, meaning "in the mouth of the wolf," reserved for opera singers to show the man that he was indeed an opera singer this night.

"*Crepi*," whispered the leading lady, an abbreviated response for "Kill the wolf."

As the curtain rose, there was complete silence. A real compliment from this audience. Pietro smiled, infinitely proud of what his men had accomplished. Silence. The international sound of an audience's attention gave the actors such a boost, his lead's shaking lips smoothed into a smile.

After a few nervous warbles from the white-powdered face of Cio-Cio-San, she/he drank in the rapt audience and went from amateur to budding pro. Pietro felt his smile spread from ear to ear. There was nothing more powerful than captivating an audience. When had he forgotten that? Ah, yes! It was sometime between a Sudanese tree, six months in hospital, a soul-destroying prison camp and three weeks in the underbelly of a luxury liner!

And then it was time for B.F. Pinkerton, lieutenant from the United States Navy, to make his South African debut—with an Italian accent, of course.

Pietro entered stage right, and the easy familiarity turned to exuberant joy to be doing this ... the only thing he knew.

The audience was every bit as entranced as Pietro had

hoped. You could hear a pin drop until seconds after each act, and then they stood in unison: officers, NCOs and prisoners alike, cheering and whistling and shouting and stamping their feet. A celebration of appreciation.

There was one disturbance. It was after his opening aria, when the back door of their "auditorium" was pushed open with exaggerated force, and thanks to the far-from-adequate stage lighting, Pietro could make out Tap Tap storming out, his whip beating his leg as if it were an ill-tempered horse.

When everyone had left and they were cleaning up the hall, Antonio sought out Pietro. "They picked up their programs, Pietro. From the floor. They picked them up afterward and took them away with them." The square man's face was alight with awe.

"Well, they wouldn't have done that if they weren't works of art, Antonio." It was Antonio who had painstakingly copied each program from Pietro's original, a hundred or more by his own hand.

"They wouldn't have done that if our opera didn't mean anything to them." Antonio's articulation stunned and delighted Pietro.

"How right you are, my friend. But I will need you to go to work again. Colonel has asked for a repeat performance tomorrow night. Perhaps this time we will write a short piece on each act, so they will enjoy the story as well as the art!"

"A second night? A repeat performance? By request?" Antonio thought he was hearing things.

When Pietro nodded, Antonio threw back his head shouting as if to God, "Grazie! Grazie!" If there was a prize of prizes, it was that his dim friend had found some brightness. Well, that, and his first step toward Mia Rossa had been accomplished. The second step would be taken after tomorrow night.

Pietro had been waiting for the colonel since the doors opened at 6 a.m. It was 9:30 a.m. At least three times, Rogers had told Pietro he was wearing a permanent trench in the parquet floor.

The big man arrived but made Pietro wait outside another fifteen minutes while Rogers debriefed him on war issues or some such officiousness.

At last!

"Excellent job, Pietro. You are a man of your word. You produced, and then some. I do believe we have converted the full army contingent from never seeing an opera to ardent lovers of this great art. Well done."

"Grazie, sir. Whole camp help."

"Yes. A real team effort with you at the helm."

"Colonel, I have, how you say, idea?"

"Hmmm?"

"What if you take *Madam Butterfly* to *centro* ... town?"

"No. There are too many naysayers out there."

What the hell was he saying? All his strange colonialisms drove Pietro crazy. "Naysayers?"

"Those who don't buy what you are selling."

"But we are no longer enemies, Colonel."

"As I told you, Pietro, you are the enemy to us until the war ends. No ifs, ands or buts."

"But ... " Damn it. The man had to listen to him.

"Stop. Enough. Answer's 'no,' Pietro."

There was a knock on the door. "Come," barked the colonel.

Sergeant Rogers's head appeared. "Sorry to interrupt, Colonel, but good news. Message from Natal Command. Brigadier Powers sends his congratulations on an exemplary war relations effort. Says everyone is gung-ho about the opera. Brigadier says he hopes you caught the Japanese pun, sir. He says he's too busy for you to return the call, just keep up the good work and spread the music. It eases the hatred."

Pietro watched the colonel's face actually glow with pride. His cheeks spread, and Pietro swore his teeth sparkled.

"Ha! Powers, no less. Thank you, Rogers. Who knew he was such a liberal? Perhaps just an opera fan. Now, Pietro, let's talk about a concert, and let's get you out there to show these Martitzburgers how it's done. I'd love to do the whole 'Butterfly' bit, but it's a security nightmare. Let me ponder. Dismissed."

Enzo knelt on the floor of their new church, marveling at the detailed work of his fellow camp-dwellers. Their church had been built from stone—quarried and cut by his fellow prisoners. Under supervision, of course. It was a work of art. Inside, the woodwork all around him was magnificent. His very own Jesus was before him. It took Enzo hundreds of hours to carve the life-size Christ on the cross, which was the backdrop of the pulpit. He knew pride was a sin, but here he was, in their newly built Catholic church, feeling good about his own Jesus. He'd better get busy and ask forgiveness for his cardinal sin of pride. But what was the use? He was about to tell some whopping lies in this place of worship, so what the hell? He sat back on the pew. Next to him was his first carving of the Virgin Mary that had lived happily for a year in their tent.

The church door opened, and a private entered, looking left and right guiltily.

The man slid into the pew in front of Enzo. He sure was jittery.

"It's done," the private promised.

"Nobody hear you?" Enzo's voice, loud with intent, made them both jump.

"No."

"Rogers believe you big brass?"

"I'm a good mimic. I used to report to Powers. OK, down the chain, but still, I heard him many times. I made it clear to Rogers that there was to be no further discussion." He paused for no more than three seconds. "Can I have it now?"

The private strained his neck to see the Virgin Mary sitting next to Enzo.

Enzo moved the carving about an inch out of the private's sight.

"You understand you don't mess with Mother Mary? Especially she, who has been blessed by the pope in The Vatican?" It was, after all, his first Mary's *je ne sais quoi*.

The private's head moved up and down with gusto.

"You take this, and in the name of The Holy Mother, you use it to help your sick sister. You never ever talk of this. Ever."

The private crossed himself. "I understand. I will do anything to help her. Anything."

Enzo picked up Mary and held her in sight but just out of reach. "This is direct connection to God, you understand?"

The private, nodding vigorously, crossed himself and kissed his fingers before reaching for the carving.

"God bless your sister," said Enzo, meaning it.

The private could barely nod as tears poured down his cheeks. He rose, dipped humbly in front of Jesus, crossed himself and hurried out, Mother Mary clutched to his heart.

"Forgive us our trespasses ... " Enzo was on his knees, crossing himself in earnest. "Please, Jesus, forgive me. If white lies told for the good of another are really forgiven, then let this be one. Amen. Oh, and God? Please heal his sister."

The front page of the *Pietermaritzburg Gazette* dated 9 October 1944 was plastered on every lamp post in town. The headline in bold read: "Italy Declares War on Germany," and the article continued: "Just one month after Italy surrendered to Allied forces ... "

The first time Iris saw it, her heart lodged in her trachea. *What does it mean? Does it mean my Pietro is free or that he will be sent home and out of my life forever?*

FINALLY!

29th September, 1943 (received 20 October 1943)

Darling Sunshine,

I got back from my many sorties and found a slew of letters from you and half the number from Mom. Buggers kept me moving around so much, they couldn't forward letters, so they kept my post at the base. Ah, the glamorous life of an aerial photographer. I missed you, you little imp. I sincerely apologize for not writing while I was hither and thither. I always thought "I'll write when I get there" and it was so remote there was hardly a long drop to poop in, let alone a postal facility.

Your letters bring me home and give me enormous pleasure.

It sounds to me like you are soft on a someone. I know you'll tell me when you're ready. Though I really want to know NOW.

But most importantly, I am so damned proud of you! I knew my little sister would one day accomplish great things. And you have! America! Hollywood, no less. I think I burst several buttons on my uniform with the swell of my chest on reading about your invite to join a celebrated fashion clan. Don't you dare bloody hesitate. Just send your acceptance already! Hell, steal the money for your Trans-

American if you have to, just send the blooming thing! There is a slim to none chance that this opportunity will ever, ever present itself again. Do it now! Mother will survive without you till I get home. Hey, and don't get too soft on that boy and have that hinder your adventure. I know. I am psychic. I could hear by your tone something was curdling romantically. Under no circumstances let that stop you, do you hear me?

The Yanks have arrived in full force and have replenished our resolve. We're tired, Sis. We've been fighting forever! Perhaps with this injection of manpower on our end, we can finish this bloody thing sooner than later! In the midst of it, we can't help but wonder what the hell we're fighting for. Then we lose some good men and a plane or five and we remember.

The news, Kiddo (see? I speak Yank now!), is there are some good Americans. Yes, they're showy, sometimes arrogant, they talk funny and eat with one hand, but they're smart, amusing, and under their bravado I've found really decent guys. So, don't hold back. Whoever you're soft on can soon be replaced by a rich Yank in Hollywood.

This is a quickie, just to let you know I am safely back at base and ready for another of your written gems, so get to it! My news is war-war-war. Yours is my delight.

I love you my Sunshine.

G xx

20th October, 1943.

YAY, Finally!

Hi dear Brother,

Boy! Did you have me worried. Next time, stop in at civilization somewhere won't you, and post me a bloody letter?

Well, now you are legally allowed to have an Italian lover, I believe, with Italy joining the Allies. Though from what I've heard, it's still taboo to mingle. Certainly here. The POWs are considered vermin by most because so many RAF and SAF men were killed by them. I read they will be considered POWs till the war ends. Can't help but feel sorry for them, locked in a cage like animals, though a better cage with the new colonel in charge. Under Julian's charge it was purgatory, not surprising.

I have attempted to write my acceptance letter to America a dozen times, but something happens when I am just about to put pen to paper and I put it off again. But I WILL, Brother—I have plenty of time. Six months or so. Don't fret. I will DO it. I know it's a once-in-a-lifetime shot. Promise.

Guess what I saw plastered to a pole outside my store? A poster: "The South African Army cordially invites you to a cultural evening. Wear your finery and meet Colonel Cairns. Tickets will aid Red Cross War efforts."

Manna from heaven, I tell you! So, I bought two tickets with my precious savings and am presently whipping up a chocolate-colored dress for mother to which I will strategically pin a gathering of fresh roses.

But there is a wee bit of a problem. I found out that the colonel is not widowed, but DIVORCED. How easy do you think it is to get an annulment?

I suppose I am putting the cart before the horse, or the marriage before the mother, or some such foolishness.

Gregg, you're your usual perceptive self. Yes! I've fallen for somebody. I can't get him out of my head. It's complicated and unrealistic and ridiculously impossible so don't worry—nothing will happen. And no, he's NOT married, silly. But I doubt with all that is true that I will ever find somebody who stirs me to the very core like he does, no matter what continent I'm on.

I am bursting and had to tell somebody. Who better than my BEST somebody?

Still freckled, but looked up cures in the library last week. How about the meat of a crocodile? Or the gallbladder of a hyena? Hmm, I was thinking about this fellow I'm sweet on, while at the library, so I may have been so distracted I mixed up these old cures. Perchance they're for dysentery or flatulence. Oops! I'd better check before I go crocodile hunting, in case it's all in vain!

I love you forever,

The Aspiring Match Maker. xx

P.S. WRITE!!

The Fuller women looked spectacular, and they knew it.

Iris wore pure white. She'd used too much from her precious savings on luxurious material for her mother's chocolate creation and the tickets for new material to be an option for her own dress. But luckily she remembered her white catechism dress wrapped in sheets under the bed. She felt a wee bit blasphemous as she skillfully converted the frothy purity into a daring little number. Respectable enough for a cultural evening, with its non-conforming inch above the knee, it was audacious enough to be remembered. (Truth was, she'd been a whole lot shorter when she first needed the dress.) To complete the young-and-free look, and contra to fashion, she'd left her wild hair loose, and it hung thick and long over her shoulders.

Iris herded her mother toward the beacon of light in the night: Colonel Cairns, in full dress uniform, looking exceedingly dapper. He was in high demand, especially with the women. Ears straining, she heard snippets of conversation.

"Oh, Colonel. We've been starved of sophistication for so long, why, anything would delight us." Iris rolled her eyes. Pretentious old bisms. Surprisingly, the colonel seemed quite modest and unaware of the hullaballoo he was causing. Encouraged, she took her mother by the hand and led her toward this center of attraction.

"Colonel, my name is Iris Fuller. My mother, Margaret." She paused for a dramatic moment. "Margaret Alana Fuller." She enunciated the "M" and the "A" and the "F" so loudly, he might think she had a speech impediment. What he thought about her didn't matter. "I was at the camp to help inoculate the prisoners." She gestured to her mother. "Mom's idea. She encourages these acts of selflessness." She stopped as she realized his eyes had lost contact with hers and yes, yes, yes, had captured her mother's.

Good golly, her mother was blatantly batting her eyelashes at him, and his face was shiny with interest. Iris swore she saw something click behind his intelligent eyes.

"Margaret A. Fuller?" he asked, and her mother nodded, smiling coyly. His eyes followed the languid flow of the chocolate-colored sheath, stopping at the fresh roses caught on her hip.

"Chocolate and roses," he whispered and pulled reluctant eyes back up to MAF's eager face. *Oh, yes!*

"Have we met before, Colonel? Does my name ring a bell?" Her mother's face flushed with deep interest. Ha! This could just work.

Colonel's grin was laced with charm. "No, but I think it's about time." He took her mother's hand and kissed it. "Peter Cairns."

Margaret Fuller was flushed. "Well, Colonel. It seems charm comes easily to you."

His face went quite red. "Quite the contrary, Mar—may I call you Margaret?"

She nodded, and he suddenly looked like a little boy. "I'm desperately shy with women, truth be told, but your warmth and kindness was unexpected and a marvelous welcome."

Before her mother could digest this strange response, Iris chipped in, "Is your wife with you this evening, Colonel?"

"I am sans wife. For four years now."

The starting-gong sounded, but her mother was enraptured. "Widowed? Oh, it's so hard. Me, too."

"Divorced." His stare was intense, but her mother broke eye contact immediately. "We need to secure our seats. Good evening, Colonel." Nose aloft, her mother led the way into the hall.

Once seated, Iris burst: "Mom, I have one word for you."

"What are you on about, Iris?" Her mother waved royally to this one and that in the buzzing auditorium.

"One word that will change everything for you, Mom. Everything."

"Oh, for Pete's sake. Spit it out, and let's read the program."

"Annulment," said Iris, pulling her mother's arm to urge her to look at her. "He's handsome and larger than life, isn't he?"

"Like Philemon from the petrol station," said her mother, straight-faced.

Mother and daughter collapsed with laughter in a most unladylike fashion.

18

LOVE AT SECOND SIGHT

8 December 1943

By this time, he should be used to disappointment. But it seemed he wasn't quite yet.

The anticipation he'd felt that day in the colonel's office after the first concert had fizzled to this dismal compromise.

There was no doubt the prisoners were prisoners, in spite of the alliance overseas, so he should be grateful for this small mercy.

And *small* it was! He had to share the bill with Scottish dancers doing the highland fling, "fling" being the operative word; a pas de deux during which the male dancer dropped the loudly protesting ballerina; a fairly gifted *uomo macho* wearing a kilt and playing the bagpipes; and, he had to admit, a surprisingly well-acted snippet from *Romeo and Juliet*.

If the merest hint of possibility of getting word to Iris existed, then every dropped ballerina would be worth it. *You have to roll a lot of shit and look at the stars to eventually find the way to your woman.* Life lessons according to the dung beetle.

The primary-school cello player was nearing the end of his piece.

Pietro, flanked by Sergeant Rogers on one side and the beefy Burbero on the other, looked down at his handcuffed wrists. "This off for performance?" he asked Rogers.

The cello player's chair pushed back. Polite applause.

If only I could have got word to Iris that I would be here. The orchestra began the overture to his aria. *Orchestra? This is nothing but a band a tenth the size of the camp's orchestra. These people have no idea what they're missing.*

Cuffs off chafed wrists, he walked into the spotlight. He was on a real stage. Damn it, he would make the most of it, and perhaps word would get to her. Finding a way to communicate with her plagued his sleepless nights, as did his need for her.

The overture was over. He closed his eyes, took a deep breath and indicated with a subtle nod for them to begin. He opened his mouth to sing the very first note. Not surprising, the vision of her—like an angel—appeared in the third row, her red hair glowing like a halo. He imagined her everywhere. She was his reason.

No. No. Couldn't be.

Yes. Yes. Yes! There she was! Mia Rossa! Third row. In the flesh. In white. His angel.

It was as if she wore a brilliant aura. It was a trick of light. No! She was *his* angel. Was he really singing while her vision consumed him? God, he was smitten. He could see her hand on her throat. She was leaning forward. Her face was shocked, and in a split second he realized she had no idea he would be here.

He smiled.

Nobody but she knew it was for her.

He was only vaguely aware of rows of people making a show of leaving the auditorium in protest of an Italian—an enemy—

gracing the stage. The steel door slammed. He didn't care. His voice had done its job. It brought him into her presence.

Pietro knew that his future with this woman of his heart depended on this performance for a million reasons. When he dragged his eyes away from hers for a second, he saw that the stampede for the exit had ceased and that all eyes were upon him. But it was impossible to keep his eyes from hers ... she was all that mattered. His eyes returned to her, and there her eyes were, waiting for him. Bright, beautiful and beguiling.

The mournful Italian lyrics he sang, so familiar to him, were not what he wanted to say, but since she didn't understand he pretended they were filled with words of longing and promised love and he sang to her, and her alone. He finished with a flourish.

The silence that followed was disconcerting under these circumstances.

He looked back to Iris for reassurance, and it was there, in her dazzling smile. He thought he saw tears glistening on her cheeks. He felt her pride and was pathetically grateful. He had pleased her. Nothing else mattered, and he realized in that split second that nothing else ever would.

The silence was broken by an eruption of applause.

En masse, the audience leapt to its feet, shouting: "Bravo. Bravo. Bravo! Encore!" He had underestimated them. They knew how to commend a worthy performance. But the thought was not laden with vanity, just fact, because he felt profoundly grateful and sublimely humbled.

He found her eyes again, and they smiled at each other. Smiles that were as familiar as they were new.

Then he bowed deeply.

The standing ovation and demand for more continued, but the guards appeared on either side of Pietro, and he was escorted offstage. But not even this very public humiliation could mar his exhilaration at seeing her exquisite face. Feeling her pride.

19

FLUSTERED AND FEARLESS, CHAINED AND CHARMING

Iris's mind was reeling, her heart was thudding, her hands were wet and trembling. Her Savior. She couldn't digest it all. Her mind and body were simultaneously on overload.

On top of all that, he sings like Caruso? Thoughts of his gaze on her while his velvet voice massaged her heart, her ear drums and every wee corner of her sensory system, made her knees weak.

"Are you *coming*, Iris?" The impatience in that voice implied that her mother had noticed, in the now empty hall, that Iris had tried unsuccessfully to get out of her seat three times. Damned if she wasn't coming down with something. Lena would say she had "Love Legs."

Once outside, her mother socialized with friends from her bridge and tennis clubs. Iris was relieved she was required to do nothing but smile because it came easily. Iris was struck by the prattle of praise for her savior and felt an inordinate sense of pride, as if she alone was responsible for his great talent.

He was so near and yet, so far.

Damn it! She couldn't let him be so close and not do anything about it. And *he* couldn't come to *her*.

"Excuse me. Mom?" Her mother looked at her and smiled. "I'm off to the loo. I will be a while. Enjoy!" She gestured to the women and their husbands in her mother's circle.

Out of sight, she ran like hell and rounded the back of the Town Hall.

And stopped dead.

Shackles, reserved for psychopaths and serial killers, trapped his wrists and ankles. She felt her heart clench as sadness burned her chest. The dancing monkey, having filled the talentless musician's cup with coin, was now locked back in his cage.

She shouted, "Sergeant Rogers?" Oh, God, she hoped it was him. "Remember me? The cake delivery girl?" The uniformed man turned, and she thought she glimpsed a quick smile before he stood in front of her Pietro, shielding her from his ... Italianness? His supreme musical talent? His good looks?

The big beefy guard was holding Pietro away from her, so he couldn't what? Pounce on her? Oh! Now *that* would be just lovely!

"Sergeant, may I have this man's autograph? Please?" Thank God she still had the program, rolled up in her hand. "I'm a great Caruso fan. He sounds so much like him."

"That would be, well, unacceptable, Miss."

"Unacceptable, Sergeant?" Her notorious red temper flared.

"He's a prisoner."

"He's a prisoner of war, Sergeant. There's a difference. He didn't rob anyone. He didn't murder anyone. All he did was follow orders to fight for his own country, a country now fighting *with* us, for God's sake. Now all I want is to have him sign my bloody program!"

She was surprised to see her tone worked. Though the chains were still in place, the beefy guard released his tight hold on Pietro, and he was able to turn toward her. His smile was radiant. She smiled, moving boldly toward him.

Before the beefy guard pulled him back, she extended the program toward Pietro and barked at the less intimidating of the two: "Sergeant, do you have a pencil in your pocket?"

The beefy guard smiled, being silly: "No, Sergeant's just happy to see you."

"Well, shame on you, Sir! Where are your manners?" The burly one zipped his mouth closed as she turned her best smile toward the more familiar one. "Sergeant? Rogers, isn't it? A pencil, please?"

Without further ado, a pencil appeared, and she was face to face with Pietro.

"Please, sir. Would you sign this for me?"

"My please, my delight, my lady." *God, he's gorgeous.*

Her Pietro took the proffered pencil and, for the second time, their fingers touched. This time, they were prepared. They welcomed the electricity igniting from their touch and never lost eye contact as the current ran from their fingers to their eyes, to their mouths. Both experienced a rush of saliva, as if, while starving, they dreamed of opening their mouths wide for a greedy, sinful bite into the most delicious, succulent, forbidden fruit.

The big guard grabbed Pietro's shoulder. "Hurry up!" Big Beef barked.

Pietro hurriedly wrote something as Iris studied his face. Her eyes were fixated on his lips. His wide mouth. And as he looked up and smiled, she almost felt relief when she saw his front tooth's slight overlap again. It gave him character. Whew! He was sexy as hell. She managed to lock her eyes with his in an electrifying moment before the noise of the shackles jarred them and he was shuffled away from her. Into the darkness.

On the way home in the taxi, her mother said: "Perhaps we should clean the top of the fridge, just in case. He's rather tall."

Iris jumped, guilty as hell. Was Pietro tall enough to see the dust on top of the fridge?

"He wears his uniform rather well, don't you think? And he seemed quite taken with me, I thought. And perhaps annulment wouldn't be a bad ... "

Oh, Mother, how simple your problem of mere annulment. Imagine my problem, Mother.

The man with whom I am smitten wears shackles and chains!

Then Iris remembered. She opened her program deftly so her mother couldn't read it.

"It's love that makes me sing this time. And only for you. P."

Her heart throbbed hard against her chest. Good God. How would she ever live without these massive feelings he provoked in her? She had no idea you could feel so much. But how? How in God's name would she ever be with him? It was impossible.

Hollywood. Think Hollywood. It's your dream come true. Your only reality. Pietro is just fantasy. It can never be.

"Why on earth are you crying, child?"

Iris wiped quickly at the tears she had no idea were pouring down. Pouring down in mourning for the love she'd never have. The acute passion she'd never be able to feel. Perhaps she'd meet her Pietro in yet another lifetime. It was so bloody long to wait. But it felt like she'd waited for him before. Maybe she could do it again. She'd have to.

"I'm just happy you've shown interest in a man, Mother. It's about time. I give you my full permission to have a dalliance with the colonel."

Her mother's response was a sly grin.

Burbero unlocked the second gate behind them and left to patrol the tents. Sergeant Rogers first unlocked the cuffs on Pietro's feet and let them fall, then worked on the handcuffs. Pietro was bedazzled. His entire body was alive. It was as if his every nerve was exposed and electrified.

"Sarge, did you see her?"

Rogers said nothing. Pietro tried specifics. "My redhead *visione* in white."

"She was a hard one to miss, Pietro. Quite a fireball, I would say."

"How will I see her again, Sarge? How? Help me. Please."

"It is too dangerous for her. You have to stay away. For her sake. She could go to jail."

Pietro wrapped his arms around his head in a childish fashion to block out what he knew to be true.

"Of course, you would be shot by firing squad for escaping from a prison camp, but I don't think you'd care. But think about her. It's too dangerous for her."

Rogers turned away and triple-locked the gate behind him, leaving Pietro filled to capacity with joy and hopelessness. The latter he was used to ... but joy? A brand-new sensation.

ALLY

Pietro was morose.

His dizzy high at seeing Iris had lasted a week, but Rogers's warning finally won through, causing the deepest despair at the hopelessness of the situation.

Sergeant Rogers was right. He couldn't risk her life. It was a life too vibrant, too hot, too interesting: like a fire you could watch forever, mesmerized.

He felt a jolt. Iris was the first woman whose destiny he'd ever considered over his own. *Dio mio.* He had to move a continent from his birth to find his own unselfishness?

He never had to work at getting women, and he'd certainly never been prepared to work at keeping them. Until now. He could smell her very essence. How would he, how *could* he cover her raging flames with his body to absorb her warmth? It was as if she'd always been an integral part of his heart that he'd only just discovered had been missing all his years. Was she a kindred spirit? A many lifetimes' love, perhaps? He didn't know. How could he? It was a feeling beyond reason or sensibility. But it was, without a shadow of a doubt, the strongest feeling he'd ever had for another human being. It wasn't a feeling. It was a consummation.

What was he to do? He laughed dryly and out loud as he realized that this morbid, implausible situation, fraught with devastating heartbreak, was perfect fodder for a new opera.

How Antonio had loved the opera at the camp. He'd come alive again, but as soon as the sets of the Japanese house with the view of the sea were torn down, Antonio seemed to regress.

Fortunately, Pietro had just the cure.

He found Antonio sitting on his bed again, rocking.

"Antonio. Antonio, look at me."

The square man's eyes opened lethargically.

"We will do another concert. Soon. I promise. But in the meantime, I have a present for you. It's something only you could appreciate because you, my friend, are the only mechanical genius I know. "

He passed the nondescript sack to Antonio. One look inside, and Pietro was rewarded with a smile as big as Italy herself. He started, "Look inside, Antonio-second-only-to-Marconi-himself ... "

"Radio!" Antonio's voice was raspy with joy and disbelief. He hugged Pietro so hard he thought one of them might blow a gasket. Pietro had never given a gift that resulted in so much unadulterated joy. Antonio came alive. His fingers were nimble and swift, and three hours later, the radio was picking up more stations than the thing was designed for. English, Afrikaans, Portuguese babbled as the dial was turned, even Mother Italy herself in spurts. And all kinds of music. To see Antonio's eyes come back from an off-key sonata to a perfect operatic performance was a gift unto itself.

They'd carved a deep hole under the spot where Antonio's bed was positioned, lined it with waterproof fabric courtesy of the Red Cross's entertainment donations, and Enzo had created a wooden trap door they covered with straw. Voila!

Antonio, who was permanently glued to the box, ear against the mesh to keep it as quiet as possible, became The War Source, and their tent was no longer where you came just for your to-go atonement courtesy of Enzo's religious whittling skill, but where you came for up-to-the-minute war news and a melody or two.

The men were all relieved that despite his being Italian, Caruso was the staple of classical music, no matter which continent you were on.

Though Stef would rather be practicing his violin than listening to his old friend's fanciful delusions, Enzo never tired of debating a new idea for Pietro to see Iris again.

Based on his glimpses of her, Enzo whittled an exquisite bust of Iris out of a thick piece of mahogany, courtesy of the new chapel's ceiling.

It was the first time Pietro had shown any animation in weeks. The redhead's bust was the most precious possession he'd ever owned, even at the zenith of his wealth. But it was like hiding a stowaway. The bust had to be kept hidden, lest any one of the guards would recognize her. Ridiculously, Pietro sneaked looks at the damned piece of wood whenever he could.

Pietro felt Sergeant Rogers's eyes on him quite often in a kind way, as if he felt Pietro's frustration.

Thank the Lord, Colonel's "Let Me Call You Sweetheart" days had fizzled out after Pietro's town debut. He was grateful, but Pietro quite missed Rogers's company to and from the officer's mess. When Rogers approached Pietro three weeks after the concert, Pietro was happy to see him.

But Rogers was glum. "There will be no more town performances."

Pietro's heart stopped dead. "Why?"

"Big brass, Powers, nixed it. Said he'd only allow concerts inside the camp."

A heavy boot filled with disappointment kicked Pietro in the gut.

"Do you want to see her again?" Rogers asked softly.

Pietro thought he was hearing things, but Rogers repeated the question.

"True? Really? *Si. Si. Si.* Please. Please." His beating heart drowned out Rogers's voice.

"Scusa?"

"I am calling a meeting at three in the mess. Be there."

Enzo, Stef and Antonio, jostled by Pietro, were in prime position at least an hour early for the meeting. The mess hall filled up quickly.

At last, Rogers jumped up on the stage. "Good news. Start your creative engines, boys. Colonel has agreed for you to stage the next opera."

There was hooting and hollering and clapping and foot-stomping, but no yell of glee was louder than Antonio's.

"I'm sure your stock is low. But the Red Cross has given us funds for supplies. I need a volunteer to come to town to pick up odds and ends you need." He pointedly looked at Pietro.

Pietro's arm was up in a flash. "Me, Sergeant. Me."

He pointed to Pietro. "Tomorrow. Nine. At the gate with your list."

FACE TO FACE

8 January, 1944

Customers dribbled into the store at a snail's pace. Even the upper class, with their brick double-story homes on the surrounding hills, nestled on acres of park-like land with gardens and waterfalls and swimming pools and tennis courts, had cut back on spending. Their seamstresses who chose materials and talked designs with Iris were few and far between. Times were hard.

She had a golden opportunity in a thriving industry just waiting for her. Her money for her trip from New York to Los Angeles was entirely saved and ready to go, hidden in the undercarriage of her sewing machine. She'd always hated limbo, but here she was, creating her own. Each time she went to write her acceptance to her dream designer, she just couldn't do it.

Was it her guilt? Was it fear of being on her own in a new country? Of not being good enough once she got there? Probably all three, but it was more than that. It was giving up ... her Pietro. Facing that fact was clearly preposterous. Whether she was eight miles from him or twelve thousand, the odds of seeing him were the same. The odds of being with him were, without doubt, quite impossible.

Oddly, "O Sole Mio" constantly played in her head. Last week, she'd looked up the English lyrics in the library.

Buffer was still growling that low warning at odd times during the night, so she was aware that somebody could be casing the house. From the outside, it was clear there was no wealth within, except of course for her hard-earned stash, committed to her new adventure. But no one knew about that!

In truth, nothing else but her Savior was on her mind.

Seeing him perform was by no means the reason for her—what was it? Infatuation? Hell, no! Infatuation didn't feel like this. This was all-consuming, all-engrossing, all-powerful. Love? How could she love someone she didn't know? Whom she'd hardly spoken to? Someone who was Gregg's enemy? Someone who lived in a prison, for God's sake. A prison fortified with barbed wire and soldiers with guns and fierce dogs, ready to tear escapees to pieces.

Her brother's face popped into her head. *And it's not because he can sing like that, either, though let's face it, falling for him after I heard him would have been easy. And damn it, Gregg, if you could have felt what I felt when I first looked into his intense eyes and into his soul, you too would be smitten.*

And then she looked up.

She blinked, sure she'd just conjured him up again, as she'd done a thousand times.

"Hello, Iris," said Pietro. *Her* Pietro.

She felt her knees go weak and her cheeks burn. She put her hand on her throat reflexively to see if she was still breathing and if this was real. If *he* was real. The throb of her pulse almost pushed her fingers off her dewy skin.

"Hello, Pietro." She barely heard herself.

"I'm buy supply?" He smiled and her ridiculous legs buckled. She clung to the counter.

He smiled, and those damned dimples put a further wobble in her knees. She desperately hoped her mouth wasn't open in awe. How could he be here?

She was lost in him, dizzy with emotion.

He handed her a list. She blinked to focus. It was a menu of sundry items, which she held on to as if it were the Holy Grail.

"For Red Cross account," he said as his eyes took in every square inch of her face, lingering on her quivering lips. She blushed as if he'd said, "I want you now!"

She felt her eyes stray to his mouth. A generous mouth, her mother would call it. To her, it was luscious perfection. She wanted to touch his overlapping tooth with her tongue, to feel its sharpness, to prove that he was real.

There was a loud "Ahem" about ten feet behind Pietro, which jolted her into real time. She looked at Sergeant Rogers and smiled as he mock-saluted and gave a hint of a smile.

She turned quickly away so the depth of Pietro's eyes wouldn't prevent her from comprehensive thought and busied herself gathering rolls of cotton, wool stuffing and the like. Every second, she felt his eyes on her. Her body was on fire, and her pesky nipples were poking at her bra, as if winter had descended on Ross & Co. She wished she had the chance to study him, but it was not to be. As soon as she had all his goodies and an invoice for him to initial, the sergeant's "Ahem" warned them of the end of this dalliance.

She looked up from the counter into Pietro's fathomless blue eyes, and she couldn't help herself. She smiled from ear to ear as the purest joy washed over her body. A smile to match hers brightened his face. They stood there, grinning as if celebrating the complete joy of finding each other in the only way they could.

The sergeant appeared at his side. "What have we here, a pair of Cheshire Cats?" But poor Rogers might have been invisible.

"Iris." She watched him run his tongue over her name like it was a rare and delicious Belgian truffle. She shivered.

"Pietro, watch how you open the dye box. Be very careful. It spills easily."

"Let's go." Sergeant grabbed the box of goodies, took Pietro by the elbow and physically faced him toward the exit, then pushed the small of his back toward the door. Pietro threw his head over his shoulder, and Iris could feel her cheeks burn as his smile mirrored her own.

She was vaguely aware that as they marched through the store, a few of the women moved hastily away, as if the man in brown had the plague and would infect them by his presence alone. Others threw down their would-be purchases and waltzed out of the emergency exit door in protest.

At the door, Pietro pulled out of Rogers's grip, turned and smiled brightly as if knowing that her smile would still be there, waiting for his.

And it was.

22

FOURFEET

The note attached to the chocolate cake with iced roses in the bakery box read: "Your beautiful chocolate-colored dress adorned with rosebuds was not lost on me. Because of you, Pietermaritzburg is already feeling like home. Thank you and enjoy. PSC."

Iris's cheeks were on fire.

"What on earth?" Her mother was flabbergasted.

"Do you know who it's from, Mom?"

"Haven't a clue." Her mother tried to sound dismissive, but Iris could see her face flushed with pleasure.

Go for it, Iris. Now's your chance. "Lena, get over here. Let's put our heads together."

The three women huddled around the kitchen table, the edible work of art in the center of the solid pine surface. Buffer circumvented the table on the off chance that someone would eventually eat the thing and the odd crumb would fall.

"So, you were wearing your new chocolate-colored number at the Colonel's ... " Iris began and then thought better of it as she watched her mother circle the cake. The elder's head tilted this way and that, like Buffer's, as she examined the cake from every angle for clues.

"I say it's from the handsome Colonel Cairns!" Iris thought she should force the issue lest her mother collapse from dizziness since this was her fourth time around the table.

"Don't be silly, Iris." But her mother's cheeks were pink.

"Well, his name is Peter Cairns. Only an "S" stands in the way of confirmation."

"Well, I can't thank him if I don't know for sure he sent it."

"Mother, he was the only male I saw, other than the taxi driver, who enjoyed your chocolate sheath."

Iris wound the handle on the black contraption on the wall and picked up the earpiece. The voice was chipper. "Operator."

"Jurita Bakery, please." She waited a second. "Ah, good morning. Did you perhaps deliver a cake to 32 Ewing Street this morning?"

Her mother and Lena were all ears. Buffer was all taste buds.

"So the order came from the army base, but you don't know who?"

The two women were straining to listen, but Iris held the phone too close to her ear.

"Thanks so much."

Her mother jumped up and down like a child. "What did she say, Jinx? What?"

"Sergeant Rogers paid for it."

"Well, it can't be Sergeant Rogers, because the initials don't match." God, her mother could be so dense.

"Mom, he is the colonel's right-hand man. You don't have to be a psychic. The colonel was clearly taken with you, and his initials match!" Iris was already late for work.

"But why the initials, for gosh sakes?"

"Maybe he likes a little mystery. You should phone and

thank him. Then, if it's not him, he'll feel bad he didn't think of it."

"Are you trying to push me off on somebody so you can go to America, guilt-free?"

The thing about mothers—they saw right through you.

"Mom, I would love you to find happiness with a fabulous man who adores you, and I would feel better about leaving if I knew your life was filled with promise. But as talented as I may be," she winked at her mother, "even I can't make somebody fancy you. They have to do that all on their own."

"Well? What shall I do?"

"Eikona, Missus. You do niks. Nothing." The Fuller women looked at Lena waggling her index finger left and right. "If cake man want you to know is him, he sign his name proper."

"Good thinking, Lena. If he's that keen, he'll expose himself," Iris exclaimed, looking at the kitchen clock. A little bit of anticipation would keep her mother occupied, and Iris had to get to work.

"Oh, God forbid. I am not ready for anyone exposing themselves quite yet!" Her mother flushed, and the three laughed together as Iris inched out of the back door.

"Bon appétit!" Iris shouted, and Buffer licked his lips. The dog was multilingual.

"Morning, Klein Miesies," Fourfeet greeted Iris as she hurried down the path.

"Hi, Fourfeet."

Fourfeet's voice followed her clipping heels down the Fullers' walkway in the midst of the tired garden. "I saw Singingman when I come to work today, Klein Miesies."

Iris stopped dead and turned to him.

Fourfeet warbled an odd version of her Pietro's aria. Her stomach lurched. He'd caught the melody exactly, with lots of humming and three words that vaguely resembled a European language. "How do you know Singingman, Fourfeet?" She smiled with what she hoped was encouragement so he might share every nuance.

"Concert. I clean town hall after show. I come early. I hear." And off he went in C key.

Iris bounced on her tippy-toes like an impatient boxer. "Today. Where was Singingman today, Fourfeet?"

"Fixing road. With other men. All happy."

"How come you went that way, Fourfeet?"

"I have found girl in my mother's old kraal. She's pretty. I go see her."

"Are they nice to you when you pass? The men, I mean. The men in brown."

His grin was guileless and wide. "Oh, yes, Klein Miesies. All of them. Except Tap Tap."

She asked casually, "Tap Tap?"

"He come here for you, Klein Miesies." He gave an all-too-lifelike Julian-with-a-whip impersonation. "Solomon call him Tap Tap. Same as men in camp. Tap Tap not there today."

It was a gift from heaven. "Fourfeet, do you think you could take my bike and deliver a message to the Singingman without anyone really noticing?"

"On your *bike*?" The young man was awestruck by the very thought but quick as a flash said: "Easy on your bike, Klein Miesies."

Iris recalled that when she was seeing Julian, she was walking him to his car, and Fourfeet came bounding over the hedge bordering their yard.

"You all right, Fourfeet?" she'd asked.

"Ja, Klein Miesies, thank you. I want to ask colonel about faraway white people in camp. Ugogo* says they from phezu kwamanzi?"**

Julian had stepped back from the young man, spreading

his arms to "shield" Iris from the encounter. Iris had swatted his protective hands away. Julian pulled himself up to full height and looked at the young Zulu as if he'd just found the source of a nasty smell. "It's not for you to ask. It's for you to do. Get back to work!" And he'd turned away, smiling sweetly at Iris.

"Fourfeet, I am so sorry this man is so rude. I apologize for him." She'd been appalled.

It was the day before she broke up with Julian.

No wonder Fourfeet was eager to defy Tap Tap now.

She hastily wrote a note, folding it into a tiny square, and handed it to Fourfeet. "Take my bike and come back as soon as you can." The young man's white, straight teeth dazzled.

An hour and a half later, she was very late for work, and Iris had paced the kitchen floor for the fifty-second time. She swore she was two inches shorter. Thank God her mother was contemplating her cake, no doubt, in her bedroom.

And there, at last, came Fourfeet, limping up the path. She ran toward him. "Oh, no, Fourfeet. What on earth happened?"

His shiny face was dark with blood, and his shirt was torn. Iris took his hand and led him into the kitchen, where she lit the kettle to make him a hot cup of tea. She went to work cleaning him up, adding six sugars to his tea to calm his nerves and serving him a huge slice of Melktert, the thick milk custard tart, sprinkled lightly with cinnamon in a brittle crust Jurita baked so well. "Now tell me everything."

"I go very slow. I stop to say hello to few people so no suspicious."

"Clever man!" Iris encouraged.

"Then I see Zacile. Next to Singingman."

She put up her hand, confused. "Zacile?"

"Skinny means Zacile in Zulu, Klein Miesies. Singingman smile at me. I make big eyes and show note quickly in my hand.

Skinny very quick. He make like he shake my hand, and he take note."

"Oh, Fourfeet, you are so clever and brave. Then what?"

"A jeep comes quick—too fast—with Tokolosh. Tap Tap jump out with shambok." Fourfeet gave a demonstration of the whip's quick, vicious movements. Fourfeet lurched into mimic mode, breaking character only to flinch for Iris's wound administrations. He motioned Julian hitting the side of his leg with his whip.

His impersonations were so true to life, and Iris's interest so keen, Fourfeet's level of performance got better and better.

He was Julian, sauntering up the road. "Whose bike is this?"

"I borrow it, Baas." (Himself.)

"From whom?" (Julian.) He elongated the "oo" and ended in a triple "m."

"From my Klein Miesies." (Himself.)

"Bullshit! I know your Klein Miesies. You stole this bloody bicycle." Fourfeet wordlessly demonstrated the beating with the whip.

Iris's eyes were moist. She felt dreadful, putting this poor man in harm's way for her own intentions. Shame on her.

He held the "whip" motionless. "Beating stops. I see Singingman holding shambok high so Tap Tap cannot beat me anymore. Then Zacile, Skinny, he pushes me. He say, 'Run, run, run,' and I listen and run. But I hear Tap Tap shout, 'Ignorant piece of shit.' 'Scuse me, Klein Miesies. 'You piece of macaroni. You fucking Eye-Tie.' 'Scuse me again, Klein Miesies. And then when I turn in my running away, I see Tap Tap kick Singingman, who lies in dirt. He kick him in his side, over and over and over."

Fourfeet was on the ground writhing in a fetal position to demonstrate her Pietro's pain.

Iris's hand was over her mouth. Her heart beat a million times a minute. "No. No. No."

Fourfeet sat up, concerned. "You OK, Klein Miesies?"

She really didn't know.

Ugogo: Zulu for Grandmother or, in this case, one perceived as grandmother.

**Phezu kwamanz: Far away across the water.*

23

WORTHWHILE CONSEQUENCES

Antonio was the busiest nurse south of the equator. He was entirely focused on the mission of mopping Pietro's sweating head and gently massaging the right side of his lower belly with some stinky gunk.

Pietro sniffed and opened one eye. "What the hell you doing, Antonio?"

"One of the Zulus gave it to me. Said it would take away your bruising."

"I hope you didn't trade anything valuable for it. It smells like regular horse shit."

Antonio sighed loudly. Oh, to be an unappreciated nurse. Pietro called loudly for Enzo. The elder's head bobbed between the flaps.

"Where is it?" Pietro yelled.

"Where is what?" Enzo teased from outside the tent flap.

"Enzo gave it to me, and I lost it." Stef's voice was somber, ending with a sob.

"Enough, you two! Can't you see I am in enough pain already?" He winced for effect as they ducked through the tent flap.

Stef laughed joyfully at the absurdity of it all. The innocence of Stef's laughter struck a chord in Pietro as he realized how much he'd missed the familiar sound. Stef laughed so little these days ... the note! Good God, nothing was more important than The Note!

"Enzo, damn it!"

Enzo took mercy and opened his clasped fist. Pietro sat up too fast and cried out in pain, causing Nurse Antonio to hover over him. Pietro grabbed his prize. He read it, then closed his eyes, trying to smell her, but too many hands had touched the grubby note. He read it again.

"Tell us," said Enzo. "We're in this together, remember?"

"Please, please," Antonio begged.

"All right, you horny bastards. Stef, read it to my brides-maids, will you?"

Stef grabbed the note and cleared his throat: "I don't know why, I don't know how, I don't know where ... but I *must* see you. Iris."

"Again. Please. Please, my friend, it's the most beautiful lyric in the universe."

After five times, Enzo yelled, "Enough! What will you do?"

"So what *will* we do?" asked Antonio, wringing his hands.

"I must make Rogers take me to town again."

Stef stirred the pot. "Is that what she meant? A monitored minute, with a counter between you and a guard hanging on your arm?"

"Then what? Damn it. Then what. How?" Pietro felt desperate.

"All that matters is 'why.' " Stef the philosopher.

"Because I have loved her since I was born. Maybe before."

Leg extended and toe pointed with a lavish wave of his arm, Enzo bowed low. "This is where I come in. With your determination, and my good looks, as well as my excellent pre-army skills as a pussy thief ... "

"Pussy thief?" Pietro was perplexed.

"Cat burglar! It was *you* who was the *real* pussy thief, Pietro!" Stef's guileless laughter rang out again.

"Stop. This is serious now. The most serious thing in my life!" Pietro suddenly felt hope surge in a hot flush from his toes all the way to the top of his head. His head was pulsing. "You can get me out of here?"

"More important, I can get you back in so nobody will know you've left," Enzo bragged.

"You're that good?" Pietro was impressed.

"I am only as good as my students are eager to learn. In your case, you have everything to lose, so I think your passing score will be off the charts."

"What's in this for you?"

"The biggest challenge of my life. An adrenaline rush so big it will rid the cobwebs."

"And if I get caught, it's only on me." Pietro didn't want anyone else to be in jeopardy.

"You understand the risk?" asked Enzo solemnly.

"Death by firing squad. The price of escape," Pietro answered.

"Death would be the merciful punishment if Tap Tap has anything to do with it." Stef's voice was somber. Pietro noticed but was too excited to delve into Stef's ominous tone.

"But what if Iris is caught with me? What will happen to her?" The thought churned Pietro's stomach in fear.

"It's treasonous to fraternize with a prisoner. It says so in the rules that are soldered onto the metal sheet in the mess hall for the guards to see." Antonio was happy to contribute.

"What is the South African punishment for treason?" Pietro was afraid to hear the reply.

"Death or life imprisonment, depending on the extent of the crime." Antonio had studied.

"*Dio mio.* Mia Cara Rossa," Pietro whispered.

Enzo sobered. "You must prepare yourself for the worst consequences. It's the only way your precaution will be at its optimum. You must prepare Iris the same way. She must know what she is getting into. This is not a game. This is your life and hers. And the end of both, if you're caught."

"I understand. I understand. But, goddamn it, Enzo, no matter what the price, she's worth it. Nothing has ever mattered more, nor will it ever again." Pietro's voice was quiet.

"It's true, Enzo." Stef was earnest. "He could have any woman in the world. He charmed them, bedded them, and didn't give a shit for any of them. Never seen him this obsessed."

Enzo was unsmiling. "Just focus on the hell that will be yours if you are discovered. Tell me after you have digested the worst that can happen that you are still ready."

Pietro lost no time in responding: "I have discovered hell. I have tasted it. I have smelled it. I have had it pushed down my throat, and I have swallowed it. All for this war. This time it will be for myself. I choose hell over complacency and have no regrets. But it is not about me. I must understand that my Iris knows the consequences. Only then can I move forward."

And for the first time, Pietro's passion and excitement was overridden by palpable fear. What if she was too afraid? What if she wasn't afraid enough?

24

DYE FOR YOU

Her eyes had been glued to the store's entrance since she'd sent the note. She became quite efficient at doing her job with only a glance. Her *real* job was watching the door.

Two days after Fourfeet was beaten, Iris saw Sergeant Rogers enter the store, and her heart stopped. Dare she hope?

At last. Praise be. Behind him were Pietro and a skinny older man, both grinning.

"Ah," she thought. "There's Fourfeet's 'Zacile.' Skinny." Joy and anticipation, tenderness and excitement welled through her every pore. And then relief. He was walking, albeit with a little stoop. That bastard Julian.

Then they were at her counter. Pietro handed her empty boxes of dye. She put them down dismissively, but there was panic in his eyes.

"Please put dye in same boxes, Iris." He smiled at her. "We need lots of colors for opera, so this way we will be, how you say, thrifty? Same box, same color." That blooming smile of his made her breathless.

"Of course, makes sense," said Iris as she opened one of the boxes and almost dropped it.

A note.

She looked first at Rogers, who was deliberately looking anywhere *but* her counter. She thanked him silently, pocketed the note, then filled the dye box. Her hand was shaking.

And then she felt his hand on hers, just for an instant, to make her look at him. Her knees gave way. Steadying herself, she looked into his eyes and she was lost. Again.

He whispered, "Check all the boxes. Only say yes if you understand the danger."

The skinny guy cleared his throat. She pocketed three more notes and busied herself with completing her task, though she spilled more than she managed to get into the box.

"How are we doing, chaps? Sorry this is taking so long, Miss." Rogers was definitely on board. She felt a thrill of relief that her Pietro had allies in this quest.

"N-n-not at all, Sergeant. This is my job. Anything else you need?"

Rogers looked pointedly at Enzo, who sprang to attention, then grinned with pride. "I am show manager."

"That's impressive." Iris smiled before Enzo rattled off more items they needed.

During this business exchange, Pietro watched Iris's every move. She felt his fathomless eyes on her, and it warmed her from within. She dared not look at him, because her stupid legs would give way. But when the sergeant spoke, she knew Pietro's eyes had left her, and she felt complete abandonment and great loss.

" ... For the Red Cross account. Thank you, Miss."

She managed a "My pleasure, Sergeant," and was relieved he turned away, as did Enzo. It was as if they were giving the two a moment, although she caught the sergeant and Skinny sniffing the air. Her store's fancy tea room's baked "delectables" must be torture to these starved men, she thought fleetingly, but later she realized under Colonel Cairns' rule, they were much healthier than she'd seen them. She'd splurge and buy a tin of Humbugs to keep under her counter so she could give them a little treat when next they came in.

Pietro placed his hand palm-up on the counter. Everything else, everyone else, disappeared from thought. She lightly ran the very tips of her fingers from his fingertips down his dry palm to his wrist. Her nerve ends were zinging. It was a sexy invitation and a sensuous response. She'd surprised herself, later—now she was just doing what came naturally.

"Iris." His voice was a whisper.

"Pietro." Hers, breathless.

"Let's go, let's GO." Rogers voice made her jump and glance up, and when her eyes sought Pietro out again, she saw just his back, moving toward the exit.

But in spite of Rogers's jostling, just inside the door, Pietro stood rooted, looking past all the bustling shoppers and right at her, no, *into* her. She looked at him, into him, and her world stood still, an exquisite moment in time suspended because of her heightened senses. Then a skinny arm reached in and pulled him away.

She opened the notes, and it was then her knees buckled all the way, as they'd been promising to do since he appeared in front of her, like a vision. She sat on the red carpet beneath her, her breath coming hard and fast as her heart thudded. *Is it really possible that I'll see him alone? Just us two? At night?*

She felt a rush of heat pulse through her entire body, as if it had only just awakened. She pulled a pair of the store's most expensive red gloves from the drawer, pulled them on and placed her gloved hands palms-down on the counter, to trap the sensation of his palm on the tip of her fingers. She closed her eyes. Right there in the store, she allowed herself to enjoy the new sensuality coursing through her body. As Pietro's face invaded closed lids, she began to feel the full effects of what Lena promised. *This feeling ... oh, God ... this feeling ...*

"Miss?" Iris heard the sound, but it was far off.

"MISS?"

Iris jumped to attention, blinking to focus and guilty as hell. "So sorry, madam. Unexpected women issues," Iris whispered, a little breathlessly.

The woman's head bent forward, and Iris moved hers back as much as she dared, preparing herself for the inevitable wrath and uproar. She really couldn't afford to get fired.

The woman patted Iris's gloved hand and smiled wickedly. "I'll take a pair in every color, miss." She pointed to the red gloves and winked. "They seem to harness all sorts of delicious mysteries."

If only she knew how right she was! It was Iris's biggest sale of the week.

25

PRACTICE, PRACTICE, PRACTICE

1944

Pietro's first note to Iris had read: "Meet at 9:45 p.m. 18th March, old dead-end dirt road, west side of camp." Second one said: "I will be waiting." The third: "I will understand if you can't come. Very, very danger for you."

Enzo, Stef and Antonio secretly managed to convince Rogers to take them in to pick up a large volume of stage goods they needed. They deliberately left Pietro at the camp because the two would-be lovers couldn't look anywhere but at each other, and they had important business to discuss with her. They wanted no blood on their friend's hands.

They felt bad when they saw Iris craning her neck to watch for Pietro's arrival, then felt her grave disappointment when he never appeared.

Stef led the way. Thankfully, Rogers was chatting to some lady he knew a few counters over. "Iris, I am Stef, Pietro's old friend. From Italy," the slight man with the kind face said.

"Delighted." Iris smiled. "Is he ... coming today?"

"Just we," he indicated the three of them, "wanted to talk. Private. Our friend is ... " He twirled his finger above his left ear. "Crazy for Iris." She'd touched her throat and blushed.

Stef's voice dropped to a whisper. "If you agree see him ... "

"Agree?" She was horrified that her commitment was in doubt. Angry even. Stef knew from experience, you didn't mess with a redhead.

"If you do what you want, you two—it is very, very dangerous for both. He does not care for himself. He cares for your good, your safe. If you catch—big trouble."

She nodded, businesslike. This was clearly not news to her. She'd thought about it. She'd accepted it. Her stance told them everything they needed to know. She was strong. She was ready and she was aware. Not a giggly schoolgirl. A woman with a mission. A woman in love.

"I am more afraid for Pietro than for me. We are adults. We know what we want. We understand the consequences. You've done your duty to your friend. I promise." Then she smiled, and their worlds were brightened and their hearts were calmer.

"I. Antonio," the square man said warmly.

Iris put out her hand. "I am delighted to meet you." They shook formally.

"I have something for you." She bent down behind her counter and came up with a tin. She went close to them, now in a tidy row against her counter, and opened the Humbug lid so they could smell the waves of peppermint and molasses.

"Help yourself," she said, offering the can to each. They took as many as they could without being impolite.

"And ... wait ... " She went off to the other side of the counter with the heaven-sent tin. When she came back, she handed Stef one of her invoices, which covered some humbugs. He could feel the round bottom and flat top of the sinful sweets. "For Pietro," she said, smiling.

"Sergeant, would you like a humbug?" she asked.

As Rogers helped himself, the opera team got down to business, accumulating the items they needed.

———

Pietro had not seen her since the day in the store when they'd set the time. He would've been climbing the fence to get to her by now, if it weren't for this ultimate goal.

To see her alone? Oh, God, he must have been good in his last life.

He had been unaware his friends had auditioned her for their planned caper until they returned grinning with a hot sticky piece of paper covering some delicious peppermint treats. He was further surprised when he saw her writing on the inside. Thrilled, he licked the goo off and read, "I have never been more ready for anything. Tell your friends all is well. Soon, your Iris."

No matter what happened, knowing she felt as he did was worth every possible consequence, and then he added, in case God was listening, "As long as it's mine to bear."

Enzo was an expert planner. No stone was left unturned.

The elder had worked out everything: from the new moon for the maximum darkness for his first time out, to explicit timing. They had half an hour to get Pietro from the safety of the camp to the dense, wild undergrowth on the other side.

The most unpredictable factor was Tap Tap.

Though a whittled, mini Virgin Mary had paid an army clerk to find and copy Tap Tap's schedule, the butcher was indeed a law unto himself.

Since Tap Tap worked mostly nights, they needed a way to lure him away from Enzo's training spot, from which teacher and student could observe guards' routines and other essential components of "The Great Break Out, Break In" caper.

"I will take care of him," Stef said stoically.

"How?" Pietro wanted to know, ever-protective of Stef.

"He has a strange fascination with the violin. I will watch for him and, if necessary, lure him in the opposite direction with my instrument."

"God, be careful, Stef. The butcher is unpredictable. I doubt music will be enough to quiet the demon that rages within him."

"Pietro. You know that I am the wisest of us two. Always have been." He grinned. "Trust me with leading this motherfucker away, like the Pied Piper lured the vermin."

"We four are conspirators. We must all have a part. I have mine planned." Antonio's input touched Pietro enough to bring tears to his eyes.

The phases of the moon and where to enter and exit for best concealment was a huge factor. They lay in the darkness after lights-out, watching the guards' movements, which thankfully followed military precision. Enzo observed the crossover point where, coming from opposite directions, the two guards would exchange pleasantries or weather complaints while their dogs inspected each other's bums.

Enzo then picked a spot farthest away from the camp, at the elongated end of the wire enclosure, which would render that stretch the farthest to get to from the guard house.

Camp perimeter lights were used sparsely to save the generator, and this chosen spot was so far from the source, the light would only go on when an emergency dictated such a wasteful surge of forced power.

"You, my eager young buck, need all the time I can buy you. The distance between the inner and outer fence here is about twenty feet. A paralyzing long way, considering what you have to do in a narrow time window, in the dark. Are you ready for this? Do you know how much can go wrong?"

"You don't scare me, friend. Iris's lovely face wipes out all my fears and uncertainties."

"God help you, you horny young fool."

Unlike Pietro's own, Enzo's patience was endless.

Every second or third night, they stole crusts of bread soaked in gravy from dinner plates, then lobbed the treats over the fence and onto the guards' path. Once a pattern was set for the dogs to go ballistic at that specific spot, Enzo snuck down to the fence with wire cutters. Pietro gave thanks to the Red Cross for their generous and most useful tool, donated for stage sets.

Enzo cut through the barbed wire at the base of the inside fence. It was no easy feat, since the expensive roll of wire was pulled taut to cover a huge area, and once cut, it would disappear like a tightly-wound spring. Enzo knelt on one end of the wire as he held tightly to the other end, and Pietro reckoned he was bending the wire into a sturdy hook, as planned. His wiry frame stepped on the opposite side of the wire and reattached the ends. Pietro watched him in the moonlight, which furnished the bright light needed for his intricate setup. Enzo's stance showed his satisfaction. He'd promised Pietro he would make the ingress and egress look like a design flaw so no attention would be drawn to the escape route.

Enzo reached the inside perimeter fence, did some measured pacing, and then, on his knees, he nipped a rectangle in the three-story fence. No doubt big enough for a more solid man than his wiry self.

Pietro was nervous. Enzo seemed to be taking a hell of a long time. He was so precise, and that's exactly what was needed, but holy shit, the guards would be back soon.

Finally, he wiggled easily through the opening. *Whew. OK, you did it. But get out, Enzo. Get out, now!* Enzo casually fished into his pocket, and Pietro saw the cloth in the moonlight and knew the elder was finding an appropriate place for the gravy-soaked bread.

You've done it halfway. Come back now. Please. Please, Enzo.

Far too slowly for the sake of Pietro's nerves, Enzo wiggled back through the opening in the fence and spent some time reattaching it and then cautiously tiptoed, avoiding the lethal barbed-wire jabs, toward his hook and eye. Dogs started to bark from either side of Enzo, though they were still far away. Pietro jumped at least six inches off the ground. *Come. Come. Come.*

Enzo no sooner lay down next to him when the dogs were in sight.

"You have nerves of steel. Thank you, my friend." Pietro put his hand on the elder's skinny shoulder and squeezed. He loved this man. When had that happened?

Pietro thought his heart would stop when he first spotted the Dobermans' gaits change as they sniffed the air, four hundred yards apart. By the 200-yard mark, the dogs began to hurry their guards along, drawn by the smell of "people" food and toward the crossover point Enzo had forced.

Oh, God, Pietro desperately hoped it was the gravy-bread they were smelling and not his brave friend.

The left guard let his dogs pull him along. "What are you guys doing? What the hell are you smelling? Something strange out there?" he rhetorically asked of his pair, while the guy on the right, yelling commands, used all his alpha control to keep his dogs walking at the pace he dictated. Two canine noses were millimeters from the ground when the first of the lean dogs found the treasure. A few snarls ensued, as the other tried to taste the nugget of gravy left on his partner's jowls.

"What's with you two lately?" the guard grumbled as he tugged on their leashes to make a point, but then let them sniff. They were right beneath the ridge on which Pietro and Enzo flattened themselves to become invisible. The guard continued to grumble: "Bloody meerkat poop again? You guys get enough. No need to eat shit."

The second guard came tripping along behind his pair of pooches. "Man! What's up with the dogs?" the second arrival asked the first.

"Bloody meerkats. Those little buggers must shit boerewors." The two shared a hearty laugh at the thought of delicious South African sausage being defecated by a family of feral meerkats.

Once the guard teams went off in their own directions, they slowed down to a snail's pace. Both military men, Pietro and Enzo knew that guard duty, though inevitable, was the worst part of military service, and the slower they sauntered, the faster their interminable night ended.

Pietro was suddenly overcome. He'd never been more relieved, or more proud, or more moved that one human being would willingly risk so much for another. Certainly no one had ever done this much, and so unconditionally, for him.

Pietro squeezed Enzo's shoulder, whispering, "Thank you, my friend. Thank you." His voice broke. This risk was by no means Pietro's alone.

Two nights later Enzo repeated the daring feat, going all the way. With Enzo's relentless schooling, Pietro could recite the route in his sleep: "Directly down from our ridge to the barbed wire. Unhook. Hold. Hook behind you. Step three feet to the left, carefully; straight ahead to the rectangle. Unhook. Wiggle through. Hook. Drop the bread. Pace seven feet to the left against the fence. Leopard crawl straight ahead. Find rectangle. Unhook, wiggle, hook. Three feet to left, then straight ahead, find hook and eye on barbed wire. Unhook, re-hook. IRIS!"

Even when they weren't practicing, the dogs got their gravy treats, but on odd nights, so their canine expectations were constantly high, they were randomly rewarded.

Enzo created duplicates of the hooks and eyes he had made

for the barbed wire as well as replicas of each fence rectangle, showing where to find each hook. Pietro's job was to learn the feel of each, until he could literally open and close them with his eyes shut.

During the training, they'd twice heard the mournful sound of Stef's violin, and they knew their very own Pied Piper was dealing with the vermin, Julian. Pietro prayed that Tap Tap was calmed by Stef's skill and that his old friend was safe. Stef never complained, and there were no marks to show that Tap Tap had beaten Stef, and if anyone could delight and calm with his skill on the exquisite instrument, it was Stef. So though Pietro's concern about Stef's safety lingered, it was in the back of his mind. He had to concentrate on the most important mission of his life.

And then it was Pietro's turn.

He'd never been so afraid. But he had to keep his eye on the prize.

He was ridiculously grateful for Enzo's watchful eye from the ridge, though he made Enzo promise that if Pietro was caught, he would do nothing but run back to the tent.

Pietro traversed quite well the path Enzo had so skillfully created, propelled by thoughts of being with her. *Unhook. Hold. Hook. Step three to the left, carefully, straight ahead. Rectangle. Unhook. Wiggle. Drop the bread.* He got all the way to the other side. Freedom. Iris. Mia Cara Rossa.

But he was too slow.

He heard the dogs just moments before he heard Enzo's alarm call imitating the bird: "Haa-haa-haa-de-dah," and knew he wouldn't make it back to safety. He was trapped on the outside of the camp. *Dio mio.* What to do? They hadn't prepared for this.

A two-foot trench for drainage surrounded the entire camp. It wasn't a lot, but Pietro hoped to God it was enough. He flattened himself into the ground. Praise be, it was dry season. He knew enough about the wild animals, courtesy of Sergeant Rogers, to know that where there was noise was not where they wanted to be, so, ironically, the dogs kept him safe in his vulnerable position.

He heard the dogs come from both ends and knew the guards were hanging on for dear life, because it sounded like they had canine respiratory issues with the strain on their choke collars. The goal was to reach the gravy spot first. Pietro swore the first responder gloated as the other three sniffed around the bread spot.

Then, without warning, all four converged on the barbed wire, close to him.

He was ashamed as he realized he'd soiled himself. Just a little, but enough, before he remembered he was protected from their snarling teeth by two sets of barbed wire and a perimeter fence.

The guards shouted at each other to be heard over the barking dogs. Once Pietro realized he was protected from the lethal, yellow teeth, he could concentrate on the guards.

"Quiet, you buggers! Shit, man. It's bloody hot again," one guard complained. Pietro couldn't believe his ears. They were talking about the weather?

"Man, those meerkats drive the dogs mad. I think they've made a burrow under the wire. Maybe they've been kicked out of their home by a snake."

Oh, God! They were looking his way. Then he realized Enzo's genius in staggering the trapdoors and exits. They were looking at where the dogs were barking, straight ahead, and not near where he was lying.

"Bitch wife kicked *me* out for a new snake, too. Sounds like home." The men laughed easily, taking no notice of the snarling dogs, who were sniffing and running back and forth as far as their leashes would allow, but far enough away from Pietro.

"Man, these meerkats must be shitting boerewors again to make these guys so excited." The guards laughed. Seemed there was little need for new material when the old stuff worked.

"Or a meerkat's on heat to cause all this excitement!"

They clapped each other on the shoulder and moved along in their respective directions. Pietro wondered how many meerkat jokes he'd hear in the nights to come. As long as there *were* nights to come, he didn't care.

He counted to ten once their backs were sucked in by the darkness and made his way back to Enzo. Never in his life had he felt such a sense of accomplishment, made all the sweeter by Enzo's grin of fatherly pride. "You made it, son. But more practice. You have to double the time. You felt the worst of it, and still you made it."

Pietro felt ridiculously proud and as quickly was overcome by shame: "Not without shitting myself."

"We all shit ourselves, Pietro. It's just the degree that varies."

26

GETTING THERE

"They have a huge batch of wounded soldiers coming in, Mom. Not sure when I'll be home, just don't worry." It was a miracle she got any words out at all. Her throat was thick with anticipation and fear and excitement and apprehension. Thank goodness her mother never looked up from her needlepoint, because she would surely have seen her daughter's lie, planted squarely on her carefully made-up face.

She'd chosen her yellow dress. She figured he needed a dose of sunshine after all he'd likely go through just to get to their rendezvous. The hemline was provocatively above the knee, a style she favored. Her naked lips kissed her mother's soft cheek. "Sleep tight. Don't wait up."

Her mother smiled, still immersed in her cross stitch. "Be safe, Jinx." Her long-lost nickname's resurgence was standard lately, but it never went unappreciated.

She added the bright red lipstick in the hall mirror, shrugged off her dull rain jacket, checked her watch, bent down to give her Buffer a hug, and slipped out of the door with wings on her high heels.

Pietro. She loved the sound of his name in her head, where it had to stay.

The taxi was waiting, and Iris immediately went to work as she slid into the back seat.

"My name is Iris."

"I am Sanjay."

"Sanjay, I need to trust you with my life. I want only you to be my taxi driver on these evening trips. I am conducting a covert survey for the government, so I need you to keep these trips top secret. My life and yours depend on it."

The young man swallowed, his eyes big.

"What will it cost me for sixteen miles and three hours of your time?" she asked.

"Well, Iris. Considering this is a secret mission, I will have to charge danger pay."

"How much will that be?" She dreaded his answer, imagining her overseas stash diminishing drastically. "Thirty pounds, please," Sanjay said.

She was furious. "Are you out of your bloody mind? That's more than I earn in three months."

But Sanjay was no fool. "If it's a government assignment, then they will pay." He avoided her eyes in the rearview mirror.

"Not that much. I will give you ten. It's more than I have authorization for," Iris said flippantly. God, how many taxis would she have to share her story with to afford her trysts? She was sure there would be more. And then at what risk? Damn this businessman in front of her.

Precious time was wasting, and she quickly agreed to twenty pounds, which was two-tenths of her trans-America ticket. She waited for a hint of regret for spending the money allocated to her professional dream, but it never came.

Pietro shook out his best brown POW shirt and inspected it closely. It would do. He smelled his armpit and did a double take. He'd been on road repair until they walked back in the beating tropical heat and straight to supper. A shower would cause suspicion.

"Antonio has a surprise for you." Enzo hinted to Antonio that it was time.

"Remember I said that we four are conspirators? We must all have a part. Here is mine."

Like a skilled magician, the beaming square man whipped off a cloth hiding a bucket of fresh water behind his cot. Pietro took Antonio's glowing face in his hands, kissed both cheeks, gave him a bear hug, then stripped naked to wash every square inch of himself. A whore's bath. He had seen it done many, many times.

A half-hour later, Pietro and Enzo lay as close to the fence as possible. Their nerves were equally heightened.

"Now remember ... "

Pietro touched his friend's arm. "How can I forget anything you taught me? Galileo himself could not have been more scientific."

"Perhaps you can teach me *your* pussy skills to use when the war is done. Just tell me, don't show me, for goodness' sake."

"You're handsome, Enzo, in a sinewy kind of way, but not that handsome." Pietro smiled and flicked the elder lightly across the ear. There was enough light to see the other's grin. Just the right amount of light from the stars, as the master had planned.

The guards and dogs arrived, and the dogs' noses were sniffing madly. The guards took no heed, yanked on choker chains when they'd run out of conversation, and moved on in opposite directions.

Enzo counted down from ten and squeezed Pietro's shoulder. "Go."

The razor wire and the first fence were easy. Enzo's relentless training worked. Pietro recited his directional mantra, then crawled between the fences. He took the briefest moment to turn and give his "invisible" friend on the ridge the thumbs-up.

But the second fucking fence ...

Nerves thickened fingers, which became thumbs. Why was it so damnably difficult? He shook his hands and tried again. He could hear the dogs in the distance, but thank God, far enough away.

For now.

He'd unhooked and re-hooked the damned thing a thousand times on the mockup Enzo made for him, ten times blindfolded and twice in practice. Panic rose from his tight stomach upward ... upward ...

NO! This was the greatest challenge of his life. He'd had an insurmountable challenge before on the stage of La Fenice, convincing a pompous audience to fall in love with a newcomer. The stakes were higher than he ever thought possible then. They were higher now, but when had that stopped him? He slapped himself. Hard.

He dropped his arms, closed his eyes and breathed in slowly. And he thought of her exquisite face. Not perfect. He'd had perfect. But for the first time, perfect for him.

Life would never be the same without her, no matter where in the world he was. *Carpe diem, my Iris.* He bent down and unhooked the rectangle. The loosened wire sprang off the taut expanse, and he crawled through easily, calmly reattaching steel pieces. He pulled two tiny pieces of gravy-soaked bread from his pocket and threw them through the wire, in opposite directions.

He only had the razor wire on the freedom side to go.

It snapped free.

The dogs were getting closer. He could hear them sniffing and their guards' scolding.

Panic hit him like a sledgehammer.

He forced himself back into a state of composure. "O Sole Mio" rang in his head as he held the ends of the barbed wire, then connected hook with eye on the second try.

But he'd taken too long. He knew better. There was no room for hesitation. He could see the dogs. They were so close he could see spittle flying. *Dio mio.*

He leapt like Nijinsky and launched himself over the lip of the ridge, flattening himself into the rain catchment he'd found invisibility in before. He closed his eyes tightly so he couldn't see his fate as he heard the dogs converge on the other side of the fence. It was Enzo's brilliance to up the ante with two pieces of bread to cause more pandemonium than usual.

But what if...

When prayer didn't work, he let her face fill his head as he forced himself to silently sing "O Sole Mio" in English. "What a wonderful thing, a sunny day ... "

When he opened his eyes and peeped over the ridge, the guards' backs were moving farther and farther away from each other. He blinked, not believing his good fortune. *Dio mio, Enzo must have shit himself.* Thank the lord, Pietro had not—this time. That would certainly have hampered his first date with the woman of his heart!

He raised up to a crouch and froze.

Fuck.

Right guard turned around, and the dogs were pulling him back toward Pietro. Standing, with his back hunched, he froze, daring not even to blink. Even his heart stopped, he was sure.

The trio was coming toward him in slow motion. "Wait! Slow! Stop!" The dogs responded, though still straining on the leashes. They were twenty yards from Pietro. *Dio mio.*

I hope the whites of my eyes aren't shining in the moonlight. His limbs were aching from his frozen position. *I will be shot. I will never know her. She who is my soul mate. My perfection.*

"You guys are not going to sniff those bloody meerkats. Forget it. Next time, OK?" The guard rounded his back, struck a match and lit a cigarette, shielding the flame from the wind. As soon as the tobacco tip glowed, the guard pulled the reluctant dogs around and followed his usual path, away from Pietro.

Sweat poured down Pietro's face and body as he stayed rigid until the guard was out of sight. Then, still crouching, he slithered into the undergrowth. He heard Enzo's "Hah-dee-dah" call of good luck and he smiled.

There was a vague foot path worn by Zulus who trudged up and down to their kraals on occasion, so thank God it wasn't complete jungle. His mind slipped to one of the spiders the size of a kitten that Antonio had shown him just yesterday on their way back to camp.

To hell with the spider. I am the dung beetle. My mission is Iris. Iris. Iris.

He slipped and slid on turf unknown in the dim moonlight, but he and Enzo had been over the route a hundred times from a vantage point they'd found from their construction of the very road he was headed toward, so he knew he was going in the right direction.

At last the clearing, then the road and a mercifully dry drainage ditch. Hmm, on the other hand, a fresh dip in rainwater may have been exactly what he needed to ingratiate himself to his love. He lowered himself into the ditch and marveled at the night light—bright enough to see, but not bright enough to see far. His pussy thief had way exceeded expectation.

Car lights. His heart beat loudly in his chest cavity.

He peered over the lip of the ditch, then quickly ducked

down. What if it was Tap … ? No. He couldn't let his mind go there.

He peeped again. A taxi? No. Couldn't be. Which passenger in their right mind would pay a taxi to traverse off the tar and farther down this shale-covered bumpy stretch leading to nothing but a dead end? More to the point, who would trust another human being, a taxi driver, with this treasonous rendezvous? The road was only for back access to the west side of the camp and only used during the day for deliveries, way down the other end, where the tar ended. Nobody had cause to linger here. The few Zulus who used it were only ever on foot, and never at night, because of their feared Tokolosh.

Perhaps the taxi had taken a wrong turn. But no, it stopped. Headlights were turned off.

He waited all of thirty seconds to let his eyes adjust, then decided to go for broke and vaulted out of the ditch as if propelled by a trampoline. He crouched, ready to attack … what?

The taxi door opened. Long legs unfolded and touched the ground, followed by the most beautiful woman in the world, in the sunniest of yellow dresses. The stars made her seem luminous. Divine. And he was entirely smitten all over again.

TOGETHER AT LAST

He was here. She was here. She was the luckiest girl in the world. His face was shiny. A wet lock of his wavy black hair fell over his forehead. He was magnificent. What he'd risked for her. What he'd done to be here. She could only imagine.

He moved into the thicket off the edge of the road and out of sight of the taxi. He put out his arms to her.

She was overwhelmed by a love so raw, so hungry, so powerful, she ached to touch him. Her feet closed the twenty-foot distance between them before she'd made a conscious decision to move. Somewhere in that twenty-foot gap, she accepted that there was no time for coyness or mind games. Every second was precious.

Her body melded into him like a perfectly fitting jigsaw piece. His strong arms wrapped tightly around her waist, up her back, pulling her so close, she could feel his warmth gently pushing through every inch of her yellow dress. She felt at once comforted, safe and incredibly sexy. He smelled musky and sweaty and all-male, and his closeness made her body pliable and entirely at his mercy. She lifted her head, and his breath was hot on her face.

He smelled like he belonged to her.

God, this man was the essence of desires she didn't know existed.

She tilted her head up further, then opened her mouth so she could inhale him.

What an odd thing to do, but so it was. She wanted to breathe his breath, to consume him in the basest way.

She didn't know how long they stood like that: eyes locked, mouths open, devouring without touching. It was as it had been when she'd first seen him up close during their first encounter but closer, more delicious because now their lips could touch and they could taste each other. And still they breathed each other, savoring their heady closeness, anticipating the divine, intimate touch of lips and tongues.

Was it seconds? An hour? A lost lifetime? It didn't matter. It was necessary. And satisfying. At first.

His hands held each side of her face, and he pulled her a half inch closer.

His lips expertly covered hers, and she felt her own slightly parted lips swell as he sucked ever so gently on them until he coaxed her tongue, tentatively, shyly, into his warm mouth. The deeper she went, the more frantic her tongue became in search of his own. The fleeting touch of his tongue, at last on hers, sent a surge of blatant lust from her mouth all the way down.

She coaxed him deeper, wanting him desperately to explore her, showing him it was okay, it was what she wanted, and she urged him to find solace there. And he did.

The kiss was not just a kiss. It was a discovery. Yet a familiarity. It was a reunion of souls. It was an explosion of acute yearning. It was, perhaps, a celebration of being reunited after lifetimes apart.

It was the mother of all kisses.

And it was enough. For the moment.

NOTHING IN COMMON?

Pietro had been taught by many lovers. He knew how to make women quiver. It was his delight and his duty as a bon vivant.

He used this skill to tantalize and tease and please more women than he could count, but none of them had ever made him want to repeat his performance more than a dozen times. The novelty wore off quickly. He thanked his heartless mother for that.

His work, and the places it took him, were the perfect excuse to get the hell out of whatever it was the women were hoping for. Once he became famous, women never expected him to become attached.

So the intensity of this all-consuming feeling he had from the very moment he locked eyes with Iris was a gift, or an inescapable curse, he'd never expected. It humbled and excited him. The thrill of performing in Europe's famous opera houses paled in comparison to the rapture he felt in this stunning woman's presence.

Iris. His Iris. She smelled like flowers. She would taste like them, too. But when he stood breathing her in, he was unprepared for the enormity of what she was to him. She was sunshine. The very essence of life. His life. *If I hadn't found you, the seed of my life would have dried up and caught the wind, sailing into oblivion.*

She fit into him so perfectly. They were where they were meant to be. Attached. Together. Overcoming all the ill forces of man and their wars and giving in to their inevitable, perfect union. He allowed himself at last to encapsulate her mouth with his own and was surprised by yet another new sensation: home. She tasted like everything familiar and comforting and safe. Home. A place he'd never known. A place he'd never realized he'd missed, until now. And he couldn't get enough.

But then there was the yearning physical need to consume her. To become one with her. To languish in all her elixir and to share his with her.

The tip of her tongue tentatively touched the inside of his upper lip, and he understood, as Gibran had, the pain of too much tenderness.

And then his manhood responded with a throb. He didn't want to scare her.

He worked hard to let her explore in her own way, when he longed to use his tongue to show her how much he wanted her.

Her passion was at the same time hot and sweet. Just like the rest of her. A contradiction. A surprise at every turn. Just one word could never sum her up. She was as he'd expected her to be in part, and the other parts were deliciously and entirely unpredictable.

God, she was getting bold.

He knew the longer he held back, the more exquisite the union, and he allowed himself to be explored. Her tongue was hard and urgent now, searching, searching.

And when he could no longer ignore her demands, he closed his lips over her tongue and sucked. He felt her body jolt and an intake of her breath, but she didn't pull away. Quite the contrary. Her nipples poked into his chest; her hips, unguided by his hands, pushed into his own.

Then his tongue and hers danced and stroked and interlocked and suckled, and he'd never been so turned on by a kiss in all his long life.

She was ready to give herself to him.

Damn it. That's why he had to stop this. Now!

His hands, which were gently still bracketing her face, slowly pulled her mouth from his. He gently held her cheeks, gazing at her and waiting for her eyes to open. Then he kissed her softly on the lips and on the tip of her nose.

He felt the warmth of her cheeks grow hot as her eyes faltered and fell from his.

He knew her body had taken her places her finesse and upbringing would never have allowed her to offer the boy next door, let alone a prisoner of war.

She shook her head slightly, partly in denial at what she'd just done and partly to shake his hands away, but he held fast to her burning cheeks.

"Iris."

She looked up at him. He saw confusion and a touch of shame in the green orbs.

"I am whore's son."

He had no idea *that* was coming. Nor, apparently, did she.

Shock changed her face. No, it was worse. It was disappointment.

Her reaction told him she'd fantasized about his birth to loving parents, singing lilting lullabies as his pink, healthy gums held fast to one of many newly engraved silver spoons.

He understood now that to her, being self-taught was less acceptable than rich parents paying somebody to develop a weak talent.

In that instant, he realized that the chasm between them was greater than POW and enemy. It was Italian and English. Street-reared versus excellent, pompous schooling.

But he didn't care. What he felt emotionally, spiritually and physically for this woman was outside reason. She filled in all his gaps. Where she was hard, he was soft and vice versa. No chasm was wide enough to matter. Even without the bridge they might someday need to build, she welcomed him home.

Her intense stare brought him back. She'd waited patiently for his explanation.

"Lucky for talent take me out of slums and learn culture. You are woman born of class. I cannot take ... vantaggio ... " He struggled. "Advantage. I must *know* you." He tapped his fore-head. "I desire you there." He touched his temple again. "Please, I desire you all over." He fanned his open palms down her curvy sides, then tapped his head again. "But here, here is important forever."

Her head cocked this way and that as she concentrated on his English, broken by nerves and the urgency to express himself. *Dio mio,* even the tilt of her head was titillating.

"You are my forever." As the words tumbled out, he knew with certainty that what he said was absolutely true.

Her green eyes twinkled, and his relief was immense. Tension left his body.

But she took a step back, and he felt cold and alone without the heat of her.

Then she smiled, and the sun came out again. "And I think, however strange this may be, that you are my forever," said Iris.

And he ate his words of cerebral need over physical and pulled her roughly to him, devouring her mouth with his own.

THE SEX SONG

They sat very close together on a huge log termites had feasted on for many generations.

Behind them, the taxi was dark and silent. Ahead of them, forest-like undergrowth. He studied her fingers, one by one in the pale moonlight, as if each digit was some incredible find. He, the treasure hunter, she, the treasure.

How long had they been talking? It was so easy with him. She'd spilled out all her hurt when her dad died, and how her brother and her Zulu friends had saved her. She'd never talked of this to another living soul.

He told her of his strange upbringing and how, with the help of Stef, he'd followed his dream. He told her of the crash and the prison camp.

Something made her hold back from telling him about her dream job in America. It was the only thing that was off limits to him. Perhaps she feared that he would have let her go before they started so as not to bind her to him, so that she would live her dream and not feel torn between him and a career. She felt that already he cared more about her happiness than his own. And she wasn't taking that chance. She would make that decision when she had to and not a moment sooner. And only *she* would make it. Selfishly.

Though they were hungry to learn about the other's lives, they were hungrier still to touch and explore each other's bodies. But she almost appreciated his holding back from taking her, right there and then. He was being respectful, though she'd thrown every ounce of her decorum out of the taxi window, en route to their rendezvous.

He lifted her left hand and kissed each finger tenderly. By the fourth finger, she wanted desperately to participate. He must have sensed it, and his light pressure stopped her. Holding her finger, he traced the tip over his sensual top lip, then, letting it go, he caught it between his lips. She felt herself shiver as the tip of his tongue tickled the sensitive end. *Imagine if he was doing this to ...*

Her eyes felt as if there was a film of lust over the orbs, and she couldn't stop the urge to lick her lips.

Would she ever tire of looking at him? Thick lashes outlined his deep, hungry stare, which never wavered from her face as he softly, so excruciatingly softly, used his lips to take her entire finger into his hot mouth.

She welcomed the feeling of being encased, trapped by him, so deep into his mouth, she felt his lips brush her knuckle. The silky warmth and light suction became a searing vacuum and made her gasp. His eyes never left hers as he sucked harder and harder. The tension of the delicious pressure he created made her feel hot, tense and wet with desire.

Just when she thought she would explode with longing, he drew back his head ever so slowly, and she felt the night breeze on her wet finger. The contrast was exquisite.

God, he was sexy. Sensuous full lips. Black, wavy hair falling over his forehead. His blue eyes looked dark, maybe because of the bright stars above; or maybe his lust, which matched her own, darkened his deep blue orbs. Her nipples strained against her bra. *Damn the thing. I'll go without one next time. Less is more. Less I wear, the more I'll feel his closeness. Braless? Mother would die of shock!*

He softly kissed her fingertip and took her hand in his, studying her face again. It was as if she fascinated him. Amazing as that was.

"You really know women." She was not criticizing, just stating a fact.

"Si. But I have never love any."

He held up his hand. He had more to say. *"Ancora.* How you say ... yet?"

"Yet?" she asked, and he nodded slowly.

His kiss was soft. A whisper. A promise?

She pulled away and put her hands in her lap, studying them. It had to be said. "My brother is fighting in Italy."

Silence.

"He is a pilot," she said, without looking at him.

"Like me." His voice was flat.

She kept her head down. "Yes. But on the opposite side." That wasn't necessary, but she had to say it, to bring herself back down to earth. Self-inflicted pain.

"There is not lot of fight in Italy now. Germans in one place. Safer for him than other Europe." It was a matter of fact. And why not? It's not like he should apologize for the war.

He glanced behind them at the silent taxi. "Why taxi?"

"We don't have a car."

"How you keep driver ... how you say, secret?"

"I paid him. Handsomely."

"He is good-looking?"

She laughed so hard, she nearly fell off the log. He joined in, and they knocked into each other, they laughed so freely. They both ended up on the mossy earth, holding their stomachs. His eyes were streaming with tears now, but he'd stopped laughing. Indeed, there was nothing to laugh about. How could they love within this vortex of opposites? Opposite upbringings? Opposite sides of the war?

But when he took her hand again, his once women-jaded heart, the state of the world and who was on whose side made no difference whatsoever. Nothing mattered but him. His spirit. His kindness. His humor. His familiarity. His ravishing face. His soothing voice. His expert hands. His hot tongue. But most of all, the way he made her feel.

She shivered, and his arm protectively encircled her.

"I have some money to help you pay taxi." He pulled out ten shillings.

"What? That's all the pocket money you get for being a prisoner? That's just rude. I'll have my mother speak to the colonel."

"Your mama know new colonel?"

"My mother doesn't know it yet, but she fancies the colonel."

"Oh. Oh," Pietro said ominously.

"What? What's wrong?"

"Every week I play ... " He moved nimble fingers across an imaginary piano. "For colonel and his lady."

"Lady? Oh no! He has a girlfriend? There goes that plan!"

"No. No. No." He shook his head vigorously, then touched his heart, then made an "X" with his finger and enunciated, "No girlfriend. Lady friend." He mimed big boobs, an hourglass figure, and then he rubbed his thumb against the inside of his forefinger.

"Money?" And then it dawned on her. "No! A prostitute? I didn't know Pietermaritzburg had such things."

"Everywhere has such things!" He grinned at her.

She was fascinated. "Where does this happen?"

"Officer's mess. On stage. Inside curtains." He mimed drawing curtains. "Door lock."

"Oh, my." She was mesmerized. Scandalized. Morbidly interested.

"I play, I sing 'Let Me Call You Sweetheart' sixteen times, tops, then must run," and he mimed running, stopping, then looking up as he pulled the cord to release the water from the shower, and relief, as he watched the water hit his body and he washed away the colonel's tryst. She was at the same time entertained and horrified.

She was almost too afraid to ask. "What do they do?"

His ability to perform was evidenced in his vivid reenactment of the lovers' couch time. She was transfixed by his distinct masculine and feminine portrayals of entwined passion.

When he lay back demonstrating their satisfaction, her folded knees rolled her over in another bout of delicious laughter.

When she'd recovered, she asked, "How do you see this?"

"Piano is very chi-ney."

"The reflection. Oh, my God. Would he die if he knew you could see them so well?"

Pietro mimicked Colonel's horror to a "T."

"Sing it to me."

"What?"

"Let Me Call You Sweetheart."

His face was shocked. "No, no."

She felt her laugh bubbling up again. "Why not?"

He shook his head. "It colonel's sex song. Not for you."

She felt a niggle of worry that she'd set her mother up with a sex maniac, but other things dominated. She'd had more interesting conversation and been more entertained by this man, a whore's son with no education who spoke less than perfect English and was a prisoner of war, than any man she'd ever met. Besides her loquacious brother, natch!

In fact, she'd never understood anyone more clearly.

He stood up. She knew it was time and felt her disappointment. He put his hand out to her, and as soon as she stood, he pulled her into his arms and held her tightly, as if he'd never let her go. She felt real tears tickle her cheeks. She was at once deliriously happy and abysmally sad.

He loosened his tight grip and held her as if they were on a mahogany dance floor, crystal chandeliers overhead, and he sang softly into her ear. She closed her eyes, and her head felt like it was filled with champagne bubbles as they danced on the uneven, shale-filled road, oblivious to the pesky pebbles beneath their feet. Perhaps they were dancing on air.

During his tender kiss, Iris felt dread at him leaving. She knew this was goodbye, and for how long? Who knew. She needed him like her body needed food or her lungs needed air. When any part of her body was attached to his, there was no distinction where Pietro started and Iris ended. One was integral to the other. Together they made sense.

He drew away suddenly. She shivered, keeping her eyes closed.

He gently kissed the tip of her nose and whispered, "Iris, Mia Cara Rossa," and her head spun at the sound of his voice.

She shivered and opened her eyes. Only the shifting shapes of the undergrowth on the other side of the ditch hinted at his departure.

She stood alone. Deliriously happy and desperately sad.

30

PICCOLO AND AXLE GREASE

How the hell had he managed to exercise such restraint?

He knew how.

She was the first woman from whom he didn't just want sex. He wanted her heart, her soul, her laughter, her joy. She was his first, his only, unselfish love. She'd conjured up such protectiveness in him that it overcame his need to make love to her.

Shockingly, Iris had turned his very understanding of the world upside down.

He so relished the smell, the taste and the touch of her that the dense undergrowth and dangerous creatures that lurked there were of no consequence to him. His mission was just to get back to the camp without incident so as not jeopardize the chance of doing this again. And again.

And then he heard it.

A pitiful little whine.

He stopped. Listening.

Again. He was relieved it wasn't human and thankful the noise was so pathetic it wasn't going to harm him, so he could get back to the camp. But the noise was closer now, following him. He was suddenly afraid. Perhaps this was a small version of the gargantuan parent who followed. Sweat broke out all over his body. Please. *Don't let anything jeopardize this incredible privilege. I can't die yet, not now that I have just found her ... again.*

Surely God couldn't be that cruel? Damn it, he knew he could. Pietro shivered.

And then a head popped through a thick-leafed fern. His heart stopped until his mind came to terms with what was before him.

In the intermittent starlight filtering between the trees, he saw a little mutt, mostly fox terrier, with the saddest eyes and a wet blob where once an ear was attached. A big chunk had also been taken out of his right buttock. The little guy looked at him so pathetically, his heart softened. He knew whose life this little mite could brighten. Stef was so withdrawn of late.

He heard Enzo's voice. *NO! Don't be stupid!*

The dog wearily inched closer, and when Pietro didn't beat him, the little guy's tail wagged at ninety miles a minute.

Pietro was done for.

He bent down and picked up the mutt, who nuzzled into his armpit. "You're brave to stick your nose in there after you made me sweat like that!" As he spoke, the little dog stretched out his front paws to get a good look at Pietro and cocked his head this way and that, trying desperately to understand with just one ear. Pietro thought of Iris's head turning to catch his words through his thick accent, and he switched to English. "You no Italian?" He smiled at the little dog, whose head moved the same way in both languages, so Pietro switched back. Every sound must be amplified without the protection of the covering of an ear, Pietro supposed.

See Enzo? This little guy is an asset.

"I must be mad." He tucked the dog under his arm and moved toward the perimeter lights of the camp, knowing full well he'd just made an essential excuse for taking this unnecessary risk when so many lives depended on his successful re-entry. The camp would become a bona fide war camp again, no concerts ... the thought of letting Antonio down broke his heart.

At a vantage point where he could safely see the whole camp and perimeter, he lay down with the dog lying quietly next to him. "After all this, you'd better cheer up my friend, do you hear? It's your job." The little head moved from side to side as he gazed at his savior with intelligent, gleaming eyes. He was mercifully quiet. "Piccolo," Pietro whispered. "Your name is Piccolo."

Dog under his arm, he crouched down and made his way through the edge of the brush closest to the guards' forced cross-over point. With Piccolo now in close range, the Dobermans were more restless than ever on the approach. But their degree of skittishness at this same spot was so commonplace, it wasn't a red flag to the guards.

Piccolo passed the test. In spite of the dogs, whose scent he clearly caught because of his wet, twitching nose, the little dog was silent. The little guy had come up trumps, and it was time to break back in.

As soon as the guards disappeared around their separate corners, with Piccolo tucked under his arm, Pietro crawled on one arm and two legs to the barbed wire fence. He fiddled with the secret latch on the barbed wire, which thankfully sprang free. It was awkward with Piccolo under his arm, but he did it. He swore Iris had given his fingers the speed and accuracy he needed, and the thought of cheering Stef with this damaged little dog, who clearly loved love, gave him purpose.

He protected Piccolo with his body as he made it to the perimeter fence, unhooked it and began to crawl through. Protecting the dog with his body so he didn't get jabbed by the fence bulked Pietro up, and the squeeze was really tight.

On the other side, he quickly fastened the fence, and crouching, they dashed to the next.

He heard a shout. The timber of the voice was vaguely familiar.

His fingers thickened.

But the shout was far away. Perhaps a fellow prisoner having nightmares about Tap Tap? He hoped to God that's all it was.

He thought of Iris, and his fingers became nimble and quick. He pushed through more easily this time, but when he tried to reattach the wire to the fence, it kept jumping back up. He still had the razor wire to attach, too, so time was tight. So much so that he heard the dogs only after he felt Piccolo stiffen in his arms.

He couldn't stop now. It was just too late. He had nowhere to hide. "O Sole Mio..." he whispered, and just as the guards rounded the corners from opposite sides, he latched it closed.

He still had twenty yards to safety.

"O Sole Mio ... " He unhooked, stepped through, re-hooked the barbed wire and sped away from the scene of the crime, still singing in his head, with Piccolo, trusting, under his arm.

The inside of their tent was pitch dark. "Stef. Stef."

Enzo and Antonio were awake, like they'd been waiting for him, which likely they had. Pietro felt he had two guardian angels now. It was both annoying and comforting.

"How was it?" Enzo was anxious for details.

"Did she like your clean smell?" Antonio's mission contribution was of high importance.

"Yes, she did, thank you, Antonio. I brought something for Stef. Where is he?"

The tent opened a fraction, and Pietro felt his heart stop.

Then Stef's face pushed between the canvas edges.

"Fuck, Stef. Where were you?" Pietro's fury was induced by fear, and Stef looked guilty as hell. Pietro was disappointed that his friend was not where he should be to enjoy the surprise he'd planned at such great risk.

Stef was all the way in. "I was in the bathroom. Why are you looking for me?"

"I thought I found you a girlfriend, but sadly, it's not."

"What the fuck?" Stef was befuddled.

Pietro lifted the dog from under his shirt and held it out at chest height for all to see. Even in the dim light, Piccolo's fine set of jewels was evident.

"Sadly it's not a *girl* friend, but he's cute anyway. His name is Piccolo." He held his offering toward his old friend.

Stef's grin was wide as he scooped up the little dog. Its tail wagged as it showered Stef with a thousand kisses. "He's perfect. Piccolo. Thank you, my friend. Thank you." There were tears on Stef's cheeks. The little guy flinched and made his first noise. "Oh, no. He's hurt."

"Yes. He lost an ear, and his bum looks bitten. But he was so determined to get to you, he didn't say a word." Pietro's heart was unduly soft for this pair before him.

Enzo was livid. "And at what risk, you fool?"

"Look at them, Enzo. It was all worth it, and he was as good as gold." Enzo's sharp retort was cut short by a solid beam of bright light that illuminated the tent.

Every stomach lurched, then dropped to weak knees.

The big bulk of Burbero, the surly guard, followed the beam he shone through the tent flap. Their collective relief that it wasn't Tap Tap was short-lived. This guy was huge, and he'd been Tap Tap's right-hand man. His scare tactic: his brawn.

And he was here, in their tent.

"What the blerry hell is the noise in here, hey?" The guard was angry.

The light shone in each of their faces.

"One, two, free, four ... " He counted before, to the men's horror, Piccolo wriggled out of Stef's awkward hold behind his back and plopped to the floor.

Not a muscle moved as they watched, frozen in sheer terror, as Piccolo, soon be Stef's short-lived new friend, trotted confidently toward the big hulk.

The eager little dog sat down and looked up at the big man. Seconds seemed like hours. Then Burbero bent down slowly, as giant men often do, and each inch was torture for the men who stood helplessly and waited for the inevitable "crunch."

Once in reach, as eyes fluttered closed to avoid seeing the cruelty, the surly guard scooped up the little dog and giggled with delight as Piccolo showered him with canine kisses.

Their collective relief was palpable. Pietro and Stef faced one another and shared a look reserved only for childhood friends who'd seen the worst of humanity but made it through because they had each other. Piccolo bounded back into Stef's arms, and the moment was gone, but not lost.

Dio mio. Not only had Piccolo received an unexpected welcome, but in the excitement the big guy hadn't noticed Pietro was clothed. He took the chance to creep slowly toward his cot and cover himself, boots and all, with his blanket.

Burbero's voice bellowed: "I'll get axle grease for his bum and ear. I'll say he's mine. But he's really yours." He nodded to Stef and grinned. "I'll fix the little bugger."

31

SIBLING REPORT AND HAMMOCK SANDWICH

31st March, 1944

Hi Brother Mine,

Okay. I know now to be patient. I will no longer panic because there's no letter from you. I'll know you're being a South African hero, nay a World War II hero, somewhere.

You'll always be mine.

So! I think my matchmaking ruse might be working! Mother went on a date with Colonel Cairns. She was all a-twitter, either because she was thrilled to see him or embarrassed there was such a sendoff with Lena, Sofie, Buffer and me sizing up the situation and crowding the hall. She made her exit on his arm like only our mother can—with style, poise, confidence and a royal wave of dismissal of her subjects in the hall from her gloved hand.

I must tell you that a secret source (don't I sound like Mata Hari?) told me—wait for this—that our mother's colonel was seeing a prostitute on a regular basis at the camp! What scandal. If mother knew, it would be the end of a beautiful thing. Selfishly, I can't tell her, because other than him dipping his pen into a naughty inkpot, he's perfect for Mom. I told Lena that I was afraid Mom would get a disease, and she said, "Even most beautiful fig may contain worm, my child. Better worm likes ubulili more than hitting." She has a point. Much better to enjoy having sex than to enjoy giving beatings. Small mercies and all that. Besides, I may have a contact for a penicillin shot or two. Tee hee.

I suppose prostitution is as old as time—but our mother's beau partaking? But then, mother needs a man, perchance a husband, so my new mantra? "Think of the worm in the fig, Iris. The worm in the fig!"

How I'll miss those Zulu proverbs when I am in Hollywood.

We waited endlessly for mother's reappearance. I know now what it must be like having a teenage child. One can worry oneself sick! The front door finally opened, around midnight no less, and one glowing mother sashayed into the foyer. I believe we all mentally examined her for signs of deflowering.

"Well? What did you do? Where did you go? What did he do to you?" I asked way too eagerly. And here was our mother's response: "Iris Mary Fuller." But she was smiling brightly, her face flushed. "We went to a little restaurant. He was charming and delightful."

"Now, mom, you didn't kiss him, did you?"

And you know what our prim and proper mother did, Gregg? She kicked off her shoes and, like an eager teenager, sat down right there in the hallway where we all joined her. It felt like sharing with best friends after a naughty night out with a cute boy. Hmm. How would I know? I never had any best friends. You were it, my brother! Oh, dear, I never had a naughty night out with a cute boy, hell any boy, in those days either!

"Well, he was very persuasive," our mother said, avoiding eye contact.

"And? Was it The Kiss as described at the card table?" I asked.

"Let's just say it had huge potential." She fairly glowed, Gregg!

"Don't you think you should take this slowly? At your age it's not good to rush into anything. You don't know what he's been up to—or who he's been up to—"

"Iris! That's not ladylike. In fact, it's downright crude. He's a perfectly decent man. A gentleman of note. A compassionate humanitarian. I like him. I have not liked a man since your father, and he left me eleven years, three months and four days ago. And he's not coming back. Now excuse me, please. I am going to bed."

Now. You tell me if matchmaking isn't my new calling!

So, my dearest sibling (and that you'd be, even if you weren't the only!), I'll keep you posted on all the developments of our mother's romance.

Please God that you are safe. I miss you every day.

Your ever-loving, I. xx

What Iris didn't tell her brother was the conversation at 32 Ewing Street while they waited for the wayward mother to return from her date.

Three women and a dog lay the wrong way on the hammock. Their torsos relaxed in the twine swing, gazing at the stars, as their legs dangled off the woven edge. Every now and then, someone risked upending them by using tippy toes to give a push.

Iris was sandwiched between the two Zulu women, and she couldn't have felt more comfortable. Buffer lay like a hat made for three, lengthwise, completing her nucleus. Well, except for Gregg. There would always be something missing without him.

"Eich. We miss you so much when you go to America." Lena roughly wiped her eyes.

"I'll miss you, too. Promise to look after Buffer for me?" Iris begged.

"You want to go?" There were no flies on Sofie.

"Designing has been my dream since I wore my nappy at a jaunty angle. I should go, ladies. It's what I've always wanted."

"What of Singingman?" Lena asked softly.

Guilt burned hot on Iris's cheeks. "Oh, Lena, I wanted so much to tell you. But I had nothing to tell until a few nights ago," she burst. The ladies simply waited for her to continue. "I first saw him at the prisoner camp. My heart knew his heart. I saw him again at the concert when he became my Singingman. Singingman's been in to the store to buy supplies. Then I saw him. Just us two. Secretly. At night."

The revelations that spewed forth were greeted with silence.

Lena was hurt and Sofie, just plain annoyed that she was the last to know.

"Fourfeet must have told you that we have been sending notes. Little shit for telling you before I could," Iris complained to mask her guilt. "Please, you have to understand, I didn't know what my heart was feeling. I didn't know how to tell you that I had fallen for Gregg's enemy."

"Ibhubesi. Love, like rain, does not choose the grass on which it falls," Lena said wistfully. Iris would have preferred her Zulu mother's wrath over her sublime kindness. It made her feel guiltier than ever.

Then Iris realized, like the true mother she was, Lena's worry was for her child's feelings over her own. Iris threw her arms around Lena and hugged her as they both cried. Sofie, not to be outdone, joined in, and Buffer leapt up to protect his mistress. The whole contingent went sprawling onto the patchy grass below. And they laughed. They laughed until they cried and then they laughed again.

Out of the corner of her eye, Iris saw Buffer crouch and give a long, low growl, but she was too relieved, having confided in these beloved women, to really worry about the cause.

When they came up for breath: "Ladies, may I hereby announce that Singingman is my Philemon from the petrol station."

"*Eich!* Two Fuller women with Philemons!" Sofie was impressed.

They resumed their laughter, shrieking with glee, and Lena slapped plump knees.

"Oh, ladies, I *can't* stop thinking about him, longing for him." She felt abysmally sad again, and her tone sobered them all.

"Very big danger, Ibhubesi," cautioned Sofie, none too gently.

Lena's beloved face creased with grave concern. "You be careful, Ibhubesi. *Your* Philemon make you go to jail."

LUST OR ANGER; ANGER OR LUST?

Julian Kaiser settled himself in his usual place for a bird's-eye view of the back yard.

He had already nestled a worn patch, such were the frequency of his visits, though catching her outside late at night was a rare bonus. He could see her window from here, too. He congratulated himself on the perfect vantage point. The wild ferns had become ground cover from the weight of his body. If anyone had looked, there would be hard evidence of his voyeuristic intentions. But the yard was so unkempt, clearly no one had the inclination.

She looked like a child this night.

He felt his arousal.

She was dressed in long socks and a man's thick, long jersey. He wished she'd worn her silky pajamas. Then he could see the outline of her nipples.

He felt the darkness of anger creeping in as he watched three women and that fucking dog on the hammock. What was it with her and her liberal ways? She was lying with black bitches on either side of her. Have you ever? She needed to be severely chastised. He needed to beat her senseless. Then he would fuck her.

No, no, not yet. He had to talk himself down. Literally.

Hearing their chatter was touch and go from where he sat. It literally depended on which way the wind blew. Occasionally he could catch snippets, but he wasn't here for the conversation.

The longer he stayed, the more he was rewarded by the flashes of milky thigh between the long jersey and the high socks, as the hammock swayed this way and that.

Ah, a prize for his first hour of vigilance: Iris laughed so hard, she opened her legs. He thought he would come right then.

Then they all fell off the hammock.

That was close. He had to breathe deeply to calm his arousal.

Damn. He must have moved. The damned dog was crouched, growling.

He concentrated on being still, which quieted his erection for a bit. Good. He could stay longer. The longer he could make this last before he satisfied himself, the better. He was off tonight, so he had all the time in the world.

She sang, *"La donna è mobile, Qual piuma al vento, Muta d'accento—e di pensiero"* and ended with, "That's all I've learned so far."

Why the hell was it so familiar? Where the hell had he heard that before? And why the hell did it fill him with such white-hot anger?

There was great laughter as those other two tried to wrap their wretched Zulu tongues around the strange lyrics.

Then it came back to him. He'd seen her at the stupid concert where "the colonel" insisted the Eye-Tie sing. He spat. He was long gone from the town hall before the bloody song ended, but he remembered the tune and the bastard who fancied himself an opera pundit. Nancy Boy. Hmm. He wanted to squeeze the opera out of him. That would feel so good.

Damn. He wished he could creep closer and put a hurt on all of them and the dog. The damned dog.

The anger was coming before the relief. What now?

And then they took away the decision from him. They went inside. The dog crept toward him, low to the ground. Growling. Coming closer. He'd like to snap its ...

"Buffer," she called from the patio's French doors. And like the dog he was, he obeyed. That was the trouble. She knew *he* would never obey her. That's why she didn't want him. She lifted him up and then threw him away. She said his hand didn't matter, but by God, it did. Curse that bloody violin.

They were all inside. If only he had done to her what she deserved. He had the chance months ago when they were alone so often. He blew it. He would make sure he didn't blow it the next time, and by God, he would find a next time. And she'd pay. He'd push her legs apart ...

No. No. Down, boy.

He had to find real satisfaction tonight. His anger needed to be stilled. The night was young. He could get to the camp to snuff the opera out of the Eye-Tie so *his* girl would never sing the bastard's songs again. And then ... and then he could have his sweet release. It would be well earned.

33

SATISFACTION

He knew the singing macaroni was in the same tent as the moron he'd used as a guinea pig for his monument, The Hole.

What a rush that'd been.

His legacy still stood at the far end of the camp. The brick hell hole was all he had left of his time in charge. But wasn't that the most notable building around? It contrasted so well with the macaroni church. Hell and heaven. Which would these bastards remember longest after this war? Making those fucking Eye-Ties build the very walls that would punish them so cruelly was pure genius.

He'd told the guards he'd be checking on the camp himself. He did that sometimes when he needed time to himself. He was in his civvies, but the night staff didn't care. They were just relieved to have down time in the middle of the night.

He'd checked the tent roster and the tent layout as to where he'd find the moron. He remembered his name was Antonio, because the fools chanted it when their half-wit came out well-cooked. That's when he'd earned his "master chef" title. Rarely those idiots made sense, but this was such a time. *Macellaio.* He thought it fitting.

Then he was outside the right tent. The confident fucks left their flaps unfastened now. Weak. That's what he was, that new fucking colonel. Ha! He felt the cool chill on his teeth. After tonight, all flaps in the camp would be tightly sealed.

He peeped inside, holding the rest of the flap closed so as not to let in any light, and slipped in. He stood still, allowing his eyes to adjust. Everyone was asleep.

Jackpot! There was the big square form of the moron, mouth open, snoring.

He could make out the skinny one who hardly made a dent in his own bed, and the one with the violin, curled up in a fetal position. Then there he was. The one Julian was looking for.

A slither of the tune Iris had sung from the hammock came into his head, making his nostrils flare as anger fired deep within.

Was this the same one who had stopped him from hitting the fucking Zulu on the bicycle? They all looked the same.

He crept toward the prick's bed. He had a cocky way about him even in sleep. He'd end that tonight. There would be no more reason for Iris to sing one of his goddamned songs again. Hadn't he always said "NO SINGING"? See? This was the kind of shit it brought on!

His whip felt searing hot through his gloves. Straight from the embers of hell, it was balled between his two strong hands, an inch from the throat, spaced just enough to cover the prick's larynx. The very throat which had pleasured his girlfriend. *His* girlfriend. The girl he would marry, then beat into submission.

He delayed the pleasure just a moment before he struck, and as he felt the familiar throbbing in his crotch, he went to crush those fucking vocal cords so they wouldn't emit anything but a whisper ever again.

Unexpectedly, the opaque whites of both frightened eyes

were upon him, and he thrust bone-hard leather into the larynx with all his might—but not before the prick made a noise. A grunt. Enough in these close confines. He woke the others. How could a dog be barking so close?

He pushed harder, concentrating on his mission, blocking out the peripheral noise so he could enjoy this deliciously vicious moment. Vaguely he heard screaming outside the tent. But he knew they were too chicken-shit to try to stop him. By the time someone of authority came to the prick's defense, his work would be done. The larynx would be damaged beyond repair.

Damn. The prick was strong. The new fucking colonel didn't understand the advantage of keeping them hungry and weak.

Prick was trying to push the whip up and away from his precious throat, flailing. Oh, he loved it when they did that. How'd the bastard get his fingers under the whip to protect his throat? It didn't matter. His wicked whip was strong enough to cut through both.

He pushed in little, unpredictable bursts until he was squashing fingers and larynx all at the same time. Hot, intense, bloodshot, bulging eyes looked like the devil incarnate, and for an instant, he recognized himself there. How dare this fucking Eye-Tie, *his* prisoner, be anything but submissive under his tight leather?

He pushed harder.

The flap flew open.

"Captain!" He recognized Rogers's voice. How quickly that one had changed his allegiance.

Julian used his "colonel" voice: "I will not tolerate insolence from a prisoner. He must be punished. Get him into The Hole. NOW!" Damn him. He was forced to release his advantage.

"Good idea to get him into the *hospital* now, sir."

"No, you deaf idiot. In The *Hole,* now!"

"Right away, sir. In the hospital he goes." And all of a sudden six men were in that tent pushing him aside to carry the bastard outside and toward the new camp triage.

Damn them all to hell.

34

PICCOLO'S PERFORMANCE

April 1944

The men of his tent were more informed in the minutiae of the war than most South Africans, Pietro would bet. Since he'd last seen Iris, German troops were occupying Hungary, and the U.S.S.R. had retaken Odessa. If nothing else, the war was representative of how long nearly six weeks really were. That's how long since he'd laid eyes on his Iris.

It was opening night of *The Barber of Seville.*

A flurry of exuberance ensued in the mess hall. Pietro could hear it from the stage. A brilliantly real Italian street scene smelled of fresh paint. He was so damn proud of them all. Behind the closed curtains, men as men and men as women practiced with falsettos to match their costumes. Pietro lightly touched his bruised throat and flinched. The only good thing was, without him, his actors and singers could shine in their own light.

Iris. *Dio mio.* How he longed for her. Each day without the touch of her skin was torture. He'd take Tap Tap's vile abuse over being deprived of Cara Rossa any hour of the day.

He thought he heard her lilting accent and turned his head too fast. She was everywhere and nowhere. Damn, his neck muscles shouted their objection. That motherfucker had never been held accountable, on Pietro's insistence. He'd begged Rogers, Doc and the guards not to report the son of a bitch. He couldn't afford to draw attention to himself. Another reason it was good he was sans voice. Better he was a *persona non grata*. Bah! Who was he kidding? Once a ham, always a ham. Though his "glaze" had been dormant before Iris had rekindled its sheen. One look at his Iris, she became his reason for everything: breathing, living, music, ridiculous risk-taking.

The soonest he could get to her was two weeks ago, when Pietro had refreshed his eyes and replenished his heart with the sight of her. The note in the dye box he passed her read, "See you at 9:45 on 17 April? My heart needs you. My mind needs you. My body longs for you."

She'd asked about his hoarse whisper, and he told her he had laryngitis.

Their hands had touched between the material they pretended to be discussing. It became an exquisitely sensuous form of foreplay: his hand, blindly seeking hers, finding it but never being able to touch her skin because of the satin layers that separated them.

She busily piled reams of fabric on top of their eager hands to hide their union. He gently separated her fingers and then interlaced his with hers. He was rewarded by her enigmatic smile and a modest flush of her cheeks, and as she squeezed his hand, he saw a pulse in her suprasternal notch. Very early in his life he'd learned what an erogenous zone that tiny area could be. To see her throbbing from that very source made him want her desperately. Right there. On her glass counter.

A willing student, she followed his lead and did the same to his fingers as he did to hers through their slippery prophylactic. They stroked and touched until her face flushed with pleasure, and she gave a little gasp as her pupils dilated. God, she was divine.

This give and take, this ultimate in sensory stimulation came easily. The skill, however, lay in conducting a dull conversation on the merits of the material and its multiple uses.

Fortunately, Enzo was engaging Rogers with what could be nothing less than a fascinating tale, and the cunning old fox had managed to manipulate the sergeant to face away from the counter, giving the lovers time to explore.

"The color looks so dull at first, but then you touch it."

"Touch always ... how you say ... *determine di qualita.* Determines quality."

"Do you think it feels too slippery?"

"Never too slippery. It feel ..." he was thinking of the right word.

"Moist? You're so right. I feel it, too." Her voice was breathy.

Thank the lord Enzo's animated story was a long one and the store was quiet in the early morning, otherwise Pietro and Iris would both have been jailed on the spot for indecent use of satin and locked up for treasonous finger-fondling.

An exceedingly loud, off-key soprano blasted forth a practice scale, severely disrupting Pietro's musical sensibilities, but it certainly worked to bring him back from his Iris-reverie.

Piccolo was made for the stage. He wandered around playing the Stray, greeting everybody, his stubby tail wagging so fast, it was a constant blur. The baboon bite in his hind quarters was well healed thanks to Burbero's loving administrations of axle grease.

The mongrel was in full costume, sporting a wig fashioned from bright yellow wool that resembled uneven bangs down to his eyes and long braids that hung nearly to the floor. The earless side's braid kept falling forward, so their costume department had created a fake ear with bobby clips to hold it back. The sight of him brought delight to all, and Pietro swore their laughter could be heard in Milan.

Piccolo had become the most beloved dog in the southern hemisphere. He was carefully hidden when Tap Tap was on duty, though there wasn't a man inside or outside the camp who wouldn't have faced Tap Tap's wrath or gone to the gallows to protect little Piccolo. Stef was smitten with the little guy. And if Stef was Piccolo's doting father, then Burbero was his godfather.

"Break a leg," Pietro shouted to his motley crew before he slipped from the stage into the hall to watch the show. He was thinking about the silly English good-luck-wish he'd used, when Enzo took his place on stage, a finger to his lips. The crowd miraculously obeyed, as the wiry man placed a chair outside the curtains, back to the audience at an angle.

Pietro allowed himself a moment of immense pride as he looked behind him to see rapt faces from every rank and station from both sides of the war together for two hours of escape and roaring delight.

"Ladee ... ahem! Gentlemen. I give you Stef and Piccolo!" Enzo announced proudly.

Stef slipped through the stage curtains, sat with his back to the crowd and whistled.

Out came Piccolo. He did a lap around the front of the stage, legs pumping, braids swinging, pink bum swaying, false ear at an angle, and Pietro marveled how well Stef had taught him to milk a crowd. Wild wolf whistles and loud clapping erupted. The little dog stopped in front of Stef.

As Stef positioned his violin under his chin, front paws involuntarily lifted off the floor in frenzied anticipation. One note was all it took.

Stef began a complex violin solo. Piccolo got up onto his hind legs, lifted his nose to the rafters, and let out a mournful, continuous howl. It went on and on, in different keys, mouth open, mouth closed, head this way, then that, so immersed in the music was he.

The audience rolled about, laughing.

Stef stopped playing, and Piccolo, still on his hind legs, stopped too, though his eyes were closed and his mouth open, waiting. *Damned if he didn't know when the sonata was not yet complete.* Stef made the violin squawk, which drew a similar but amplified squawk from Piccolo, who held the note, eyes closed, as long as Stef did. Then he continued to play, and the dog was confidently back into his groove, braids swinging.

The closer they got to the end of their show, the more the canine howling intensified, until violin and howl collectively ended with a flourish, matched by the audience's howl of appreciation, loud enough to raise the roof.

Stef put his violin down, stood and bowed. Piccolo dropped his head too.

Then, in the front row, Burbero stood, turned to the audience and bowed, looking as grim as usual. Piccolo scampered to the edge of the stage and jumped into the big, waiting arms, where he stayed, cradled, braids and all, for the rest of the show.

35

SECOND RENDEZVOUS?

17 April 1944

It was early—far too early for a girl who had a late date tonight with a dark-haired, blue-eyed prince—to be interrupted by a loud knocking on the front door. Buffer was barking viciously. Iris heard a man's voice and, on her way to the hall, she heard her mother make a peculiar sound. Rushing, she took in the scene and her heart fluttered, then burned with fear. A down-mouthed Rogers and next to him, the Colonel, stern-faced, lunged forward to catch her mother, who reeled toward the hard parquet floor like a puppet whose strings were viciously cut.

"What's wrong?" Iris asked as she knelt down next to her mother.

"He's gone. Gone. Gone."

"Who, Mom, who? For God's sake, who?"

Sergeant Rogers stepped forward and held Iris's shoulders. She looked at him mournfully, shaking her head no. No. NO! Not Pietro. Please God, not her Pietro.

"Your brother, Miss Fuller. Gregg. London has confirmed his

plane was shot down four weeks ago. He is missing in action over Italy. Presumed dead."

Iris's shame was so deep, she heaved, so as to eject it from her body. Gregg. *Oh God, forgive me, Gregg, forgive me. I didn't even think of you.*

She tried to cover up her dishonor with an aggressive tone: "Can't be bad news. Where's the chaplain?"

"We didn't think we needed one since we know your family," said the colonel gently.

She reeled away from the tragic tableau, her arms over her head, shrouded in mortification so black, so appalling, she couldn't stand to poison these kind people who had never wavered from being on the right side of the war. So obsessed with Pietro was she, her brother had become secondary. He who fought for her country against Pietro's kind, to protect her, to keep her and her country safe. Oh God, what had she done? It was all her fault.

She heard a primal wail and recognized it as the sound of her own pain.

Her fault. She had made a deal with God, and she was pretty clear about the payment of her hospital time in lieu of her brother's safety. But she'd underpaid. She herself had let her brother down, not God.

Her forehead rested on the hard floor of the hall. Buffer stood over her. Her mother's properness came to her: "It's unladylike to kneel on the floor and, God forbid, put your head down and leave your bum in the air in front of men you don't know, in your pajamas no less." But then Iris realized Gregg's mother was screaming with her own desolate despair and grief, and Iris? Well, Iris no longer mattered. Bum in the air or not. Invisible. Unimportant.

The length, breadth and depth of her culpability was all-consuming. At a loss, she ran outside. She wanted to beat herself up. Pummel herself until she was black and blue. Instead she fell into the hammock, and Buffer followed. She wished Buffer would bite her hand instead of licking it. But then she looked into his sage, brown eyes, and she figured he understood, perhaps better than she, what she needed from him.

Sergeant Rogers had obviously been dispatched to find her, because he rounded the corner of the house, his face grave with concern. He handed her a perfectly clean handkerchief.

"My brother is dead, Sergeant."

"We don't know that for sure."

She felt hope surge hot through cold veins and clutched his forearms to tell her more.

"Only if we find a body or identifiable remains can we acknowledge death." The sergeant's tone was gentle but matter of fact.

"How thorough can you be in a war zone? How closely are they able to look for ... remains? His plane was shot down! What chance of finding a piece of him to put to rest?"

They were all rhetorical questions. She knew. He knew, and he just shook his head from side to side until water seeped from his eyes. Like her, he was at a loss for words.

She hid her head with her arms as if to shield herself from the ferocity of the blows she deserved. She rocked back and forth. "It's my fault, Sergeant. My fault. My fault." The rhythm lulled the magnitude of her words.

Rogers gently took hold of her shoulders, but she shrugged him off and ran back inside.

Lena and Sofie came into her room to comfort her, but she didn't want, no, she didn't *deserve* comforting, so she begged them to leave. Her mother? She didn't know. She had the colonel. Under her covers with Buffer pushing himself into her form to protect her, she cried and cried and cried, because she didn't have the courage to kill herself.

Three hours later, she knew what she had to do.

She retrieved the letter of acceptance she'd written four minutes after she'd read her invitation to Hollywood for the fifth time. It seemed a lifetime ago. She'd left the letter undated at the time but had no idea why. But now she knew. The job prospect, all she'd dreamed of and more, had come shortly before she saw Pietro for the first time on the barbed wire fence, rescuing a pigeon.

She would sign the bloody letter tonight and post it off in plenty of time for her July 31, 1944, deadline, and she would have a year to embark on her voyage to America. A new life. A life where she wouldn't live in hopeful expectation of having her brother back. A life where the void he left would be less painful because she wasn't home.

A life without Pietro.

She felt a physical stab in her heart. She could never see him again. She'd never felt more bereft. "I've lost two men I love on one day." She curled up again and wept until she couldn't any more.

Later, she put pen to paper, wrote in the date—but looked away as she signed the solid stock, as if to detach herself from the act of separation.

36

THORNS

Pietro created a moat fit for a large castle with his pacing outside their tent.

What the hell was he going to do? How could he see her? A note? She'd throw the thing away. Unread. She wasn't at her store; he'd tried three times to lie about supplies he needed and was greeted by a very gay and very charming replacement.

He thought how he'd felt, alone in the ditch on pins and needles for hours and hours that night of 17th April. Thinking the worst. Thinking she was hurt or, God forbid, their tryst discovered and that somehow she'd protected him because they weren't here to arrest him, but he wished they'd come and lock him away because living without her was not living at all. He knew this now as surely as he knew Stef was born to play the violin. His love for her was not a fanciful way to pass time. His love for her was fucking essential to his heart beating.

Then Rogers delivered the news to Pietro in whispers during the Sunday morning mass. Iris's brother was presumed dead in Italy. He was pathetically relieved it wasn't something he'd done to cause her not to come to their rendezvous. *Forgive me, Father, for I have sinned.* How could he be so self-centered? *Take his soul into your keeping ...*

Italy, of all places. He knew full well that she was angry with Pietro because of *where* her brother had died. He understood that the very act of fraternizing with the enemy of her brother would be reason enough in her mind to bring down the wrath of God himself.

It was all very complicated, and there was hardly an opportunity for Pietro and Rogers to sit in the sunshine together and contemplate the whys and wherefores.

The world simply wouldn't let him and Iris feel what they felt. He knew that if she blamed him, he might well lose her. He knew that if she blamed herself, that would take even more convincing. He also knew that if he lost her, he would lose his soul, this time for good.

He had to make her see him.

As he crept through his two secret trap doors and the barbed wire that night, he was on automatic; there was no thought of his own danger.

All he could think about was that if she refused to see him, he might just wander the hillside till the authorities caught up with him. Then he would run so they would shoot him in the back, and the misery would be over.

He surprised himself. In his worst hours, and there had been many, he had never contemplated death as an alternative. Until now. Until Iris. He half-walked, half-ran down "their" road. Her face was the impetus that kept his legs pumping in spite of the acute pain in his left side. Miles and miles he ran toward the lights, following the road they'd built. He was glad there was cloud cover over the abundant stars to camouflage his movements out of the camp's perimeter, until he got close to town; then electricity was a blessing and a curse. The lights helped him to see, but his uniform was like a target on his back. It would take but one person to recognize him as a prisoner, and he was done for. But those were the least of his fears when he had Iris to worry about.

He had no idea how he would find her house.

He knew she walked to work, so she had to live within a mile of the department store. He would just peep into houses until he found the right one. Desperate times called for desperate measures. And this was indeed such a time.

It took him three hours. Adrenaline kept his feet moving from house to house. Had he been caught, his punishment for being a peeping Tom might have exceeded that of falling in love with the enemy. He smiled to himself. English society!

Then he saw her.

His heart somersaulted.

Her bedroom faced the front of the house. There *was* a God!

The light was on, and the curtain was halfheartedly pulled closed, leaving a gap of half an inch. He peeped in, and his heart stopped. There she lay, a big dog beside her. The beast was panting, probably from the heat of her body, since he was lying so close. Her dog quickly looked toward the window and snarled. Pietro jumped back instinctively and fell into a bed of wildly climbing roses that pricked the hell out of him.

Her light went off. He stayed where he was on his butt, leaning on his elbows. Her face appeared at the window, the dog's snarling face next to hers.

Her face registered complete surprise as she saw him in the dim light cast from the street lamp. Ridiculously, he waved and smiled. She smiled back for an instant, before her face fell and she pulled the curtains together tightly.

He was stunned. Disappointed. Heartbroken. He didn't move from the prickly bed. It must be the Catholic in him, self-flagellation of sorts. He convinced himself that if she looked out again and saw the absurdity of his predicament, her beautiful laugh would ring out, and all would be well and all the thorns would be worth it.

Come to the window, Mia Cara Rossa. Thorns became daggers, and muscles felt like they'd been wrapped tightly around the handle of the blade. His left side beat loudly, like a monotonous bass drum.

She really was punishing him.

But still he didn't move.

Finally.

She peeped out again. She and her dog.

He smiled and waved. As he'd desperately hoped, the absurdity tickled her, and in spite of herself, she smiled slightly. It wasn't a laugh, but he'd take it.

It was all the incentive he needed. He tried to jump up, but his muscles had knotted, and he fell back down. It hurt like hell as new thorns penetrated his cotton uniform. But it was worth it because, finally, she threw her head back and laughed.

She pointed to her left and drew the curtains.

Aching and itchy, but too excited to care, he scrambled out of the climbing roses and went to the right of the house, unsure what he needed to do.

He wove through the overgrown yard, saw an odd, worn patch in the grass and wondered fleetingly what that was, then she appeared in front of him, holding fast to her tooth-bearing dog.

"Put out your hand, palm up." She demonstrated, and he did as he was told. The dog sniffed, and at least his teeth disappeared.

He longed to embrace her, but he felt her distance, and it broke his heart. She sat, cross-legged on the grass, the farthest spot away from the house. He sat, legs in front of him, leaning back on his elbows. The dog sat next to her, eyes boring into his own.

"This is Buffer," she said as she scratched his neck.

"Buffer." He put his palm out again, and the dog humored him with another quick sniff.

She smiled for an instant. "He doesn't like men, but he's OK with you."

"Trust your dog." He smiled, but she dipped her head, avoiding his eyes.

He was glad they were both whispering so she wouldn't notice his voice still gone.

"Iris."

She refused to look at him.

"Your brother. I am so terrible apologetic. Please accept my *condoglianze* for you lost."

When she finally looked at him, her eyes were red and wet.

"It was my fault."

"Why? *Dio mio,* Iris. Why?" It was the first squeak emitted from his throat since Julian's stick did its worst.

"Because of you."

She stood up. He was dismissed. Damn it! He couldn't give up so easily. He wouldn't.

"Blame me. Yes, it's me fault I Italian." She still wouldn't look at him.

"But just as you brother didn't shoot down mines plane. I did not shoot down hims." He didn't give a shit that his pronouns were discombobulated. So was his heart. And he only realized after he'd made the mistakes. She understood. That's all that mattered. He'd worry about how his English teacher, Rogers, would be shamed later.

"If I could bring hims back, I will for you. Believe what I say to truth, *Mia Cara Bella.*"

She refused to look at him, and she turned.

"Wait, Iris!" He felt real panic, but thankfully she and the dog both turned to him. He held out the letter he had painstakingly written. "Please. Read." His anguish shocked him. She leaned forward so as not to touch him, took the note and went inside with Buffer in tow.

In all his life, he had never, ever felt so alone.

His side hurt like hell, but it was a pain he could bear. Damn it. He wouldn't lose the only woman he'd ever loved. He couldn't if he were to live at all.

He felt a resolve so thick, it filled his chest. *I cannot wander around waiting to be shot in the back when I must be strong for her. I am the only man she has left to protect her. I must live. And if I live, I stand the chance of persuading her that she is not responsible for God or the devil or war ripping her brother from her.*

How close to dawn it was, he wasn't sure. The clouds were gone now. At least the star-studded heavens promised him some time to get through his escape hatches before the sun rose, but it increased his risk of being seen while sneaking back into camp. Shit.

He walked quickly along the Zulu footpath. *Not long now.* He heard baboons bark in the distance. Thanks to his stint watching over Antonio in The Hole, and Rogers's vivid description of the animals he heard during his vigil, he could identify the night sounds.

He saw something in his path.

He stopped.

A mere thirty feet in front of him, a leopard crouched, ready to spring.

He felt his bowels churn in fear.

Rogers had told him always to stand dead still in the face of a wild animal. He did, though he wanted to run like hell. He could make out the golden-brown base coloring, black spots and rosettes. If he wasn't so damned scared, he would have marveled at the leopard's exquisite beauty.

He stood motionless, focused, his eyes unblinking on the crouching animal, just as Rogers told him to do.

But then the rest of Rogers's words tumbled through his head: "The leopard's fearless. It has no qualms killing animals far larger than itself. Sleek and muscular, it reaches immense speeds, for usually only short distances. Its explosive jumping power can propel it over an elephant from a standing start. Its neck and jaws are so strong, it can haul its kill, the size of a large buck, up a tree. Actually, that's its preferred dining room, so it can eat at leisure, without lions or a large pack of hyenas stealing its loot."

"Goodbye, Iris, Mia Cara Rossa. I go having loved. Forgive me, big brother, for not being able to shield her from life's harms."

The leopard's yellow eyes were boring into his own.

His fear was gone. He wondered fleetingly if that was always so when you faced the worst of what death could dream up.

The baboons' barks were louder. They were close. And so was the fucking leopard.

One more step toward him. Pietro refused to blink. David facing the leopard's Goliath.

And then a miracle! As if in a dream, the leopard was gone! Sounds of long, resistant grass bending quickly away from a powerful body whooshed past him in the dark bush as baboons' cries screeched louder and higher and then the ear-piercing scream, which sounded exactly like a human baby followed shortly by its devastated mother's heartbreaking howl.

The leopard chose baboons in favor of the bigger, unblinking challenge that was Pietro. *Sergeant Rogers, you beauty!* But no sooner had the thought left him when adrenaline ebbed and fear flowed in, wracking his body with merciless shakes.

37

ENGLISH TEA, ONE CRICKET AND TWO SWANS

Iris forced herself to stand straight like the nuns had taught her while holding a pencil between her shoulder blades, point-side in. She desperately wanted to lie down under her counter in a fetal position.

She couldn't look at her grieving mother without feeling guilt, which was even worse than the abhorrent truth that her brother was never, ever, ever coming home. Thank God there were people around to comfort her mother. The colonel. Her mother's tennis cronies. She wanted none of it. She didn't deserve comfort. Not even from her surrogate mothers. Mostly because they just told her what she knew to be false truths. *Of course* it was she, Iris Mary Fuller, who was to blame.

The fact that she mourned Pietro as much as she mourned her brother—God forbid, maybe even more—did nothing to ease her heavy burden. She just got madder with Pietro because she could. Because he was still alive.

Her heart lurched when she saw Sergeant Rogers come in to the store. She looked behind him, and her heart fell. No Pietro. Devastating disappointment. Then double the guilt.

"Good morning, Miss Fuller."

"Sergeant." She refused to meet his eyes.

"When is your lunch hour?"

"I don't get one."

"Well, I will have to lodge a formal complaint to your management on behalf of the South African Workers Union."

She couldn't take the chance that he'd just made that up. She couldn't bear any fuss.

"At noon." She still couldn't look at him.

"Please join me at the park on Main. I have two sandwiches and a flask of tea."

She had no desire whatsoever to dine, even on sandwiches, with Rogers or anyone else. But he'd been immensely kind on that dreadful day, and she couldn't be rude. Again.

She dragged heavy legs toward the park. She saw Rogers look at her legs and was disappointed for a minute before she realized he was gazing at the hem, which had come out the last time she wore this dress, and she hadn't bothered to fix. Who cared?

She sat on the far end of the bench. Between them, Sergeant placed a large, brilliant-white, starched serviette. Iris blinked. The brightness seemed to invade her dark place, where she deserved to stay.

He carefully placed two thick sandwiches on the whiteness and poured milk-tinged, pre-sugared tea from a flask into two cups. She sipped the hot, sweet liquid but left the second sandwich untouched.

"You need to eat. You're wasting away."

She willed herself not to look at the magnificent white swans on the pond. She didn't deserve to feel any pleasure. Instead, she watched a grass-colored cricket, still as a stick, a foot away from her shoe. Even the cheerful green of the insect offended her deserved darkness.

Staring straight ahead, Rogers sipped his tea and took a

hefty bite of his sandwich and masticated, closed-mouthed and polite. After two bites and another sip of tea, his voice was quiet and even-toned. He didn't look at her.

"First and foremost, your feelings for Pietro have nothing to do with losing your brother."

She felt her body go back to rigid as she laid down her cup and covered her ears.

To no avail. She still heard him: "You are not to blame for loving him. He is not to blame for loving you. It just happened. I saw it happen before my own eyes. Neither of you could help what you felt. It was as if you were just waiting to find each other, and when you did, it was divine. Reverent. Hmmm. Where did those words come from?" He laughed dryly. "Not my standard seven education! Put it this way, I've seen a lot, but I've never seen anything more—well, preordained." She found herself watching him, unconsciously reading his lips.

He smiled as he saw her watching him. Iris turned quickly away, eyes streaming. She sat on her hands so as not to wipe her face and bring attention to herself.

"Probably what you are feeling is pure guilt, because what you feel for him and him for you is taboo. Your feelings at this time, in this place, are not allowed."

She bristled and held her head high. Of course she knew her feelings for him were wrong. She didn't need her nose rubbed in it. She prepared to leave.

The volume of his voice increased. "You cannot share your thoughts about Pietro with anyone else. You will, without question, be cast out of this town. Your mother will be ruined. Your family will lose their place in society. Promise me you will not talk about Pietro under any circumstances, because it will only hurt those you love."

For the first time in months, she felt something.

It was white-hot anger.

"You came here to tell me not to get Pietro into trouble?" she spat at him.

Wisely, he was silent. He just sipped his tea and meticulously ate his sandwich.

He was bloody infuriating. "Did he send you here to silence me?"

He swilled down his bite with a long sip of tea. "Oh heavens, no. He would die if he knew I had said what just poured out of my mouth. But he did send me to ask how he could help you. He's desperately worried about you and your grief. He says if you want to blame him because he's the enemy, or because your brother was shot down in Italy, he understands. He will take the blame. But he can't take your coldness. He asked me to tell you that people who love each other help each other in times of need. They don't turn away. He also said he has just learned this, because he loves for the first time in his life."

Unbidden, unacceptably, she felt her heart flip and quicken. He loved her. Could that really be, or was it just the sergeant's turn of phrase? She took it anyway, so starved was she.

"My brother is dead, Sergeant, and I am to blame."

"How can that possibly be, Iris?" Her first name rolled off his tongue.

"I must take the blame for being distracted, losing focus, straying from my promises to keep my brother safe because of my own desires. That's what caused him harm."

"Then if you must, go to confession and let a priest absolve you or whatever it is they do, but cutting out the middle man for a moment, let me tell you something. My God would never punish you for the love I see transforming your face when you look at Pietro or he looks at you."

"But I made a deal with ... "

"Sorry, girly, you've got it all wrong. My God would never

penalize you or, heaven forbid, kill your brother because you gave up three shifts at the hospital."

"How do you know?"

"It's a small town," Rogers said. "And *my* God doesn't count."

Her face was one wet, shiny, slimy blob. She removed the remaining sandwich and placed it over her cold cup of tea and lifted the lovely white serviette that doubled as their picnic tablecloth, put it to her nose and blew with gusto. She sat quietly a moment and then remembered how broken her world was, and she let out the wail of a wounded animal.

When Rogers's quiet, even tone resumed, she looked at him for an instant, wondering where she was, and she saw that his eyes were misted and red. He'd cried twice in her presence. Now that was a *real* man, in her humble opinion. Mrs. Rogers was a lucky woman.

"For a solid year you worked tirelessly in that hospital, making a difference."

"Sergeant! I didn't hold their hands when they passed away or use words to paint pretty pictures for blind men. I emptied bloody bedpans and rolled bandages and emptied buckets of vomit and pee. I was hardly Florence Nightingale. I wanted to be all of those important things to those sick men, but that wasn't the deal. No satisfaction for me. I was paying my penance."

"Iris, your God is one mean son of a bitch. Excuse my language. What church do you go to that has such little joy?"

"I gave up church when even being Catholic couldn't save my dad."

"So, by your own judgment, if you happen to shrug off your penance now and then, it results in your only brother losing his life six thousand miles away in a *war,* for chrissakes?"

"Apparently."

"Good gracious. Is this all your faith has brought you?"

"As I said, we're Catholic by association, not attendance."

"And perhaps, my dear, therein lies the problem. You only remember half the story. The dark half."

She was quiet. Still in body and mind for the first time in a month.

"My Sunday school teacher was a hell of a lot more optimistic than the last priest you knew. Fire and brimstone is the least of it. Hope and light and comfort and joy are what keep people going back every Sunday. Iris, you didn't do anything wrong. You did your best. Your brother died because it was his time, not because you haven't thought of him for a month."

How the hell did he know? "You should be a priest."

"Heaven forbid."

"Well, all right, a minister or whatever. Maybe a psychiatrist."

She contemplated what he'd said as they sat in companionable silence.

Eventually she picked up the uneaten sandwich and took a bite.

"The war is nearly over. Make the most of the time you have with him. Regret is a sorry thing. It destroys you, and nothing can retrieve time lost. You can never, ever go back."

He stared straight ahead, and she knew then that he was a child of regret. A man of what-ifs. That's why he was here. She allowed herself to watch the exquisite swans, necks in impossible positions so they could lovingly look at each other. Love wasn't always comfortable.

And the letter in his untidy hand lined her pocket, and she held fast to it. Perhaps for that reason, "O Sole Mio" resounded in her head, and she felt a sense of quiet peace for the first time in months.

38

LITTLE WHITE DOTS

Doc touched the left side of Pietro's torso. A slew of Italian swearwords ensued.

"Oh, boy! Here we have a very angry appendix. Did you get injured on that side?"

Pietro had a vision of lying on his side on the tar after stopping Tap Tap's whip from doing real damage to Mercury, his winged messenger, who brought the note that changed his life. The hard steel toe of those magnificent Italian leather boots had kicked him repeatedly in the right side. *She* was worth it. Pietro shrugged. What was the use of telling the tale of Tap Tap's Italian boot?

The pain had never gone away after that, and in truth, it'd been getting worse. Perhaps it was psychosomatic. His heart was the place Pietro wished Doc could heal.

"It would be smart to have it out," advised the doctor.

"How long in hospital?" Pietro asked.

"Ten days if all goes well and you're lucky, then no activity for six weeks."

"No activity?" Pietro asked incredulously.

"Just your tent, maybe the mess hall and back to your bunk. I will monitor you closely."

"And if I go farther without you know?" Pietro had to ask.

"You will die. First figuratively from the pain, then literally, when you tear open the wound from the inside and you bleed to death," Doc said matter-of-factly.

"Not possible for operation." He couldn't be out of commission for two months or more. Doc was quite mad. An eternity already without seeing his Iris. He'd waited so long to be with her again, to begin mending the bridge the death of her brother had blasted to hell.

Rogers had done his work. Now he waited for her to make a move. If she did, and he didn't respond for nearly two months, perhaps the war would be over and he'd never see her again! He couldn't risk that. No. His pain was bearable. Never spending time with her was not.

"Then Pietro, if you want that appendix to stay quiet, you will not run, just walk. Don't lift anything heavy. We will try and help it stay dormant. Just don't push yourself physically in any way, or it could burst."

Doc's voice interrupted his meanderings. "Ready to tell me confidentially what happened to your throat?" the physician asked. Pietro instinctively used his hand to hide the dark purple bruises still visible on his neck.

"Prick with stick."

Doc nodded slightly.

He handed Pietro a packet. Pietro looked inside. Little white dots.

"Propyphenazone. It's a somewhat experimental pill that should help take the fire out of your appendix. Take them religiously. They'll keep your appendix quiet until—well, maybe the war will end soon and you can go home and have it out there. *Do not skip a pill.* They will be keeping you from immediate surgery. I'll also give you castor oil for an oil pack that will reduce inflammation. Eat garlic and ginger, chew mint leaves for nausea and vomiting; yes, there will be quite a bit of that, and chew raw basil leaves. I'll tell cook I want you to get a bottle of honey to keep with you. You should have come to me sooner for this throat of yours. Take honey every two hours to soothe it. Local stuff's amazing. It will penetrate and not only soothe your throat but also your appendix, and will keep it moist, as well as give you a natural protective barrier to prevent infection. It will even attempt to repair your wounds."

"Thanks, Doc. Grazie," Pietro said and shook his hand.

Just before he left the room, Doc said, "I have treated many who have suffered by his immoral whip. We doctors know, but we don't share. Usually. Stay well away from that bastard."

39

ZULU TRUTHS

In the weeks that followed the luncheon with Rogers, Iris thought long and hard about their discussion. Worst of all, she longed for her Pietro with every fiber of her being.

As was her habit, such was her *need*, she sought the wisdom of her surrogate mothers. They sat on Lena's rickety single bed, waiting for Sofie. Buffer lay at their feet. A single kerosene lamp burned in the corner.

"How do you sleep on this thing?" Iris's vivid imagination had large Lena spewing over the sides of the bed like wet dough flapping over the edge of a pie pan.

Lena sniffed indignantly. "I am perfectly comfortable, thank you," she said, imitating the mother's most haughty voice. As was the Zulu custom, her bed was elevated with bricks so, as folklore had it, the Tokolosh, who was small in stature, couldn't reach Lena to cause his havoc.

"I see you, Ibhubesi." Sofie creaked open the door and came inside. Buffer nudged her with his nose until she patted him. She hadn't been around for a while because old Mr. van Niekerk was dying and needed her day and night. She'd snuck away for this important meeting, called by their white child. Iris hugged her, and Sofie's eyes shone with joy.

All seated on the bed, the Zulu ladies waited for the inevitable, and it didn't take long.

"My Gregg." It was all she could get out before her face crumpled in pain, and she wept until she heaved. In the presence of these beloved women, there was never any pretense.

Four black hands patted her back as she wept, and one canine tongue licked her bare feet, all in an effort to comfort this girl they loved. Iris became acutely aware of the unconditional love surrounding her, and the volume of her howls increased, such was her gratitude to all three.

When the waterworks stopped, Sofie broke the mood with a disapproving, "I see you sew for snotty lady on the hill." Iris smiled. Taking the mind off the problem using conflict regarding something else entirely was Sofie's best way to get tears all dried up.

"I had no option. I had to make money for my part of the fare and money for my first month there."

"So you work for that fat cow on the hill when Sofie and Lena have no new clothes?"

"It was for big money, Sofie. Her seamstress was away, and the cow needed a ball gown. It was awful. Gold, fussy and old-fashioned. She gave me chocolates to make me finish it in time. You know how I love chocolates, ladies, but not even the sweeties were tempting enough for me to ever do it again."

"And chocolates are where?" Sofie asked, looking down her nose solemnly.

"I kept one for each of you." She fished in her pocket, gave one to each. They opened them slowly and popped chocolates into their mouths.

"Ibhubesi, you go for sure to America?" Lena looked stricken.

Iris nodded. She was so very sad. "There is nothing to keep me here. Gregg won't be back, Mom has colonel, Buffer ... "

"We will love and take care of Buffer," Lena promised as Iris's arms embraced her beloved dog, who'd managed to reduce himself to the size of a puppy to fit into the tiny room.

"What about Singingman?" asked Sofie. Iris smelled divine chocolate. Her mouth watered.

"Yebo, Ingane. You must not be angry with Singingman," Lena was quick to emphasize.

"Why not?" Iris asked, hearing her own brittle voice. But Lena's big arm went around her and stroked her head, and she knew she would never be too old for this woman's affection.

"He not choose to fight. His king makes him." Sofie was fairly bursting to show off her news of the world.

"And if he never fight, he never meet our Ibhubesi!" said Lena with emphasis.

"So you don't think it's me who caused all this khathaza?" Iris begged their endorsement.

"Eich. Eikona," the ladies said together, followed by "clucks" from the suction between tongue and roof of mouth, made in typical Zulu disagreement.

Sofie started to laugh. She laughed so hard she held tight to her side, which was clearly splitting with a stitch. Iris was shocked.

"You think you are so important?" Sofie's face was incredulous between guffaws.

Perplexity made Iris's face twitch. She hadn't expected this.

"It be God's plan. Not Ibhubesi's. Not Gregg's. He made your life plans before you were born." Sofie had taken up Christianity but had adapted it to suit, with a Zulu twist.

"So you think that Gregg would have d—this would have happened no matter what I did? What I didn't do?" The thought that she wasn't important enough to cause any massive shift in someone else's destiny had never occurred to her.

Lena had an inherent, intuitive sense of spiritual things, taught by generations of Zulus.

"Yes, my Ibhubesi. It is so. And Singingman had to be prisoner who suffered before he got to you. Our lives are mapped by our ancestors before we birth, and everything happens when it happens. How it must happen. And remember, Ibhubesi, love, like rain, does not choose the grass on which it falls." Lena enfolded Iris within her generous layers.

"We would have told you what we think many months before," Sofie complained, "if you only think us worthy of your ears."

"I'm sorry, ladies. Perhaps I wasn't ready to hear."

"Family is like forest, Ibhubesi. When you outside, it is dense. When you inside, you see each tree has a place," said Sofie, and Lena nodded sagely.

Iris couldn't help teasing Sofie. "Is that Old or New Testament, Sofie?"

Her grin was intoxicating. "Just clever Zulu bible."

They laughed, and Iris felt a lightness she hadn't for months.

"So what do you think I should do?" she asked them, dry-eyed now.

Lena's sound philosophy prevailed. "He who receives a gift does not measure, my child. It does not matter what he is but how happy he makes you. See him. Let him be your Philemon from the petrol station."

"And when the war ends and he goes away?" Why wasn't she dehydrated? She sniffed and wiped at her eyes.

"Then patience is the mother of a beautiful child," said Lena sagely.

"You wait for him. Him wait for you," Sofie interpreted.

"Genesis?" she asked Sofie, mocking just a little.

"First book of Zulu." They chuckled.

The three women joined arms and balanced themselves on the bed. Heads together, the three silently considered this unpredictable life. They knew their precious time together was as fragile as a small spider's intricate web in the way of an oncoming crash of rhinos.

SPEAKING COSTUMES

Pietro left the hall after rehearsals on Nov. 23, 1944, and found men oozing into his tent.

He pushed his way inside and was amazed their small space could hold so many. Antonio's invitation via the grapevine to listen to "big news" had spread like the invitation to Pietro's impromptu carnival a lifetime ago.

Churchill's dry monotone to the American people on Thanksgiving Day was one desperately needed to give his Italian friends hope. He'd come to love these men, and their happiness was important to him, in spite of his own shattered soul.

"He is thanking the Americans for joining the European war. It's going to be over soon. We will all go home. To Italy where we all belong," Antonio relayed to the newcomers. The men cheered. Antonio looked like he was personally responsible for the war winding down. His English had improved, thanks to the radio. As a war aficionado, he had a huge responsibility.

Pietro was sickened by the dread that weighed down his stomach as he heard the news. Who was he, this man in love? Torn screaming and clawing from his beloved Italy nearly four years ago, here he was plotting absurd ways to stay right where he was, thousands of miles from everything he knew and loved. Well, not quite everything.

"...When this union of action which has been forced upon us by our common hatred of tyranny, which we have maintained during these dark and fearful days, shall become a lasting union of sympathy and good feeling and loyalty and hope between all the British and American peoples ... " Churchill was at his loquacious best, and Pietro considered how confident of victory the British leader sounded, and his heart sank deeper, deeper.

He knew the only way he could truly change her mind was to be in her sights. To remind her of what he knew was their united truth: They shared a once-in-many-lifetimes love, so rare, so omnipotent, it was not to be wasted.

" ... Then, indeed, there will be a Day of Thanksgiving, and one in which all the world will share," Churchill concluded to tinny applauding in England and loud roars in his own tent.

Pietro pushed his way out into the sunlight and walked in a tight circle, then dropped to his haunches, head in his hands. How the hell would he win back the woman he loved while he was still lucky enough to be in her country?

Yes! *Dio mio,* he loved her! She, with whom he had spent all of a cumulative seven hours. He'd been counting. She, whose every freckle he could trace by heart. She, whose voice was to him more exquisite than the most sought-after soprano in Europe.

This was the only woman he could *never* give up.

He was stark raving mad. She wouldn't even speak to him, let alone agree to wait for him for years once he was deported back to Italy after the war. It was ludicrous, this being in love shit. Enzo slipped out of the tent and joined him.

"I heard what you heard," Enzo stated flatly.

"You are such a wise old fart." Pietro smiled at him absently.

"And you, such a horny young fool."

The grin they shared was one only the greatest friends know and understand.

"What will Stef do about Piccolo?" Pietro worried.

"Burbero will happily take him. Finding a home for such a talented dog will be easy."

"Like finding a loving husband for such a beautiful woman will be easy! What the hell am I going to do?"

"You are going to continue your mission."

"It's impossible."

"Impossible is turning a POW camp into the entertainment capital of South Africa. You did that!"

"She was my purpose."

"And she still is. Carpe diem, my friend. See her as often as you can. Your time is short. Don't regret a single wasted moment."

As he watched Enzo's wiry frame go back inside the tent, Pietro stood and chastised himself out loud. "Get your balls back, Pietro. Since when do you *not* go after what you want?" The image of the little black beetle pushing his pile of shit with dogged purpose gave Pietro the impetus he needed.

———

Pietro sought out Rogers every single day since he'd dispatched the sergeant to work on Iris, but the bugger (he liked that English word) wouldn't give him anything at all. *Dio mio.* As many times a day as Rogers could be found, Pietro begged him to take him to her. Rogers was clearly waiting for a sign from Iris that her sadness had quieted, but time was a precious depreciating commodity Pietro couldn't afford to squander.

Four nights before opening night and a week after Churchill's Thanksgiving speech, Pietro told Rogers that there was a costume emergency that his usual tailors couldn't handle.

He desperately needed expert help, and he'd heard that Iris, at the haberdashery counter, was the one to ask. Pietro saw that Rogers knew it was all horseshit, but he also believed Rogers fancied himself as Cupid in this love affair, and so Rogers pretended Pietro had a grand idea and Pietro was beside himself with joy.

The next day, armed with the costume of Yum-Yum from their new opera, *Mikado,* he and Rogers set off to town. It wasn't lost on Rogers, Pietro mused, that Nanki Poo, played by Pietro, was condemned to death for flirting with Yum-Yum, or so said Gilbert and Sullivan.

He'd not laid eyes on his Iris since his close encounter with the rose bushes. His longing had become more acute, his loneliness more abysmal. Down the road they walked until Pietro could stand it no longer.

"Now you can tell me everything, Sergeant."

"I'll get you there. You do the rest." Rogers took his intermediary position seriously.

And he, Pietro Saltamachio, bon vivant of Italy, was nervous as a ... he was going to say "schoolboy," because the South Africans used that expression, but he'd never known how a schoolboy felt. A virgin! That was it. He was nervous as a virgin!

As they entered the store, Rogers hung back. And wisely so, thought Pietro, who didn't know what to expect from her. He didn't care if she screamed bloody murder and turned him in for breaking out to see her. At least he would hear it firsthand and would have seen her one last time. It was better than limbo.

He watched her turn toward him as if sensing his closeness. It was uncanny this—this—thing they shared.

She was mesmerizing. Their world lapsed into slow motion. He could savor every nanosecond. He'd never seen her without makeup, and he thought his heart would break with her fragility. Without the mask of sophistication, her freckles were darker than he dared hope. He ached to trace them with his finger, then with his lips, then with his tongue.

He smiled at her. Her eyes got big as saucers, and she dropped the huge pair of scissors she was holding. He didn't hear it fall. The smile she gave him was manna from heaven. A balm for his broken heart.

"I have grave problem. Camp tailor very sick. Can you fix sleeve before tomorrow night? Before concert open?"

His favorite crevice in the base of her throat pulsed, and there appeared delicate perspiration pearls that made him want to make love to her right there.

"Of course." She blushed. "I'll do it after hours. When will you be back for it?" Her voice quivered.

He looked at Rogers, who was distinctly hovering.

"Tomorrow at three." Rogers smiled.

Pietro's eyes never wavered from her face, taking in every nuance of her graceful femininity, her surprising vulnerability. She was his perfection.

"How many nights are you playing this time?" Iris asked, her eyes taking in his face one feature at a time. She always seemed to linger on his mouth, his front tooth. He shyly put his tongue to his tooth and was surprised to see her lick her lips.

"Just two." He heard his own voice quivering. Saltamachio? Quivering?

"So then, by next Thursday same time, you can start planning your new opera or operetta?" She emphasized "next Thursday same time."

"Yes. Next Thursday." He looked at her and marveled at her courage.

"I'll make sure the sewing's done for you at the same time tomorrow," she promised, with the emphasis on the "same time," just in case he'd missed it. His girl was perfect spy material. Then she smiled and his head actually spun until a stern voice interjected: "Tell the seamstress the problem with the costume, Pietro, and let's get the hell out of here. You're scaring the natives." Rogers's voice, though take-no-nonsense, was ever so slightly laced with amusement.

"It's hem. Right side kimono ... " He indicated a vague spot under his bicep.

"Sleeve," she said and smiled at him. *Dio mio.* Her eyes were true cat's eyes. He'd seen them bright green, verging on blue, teal when they were kissing. Today they were the color of newly cut emeralds.

"Good day, Miss Fuller." Rogers tipped his cap and herded Pietro away quickly before she changed her mind.

———

Iris watched them leave. There was no way on God's green earth she could wait to touch the kimono he had touched. She looked at the right-hand-side kimono sleeve, puzzled. Then she felt it.

She nipped open the hem. The note read: "My Iris. Mia Cara Rossa. I so lonely with no you. If I cud I—Pietro—wud cambiare ... alter world for you. But I cannot. Therefore, I give you ONE THING I never use before in mine life. My love."

She found herself on her haunches behind her counter again, covered in a silk-like kimono that was stitched to perfection. All she had to do was re-sew the sleeve she'd just unpicked. And learn to have less collapsible knees, apparently, like she did before Pietro came into her life and knocked her for a six.

NEXT THURSDAY: SAME TIME

"Next Thursday, same time." Music to his ears. He swore one day he'd create a melody to those words and write a love song.

Rogers, Pietro surmised, was wary of causing alarm by Pietro's frequent visits to the store, because when Pietro sought him out to remind him the kimono needed to be picked up, Rogers said he would be going alone. Pietro was dismally disappointed. But not for long.

When the kimono was back in his eager hands, he found her note in that very sleeve.

"My Pietro," it read, and he felt like a silly virgin all over again. "I believe I am ready to call you 'My Love.' Until I see you again, my heart aches."

And here it was, 8 p.m. lights out, and he was waiting for the guards to cross over on their perimeter walk so he could fly through the wire trap doors, into the brush and into her arms.

He felt the stab of pain in his right side. He had come to know that white-hot jab as his own personal clock. A warning that time was of the essence. But at this moment, all else dimmed in comparison to the excitement gurgling through his veins.

Iris. He said her name a hundred times a day, and each time evoked a different mind or body reaction.

———————

Iris had avoided her mother for weeks and weeks. She went straight from the store to the hospital and volunteered for the most repulsive jobs. Pricking boils was fitting for her. She wondered glibly how many Hail Marys that horrid chore constituted and how many she would have to prick for fraternizing with the enemy. Oh, boy ... and then how many more for doing so even after your brother had died by that enemy's hand. *Oh, shit, Iris. You know very well your Pietro can't be responsible for every Italian and German in the world.* Hmm. Seemed her own head was talking reason to her these days, instead of her mother's. A delightful change. Her mother must be too busy with the colonel, thankfully, to fill Iris's head.

When every tear was spent and she'd bared her soul to Sergeant Rogers and been chastised by Sofie for her vanity in thinking she could force someone else's destiny, she felt surprisingly calm and peaceful. She wondered if it was Gregg from the grave or being in love that gave her the gift of forgiveness. Forgiving her mother; forgiving Pietro, though it wasn't his fault; forgiving herself. She felt cleansed in a sense. But nothing would ease the incredible pain—like an elephant standing on her chest —every time she remembered her brother wasn't coming home.

Just a week ago, the newly cleansed Iris felt the urge to put her arms around her mother. As she did so, her mother burst into tears, and soon they were both weeping and holding on tightly. Neither said a word. What more was there to say?

And here it was, 8 p.m. on Thursday. Just the thought of Pietro her made her knees go weak. And the other parts? Well! They sure as hell were reacting unbidden lately too. The girly hots. She knew what all the fuss was about, and she wanted more.

She folded her arm across her suddenly erect nipples, even though under her newly crafted blouse, tucked into her fashionable trousers, they were well covered by the coat. In the midst of summer? She hoped her mother wouldn't notice.

In the living room, the radio announcer entertained her mother: "So the end of this great war is in sight, but to keep you occupied till then, here's the man, long gone, but never forgotten —The Great Caruso ... " How cruel this blooming radio. Mentioning both the end of the war, which meant the end of her Pietro, then Caruso, who would always be her aching reminder of him, in one single breath. She shook her head to free her mind of everything but what was to come in less than half an hour.

"My taxi's here, Mom." She hugged her mother. SHE HUGGED HER MOTHER!

"Go safely, Jinx. Make somebody feel special, will you?" her mother continued with her needlework and her Churchill and, praise the Lord, never looked up.

"Oh, Mother. I surely intend to!" That had just popped out.

She nearly said "I love you" but figured it would have been a guilty reaction, so she just slipped out to the hall, hung up her coat and fled out of the front door.

HELLO AGAIN

Pietro's heart beat erratically. He knew it had nothing to do with his always-harrowing escape. He knew with certainty that this was a night that would change them both forever.

Car lights.

The bright orbs evoked mixed feelings. Her taxi? Or, God forbid, someone else?

And so he waited until the car had inched around the cul-de-sac and wobbled to a stop, facing away from the ditch. Then he saw his prize: that first long, smooth leg that unfolded from the back seat and onto the rough dirt road. God, she could make a rocky road look like a runway.

His heart lurched and helped propel him up and over the lip of the ditch.

He stood where he was, more to savor the moment than in trepidation. Iris started toward him, then stopped. Time stood still. The ten yards between them felt loaded with the weight of their obstacles. He took a step. She took a step. It was as if each stride was a conscious decision to rebuke their hurdles by stepping through them and moving forward toward the love they both knew was inevitable, in spite of the consequences.

All the while he could feel this magnet pulling him toward her, and he knew she felt the same, but they were resisting, in spite of themselves, to ensure they'd thought this through.

Pietro was acutely aware of her smell. Musk and flowers. She smelled like home.

Closer now, he could see her features, and he was determined to indelibly memorize her every expression, her every nuance.

Her smile dazzled him, made him weak.

And then they stood, with only a hair separating them. Her arms were at her side, as were his, and she lifted her head to look at him. He felt her breath, hot and fast on his neck, and he got goose bumps. She was here. *Dio mio,* he was a lucky, lucky man. He gently held her face with both his hands and looked deep into her eyes and saw a million reasons why they were so right and the world so wrong.

He tilted her head, and his mouth moved toward hers.

The touch of their lips was so electric, they pulled away with the shock of it. Then he pulled her head back and covered her mouth with his own hot one, and his desire was greater than it had ever been in his life, but he held back until she responded with a hunger equal to his. He could do nothing but consume her mouth, her neck, her ear, her secret place at the base of her throat, her eyes and move back to her impatient mouth, which he stilled with his hot tongue. He felt her shiver, and her arms went around his waist as she pressed herself into him, fitting perfectly. Her yearning matched his own, and it thrilled him to think her abandon was due to their mutual need to please each other.

Their hunger was spawned by their destiny. It was a heady, tender, lustful and all-consuming experience. A divine, preordained union. Yes. This was love.

AFRICAN SURPRISES

They sat so close together in the car, their silhouettes could have been mistaken for one.

The taxi bounced along an uneven stretch of clearing, a long way off the road.

"This bloody road is killing my car!" Sanjay's complaints did nothing to suppress the ecstatic mood in the back seat.

Iris said at last, "This is far enough not to be spotted, Sanjay. Thank you, this is perfect!"

The driver was sulky.

"I'll make it up to you, Sanjay, I promise." Iris patted the man's shoulder, and Pietro fished out all the change he'd been saving, which wasn't a great deal, but it made Sanjay smile.

Iris's face glowed with excitement. "Are you excited about your surprise?"

Pietro nodded. He felt a tenderness he'd never known existed. As long as they were together, nothing else could be more thrilling—never would be, he surmised.

She opened the car door. "Your surprise begins now!" Her smile was enigmatic, and she was out of the car before she finished her sentence.

She pulled him by the hand beyond the clearing through a copse of tall, dense, Natal mahogany trees. Pietro caught glimpses of the night sky illuminated by the Milky Way, winking between heavy branches.

They reached the edge of the precipice. Iris let go of his hand and used both of hers in a "Ta-daa" fashion, proudly showing off the finest light-show Africa had to offer.

Though he'd seen it during the vigil with Antonio, he'd never seen it with her, and everything always felt like the first time with Iris.

The Milky Way was so close, he reflexively extended his hand, palm up, to hold it in his hand. The opaque streaks of movement and white-hot dots of twinkling stars, distant yellow planets, and Mars in her red glory were clearly all showing off for him this night. The unfurled blanket of ever-changing light seemed to lift them up and enmesh them in its vastness.

As he did with most things that overwhelmed his senses, Pietro converted the heavenly spectacle into musical terms he could capture and retain forever. The swarms of old, dull, slowly blinking stars and tightly bound, bright new ones became a multi-faceted orchestra of light. Pietro saw two hundred billion stars in different stages of a rehearsal and heard varying tempos: allegro to zeloso; diverse pitches: bass, baritone, tenor, countertenor, contralto, mezzo-soprano and soprano, simultaneously performing all types of music, from opera and big band and baroque to calypso and chanting and danza and flamenco and hymns and polka, filling his senses with every note ever played on every instrument in existence.

His Iris had presented him with the ultimate musical spectacle.

The changes in color, density and brightness of the Milky Way, as mind-blowing as they were, paled in comparison with his Iris's expressive face. She was as complex, unfathomable and beautiful as their heavenly spectacle. He felt like the richest man in all the world. When a burst of shooting stars burned through the atmosphere, he squeezed her hand. Sharing this galactic wonder with her, their own, private fireworks to celebrate their love, was an immeasurable pleasure and a firm nod from the universe that had tossed them together in spite of the odds.

He'd become a sap. And he couldn't be more proud of it.

They stood as close as two bodies could, hearts beating in sync, looking up at the stars.

The sound of rhythmic drums drowned out his heavenly music celebration, and he looked down the hill for the first time.

DUM-dee-dee-DUM-dee-dee ...

On a low rise, a score or more fires burned in caldrons, illuminating a Zulu kraal dotted with clay huts topped with intricately woven grass roofs.

Glistening, half-naked bodies wove this way and that in the flickering orange light, a loose choreography of animal skins and shiny ebony figures, bare feet pounding the earth in rhythmic time to drums crafted by stretching cowhide over intricately carved wood. There were a dozen tableaus before them, each a fascination unto themselves. When bare-breasted young women shaking grass rattles began their high-pitched keening, he cocked his head to catch the unique, raw, melodic sound.

He realized she'd been watching his reaction. Then she took his hand and led him down the ridge toward the frenzy of fire and music, dancing and chanting.

The most adorned of the Zulu men, slathered in animal fat and holding court, took ten great leaps toward them, landing lightly. He wore a mighty grin.

"Singingman! Klein Miesies!" His hand was out in western greeting.

"Remember Fourfeet?" Iris beamed. "This is his wedding!" It was no wonder there was no recognition in Pietro's eyes. The gleaming, shirtless man, wearing a hint of loincloth and a leopard skin headdress, was a far cry from the fearful note-bearer at the mercy of Tap Tap's whip.

Pietro smiled warmly, and they enthusiastically shook hands.

"Many congratulation, Fourfeet. To me you are Mercurio."

"Mercury is a Greek winged messenger in our culture, Four-feet," Iris explained.

The young Zulu looked befuddled.

"You bring message from my love," Pietro explained, gazing at her and feeling giddy. He dragged his eyes back to the young man. "Thanks you, Fourfeet, for that." Then he gestured to encompass the spectacle before them. "And for these."

Mid-sweep, Pietro saw Solomon, and they waved. After Solomon's involvement in the secret note-passing, when Pietro "read" the man's arm till it nearly fell off, they were old friends.

"Come. Please. Your honor, place all ready," said Fourfeet, who was fairly treading on air in his haste to return to the action.

DUM-dee-dee-DUM-dee-dee...

They sat next to two elders on ancient, bum-smoothed tree stumps that were evidently reserved for the most important guests, because the rest of the visitors sat cross-legged on the dirt floor, no matter how old they were. Theirs were the only two white faces at the ceremony. Pietro realized that mingling must be a rare thing in these parts and felt enormously privileged to be a part of this great night.

Two middle-aged women ran up to Iris. One was a large Zulu woman whose body wobbled with joy and the other, lean as a stick. Both their smiles were as bright as the stars above, and they clearly loved his Iris. When the hugging abated, Iris said, "Pietro, this is Lena," and gestured to the joyful, wobbly one.

The woman smiled and said, "This is my baby. She mine one

week after she born." The little one waved a bony finger close to his nose and said, "I am other mother. You hurt our Ibhubesi, and I will send Tokolosh to make you frightened."

Pietro was still confused, but Iris said gently, "Pietro, these are my surrogate mothers, the ones I told you about. They are the only mothers who know about you. I so much wanted you to meet them." His Iris's face was glowing with love, so he knew just how important this introduction was to her.

He took first the wobbly one's hand and said, "Lena, If you love Iris, I love you." Then he turned to the mean little one who was still squinting up at him.

"And Sofie?" She nodded. "I no ever hurt your Iris. She mucho important to me, to my life." Sofie smiled, and Pietro felt her warmth. He hugged them both, but in a flash, a maiden, naked young breasts gleaming in the firelight, pushed the ladies off to their cheap seats on the floor then, more gently, pushed both Iris and him down on their stumps and offered Pietro a drink from a hollowed-out gourd.

He drank deeply, though he felt Iris watching him. He handed the gourd to her, and she leaned into his ear to be heard over the music. "I don't know how many cockroaches, bugs and rats were likely included in the brewing, but when in Rome, excuse me, Zululand ... " She held her nose and glugged loudly, then wiped her mouth with the back of her hand, her grin matching Pietro's. He understood her just fine, though her words were too sophisticated for him. He had a fleeting question how Rome got in the middle of it all. He prayed he had a life-time to find out.

Iris explained that the magnitude of the elders' achieve-ments and the life of adventure they'd lived were measured by the amount of paraphernalia that hung from their headdresses: porcupine quills, what looked like a giant lion's tooth, a few gnarly crocodile teeth. Something odd dangled between an old man's eyes. Iris said it looked like a half-baked science experiment and made her shudder, but Pietro thought it might be a liver and was entirely fascinated.

The bride's family had center stage, and a cow was led by the most adorned of the young women, who balanced an elaborate contraption of beads and woven grass on her small head.

"That's the bride, Elange. It means 'she who kisses.' " Iris leaned in so Pietro could hear.

"Ah, that must be what Iris mean also?" On cue, she leaned in and kissed him softly on the mouth. He was delighted that her lips lingered longer than was polite.

Fourfeet's side of the family were very few, but they too stepped forward to receive the cow. The poor animal had all of two seconds in the spotlight before it was fairly humanely culled by a *clonk* on the side of the head. A scrum of bodies huddled for a minute, then stepped back proudly to expose the cow's stomach, expertly slashed from neck to groin, the dark red, shiny contents spilling out. Iris looked a bit green, so Pietro grabbed the gourd of liquor from the elder next to him with an apologetic shrug indicating his lady love's delicate state, and Iris gratefully took a long swig.

Pietro was ridiculously enthralled. How better to experience the real Africa, and how lucky to do so with the woman he loved, whose skin color and culture was so different from them, but who clearly cared for these Zulus and enthusiastically embraced their culture. From what he'd experienced in South Africa, she was a rare breed in a very uppity, British society.

DUM-dee-dee-DUM-dee-dee ...

"She Who Kisses" had the gory job of extracting the cow's vital organs. One by one, she presented them to what must be her new in-laws, Pietro supposed. Each recipient seemed duly humbled by their gift of lungs, kidneys and so on, which they accepted by extending one flat palm over the other to form a "V" as they bent knees slightly and bowed their heads. The Zulu lady with salt and pepper hair who received the heart, was overcome with joy and even broke into a mini dance solo. Pietro felt his permanent smile widen into a delighted laugh.

Pietro guessed returning to your kraal with a vital organ was the Zulu alternative of going home with an autographed program from the opera.

Each time he was mesmerized by something new, he squeezed Iris's hand, and she responded. Sharing this spectacle with her was by far the finest gift he'd ever received, and this was the best party he'd ever been to.

The caldron of kefir beer was passed around again, and Pietro was amused that Iris had lost her qualms about the suspicious content.

The drums beat louder, and the rhythmic sound seemed to seep into the deepest part of their core. A deep, sexy sound.

DUM-dee-dee-DUM-dee-dee ...

Iris stood quickly, almost losing her balance, but Pietro was there to steady her. Then she tugged at his hand to pull him up from the stump.

She led him down, down, as fast as the beer and the terrain would allow.

DUM-dee-dee-DUM-dee-dee ...

The drums seemed as loud as they were in the kraal, but the chatter and keening became a peripheral noise, almost like a soft harmony.

Halfway down to the flat, there was a small hillock, and as they rounded it, as if she'd willed this perfect spot, appeared acres and acres of the tallest sunflowers he'd ever seen.

Their vast, yellow magnificence made them catch their breath—thousands and thousands of five-, six- and seven-foot-tall stalks, most bowing their heads in sleep, though they would reposition to face the east so they could lift their heads to greet the morning sun. Pietro loved sunflowers. They reminded him of home. *"Girasoli!"* he whispered.

"Aren't they beautiful?"

"Like you, my love."

God, she was breathtaking. Iris pulled her hand from his, and turning toward him, she pulled the hairpins from her hair. As her red mane cascaded over her shoulders and down her back, she threw away the pins, shaking her thick, wild hair free. *She was so incredibly sexy.*

Pietro melded into her waiting body, gently grabbing her wanton tresses. He covered her parted lips urgently with his own.

Pietro cupped his hands on Iris's bottom and hoisted her up. Long legs wound easily around his waist, as she pushed her mound tentatively into his crotch.

Dio mio. He wanted her so urgently, but he *must* control himself and slow her down, too. He knew she was a virgin, and his only mission was to make this spectacular for her. She would call the shots once he'd led her to the brink of what they both wanted, needed. He would make sure she never felt forced or, God forbid, scarred by the experience of giving him her most private, most sacred gift. He bit his thumb hard, so the pain detracted from his throbbing desire.

She had no idea how sexy she was. Nothing about her was contrived or rehearsed. Her very essence was instinctive. Her naiveté was real and unabashed, and her fearlessness was remarkable. This woman in his arms was a complicated contradiction, and he was never more intrigued. She was fathomless. She would likely always surprise him. A surge of love, so pure he knew it wasn't generated by his groin, made him weak. At the ripe old age of twenty-seven, after seducing and being seduced by scores and scores of women, he was a virgin this night.

He kissed her, showing her the love she'd evoked, nay,

awoken in him, and he walked her into the midst of the sunflowers. Some flowers were the same height as they were; others towered above them. He turned her slowly around so they had a 360-degree view of their fantasyland of stalks and yellow petals and the Milky Way's illumination above. Even if their senses weren't heightened to the Nth degree with lust, it was a vision they'd never forget.

DUM-dee-dee-DUM-dee-dee ...

Iris threw her head back and laughed, a delicious, carefree sound. She lowered her head in search of his waiting mouth. Their tongue-tangled kiss was fueled by the fire of desire too long denied.

Without breaking their unity, he walked her out of the world of sunflowers and into the field of short, soft grass on the perimeter. Using all his strength and still kissing her, he went down on his knees and slowly guided her head down onto the green carpet below until she was underneath him. With Iris's legs still wrapped around him, he was on all fours above her.

He closed his lips and kissed her freckled, pert nose as he applied gentle pressure to her thighs, expertly stroking them until they relaxed, releasing him. He furrowed his fingers deep into her hair and pulled his face slowly away as he looked at her. Her lips were swollen and moist and parted in anticipation.

"Take me, Pietro. Make love to me. I'm ready for you." She was so serious. And for good reason. She was offering him her virginity. Her maidenhead. Her chastity.

God, he wanted her now. No, Pietro. No! She doesn't yet know what she wants. It's your job to control this. He bit down on his thumb, and his erection subsided. Just enough.

"Still, my love. Very still," Pietro whispered. "Let me please you, Mia Cara Rossa. Let me pleasure you."

With a dozen soft, chaste kisses, he identified her most prominent freckles, whispering to her in Italian. He stroked her hair and looked at her with an aching tenderness. "My Iris," he said, surprised by the rawness in his own voice.

Tears sprang to her eyes, and he whispered to her as he kissed away her tears. Then they sought each other's mouths like they were soon to be parted, desperate, hungry, longing to be joined as deeply as they could.

She rolled away and, with a hand behind her back, tugged at the top to bottom zipper of her blouse. It caught in her long mane and, before he could help her, the blouse fell open.

She was naked underneath. Her pink nipples were round and perfect, topped with a nub of raw desire. It took everything he had not to touch them as he heard his own loud intake of breath. Oh, God, what was she doing to him? He felt a surge of hunger, so hot and strong, he once again bit hard into his thumb. The pain made his eyes well up, but at least he'd subsided his pulsing need. He gently pulled her back toward him onto the grass, and as she hastened to pull off her long, loose, trendy trousers, he caught her fingers, kissing the very tips.

"*Pazienza*. Patience, my love."

Pietro took both of her arms, catching and holding her hands above her head so they wouldn't interfere with his plan, because one touch, and he was done for.

He bent his head and softly kissed one nipple, then the other, running his tongue around each areola. They contracted even more and stood to attention. They were, like the rest of her, quite, quite lovely. He blew on them, and the dark, rosebud-pink peaks puckered. He applied pressure to her wiggling fingers. He knew they longed to participate. Back to the first, he sucked hard on the tight little nipple, and her back arched with pleasure. His hot tongue made a path down to her belly button, which he licked and then blew on. He felt the beginning of her orgasm. Too soon. Too soon.

"Relax, my Iris. Let us *assaporare* each touch. Tonight is ours.

We must hurry not." He whispered as he lay down next to her, on his back, a few inches away, and reached for hand. He held it tight as he focused purposefully on the plethora of stars.

Letting go of his hand, she rolled on her side, knees up, hands folded as if in prayer under her head. "Pietro, don't you want me?" Her voice was timid, hurt.

"*Dio mio*, Iris. Feel how I want you." He took her hand and placed it on his hot bulge. She flinched, though she didn't remove her hand, as if she dared herself not to, a reaction that confirmed he was doing what he must. Anything more would scare her, perhaps make her fearful forever. He had to protect her at all costs. He wrapped her in his arms, holding her tight, and felt her relax. He whispered, "I cannot take you, as my body he wants. My *cuore*, my heart, will not allow. Be still my love. *Fiducia*. Trust me. Please."

Trust did not come easily to her either, another reason he was glad of his thumb and its pain. He took her face in his hands and kissed her gently until her fire reignited. He touched her nipples again to make sure. He wasn't disappointed.

Breaking off their desperate kiss, he ran his tongue down her neck, licking his favorite place between her collarbones, and then between her breasts, her stomach, to her navel. Up again, he took each of her breasts deep into his mouth and sucked. She moaned. He loved to hear her so uninhibited. His arm circled her waist, then slowly, slowly, he rolled down her trousers, slowly over her buttocks, and he, who had seen everything, saw a sight there that rendered his entire mind and body a hot, throbbing phallus.

A leaf-shaped auburn tangle lay unsheathed. He muttered in awe, and she giggled. He grinned at her and went back to work.

"Relax my Iris. Enjoy, my love. Tonight is ours. Hurry we must not." Once his whispering seemed to have the intended effect, she completely relaxed in his arms, naked and unabashed. He found her open mouth and devoured it as her back arched up, offering herself to him, and he ran his hand lightly over her triangle and squeezed her there. She groaned again, but Pietro held her tight until her body's urgency calmed, whispering all the while: "*Mia amore. Mia Cara Rossa.* My Iris. My love."

He gently laid her down with the intention of getting his clothes and boots off as quickly as he could. But she crawled onto his lap, sitting sideways, her knees up, childlike, and nestled her head under his chin. He thought his heart would break with tenderness.

"I feel cherished. Safe," she whispered. God, she would make his heart burst, one way or another. Her vulnerability was not the image she presented, and for her to expose herself like this was a gift unto itself.

But, as quickly as she'd become vulnerable, she became a siren. She pushed herself into him. Amused, Pietro leaned back on his elbows, letting her lead the way.

Iris straddled him so she could look into his eyes, and he was captured again, feeling the throb below. In the moonlight, he could see flicks of her green eyes, and they grew dark with lust as she unbuttoned his shirt. He was fascinated by her lips. Hmm. Succulent and swollen. She caught him and moved in, kissing him provocatively. When she pulled away, she moved those lips to butterfly-kiss the corners of his eyes, the sunburst scars on his mouth. She briefly licked his front tooth that overlapped, as if she had to reassure herself it was still there.

Once she'd unbuttoned his shirt, she pulled it off and rubbed the palms of her hands from waist to shoulders and back again.

"You have a beautiful body," she murmured. She tentatively touched one of his erect nipples with light fingertips. Her exploration made him shiver. She looked at him, surprised, then touched the other to make sure she could do it again. He knew his laugh was throaty. She bent her head and did to him what he'd done to her. "I love the way it hardens under my tongue." She was so enigmatic, he didn't know if her declaration was innocence or tease. His body didn't care.

She dismounted and went to work to remove his trousers but struggled with his belt. He refused to help, because that would mean touching her. They were both on fire. The anticipation was ridiculously delicious and heightened every touch, every lick. He was amused, aroused and fascinated by her tenacity as she worked on the uncooperative belt.

At last, triumphant, she was able to work on his fly buttons while trying not to touch the mound that lay beneath. Hmm, no easy feat, if he had to say so himself. He lay casually, his arms behind his head, knees bent as she pulled off his trousers, both legs at the same time, and almost toppled over backward when they slid off.

They both giggled at her inelegance. She was so childlike now. This woman, his woman was as complicated as the stars above. He could see his manhood bulging forcefully, moist against his white underpants, and was afraid that he'd scared her when he heard her suck in her breath. But she surprised him again. Her wicked smile elicited a chuckle from him, and her throaty laugh promised all sorts of willing exploration. He knew for sure that fear was as far from her mind as Italy was from his.

She touched him tentatively through the white fabric, then in one swift movement, she pulled off the last piece of his clothing, with a *voila!* like a magician. Then she studied his liberated, pulsing manhood in a curious and naughty way.

"He's standing proud and tall to admire the Milky Way," she said.

"Milky Way? He only have one eye. He only see you."

They laughed easily, and then she bent down toward his shaft. But he sat up quickly, taking a breast into his mouth to distract her, sucking hard, then harder. She forgot her quest, so he was able to control himself a while longer. He left her breast wanting more and moved to her other perfect *tetta*, to tease that into near oblivion.

She groaned, and her throat caught during a particularly sensual suck. He loved to hear her flagrant, sexual purrs. He blew around the areas where he'd licked and watched her skin pucker. Down he went between her ribcage and explored her further with his tongue. He massaged her protruding hip bones, and she arched her pelvis, showing him where she needed the most attention. Like he could forget the red triangle of divinity! How he ached for her. But this was her time, not his.

And then, he burrowed into his prize as she mewled her consent.

She had the essence of vanilla. Vanilla, sunflowers and musk.

As he got lower and closer to her sacred self, her smell was custard. An aroma so welcoming and thick, so delectable and enticing, you had first to savor it, and then greedily consume it, and afterward, lick the bowl, just to show your indelicate appreciation of something that was, simply, out of this world.

As her clitoris quivered under his tongue and her hips thrust her triangle against and away from his busy mouth in ecstasy, he moved to her slit, and his tongue darted inside her, in and out, in and out. He sucked harder and harder, and as he felt her drawstring pull together, he wove just one finger into her velvet core, and she shuddered to a climax.

God. She was the ultimate aria. Perfect innovation, perfect pitch, perfect musicality, perfect culmination. If he had two hands, he would have applauded her perfect performance.

He moved his submerged finger ever so slightly, and her sensual clutch was so strong, in addition to nearly biting off his thumb, he had to think of Sergeant Rogers, then Burbero, to quell his urge to enter her right then.

He slowly removed his finger, and though her hands tried to hold him inside her, he took them and kissed her fingertips.

And then she said the strangest thing: "So that's what the girly hots are all about." And she giggled. "You are my Philemon from the petrol station."

She might as well be speaking Zulu because it made no sense, but she was happy. And he was happy. And getting happier by the minute.

He moved upward toward her mouth, but she met him half-way. She kissed him with such wanton abandon, he thought he would come right then. Imagine! A woman making Pietro Salta-machio want to come with just a kiss!

DUM-dee-dee-DUM-dee-dee ...

She only managed a couple of minutes of quiet. She couldn't leave him alone. And he was glad. Her lips were a hair from his neck, breathing him in and murmuring her kitten sounds as her hand snuck toward his moist, silky hardness.

She lightly touched and traced, pushed and pulled, exploring and learning through his reaction. He was motionless, apart from the area upon which she operated.

He bit his opposite thumb. The other one was already numb.

Her fingers led her to a drop of moisture at the tip of his shaft, and as he groaned, she seemed to let her instinct take over. She got on her knees and straddled him. He pulled her knees tightly into his hips, entrapping himself between her throbbing legs. She lowered herself until her clitoris rubbed the taut skin between his tight testicles and his phallus.

Her body set a rhythm as she touched him with her sensitive peak again and again, and his bouncing sack beat against her tight bottom. She lifted up, then down, up, then down, until she started to quiver, throwing her head back.

He reached up, lifted her at the waist with strong arms and lowered her very, very slowly on top of his waiting shaft.

With each half an inch, she gasped, her mouth open in ecstasy. She tried to force herself down, but he wouldn't let her.

Slowly. Slowly.

He was watching her keenly. As he felt her hymen stretch, her eyes opened, and she cried out softly.

He stopped moving, suspending her with his arms. "*Mi amore*. I hurt you?"

"No, I'm fine. Please, Pietro. I want you. I want *all* of you. The hurt is already gone. Please. *All* of you. Now!"

When at last she was sitting all the way down, with him completely inside her, he began to push his hips very, very gently into hers. Further and further.

He leaned forward, searching for her mouth. Her hot tongue slipped immediately inside, finding his. He rolled her over and, with him on top, they lost themselves in each other as their bodies heated up and found a rhythm: filling and withdrawing, thrusting and dragging as their pleasure blazed. Heat shimmered off their entwined bodies as their combined fire hit the cool air.

Her moist, velvet sheath clutched onto him for dear life, and he loved it. Clutch and release. Harder, harder they climbed toward their peak, their eyes never leaving the other's, except to study a mouth or lick moisture off an upper lip.

He looked down at her, and the love he felt was brand new. Her long red tresses were splayed beneath him. Her beautiful freckles were clear even in the darkness. Her moist, swollen mouth twitched with lust.

She opened her exquisite green eyes and smiled as she opened her legs even further and took him all in.

And as they built toward rapture, he was gentle no more.

And she loved it.

All at once, an immensely powerful release simultaneously wracked their bodies, and in the midst of their orgasms, he locked on to her open mouth. His tongue probed to find hers, and they were as entangled and close as lovers can be. He prolonged their exquisite summit, suspending them in a dual sphere of acute physical awareness and rare spiritual oblivion.

Spent, he lay on top her, his elbows cushioning her from his full weight. He was still inside her. To leave the comfort of her, to disengage their perfect fit, would bring back reality, and neither was prepared for that.

On his knees, he lifted her shoulders, clutching her to him, and rolled her on top of him, keeping them joined together in what felt like a sacred union. There they lay, both motionless for fear of being disconnected. He relished the weight of her.

"I want you to stay inside me forever. It's where you belong," she said, and his heart broke as he saw her tears shimmer in the star-studded sky.

He whispered in her ear, "Love. To be like running brook, that sings melody tonight. To know pain of too much *tenerezza*, tenderness."

She was startled. "Pietro. *The Prophet*. How did you ... ?"

"I ask Rogers to help me find Gibran book. In new colonel's office, he borrow for me. Sergeant help me read. I learn some pages word to ... word for you."

Her tender smile thrilled him. He'd taken so long to pronounce the English words and understand them. Sergeant Rogers's patience was endless. "I want to understand you happy and what *influenzato* ... "

"Influences?" Iris asked hopefully.

"Yes, yes!" He kissed her. Thrilled. "What *influenced* your thought for life. Love."

And even before her tears of gratitude came, it was her inner woman that reacted and, with one squeeze, awakened his manhood. It was barely a minute before they joined together again, and like their very first touch when her electric fingers touched his electric palm, their deep electrifying charge shuddered and jolted them into exquisite oblivion.

At last they lay together in the moonlight, naked and spent.

"I know forever for you desire me, Cara Rossa." He was happier than he'd ever been.

She smiled a wicked smile. "Oh, *yes*, you do!"

"All I must have...some cow... how you say, *interiora?*"

"Ah, yes," she sighed, "cow entrails will get this girl every time."

DUM-dee-dee-DUM-dee-dee ...

CAUGHT

The horizon was brighter than usual, and unease gnawed at his gut.

As Pietro reached the pinnacle of the last ridge before the camp, he dropped to his belly. Not just the perimeter lights were on full power; the whole camp, even the chapel, was awash in electric daylight. Guards moved around like busy ants.

Pietro's fear turned to bile in his mouth. It was over. He was caught. He thought of the consequences, including being blindfolded and shot, and he realized it was not that causing his overwhelming terror, but the thought of never seeing his Iris again.

He had no idea how long he lay there, agonizing. His side hurt like a bitch. In a way, he welcomed the pain. It was good preparation for what was to come.

At last, the lights went out. He stayed where he was until the sky changed color, hinting at the oncoming dawn, and he knew he'd pushed his timeline beyond its limit. But what did it matter? It was over anyway. He might as well just go back and face the consequences.

The perimeter guards and dogs were back on schedule, and

he counted as he usually did but steeled himself for the blow of the bullet in his back until his back ached.

Nobody was more surprised than he when he made it to his tent without being shot. When he slipped silently inside, Antonio screamed, imagining an apparition of Pietro and not the man himself.

"Thank God. We thought it was all over for you. The lights came on, and we were sure they had caught you." Enzo's face was more wrinkled than ever.

"Did they find me gone?'

"No. They were too busy."

"So, if not me, then who did what to whom, to warrant such a festival of light?"

Enzo and Antonio looked completely out of sorts. Discombobulated. Shocked. Confused.

"Stef," Enzo said, and his face crumpled in grief.

Pietro felt his head might explode. *"Stef?"*

Like a macabre couple of puppets, they nodded in unison.

"Why was Stef trying to escape?" He was so confused. They just stared at him blankly.

"What the fuck happened? Was it a heart attack? He was not a robust man, and he looked fit. Stef is not the sharing kind, but if he was sick, surely he would have told me? I am his oldest friend." His logical brain couldn't process this ridiculous information.

Enzo was next to him, holding his arm. Pietro shook him off.

"Hospital at camp or in town? I must ask colonel if I can see him."

Enzo gripped his arm again, and Antonio appeared on the other side of him, holding his other elbow.

Pietro looked from one to the other, confused, and then absurdly frightened.

Enzo spoke slowly. "Stef hanged himself."

The impact of the dreadful truth took minutes to penetrate, and he froze as everything stopped, including his heart. Then he pulled away from his friends and stormed out of the tent shouting, "STEF!" He gave a dry, mirthless laugh as he headed to orchestra members' tents. He pushed flaps open, shouting, "They're telling me a sick joke. You can come out now. I didn't fall for it. Not me. Come out, Stef. Stef!"

Then, confused, Pietro walked around the camp calling his friend's name until, like red-eyed zombies, the men from Stef's well-oiled orchestra encircled him.

"Where is he?" He felt like a mother bear, searching for his cub. "Where? Where? And Piccolo?"

And their arms were out, like the living dead.

"He's gone. Stef is dead. He killed himself," a crazy person with glazed eyes said.

Pietro lashed out, but they held their ground, keeping him inside their protective circle.

"NO! Not possible. He loved music. He loved Piccolo. He didn't want to die. Not here. Not even in Italy. He loved life. No. Not Stef. I know Stef. Since we were five. I know Stef. Why? No. It can't be so. It can't be so. Not my friend Stef. If he was unhappy, I would have known. Was he unhappy?" He was so confused.

Enzo pushed through the circle, breaking it. He spoke softly and calmly. "We don't know why. Come. Stef left something for you."

"Where's Piccolo?" Pietro knew he was shouting.

"He's with his godfather, Burbero," Enzo assured him, leading him back to their tent.

Inside, Enzo said, "We don't know why. Nobody knows. But he wanted you to know. He left this for you." He handed Pietro a sealed envelope.

Logic pushed through Pietro's addled brain. "Why didn't the guards take this letter?"

Enzo's voice held reverence. "Rogers found it and hid it from the authorities. He gave it to me unopened. It has your name on it."

Rogers. Pietro felt the warmth of gratitude. He took the letter with mixed emotions. This was his oldest friend's last words. What in the world could have been so bad that it prompted him to take his life? And in South Africa? No one loved Italy more than Stef. Just a few more months, and he could have been buried in Italy. What could be so bad? What? *Damn you, Stef, whatever it was, I could have helped you through it. We went through so much, you and I, this ... whatever it was, we could have overcome it together.*

"Somebody else did this." Pietro felt anger surge, and it was better than confusion. He would find out who did this and make them pay. They would fucking suffer for taking his best friend away.

"No one did this to him. He did this to himself. It was clear."

Pietro crushed the letter to his chest and, as realization hit, his legs started to give way. He pushed through the tent flap just as his legs failed him, and he fell to his knees. Starting in the pit of his stomach, giant sobs wracked his body and pushed their way up and up and up and out of his mouth, and he heard himself howl.

Between sobs, he took a deep breath and his eyes split open. Sunlight blinded him as the huge orange orb licked at the new horizon in preparation for another day.

How dare the fucking sun shine? Didn't it know Stef was dead? How dare a day just dawn as if nothing had happened?

THE MORNING AFTER

The persistent mid-morning sun forced her eyes open at last, and there was but a split second between confusion and delirious recall. Her body tingled from head to toe.

Buffer seemed to recognize the change in her and, keeping his distance at the bottom of her bed, gave her space to understand the change for herself.

"Buffer, you know, don't you? Yip. I am a bona fide woman this morning." She writhed on her back like a cat using a scratching post. "Gave myself to the man of my dreams. And it was divine. Simply divine."

Then she sat bolt upright, in a panic. "Oh my God, I hope he got back to the camp OK. It was so late."

She lay back down, moving her pillows from under her head to her chest, her mood plummeting. Buffer moved closer in case she needed him.

The war would soon be over, and he would be gone. And then what? Then what? When would boats sail to Italy again after a world war? They surely had to rebuild Europe's harbors and cities before they worried about passenger liners. Oh, God. It would take her as long to save to get there. *And will my brother forgive me for wishing myself to the place where he died, for the purpose of my own joy?* Somehow she knew Gregg would forgive her anything. And what of America? What of my dream? What of the agreement I've signed and sent? What of that? She could sail west to America, then to Italy from there after her contract expired. Pietro's face came to her as if he stood before her, but further thoughts were stopped by a loud knock on her door.

She jumped up, guilty as hell, as Buffer sprang to attention. Her mother didn't wait to be invited in.

Oh, here we go. Why are you still in bed wasting your life away ... blah blah blah. Iris could hear the words, though her mother's mouth wasn't moving. Wait! Her mother was smiling and didn't notice her daughter was deflowered and grieving all at the same time. Just as well.

"Oh, Jinx."

Iris's heart stopped for a minute. What now? But "Jinx" was a good sign.

"Please don't think ill of me." Her mother was coy as she took her daughter's hand. All she needed was her mother pregnant out of wedlock. Had Iris a morsel of good humor this morning, she would have laughed. But something niggled deep in her brain. She'd worry about that later.

"Your dad's been gone a long, long time. I've been lonely. But not anymore. I'm in love, Iris. I hope you'll find it in your heart to forgive my disloyalty. But I just can't stop smiling."

Iris's arms went around her mother. She felt it was she who was the mother, giving her child permission to be happy in spite of how Iris was feeling about life, about the world. "That's truly wonderful, Mom. You deserve to find love," Iris whispered, meaning every word.

Iris could hear the relief her mother exhaled into her own unruly, post-coital hair.

"Thank you, thank you, Jinx."

Iris kept pressure on her mom's back to keep her from seeing the tears pouring down her own cheeks. How ironic life was. Iris's plan had worked. Her mother had given her the freedom to move on. To America. Time was running out to book her cabin on that ship. It only sailed west once a month. She phoned every couple of weeks, checking in with the Harbor Master to make sure her ticket was still there and ready to be used.

"I love you, Jinx." It had only taken nearly twenty-one years to hear these precious words. But now it was the child who was old and wise, and not even this longed-for endearment could assuage Iris's fear of loss.

Then the niggle she'd felt earlier pricked again. *No! You don't fall pregnant the first time you have sex. But we made love seven times last night—well, I kind of lost count after seven.* She felt the warmth in her lower abdomen and lower still, the new sensation she'd come to welcome since she'd found Pietro. *Just in case, I'll ask Lena. She'll have a morning-after Zulu cure. Just in case.* She held her mother tighter still, rocking her as her mother cried with joy and Iris cried with a sorrow deeper than any she'd ever known. However would she live without Pietro when this war ended?

THE LETTER

28 January 1945

There was no longer a need to hide the radio from the guards. They were as interested in the progress of the war as the prisoners, so Antonio's contraption was a go-to for up-to-date news inside the camp. Just this morning Pietro heard a broadcast that added insult to injury. The end of the Battle of the Bulge saw 75,000 Americans hurt or killed. Hitler seemed doomed.

Pietro wedged himself into a corner of the old chicken coop, the same exact place he'd found the dead man whose shoes he had claimed after his very first encounter with Iris.

He held the letter with his name on it as if it was both the precious Hope diamond and the worst poison-pen letter ever written. He had run his fingers over every square inch of the envelope, up and down the seams, over the sealed flap at the back. The envelope was grimy now and Stef's handwriting, smudged. It had been seven weeks since his Stef had left him, and he hadn't had the courage to open it. The letter coupled with the tightened security of the camp, which restricted his reaching Iris in any way, plagued him every day.

He was desperately afraid of what lay within the envelope. Whatever was in it, whatever it said, the bottom line was that inside were his friend's final thoughts, and no matter the content, Pietro knew he would feel responsible in some way for letting Stef down.

Stef had always been Pietro's to protect. When they had found each other, two ragamuffins with wayward mothers and too much time on their hands, Stef had been two years older, but from the beginning, Pietro was in charge.

But Stef always called Pietro out for being less than Stef thought he should be. Pietro admired him for that. Stef was born with a moral compass in spite of the womb that carried him. Though Stef's mom was the best of the bunch, it wasn't saying much. Pietro had always been fiercely protective of Stef, who was susceptible to ridicule. With his slight frame and studious looks, he was often the butt of unkind jokes. Pietro fought more fights protecting Stef than for any other reason. It was his job to protect his friend. How had he failed him so dismally?

It was Pietro who was given a violin by the paramour of one of the dressing room ladies. The man heard Pietro sing on a number of occasions and had become quite a fan. He would send things for Pietro backstage via his lover. Pietro knew much of what the man sent him was never received, especially the money. But a good-looking suit to match his mother's only commitment to him—decent-looking shoes—found its way into his eager hands, and he felt like his pockets were heavily lined with lira when he went on stage until he outgrew the suit.

The dancer's paramour also sent back to Pietro an old violin. Looking back, the man must have thought Pietro would sound better with accompaniment.

Pietro remembered the day as clearly as if it were this morning. He thought they would get a pretty price for it, enough to go to a real opera. He'd run like the wind, bow and violin bouncing as his bare feet hit the cobbled streets, until he was at Stef's Nonna's house, pounding on the door. His profits were half Stef's. It was the way of things.

One look at Stef's face, and Pietro knew those opera tickets were done for.

His friend's face had never been more animated. He didn't even ask if it was for him, he just knew he had found his place in the world. He snatched the violin out of Pietro's hand, thanking Pietro with every fiber of his being, and he sat right down on the ground and ran his fingers lovingly over every square inch.

After ten minutes of becoming one with his new instrument, Stef looked up at Pietro. "Very soon I will make this baby talk." Stef's joy was worth more than front-row seats inside the famous Teatro di San Carlo.

At last, Pietro tore open the letter. It was like pulling off a thick scab, knowing the pain he would feel would exceed the strange feeling of the scab itself, but doing it anyway.

My Friend,

Without you, my life would have been empty and incomplete. You were, you are, better than a brother. All my life, you protected me. Promoted me. Included me. Made me feel important in your wake. That is why this will be so hard for you to read. But I have to let you know that there is nothing you could have done to stop me from doing what I did. You must believe me.

It started a long, long time ago.

But this time I was in the ablution block at the urinal in the middle of the night when Tap Tap came in. I was terrified, because we all know he's unpredictable and cruel, and I was alone. I didn't look at him, and my pissing stopped from fear. He was drunk. He boxed me in by walking back and forth in a semicircle about three feet behind me. Back and forth. I could smell booze on his breath. I didn't know what to do or what he wanted. I stood dead still with my head down. I heard his whip beating against his leg in three-four time. I wanted to shit in my pants. I didn't, thank God, because I may have needed to commit suicide sooner (joke).

I don't know how long it went on. It felt like an eternity. When he spoke, I jumped so high I saw the rafters from a new angle.

"I need you to turn around. NOW." I did so.

"On your knees, boy." What was I to do?

I heard that fucking whip beat his leg over and over, and it became a type of hypnosis. One-two-three. Two-two-three. He made me satisfy him. Then he took me in the diabolical way you would expect from Tap Tap. But my friend, this is not the horror of it all.

The horror is that my body responded. Not consciously, God knows. But it was as if I was welcoming these violent attentions, and I didn't know if it was my nature or a very basic instinct beyond my control. God knows, I was never emotionally present or invested, but my body liked what was being done to me in spite of the hatred I felt and the pain he inflicted. That's what scared me more than anything.

Forgive me. Please. I beg you.

That night was the first of many. Oh, Pietro, I so feared my physical response to the way he hideously used me that I hated myself. More and more each time. He wouldn't let me stop; he would sooner have killed me. I agonized over not telling you that I long knew I was different from you when we were boys and shared everything, but I never wanted to change things between us. When we moved to Venice, our clean start, I tried so hard to be "your normal." But it was never mine.

And then there was Tap Tap.

There is nothing, my old friend, that you could have done to stop me from doing what I did or from him doing what he did. Had you been there to protect me that night, it would have happened another time. Or another.

The war is ending. I cannot go back to Italy knowing how low I stooped. I am abysmally ashamed. Not because I am the way I am —I have long accepted that—but because of who I allowed to use me so. I ask only that no one ever knows that I debased myself with the most hateful man we have ever known.

Do me two favors:

1. Know that without your friendship, my world would have been dismal. Always remember how you enhanced my life and made it more spectacular than it was ever meant to be, and

2. Love Iris completely. In this life and the next. Once for you and once for me, like we have always done things.

I love you, Pietro. Always and forever.

Your friend,

Stef

P.S. Please make sure Burbero takes Piccolo home for keeps.

HEADLIGHTS

It was as if Antonio's damned radio become his very audible ticking time bomb just as the intermittent sharp pain in his side was his constant physical reminder. Just this morning the radio had boomed that U.S. troops had invaded Okinawa in Japan, that the Allies had surrounded more than 300,000 German troops in the Ruhr and, worst of all, that the Allied offensive in northern Italy had begun.

All of this, a frightening countdown to his time left with his Iris.

Once they'd quickly found the first place in the thicket that gave them privacy, they didn't know which part of the other they should explore first. Each heightened nerve ending needed their lover's touch more. It had been an eternity since they'd seen each other.

Her smell. Her skin. Her taste. Her face. Her hair. Her freckles. Her eyes. Her languid movements. Catlike. Fascinating.

His voice. His warmth. Oh, God, his hands! His taste. His

dimples. His full mouth. His overlapping front tooth. His command. His tongue—Oh! His mastery. His kindness. His humor.

All this, and not an item of clothing had been shed.

The week before, the surly guard came in to the store, looking not surly at all but—well, full of himself. He hugged a mangy-looking little dog, and she swore both beamed as they approached. She'd been watching the door for anyone from the camp for weeks and weeks and weeks.

"Well, Private. I see you have a new friend." Iris smiled, though her heart beat frantically.

"He's an old friend, really. But he became mine for keeps a while ago."

"Does he live at the camp?"

"Well, he used to. Now he comes home with me. Name's Piccolo." The man's grin was infectious, and Iris smiled in spite of the anxiety turning her mouth dry.

"What brings you in today?"

"Well, the camp's been on lockdown since ... hmm ... end of November."

Oh, dear God! That was the last time we saw each other.

Had he been captured after they'd made glorious love? She'd heard nothing from him, and her trusted messenger, Fourfeet, had left to integrate himself into his wife's kraal for a time. She'd even taken a taxi during the day to find someone working on the road to get word to him. No one. She was too afraid to ask the colonel anything at the camp, because it would make him suspicious. Nobody cared about the camp activities, and as far as her mother's beau was concerned, why would Iris?

She could hardly breathe. The big man continued, "Nobody's allowed out, and they have their last concert in two days and need some urgent stuff. Sergeant Rogers said, 'Ask for Iris.'"

She swore the giant could see her heart in her throat, bobbing like a pubescent boy's Adam's apple. She scratched the little dog's neck to hide her agitation.

"Lockdown?" *Oh God, please not my Pietro.*

"Ja, man. Since one of the oke's committed sewerage pipe couple of months ago."

"I'm sorry, I don't understand."

"Ag, sorry. A guy killed himself."

No. No. No. Please God, not Pietro ... surely she would know. She would feel it.

"He was a violin player. Nice enough Italian bloke. Piccolo here's dad. I'm godfather."

Iris didn't know how she kept her spine straight. She so badly wanted to collapse from relief. Her Pietro was safe.

The private stroked the top of the dog's head, and the little mongrel's neck doubled in length to receive the kindness. "Why? Nobody knows. And they are almost on the ship back to Italy. Ag, shame, man."

"And when are the ... prisoners leaving, Private?"

"Nobody knows yet, Miss. But we think the war's nearly over."

"So they tell me. So why did Rogers send you specially to me?" she asked, grateful this giant wasn't the sharpest pair of scissors in her showcase.

"He has been on leave, just got back today, said you would give the okes—sorry—the men what they need for the final concert tomorrow."

"Of course," she said blankly and began gathering items that were the staple for their concert backdrops.

"How long do you think the camp will be on lockdown, Private?" Iris asked, trying to be nonchalant.

"Ag, not long, Miss. Just a formality for a few more weeks, days even. End of the war and all."

"Makes sense. That good singer—what's his name?" She tried to be flippant.

"Pietro. He's the boss man of concerts. "

"He likes a specific fabric dye. Can you make sure he gets it and no one else?"

The large, simple man chuckled. "Ja, man, he is a fussy one. Knows what he wants!"

"Yes he does, thankfully," she whispered to herself. "OK, I'll mix it. Won't be long."

She flew to the other side of the counter, grabbed a box of dye, pulled her pencil from her bun on top of her head. She tore off the tiniest corner of her last invoice and wrote, "A week from today—Monday. I ache for you." She slipped the note into the dye box. She knew the operetta would be over by then.

The rest was a blur, but she made the private repeat three times that the special dye was to be delivered only to the music boss.

And here they were, thanks to the relaxed security as accurately predicted by Burbero—to whom Iris owed an apology for thinking him unlikely to know anything of consequence—and her own hefty dip into her savings. Sanjay's fare handsomely increased thanks to the many hours he was left in the boonies while the lovers enjoyed both the Zulu wedding and the many hours in the sunflower patch. The driver pointed out that since clearly their level of government secrets had increased because of the time they committed to them, then surely Iris' expense account had increased also. Who could argue with such perfect logic?

Could this be the very last time they saw each other?

It was more than likely. They felt not only their own ache, but that of the other. They mourned their loss now. They tried to capture every second, but time was elusive and slipped away too quickly. They wanted to touch, to talk, to explore, to kiss, to join, to weep. They wanted to learn all about each other, but the damned seconds ticked away from them.

They couldn't do it all at once, and they had to choose the most urgent need to quell, because a lifetime could not satisfy all they desperately wanted to learn about the other.

They'd started off with just three hours left to them.

And now it was two.

They were entwined, each part of their bodies touching wherever they could, to make them feel whole. They sat on their original, termite-infested log, just inside the copse.

"What will we do?"

"Each lira for each song I sing will bring my Iris close—closer to Italy."

"But when will passenger liners cross the Indian Ocean again after this devastating war?"

"Iris. My Iris. If in war we find one other—we can—we will —in peace." Afterward, she'd marvel at how his English had improved since they'd last seen each other. He'd obviously worked hard on it. Just for her.

Her wet face was against his cheek. "A letter from you will take a month or more. Oh, God, Pietro."

"Do you feel my heart?" he asked.

"Yes. Same as mine. Fast," she whispered.

"It will always beat for you these way. If prison cannot keep me afar from you, then how can a little water?"

"True. The Indian Ocean is but a bucket compared to a POW camp with crazy Julian."

He pulled away from her so quickly, she jumped in alarm. He held her hands straight down and looked into her eyes.

"You know Tap Tap? Julian?" His eyes felt wild. He didn't want to scare her.

She rolled her eyes. "Yes, but it didn't take me long to find out he was odd."

"Odd?" He was so on edge, but she seemed unperturbed.

"Strange." She laughed without mirth. "He must be strange. He didn't even really know me and he asked me to marry him."

Pietro felt the blood drain from his face. The monster was once her paramour? This fucking pig who put the fear of God into men whenever he could, who nearly broke his larynx, who fried most of Antonio's brain in a hot box and, worst of all, who forced his old friend Stef to kill himself?

"What's wrong? Pietro, I can feel your distance. What is it? Tell me," she begged.

And he did.

Every horrific detail, culminating with the cause of Stef's suicide. He trusted this woman with his life. He knew with certainty that Stef would condone his sharing with her and her alone. The men inside, Rogers and the colonel, had respectfully never asked him what Stef's letter revealed.

He felt an enormous relief in sharing Stef's reason for taking his life. He watched her carefully and loved her all the more because he knew she didn't judge his beloved friend, she only wept with him, for the loss of his Stef. Together they shed tears for all of their losses, others' humiliations and their own hurts and fears. Sometimes it was she who was the mother, placating and rocking, then he the father, patting and soothing back her hair from her forehead.

When at last they surfaced from their hurts and held each other like lovers of old, they understood the magnitude of what they'd just shared. The way both felt about these injustices was much more important than any differences.

"Oh God, Pietro. I knew he was a bit off"—she twirled a finger around the side of her head showing shades of crazy—"but I had no idea what a monster he was. You know it was my idea that he should wear gloves? His father mutilated his hand with a violin bow. It was like a piece of meat. I felt sorry for him and fitted him for gloves. I thought it would give him confidence and people wouldn't think of his horrible hand before they thought of him." Her eyes were wide with horror, and her face white as a ghost. "Oh God, Pietro. Could it be that he took out his anger on Stef because he was such a wonderful violinist? Oh, no. What did I do?" Her voice had risen, but he held her tight and stroked her arm.

"Shh. Shh. Shh. Not you, my love, no blame for you. No blame for Stef. We can only do what we think best, when things beyond—*nostra conoscenza*—happen. You thought you were helping *insicuro* man."

"He's an abomination! Oh, God, Pietro. What can I do to right this? To get redemption for all of you? Can I talk to the colonel? Get Julian thrown into a military jail? What? Anything!"

"What you can do, my love, is what you do already. Listen. Feel. Understand. He pay for everything now—or next life. I hate him for what he do to my friends. I wish him to be dead. Burn *all'inferno*." He leaned in and breathed in the smell of her hair and felt the curves of her body against him, and his hate ebbed, and love for her filled the crevices until it brought him back to her completely.

He felt his heart slow and whispered, "You, my Iris, are my forever love."

His body gave a jolt as a horrific thought hit him. He leaned his head back so he could look into her eyes; his chest pounded in anger. *"Dio mio.* Did Tap Tap hurt you, my Iris?"

She shook her head. "It lasted a few months. Four or five dates. Way too many, because I felt sorry for him. He never hurt me, my Pietro."

Relief brought him levity. "So? This is what I must expect? Perhaps I will make it to four dates and you say goodbye?" She pulled away to look into his eyes.

Her face was so serious and her eyes so intense, he saw her truth as she said, "I have never loved before now. I will only ever love once."

"So, my Iris, you love me?"

Her eyes filled with tears. "With all my heart."

He kissed her. Long and deep. Velvet on velvet. Melding of body and spirit. Her passion matched his as the tender depth of their kiss turned to unbridled hunger and he lifted her in his arms and began to walk her deeper into the woods.

As he gazed at her, car headlights came weaving toward them from a distance. He put her down roughly, turned and pulled her toward the taxi by the hand, shouting, "Inside, Iris, *now.*"

As she dived into the back seat, Pietro bashed on the driver's window, shouting, "SANJAY! Wake up! Drive, DRIVE, Sanjay. *Fast."* The lights came closer and closer.

As he dove into his ditch, he heard her passenger door lock.

Agonizing seconds passed before the taxi's engine started.

But he heard the gravel and dirt crunch and, with horror churning in the pit of his stomach, he knew with certainty it was too late.

48

MANNEKEN PIS

It was as if everything moved too quickly to process. Watching the *only* someone you love falling from a great height and not being able to catch her—like his bullet-ridden parachute, as the hard ground hurried toward him, rendering him powerless.

The weaving car screeched to a stop at an angle, blocking the narrow road.

The taxi was not going anywhere.

The car door opened, and Pietro's heart stopped dead.

Tap Tap stumbled out of the car, drunk. Pietro watched as Julian physically pulled himself together before he teetered toward the taxi like a tightrope walker.

Each uneven step closer to the taxi elevated Pietro's heartbeat.

Tap Tap pounded on Sanjay's window with his fist. Pietro could imagine the timid chap's fear. And Iris! Oh God, his Iris. What to do? What to do?

The driver's window went down two inches. Tap Tap's voice bellowed: "What are you doing here at this time of night, Coolie?"

Pietro heard stuttering but couldn't decipher the driver's soft words.

"Who do you have in the back there?" Julian tried to peer in. "Unlock the back door. Open the back door *now!* Do you fucking hear me, Coolie?"

Sanjay's dark arm moved over the back of the seat to undo the doorknob.

Tap Tap walked to the back door and yanked it open.

Iris screamed.

And Pietro couldn't do a fucking thing to help her.

"You? Iris?" Pietro could hear disbelief in Tap Tap's voice. "Why are *you* here?" He sounded sober. Shock would do that to you.

Pietro knew she was trying her best to sound annoyed at the inconvenience, but he could hear the quiver in her voice.

"What do you think you're doing ambushing us like this?" She said crossly, her voice a few decibels lower as she tried to hide her fear.

"Why are you on this dead-end road at this time of night?" Julian was accusing.

"I was at the hospital, and my taxi driver is new to the area. I must have nodded off. He must have taken a wrong turn." *Dio Mio*, his Iris was sharp.

"Well!" Julian's exclamation was menacing. Pietro knew the devil would soon rise up. "Seems you are exactly where you need to be. Get out, Iris. Let's have a chat."

"Don't be ridiculous, Julian. It's very late, and I need to get home now. My mother will be so worried. She's probably called the police already. Move your car now, please. "

Tap Tap lurched into the taxi and pulled Iris out by an arm and a leg. Pietro knew Tap Tap's strength was mighty, and his beloved Iris didn't stand a chance, in spite of her kicking and flailing, trying to hit anything she could.

And I do nothing! God forgive me. Iris forgive me.

The driver's side door flew open, and Sanjay disappeared in a blur, into the woods. *Shit.*

Pietro broke into a sweat as Tap Tap literally dropped *his* Iris on the hard road, like a doll no longer favored.

He felt her pain as she landed on the uneven shale and he flinched. The fall hurt her enough to keep her down. Her arms were grazed and bleeding.

Standing over her, Tap Tap pushed down his pants to expose himself.

Pietro jumped out of the ditch.

Though dazed, Iris must have seen him. She glared and waved her hand in a get-back motion. When he didn't move, she did it again, this time looking up at Julian to distract him away from her wild hand signals to Pietro.

"What do you want to do with that hand, Iris? Showing your true colors at last?"

With a sudden jolt, it hit Pietro. It wasn't all about Pietro Saltamachio and his consequences. It was about Iris. Not just her reputation, but fraternizing with a prisoner was a treasonous act. She could go to prison for him. *No. No. Do nothing. Listen to her. Stay where you are. Don't be macho. Think of Iris first.*

Tap Tap's voiced changed. Pietro knew the demon was loose.

Pietro saw the horrendous tableau side-on as Julian used a gloved hand to hold his penis.

"Don't worry. You'll get what you want from me. But first, a lesson in humility. You're not better than me!" He punctuated the last word, pushing out yellow pee, which arched like the famous Manneken Pis statue, and Tap Tap waved his dick this way and that so his acrid, warm urine covered as much of Iris's face as he could. Though she turned her head away, she didn't shield her face with her hand. She knew that would infuriate him further.

God, she was brave. He'd loved her before, but he knew in that moment that he'd never loved anyone more in all the lives he'd lived, nor would he, in all the lives to come.

Dio mio. He wanted so badly to get out of the ditch and kill the fucking pig.

Tap Tap pulled his pants up from around his legs and bent again to roughly haul Iris up by her arm. *She is so small. And wet and bleeding. Like my heart is bleeding, my love.*

Pietro marveled at the fact that she still said nothing. Then he knew why, and his heart nearly burst from his chest. She didn't want him to come to her rescue and be exposed.

It was as if Tap Tap's strength had tripled now that his bladder was empty. He threw her on the trunk of the taxi so hard, her head bounced twice. Pietro's own head hurt in sympathy. In an instant, the *bastardo* became like an octopus as he undid his belt and unbuttoned his fly with one gloved hand while lifting her dress and tearing off her panties with the other.

Iris screamed when Julian ripped off her panties, and he punched her in the face, hard enough to make her head loll like a rag doll's. His pants were around his hips, and Pietro saw him admire his rigid cock quickly before he spread Iris's inert legs.

No more! Fuck the consequences.

Pietro, low and lethal like the hungry leopard he'd encountered, crept over the lip of the ditch and, keeping low, he searched the ground until he found it.

Staying out of Tap Tap's vision, he took giant steps toward Iris's assailant's rigid back. Thank the lord, Julian's self-absorption dominated as he fondled himself with his black gloves before ... *no!*

Tap Tap must have felt something behind him, and as he

turned around, Pietro hit him over the head with the large stone he'd picked up.

Julian dropped to the ground like a sack of potatoes.

Pietro didn't hesitate. He pulled Iris's dress down and lifted her up as if she weighed as much as a baby and carried her to the passenger side of the car. He managed to get the door open, and he gently laid her on the front seat.

He held her face and used his shirt to wipe off as much of the urine and blood as he could. When she winced, he kissed her forehead and whispered her name. Her eyes opened and, seeing his face, she smiled for an instant and put her hand to her face. Her eyes were dark and fearful.

"You are safe, my Iris. I am here."

She sprang back. "Where is he?"

"Lying on ground behind taxi. I hit him with a stone."

"Is he dead?" Her face was expressionless.

"Just enough hit to sleep. Deep sleep."

She gently pushed at his chest to move him out of her way so she could get out of the car. Her voice was as dead as her eyes. "Then I will kill him."

Pietro barricaded her inside the car. "And then what, *m'amore*? You will go to prison for murder? How will I visit my wife in prison when I am in Italy?"

She sobered. "No," she said firmly, shaking her head, "He doesn't deserve to live. He's taken too much from too many."

"Then we find way for him pay. But you and me? We are number one. Our love must be *protezioni* ... protect. Kill him is no answer for us. Hear me, Iris. Hear me, Mia Cara."

Her body relaxed against his chest, and he held her and stroked her wet hair. "You must go while he is *inconscio*. Stay here. I find taxi man."

Closing the door, he checked that the bundle behind the car

that was Julian hadn't moved, then walked backward toward the bush, making sure she didn't leave the seat.

"Sanjay!" Pietro yelled into the copse of trees that lined the side of the road opposite to the one leading to the camp. "Safe. Come out. Help me."

At last Sanjay emerged, shaking like a leaf. Pietro took the frightened man by the arm and led him back to his taxi. "Your keys?" Pietro's heart stopped as the man looked blank.

Pietro said kindly, "For the car. Keys, please."

Fortunately, his eyes lost some of their fear, and he felt for his keys. The second pocket he tapped produced a jingle that placated them both.

"First. Help me." Pietro tugged gently at his sleeve.

Sanjay's eyes, like that of a frightened buck, kept glancing back into the forest, ready to bolt. Pietro's grip tightened so that when the driver saw Julian's blob as they rounded the car, there would be no further fleeing.

"Back seat." Pietro's decisive instruction coached Sanjay into automatic, and together they lifted the breathing dead weight and carried him to the back of the taxi. Iris had hopped out to open the back door, and they bundled Julian onto the seat. They both looked at his undone pants, his privates showing, and they looked at each other and shook their heads. No. Let him stay like that. It would add to the humiliation he deserved.

Pietro saw Iris back to her seat. Then he took Sanjay by the shoulders, walked him to the driver's side and pushed him gently down behind the wheel.

"Sanjay. Listen. No trouble if you do what I say. You go hospital. You push pig out at big door of hospital only when nobody see. You drive very fast to Iris home. You understand this?"

The shaken man was still dazed. Pietro shook him. "Do you understand? No trouble if you do what I tell. You hear?"

Sanjay nodded, and on the third try, he got the key into the

ignition and the car started. On Pietro's way to Iris around the
back of the car, he picked up her discarded panties and his rock.
He gave the former to her subtly, and when he presented her
with the rock, he said, "If he open eye or make sound, hit him.
No killing. Just hit. Please?"

She nodded. He kissed her temple softly.

"Wait, Sanjay. One minute." Pietro opened the back door and
pulled off Julian's gloves. He was repulsed by the pink mass and
understood completely why Iris had done what she'd thought
best to boost the confidence of a mutilated man.

He leaned over the seat and presented the gloves to Iris.
"Take. Burn gloves. Be free and let him be *esposti* ... exposed for
what he is. Now go, Sanjay! Quick. Be safe. Go. Go. Go." He
kissed her cheek softly and whispered, "I love you, my Iris."
Then he closed the door.

Pietro watched the car speed down the road. He contemplated what to do with Julian's car but then decided to leave it
running with the lights on. A dead battery might be the standing
ovation, even though it was much less than the bastard
deserved.

He saw the dreaded whip, like a black snake on the roadside.
Pietro went to pick it up and hurled it as high as possible into
the woods. But the folded tip hooked onto a limb of a mighty
mahogany tree and dangled there.

On his way back to the camp, he prayed in Latin, the
language reserved for God when Pietro really, really needed
help.

"Look after her, Heavenly Father. I beg you."

He stood still and opened his eyes, looking upward into what
he hoped was God's face to show him how serious the next
request was: "And please, dear Lord Jesus, sacred Mother, God
in heaven, Holy Ghost, don't let Iris kill him."

49

VIA CON DIO

Pietro couldn't believe that a whole day had passed without any sign of Tap Tap. Their rumor mill would've let them know if he was dead. Sergeant Rogers was with the colonel in Durban at a military conference—likely, Pietro considered, about what to do with the POWs after the war. They all knew the war was nearly over, so there was minimal concern that the camp was left with a light force of army brass. Perhaps Colonel had not yet heard of Julian's absence.

The sun was high on the second day when a taxi arrived at HQ bearing Tap Tap. A bandage wound around his head, and he used a hospital-issue cane to steady himself.

For a little longer than an instant, Pietro wished he'd killed him.

What hit Pietro over the head like a stone (he was mildly amused by his own joke) was that Tap Tap wore ill-fitting brown gloves. One was way too big, and the other outlined the distended mass beneath it. Pietro thought of Stef, and bile filled his mouth. *Dio mio, I should have killed him.* The thought was a whole lot longer the second time.

Tap Tap came straight into the camp, picking up a megaphone at the entrance. "Guards report to the entrance at once. Leave everything. This is an emergency. Entrance NOW!"

He used the loudspeaker. "ALL MACARONIS IN LINE FOR INSPECTION NOW!"

Prisoners were hauled out of tents, ablution blocks, mess halls, nooks and crannies.

By the time they were all lined up, not even the large megaphone could shield the spittle that spewed out like lava, along with his accusations.

"A WOP in a brown uniform did this to me." He pointed wildly at his bandaged head. "Saw one of you bastards out of the corner of my eye."

Nobody made eye contact with him.

"Come forward now, or all be damned."

Not a muscle moved.

"NOW!"

He threw down the megaphone and, with a distinct limp (Pietro bet the limp was courtesy of Iris pushing him overzealously out of the taxi at the hospital), Tap Tap began to troll the queues of prisoners.

He planted his spittle-encrusted face inches from each man's. Down one line he went. Then the next.

Tap Tap was one man away. Pietro could feel his molars lock together. *How can you possibly stop from kneeing the son of a bitch in the balls so hard they'll disappear forever? How could you watch as he threw down the woman you loved, pissed on her, hit her . . . Dio mio, then was about to...! Yes! God forbid, where were your own balls as you watched all this? What kind of a man are you?*

Then her expressive, freckle-dusted face dominated his vision, and he heard her plead: "Do it for me. Don't tell him. Where will my love go if you get hanged?"

The most hated of faces was an inch from his own.

Do it for Iris. Do it for Iris. Do it for Iris.

And then Tap Tap moved to the next man, and Pietro's jaw relaxed, leaving a dull ache to remind him how close he'd come to pulling up his knee with all his might and damning the consequences. He'd focused on Tap Tap's left ear. Had he made eye contact with his nemesis, it would have all been over.

The despicable Butcher's scrutiny went on for hours. When men fell from the fatigue of standing at attention, Tap Tap ordered them into The Hole until the place of horror would be filled beyond capacity. The lights came on, and Tap Tap started at the first row of prisoners for the eleventh time, looking for something, anything, that spelled guilt.

When he couldn't find it, he made it up.

He pulled the slightest of the men, Pietro's operatic "leading lady," from the line-up. Typical. Picking on the smallest was a testament to his cowardice.

Tap Tap lifted his cane high in the air and shouted, "It was you. I know it was you. You have it coming now. You fucking Eye-Tie bastard. Didn't have the guts or the strength to kill me, did you?"

Pietro had no idea how his legs propelled him from where he stood to where the beating was about to begin, but he managed to grab the cane on the downward motion before it delivered a bone-shattering blow.

Tap Tap looked confused for a minute, like he'd just realized that his broken head was slowing down his motor skills.

Perhaps Pietro trapping the cane's intended blows must have reminded him of the last time Pietro held the whip to protect Fourfeet, his messenger. And perhaps the pig remembered how he'd failed to completely sever Pietro's larynx.

Pietro pushed his own face into Julian's, stopping an inch away as was done to each one of them. "It was me, pig. It was me. And I would do it again." *Sorry, my Iris. So sorry.*

There was no stopping the next blows. They came, frenzied

and cruel. Pietro quickly went down on his side and into a fetal position to protect his already damaged appendix.

Then ... "It was me, pig. And I would do it again." It was Enzo's voice. Pietro's heart expanded with the love he felt for this man.

"It was me, pig. And I would do it again." That was Antonio. Pietro smiled just before he heard and felt the thick cane breaking a rib. He vaguely saw brown uniforms gather around Julian, closer, closer. "It was me, pig. And I would do it again." That was Alberto's voice, then Peppe's, and so it went on.

The beating stopped.

Pietro looked up. As far as he could see, a Lake Como of brown uniforms crowded around Tap Tap. "It was me, pig." "It was me, pig." "No. Me, Pig. I would do it again." A hundred voices chanted. They were so tightly packed, Tap Tap couldn't even lift his arm to beat his way out of the crowd.

"Guards! Guards!" he yelped. The guards were really slow in coming to the devil's aid, and when they did, they formed a barrier between the prisoners and Tap Tap so he could do them no more harm.

He barked, "Take this horde of miserable specimens. Chain them naked to the barbed wire fence. Leave them there all night. And leave the other bastards in The Hole."

The guards started rallying the crowd of rabble-rousers toward the fence. Pietro counted at least forty men, and he felt a surge of camaraderie so profound, he was moved to tears. He felt sublimely privileged to be one of them.

Their linked trek to the fence was rewarded by the entire camp's applause, hooting, shouting and whistling.

As Pietro was led to the doctor's office in handcuffs, he saw Tap Tap's mouth open wide and the vein of his neck pop out as he screamed over the megaphone, but his words went unheard over the din. The tyrant threw down the loudspeaker so hard, bits and pieces bounced in fifty directions. He also saw the men who were ordered to The Hole were merely contained in the perimeter. Nobody went inside. Thank God for that.

Ten guards tended to roping the chains between each prisoner and attaching them to the fence. Somebody shouted, "Aren't you going to strip us like he told you to?" It was Pietro's "leading lady's" voice. Always the smallest had the biggest mouth. Pietro smiled, and his heart tightened. He missed Stef in this instant so very much he felt his heart ache.

Burbero, the surly guard, now a sergeant and proud of it, had his permanent shadow, Piccolo, on his heels. He said officiously, "There is no need. Colonel would not approve. And let them out of The Hole confinement area. The colonel wouldn't approve of that either. I am instructed to follow only Colonel's orders."

The little dog spotted Pietro and bounced over to him.

"Scusi." Pietro caught the guard's arm so he could stop. He bent down and rubbed Piccolo's one ear and the nub. The little dog licked his hand tenderly.

Pietro's eyes filled with tears, and he whispered, *"Via con Dio, Stef. Via con Dio."*

50

COVER-UP

Iris woke up early to do her makeup before work. Her face was badly swollen. Her one eye was black and blue where Julian's fist had smashed into her. Thank goodness it was only slightly swollen. She could camouflage that. She looked worse today than when it happened. Buffer studied his mistress, trying to decipher why she was up before the sun.

"Please let him be safe. Please let him be safe. Please let him be safe." Her mantra started when she opened her eyes and continued until she got to the store. She knew she had to go in. It was the only place she'd learn what was happening at the camp. The camp had become the source of complete fascination now that the locals knew the Italians' time in their fair city was coming to an end. It was as if they'd come full circle. Once considered the scum of the earth and the deadliest of enemies, the men inside carried a macabre mystique. Most of the locals had, in one way or another, been charmed by the Italians. As road workers, they were cheerful and friendly. As entertainers, they were beyond any measure of excellence yet seen in South Africa, or so the rumor mill had it from "excellent" sources within the camp. Some had a taste of Pietro's vocal prowess in his only performance outside the camp a year or more ago and were still talking about his gift. As bridge builders, they had managed to impress the pants off local engineers. That shouldn't be such a stretch, considered Iris. The Italians had been building bridges more than 1800 years before anybody thought to "discover" southern Africa.

Iris turned to her attentive audience of one. "Buffer, my sweet boy, I think I have managed to cover most of it. It hurts like hell, and if you don't look too closely, you don't see it, do you?" She put her face down to his level and looked into his adoring eyes. "Thank you. I thought not."

She walked around in circles, bending and gently flexing her hurt, badly grazed knee, then picked up her handbag and tried her best to bounce out of the door as she usually did, lest her mother was watching.

At the store, one of the department managers walked past and smiled politely, and Iris tried to smile back. *Ouch.*

If only she knew what was happening. The last two days had been torture. She was desperately worried about Pietro. Her eyes filled with tears, which stung like hell. She flinched in pain, dabbed her eyes and fished into her handbag for a sleeve of Grandpa Headache Powder. How the hell was she going to get through another day without knowing? Her hand stopped its feverish search for the miracle cure when she saw Sergeant Rogers come in to her store, his legs pumping. Oh, God. Something was terribly wrong.

His words tumbled out before he reached her counter. "I was with the colonel in Durban. Julian came back with a huge bandage on his head with diagnosed concussion. He doesn't know who accosted him, but he reckons it was a prisoner because he glimpsed a brown uniform."

Iris held two fingers to her throat, feeling her heart right there—trying to break through her skin. "Did anyone confess?"

Rogers's face broke into an unexpected smile. "They all did."

It was too soon to be relieved. "Where was Julian when accosted?" she asked.

"Outside the prison on that service road—oh, you wouldn't know it. His car was still parked there, in the boonies. Battery dead as a doorknob. The car was running and lights were left on. His car was untouched, so it wasn't a robbery. Found his whip hanging from a branch too high to reach. *That's* not coming back. What a pleasure. Bet he won't be as much of a bastard without it." His face went red. "Sorry about the language."

"How puzzling. How'd he get to hospital?" It took every bit of resolve to remain poised.

"That's the odd thing. Nobody knows. Staff said they found him in a heap at the emergency door." His palms, as well as his eyebrows, lifted in puzzlement.

The obvious confusion was a gift to her. It was clear that nobody knew what the hell had happened, so she could compound the mystery by making it so murky, nobody would bother to get to the bottom of it. Word was Julian wasn't all that popular in town either, what with his pompous demeanor and his often belligerent, drunken ways.

"Hmm. Think about this, Sergeant. If a prisoner had escaped and Julian went after him, why would he do so alone? Let's face it, Julian's cruel, not brave. And then, why in the world wouldn't the prisoner, once he'd accosted Julian, not have left him there to rot and fled off in the waiting car, to continue the escape in style?"

"Well, that's the mystery, Iris. Ahem. Miss Fuller."

She was on a roll. "Well, if you ask me, Julian went on a bender, as we all know he is apt to do. He fell down drunk or stole somebody's girl. Now he's blaming the Italians."

"Could be. Could be." He nodded in agreement.

Iris dreaded asking the question but had to know. "How did he pay back the Italians for attacking him?"

"I hear he lined them up and drilled them for hours to find the guilty party."

"Sounds like him," Iris said.

"And when Julian singled out the smallest chap and started beating him, your young hero stepped in and confessed. To protect the little guy, no doubt."

Iris felt her heart twist in fear. She refused to give in to her jelly legs again but had to grab on to her counter for old times' sake. Before Pietro, that glass counter was, well, just a counter. Now it kept her upright quite bloody often when her "love legs" conked out. But it was time she bucked up and got her balls back, so to speak. RAF language and all that.

Thank God the sergeant didn't notice her clutching and un-clutching; he was too engrossed in the telling. "Julian was so angry, his head nearly exploded through the bandage. When I left to tell you, Colonel was trying to sort things out, and the fence guys—the bundle of confessors he instructed be chained to the perimeter for punishment—were being sequestered in the mess hall to try and determine the true culprit. But you can bet your last pound nobody will ever tell." He grinned almost as if he was proud of his captives' resolve.

Her voice was a whisper. "And Pietro?"

"I heard he was in hospital. Got a hell of a beating from Julian." Rogers looked down.

"Is he all right, Sergeant?"

"I heard he was okay. A few cracked ribs. He's tough. No need to worry." The sergeant smiled kindly. "I must get back before I'm missed. Pity, in a way, that the war's ending. You won't have the chance to get to know him. Hell of a guy. Hell of a guy. Bye for now, Miss Fuller." He tipped his cap.

"Thank you so much, Sergeant," Iris said to his back. Her

head buzzed. Then she knew with certainty what she had to do. She was suddenly glad her face looked worse today than the day after Julian beat her. She lifted the phone from under the counter. It was to be used only in emergencies. She rung the handle. "Colonel Cairns, please."

51

TEA FOR TWO

Iris had never been more sure of anything as she sat near the back of the small tearoom, away from the window.

As she saw his jeep screech to a halt outside, she pulled the veil over her makeup-free face. She knew her bright red lipstick would detract from what the veil didn't hide.

The colonel ducked his head as he entered the café. It was just as well the top of their fridge had never been cleaner. Poor teetering Lena saved her mother from being too messy to snag a husband. Iris couldn't believe she could be trite at a time like this!

He looked at Iris quizzically with a half smile. As he pulled out his chair, she realized he was nervous, a state that gave her an unexpected edge and endorsed her commitment.

"Miss Fuller! To what do I owe this unexpected pleasure?"

She smiled thinly, and it hurt like hell. She already had a teacup in front of her, so he ordered his own. Once the tea was poured into the dainty cup by the dainty owner, he leaned forward in the dainty chair, waiting for her answer. She'd chosen the venue carefully so he would feel oversized, bullish, a wee bit out of place and uncomfortable.

"What are your intentions, Colonel?" She had no trace of a smile.

Had he been a man of lesser breeding, he'd have spat out that first sip of his English tea.

"Intentions?" he spluttered.

"Yes." She waited.

"Well, she is an amazing woman. Fascinating in every way ... "

She waved her hand impatiently. "Your intentions?"

"Of course. Of course." He took a deep breath and squinted, trying to look earnestly into her eyes past the black veil, she guessed. He squirmed like a guilty little boy just caught cheating on a science paper.

"I—we wanted to wait for a formal get-together so we could tell you." He shook his head, struggling. "Your mother and I should be together when we do this." His cheeks were crimson.

Iris leaned forward, in charge. "Cut the bull, Colonel."

He sat back. "I asked her to marry me. She said yes."

"Wonderful." She smiled, satisfied.

"So, you are all right with this? Your mother was so nervous even though you will soon leave her for America." Huge relief dropped seven years from his strained face.

But it was time to show, not tell.

His face changed steadily from happiness to confusion to sheer shock as he watched her take off her Mandarin-style jacket, exposing the angry bruises around her neck and upper arms and the deep, tar-embedded grazes on her elbows and up her one arm. She spared him her knees. For now.

Then she lifted the veil.

His gasp was audible as he raised a hand to his mouth. She kept her one eye deliberately shut to exaggerate the engorged, navy fist-print at the lower end. So swollen was her cheekbone, the right side of her nose looked like it was dented. She knew it was shocking. It was her intention.

He hadn't blinked yet, and his mouth was open. Iris guessed he'd seen much worse in his tenure, but never on a woman. These sorts of things just didn't happen in polite society.

"Does your mother know?"

She shook her head no.

"Who in God's name did this to you?"

"Julian."

His tone was incredulous. "Our ... my ... Julian?"

"The very same."

"What the f— excuse me, hell?"

She felt a rush of apprehension about what was to come and saw him recognize a chink in her armor, though he didn't understand why. *Grab him while he's confused.*

"Pietro and I are in love," Iris blurted.

He looked like he couldn't take any more surprises and shook his head denying what he'd just thought he heard.

"Pietro?" He had a silly smile on his face like she had made a joke.

"Your prisoner. Pietro Saltamachio."

"How?" He was looking directly at her now.

"The first time we saw each other, on opposite sides of the camp fence, we knew."

"But it's just infatuation. Desire to have something unobtainable. On both sides."

"Colonel, I am my mother's daughter. Don't underestimate me."

His mouth clamped shut. Both hands fleetingly touched his ears like the hear-no-evil monkey. But he pushed through by sitting upright to prepare for this new onslaught. Brave man. She'd found her mother a good one.

"And how often have you seen each other?" he whispered,

still shaking his head. She recognized he really didn't want to know.

"Fleeting moments at my store counter when he picked up supplies, then a very few nights, outside the camp."

His eyes made him look like a nag-apie, the Afrikaans for bush baby, whose huge, wide eyes dominated small heads.

He leaned forward. "Outside?" He could barely spit out the word. He reached in his pocket and pulled out a cigar and clenched it, unlit between his teeth.

Iris passed her hand in front of her mouth slowly, indicating he should whisper.

"Just three and a smidgeon glorious nights. Enough to know. Enough to be surer than I've ever been about anything in my life."

"How ... who else was involved in this?"

"No one else knew but the taxi driver, and I took care of him. Pietro broke out of camp and back in again. I went home."

He collapsed back as if the nozzle keeping in his air had been quickly removed. "Good God." She waited for the dainty chair to give way. It might be a sign that she should shut up. But the damn thing was surprisingly sturdy.

In for a penny, in for a pound. "We love each other," she whispered.

They sat in silence. Iris held her breath, not daring to move a muscle while he processed the news, his face vacillating between shock, fear and anger.

"Julian caught you." He nodded. Understanding.

"No! Julian saw me on the camp's service road in a taxi. He didn't see Pietro. I made sure of that, though much against Pietro's grain. Julian was cruising the streets, likely looking for trouble. Perhaps he followed the taxi, lights off. I don't know. He was drunk. He found me in the back seat. I made an excuse, which he bought because his mind was ... " She disconnected her gaze from his. "Elsewhere." She was ashamed for the first time.

There'd been too much to worry about to feel the humiliation of being beaten and nearly raped. Until now.

"I am so, so sorry." She was. Truly. Not for their love or for being together, or for the chance to expose Julian for what he was, but that she had to force the Colonel into this mess when all he wanted was to glory in the end of the war and begin a new life with her mother.

His voice was surprisingly gentle. "And then what?"

"Pietro came up behind Julian, just as he was going to force ... " She could say no more. He nodded, understanding.

"Colonel. I wanted him dead. I hoped with all my heart that Pietro's blow had killed him. I wanted to bash that stone over and over again into his skull for what he did to me, to Pietro, to Stef, to Antonio ... "

He looked freshly horrified. "You *know* all these people?"

"No. No." She tried to smile again. Ouch! "Just people Pietro cares about and talks of. We didn't have prisoner parties, if that's what you are afraid of. Other than the taxi driver, nobody else knew. Promise." She guessed lying was the least of her sins of late.

"But you didn't kill him. Then what?" His voice was flat.

"The thing is, the important thing is, I *would* have killed him if it wasn't for Pietro. He stopped me from bringing the stone down on his head to really do the bastard harm. Then I would have left him there to bleed to death. But Pietro insisted the taxi take him to hospital and hurry me home. The rest of my America money was paid to the driver so he could start a new life in Durban. Away from any repercussions from Julian. He's long gone, so you don't have to worry about him. He's more afraid than any of us."

The colonel was stupefied.

"When I woke up yesterday morning, the stone was on my pillow, next to me."

"And Pietro?"

"Last I saw him, he was in Julian's car, contemplating switching the lights off so the battery wouldn't go flat." She smiled. She couldn't help it. "That's just who he is."

"He left the lights on."

"Good for him." Her genuine laugh was so unexpected for both of them that he joined in. But he stopped quickly, his humor replaced by hard anger. The pain stopped her laugh short. Her fingers massaged her aching jaw.

"Where is he now, Colonel?"

"He's recovering in the infirmary under Doc's orders. He has a few broken ribs and is pretty banged up, but he'll live. Until I get my hands on him."

She prayed his last sentence was a figure of speech.

A knot of fear twisted in her gut as she watched him get angrier. She'd expected it. He was a high-ranking colonel, and that didn't come without a hefty dose of pride. He was used to giving orders that were obeyed. Her Pietro was in dire jeopardy.

He lit his cigar, blowing a billow of smoke away from her injured face.

She'd carefully weighed her options before this meeting. She had to expose Julian for what he was, and to do that, she had to tell the colonel about Pietro. Now her biggest challenge was to save Pietro from harm.

"That little bastard took me for a fool." Words pushed through tight lips around his cigar.

"Colonel, Pietro has nothing but immense respect for you. He is eternally grateful for you letting music back into his life. He idolizes you. He would never take you for granted. He never escaped—really. He left, yes. But he went right back. He would never have shamed your status and your rank by making his escape known, even though the two of us could have run away."

Damn, playing to his ego wasn't working. She doubted he even heard her last words. His nostrils flared. Dark red and sweating, he looked like a raging bull.

"I gave him freedom to sing, and that wasn't enough for him."

"It's my fault, Colonel. He did it for me. He would never have defied you without me. It was my fault. Blame me. I begged him to meet me."

She leaned over and grabbed his arm firmly, trying to bring him down from his anger. "Please, please understand. Being apart, not being able to talk or touch, was sheer torture for us. We are completely in love, Colonel. And the war is ending. He will go home to Italy, and we have no idea when we will see each other again after this war. Please, try to understand."

He refused to meet her gaze and shook his head from side to side, removing his arm from her vise grip.

"That bastard is Hole-bound until the war ends. I don't give a shit that he's recovering."

Iris's stomach contracted. "Please, Colonel, please, I beg you. Not The Hole. Before your time, Julian threw Antonio the Marconi Man ... " He looked perplexed and confused. Clearly, he wasn't privy to all the inside information. "Well, the poor guy baked in that Hole for two weeks, and he came out half-cocked. His brain fried in that Hole. What will it do to Pietro for an indefinite period?"

"He deserves everything he gets. And then some."

Iris knew it was time to pull the ace right out of her Mandarin-style sleeve. There was no other choice. Her priority was Pietro.

"So I know you're getting married, but do you love my mother?"

"Don't use my relationship with your mother to manipulate me, young lady!"

"I'm not. This is very relevant. Are you in love with my mother?"

"Leave your mother out of it! Do you realize you could be tried for treason? And damn well convicted. Pietro is the enemy. Have you thought of that? Treason. Did you know it's punishable by death? *I* wouldn't do that to you, but it may not be up to me when all of this comes out. When I am judged for allowing, no, *encouraging* ridiculous freedoms to a prisoner. When you are judged for fraternizing with our country's enemy, over and over again. We will all have to bear the consequences of our actions."

"And where will that leave my mother?"

"Iris, it's a matter of principle, and your mother is a very principled woman. And a very British subject. She's vehemently against our enemies, especially after losing your brother."

"You intend telling my mother about all this?"

"I see no way of avoiding it. I wouldn't start a life with your mother whilst keeping such a huge secret from her."

She couldn't hold back any longer. It was time.

"You don't like secrets, Colonel?" She hoped she sounded scary.

"Absolutely not. I'll keep nothing from your mother." He was so bloody confident he took a long puff of cigar. It gave her the perverse courage she needed.

"Are you sure there is nothing that she would hear about you that would disappoint her?"

"No secrets. It's not the man I am." He looked pompous for a second, and she was braver than ever.

Iris leaned forward and stared unflinchingly. Then she hummed a familiar tune.

It took the colonel a long moment to connect the tune with Iris.

" 'Let me call you sweetheart, I'm in love with you,' " she sang softly, just to twist the knife. She didn't like it, but by God, it was necessary.

"Stop!" His voice was very quiet, and his face was red with shame.

"Well? Have you told my beloved mother about your weekly trysts with a woman of ill repute in British quarters?"

"What do you want?"

"I want you to do what you must about Julian. I don't care about my reputation. When I leave here, I am going to the police station to press charges. I will tell them it was me who knocked Julian over the head in self-defense. Talk to the Italians at the camp. Have them open up to you, knowing they are safe, and let them tell you in their own words how Julian tormented and tortured them before you came along. Let them bury their shame and tell you about the atrocities he continued committing at night while on duty, even after you were the head of the camp."

He was white and still.

Her voice was low and expressionless. "Ensure he is locked up for a long, long time. He could have killed me. He *will* kill somebody else if you don't stop him. Don't have that on your conscience."

He looked like he'd been wrung out to dry and stamped out the cigar. He was no fool. "And?"

"And don't tell my mother about Pietro and me. Find ways to endorse Pietro, so in spite of his Italian-ness, my mother starts to like him. Then find a way, Colonel, to 'introduce' me to Pietro before the war ends so Mom is prepared for what's to come, when we can afford to see each other again, after he's deported back to Italy."

"And?" he asked, his expression impassive.

"And my mother doesn't know what happened to me. Any of

it. She doesn't know that her daughter was urinated upon, bashed and nearly raped. I can hide my bruises well. The authorities will be sworn to secrecy. So if this comes out, it won't be from me. And if she finds out you knew and didn't tell her about her own daughter's trauma? Well, you know my mother, Colonel."

"And?" He was furious.

"And please don't throw Pietro in The Hole."

"Now you are pushing your luck, young lady. Pietro will go into The Hole on a charge I will drum up. For as long as this war continues."

Her eyes filled with unexpected tears. She wiped them away quickly. "The war could go on for months. Please, Colonel. Please. I beg you. Just a week. And that's a long, long time in that brick box."

"It's the start of winter. He'll be fine. It's not that hot. But he needs to spend time contemplating his mammoth misdeed. Pietro needs that Hole to understand how abysmally he violated my trust."

"Colonel. Are you prepared to compromise your obvious kindness and compassion for your ego? That doesn't sound like the kind of man my mother should marry."

"Don't manipulate me."

She tried again. "Damn it, Colonel. Nobody but you, Pietro and I know what happened. Nobody knows Pietro was ever outside the camp. It's not that you will lose face. The respect you've rightly earned will remain long after the war. You're a hell of a leader. Nobody knows that better than Pietro. And me. And my mother."

His silence scared her more than his objections. When he broke it, it was far from what she wanted to hear.

"Three weeks. It has to be long enough to teach him a lesson."

"He could lose his mind in three weeks. Shame on you to do that to another human being. You make me wonder if you're really any better than Julian."

Silence.

There was no more to be said. She pulled the veil over her eyes, picked up her handbag, and stood up, wobbling a bit on her painfully stiff leg. She leaned in to whisper in his ear ever so politely, "Colonel, what was done in the name of true love was not intended to hurt anyone. I know you will do what's right. My mother couldn't be that wrong about the man she intends to spend the rest of her life with. And as her loving daughter, I just couldn't allow her to make such a mistake."

As she limped slowly to the dainty door, she sang, "Let Me Call You Sweetheart" loud enough for him to hear. She had given her Ibhubesi best.

52

THE HOLE

Enzo was hugely comforted by Pietro's constant bursts of song from The Hole, most of the day and well after lights out. He knew that Pietro's broken ribs were likely inhibiting any kind of full aria, but the guy was making an effort, which was a relief.

As a show of solidarity, the men gathered every night around the perimeter fence that separated The Hole from the rest of the camp, and as one voice, they sang along with Pietro. Antonio well remembered Pietro's constant chatter; though he couldn't always hear the actual words, he was immensely comforted. He told all the men what his friend had done for him, and because of it, there was always someone on the perimeter, keeping Pietro sane.

The guards had all but stopped their policing of the camp. What was the use? The war was nearly over, and where you came from mattered less than what you would do to fix the mess that was the war-torn world.

In the brick building opposite the camp, plans for the men's return to Italy were well under way.

"La Donna E Mobile" they sang, and Enzo wished Pietro could see how happy Piccolo was in the arms of Burbero. The little mutt was the only one guaranteed a good home at the end of this war.

As the last notes of the song reached their zenith, Piccolo jumped down, turned his snout up to the moon and howled as he used to do when Stef played his violin. Enzo knew Pietro's eyes would be as wet as his and all the others surrounding The Hole's perimeter.

A few weeks ago, Enzo caught Pietro in a private moment, bearing down in pain. He'd been worried sick, and when the pain passed, Pietro shared the saga of his dodgy appendix and his attempt to control it from bursting. He shared Doc's remedy of the experimental pills and the herbs Doc had recommended. Pietro hoped he could postpone the inevitable until "just the right time."

Of course, Enzo—thinking himself Pietro's surrogate mother and father—scolded him severely. But Enzo knew no more stubborn, determined and, damn it, brave man.

And he simply couldn't live with himself if his friend had an attack in The Hole.

Later that night, he expertly cut a square in the fence to The Hole and snuck into the perimeter carrying two six-foot-long tubes that he found in the shack they used for props.

On the side of the brick structure that faced away from the night patrol, he began grinding the tubes into the rain-soaked ground. Then, in spite of his middle age, he was nimble enough to leverage himself up with the help of the wall and balance on the poles like he was on a pair of stilts. He successfully reached the little air vents at the very top of The Hole.

Damned if his friend wasn't catching some shuteye. It took three frantic yells while doing some serious balancing before Pietro's voice responded, startled.

"Enzo?"

"Yes. You all right, friend?"

"Never better."

"Tap Tap's in jail."

"Wahooooooo!"

"War's over. It should be official in about a week."

There was silence from The Hole.

"I brought your appendix pills. I'll throw them through the little holes."

"Enzo. You are such a good friend. Always my salvation."

Enzo smiled and nearly lost his balance. He steadied himself like a circus performer, fished in his pocket and then slowly raised his hand and pushed a small piece of knotted material through the little vent.

"I am going to get two poles up my *posteriore* if I don't get off this fucking thing now. You catch the pills?"

"Yes, yes. I have them. Thank you, Enzo. My savior."

"I love you like a son, my friend." Enzo was choked up and had to clear his throat before he continued. "Soon. Iris will be waiting for you. However long it takes. She is yours. You are hers. *Via con Dio,* Pietro."

Enzo jumped down and massaged his insteps where the poles had pushed their way through the soles of his shoes. And then he wiped away his tears.

Inside The Hole, Pietro untied the piece of cloth. He smiled as he thought of the great lengths to which his friend had gone to deliver his lifesaving pills.

In the corner of the tiny space was a deep hole in the ground. It served as a commode in these subpar accommodations. A mud hole is all it was, but distinctly an upgrade courtesy of Colonel Cairns. Until now, no one had enjoyed the improvement. He felt himself smiling. That bastard was locked away. He didn't know how that happened, but he was damned sure his Iris had something to do with it. She was fearless.

He opened up the cloth and saw the familiar tablets Doc had given him months ago, and he did to them what he had done with all the others since he'd heard the war was nearly over.

He threw them into the mud potty, where even in the sparse light, he could make out their bright whiteness dotting the perimeter of his fine new shithole.

53

CELEBRATIONS AND COMMISERATIONS

She was in the store when she heard the news.

The store manager descended the stairs and called all staff and customers together. It was most disconcerting for those who waited and those who were waited upon to stand elbow to elbow. One didn't touch the middle—or God forbid the lower—class if one could help it.

Iris didn't care, but others most certainly did. The British class system was still alive and kicking in Pietermaritzburg. The war had made a good dent, but not deep enough to amalgamate the classes of the whites, let alone incorporate their servants. Superiority was everything. "But nothing," Iris knew. She valued her Zulu surrogates' wisdom far more than her mother's or King George VI's.

The manager looked so pleased with himself, Iris thought that whatever the announcement, clearly he must be solely responsible.

She leaned her bum against the counter, preparing for a long, drawn-out speech.

"The war has ended."

"The war has ended," he said again. This life-changing news trumped his usual need for pomp and ceremony.

Far away, she heard yelps and screeches and feverish prayers of thanks as her heart sank to her patent leather shoes.

Oh, please, God. Find a way not to send him away. Don't do this to us. We must have spent many lifetimes trying to find each other. Please don't send him away. She felt she'd been punched in the stomach, and nausea threatened.

She stood up straight as she thought: "Thank God my Pietro can come out of The Hole now, and it's only been eight days since my meeting with the colonel. "

Whether or not he would have kept to his threat of three weeks in The Hole, she would never know. And perhaps he didn't, either. Iris would believe the best in the colonel.

Having used her mother flagrantly as a pawn, Iris owed them both that much.

54

SURPRISE AFTER SURPRISE

Pietro had been out of The Hole for two days. In spite of the seven showers he'd had since his release, he could still smell the stench on his person.

His side hurt like a bitch. He'd taken two pills yesterday because he'd heard it would be a week till they were ready to be shipped home. Timing was everything.

He was playing God with his own body. It was the only way. He knew the risks, but anything less would not do their love justice. He hoped to hell he knew what he was doing.

There was no explanation to anyone why Pietro was thrown in The Hole the day Julian was arrested. Pietro was prepared to take the punishment because he'd committed the crime. But nobody else besides Antonio and Enzo knew that. Not even Rogers understood why Pietro deserved such a fate.

A red, gold and yellow sunset, the magnificence of which he'd never seen, lit up the sky.

"I see you Stef. I miss you. But I see you, so I know you are here with me."

The vibrant colors were blocked out by a man's silhouette, and his heart lurched.

"Stef?" he asked hopefully.

"Pietro! You won't believe. It's your lucky day." Rogers was grinning from ear to ear, but Pietro felt desolate disappointment.

Enzo said, "What? He is going back in The Hole? Lucky, lucky Pietro!"

Rogers ignored the jibe. "Come. Colonel wants you."

As he unlocked the gates of the camp to let Pietro out, unchained and without handcuffs, he whispered: "I don't know what you did to deserve this, but man, am I happy for you!" He slapped Pietro on the back, grinning. With that, Pietro allowed his heart to quicken.

Rogers led him to a jeep that already had its lights on, ready to go. Colonel was in the passenger seat, his arm resting on the rim of the door, fingers drumming impatiently.

Pietro couldn't help himself. He grinned at the man he had become so fond of. "Colonel. Happy am I to see you."

"Just get in the damned jeep," the colonel barked.

Pietro was confused. He was the one who should be pissed. He was locked up for, as far as everyone knew, stopping a sadist's blows to an innocent man!

With Rogers at the wheel, Pietro enjoyed the wind in his hair. It had been a long time. He closed his eyes and was transported back to the time he'd ridden in the main float in the front seat of an Austro-Daimler in 1938 in the Ivrea carnival, after his performance at the opera house. For a few precious seconds, he smelled the hemp plants covering the bell tower and heard the float spectators chanting his name. But he'd looked at Stef, who said, "Get over yourself, Pietro." He felt a pang of longing for his friend and a homesickness he hadn't felt since he'd met Iris. He missed the smell of Italy, her dank walls, the sight of her fortitude in her ancient cobbled stones and crooked bridges. He knew he always would, to some degree. Roots ran deep. They shaped you. Kept you grounded. You couldn't escape them, good or bad.

Without willing it, her inquisitive face overshadowed his memories, and he felt his smile starting from the inside. He thought of her smell, so familiar. Her mesmerizing cat's eyes. Her cascading dark red hair. He thought of her easy ecstasy and her gay abandon. He thought of her humor and her bravery. He would give up anything for her. Wherever his Iris was, there would be home.

Where the hell were they going?

Incredibly, they stopped in front of Iris's house. Pietro's chest became a brick. Was this how it felt to have a heart attack? Oh, God, he must somehow have incriminated her. He would die if he was the cause of her shame or social disgrace. If it were so, he hoped there was a firing squad waiting for him inside.

The jeep switched off. He looked at the colonel's stoic profile, willing him to give a hint of what was in store. Nothing. The man wouldn't even look at him. This was serious. *Dio mio. Our Father who art in heaven ... Ha! Your God is English now.*

The colonel got out, and Sergeant Rogers stayed in the car.

"Follow me," the colonel barked at Pietro.

And he did, all the way to the front door.

The colonel's knock was opened to an attractive woman whose face shone as she gazed up at the colonel and moved into him quite naturally. And then she saw Pietro, in his prisoner browns, standing in the colonel's shadow. She blushed and moved back.

The colonel stepped sideways and gestured toward Pietro.

The brick in Pietro's chest doubled in weight.

And then there was complete confusion as the colonel smiled, as if proud. "This is Pietro Saltamachio. You heard him perform. You liked his voice."

She smiled at him. Surprised. Kind.

Good God. Iris's mother? The brick thudded against his ribcage. Remarkable resemblance. Why was she smiling? What kind of trap was this?

He glanced back at the jeep, wondering briefly if he should dash back to the safety of predictable Rogers.

"Yes. I remember." She was still smiling. The brick lifted, just a half an inch.

"Well, as I told you on the phone, Margaret, I thought it would be a humane gesture and a nod to the end of the war to bring Pietro over to chat to Iris as a kindness before his departure. He is dizzy about her, having seen her performing her nursing duties for the prisoners and on his visits to her Ross & Co. counter for supplies for the camp operas. I thought this meeting could do no harm. Almost an international 'Let bygones be bygones' kind of humanitarian token. And he's pretty much paid his dues with years in concentration camps, having been found near death in the Sudanese desert."

Pietro's mouth was wide open. He couldn't believe his ears. Boy, was he getting the hard sell. *Why in God's name? Thank you, but why?*

"As a show of peace, I agree, but let's not forget, my Gregg was killed by Italians." Margaret Fuller was serious, her smile gone.

Pietro's heavy brick burst from his chest and exposed his heart. He was no longer a third-class prisoner of war. He was Pietro Saltamachio, world-class opera star. *No!* More than that. Much more. He was Pietro Saltamachio, in love with this woman's daughter, and what he said and did next would determine his future.

He brazenly took Mrs. Fuller's hand, and the colonel reacted immediately, but she shook her head ever so slightly, giving the big man her consent for Pietro's forwardness.

"Forgive Mussolini for the side with German, Signora.

Italian people do not wish to fight. Forgive your son killed in Italy. I hope a German, not Italian, was responsible. *Molto dispiaciuto.* Sorry. Sorry. Forgive."

She let him keep holding her hand. Her eyes were full of tears. He felt his own fill up.

"You daughter, Iris. I wish to marry." The colonel put a "friendly" arm over Pietro's shoulder, squeezing it way too tightly.

"That was quick, young man!" Big fingers dug deep.

"Of course, only when I have chance to know herself." He was aware his English was faltering. He wasn't sure if it was for effect or whether nervousness had spawned it.

To Pietro's immense relief, Mrs. Fuller's mouth turned upward in a small smile. Pietro was enchanted by her. This was his Iris in twenty years. How lucky could he be?

"And how in the world do you intend to do that? She's going to America to design clothes for the movies, and you're going back to Italy," Iris's mother wanted to know.

"You love somebody enough, anything possible." His smile was automatic, but he was shocked to the quick.

America? Iris? His Iris?

"Well, you two. Don't just stand there. Come in. We'll all catch our deaths with the door open in May."

Pietro thought he was dreaming. How the hell did this happen? She gestured toward the living room. "Let's all go into the lounge. I'll call Iris to join us."

The colonel reacted like lightning. He took both of Mrs. Fuller's hands and said, very softly: "Let the youngsters have the lounge. I need you, my Margaret, alone in the kitchen. Now!" His charm was captivating, and Pietro had a moment of pure admiration for this incredible man as he watched Iris's mother melt under his soft touch and commanding air.

"Down, boy!" she chided softly, not intended for Pietro's ears.

She ushered Pietro into a comfortable, once opulent, room. "Please sit. I'll get Iris."

He must be dreaming. There was simply no possible way this could happen in real life.

Pietro sat at the edge of a worn couch, watching the door. The colonel stood just outside, still refusing to look at him.

Iris appeared at the door, and despite her resolution to get some stamina in her love legs, her knees buckled as her eyes widened in shock. She grabbed the doorframe.

"Come, my Margaret," said the colonel huskily, "to the kitchen with you, wench!" Pietro heard her giggle as they disappeared, but not before the colonel, shielding Mrs. Fuller's view with his body, gently pushed Iris in and closed the living room door.

Iris rushed toward Pietro, and before he stood up, she was in his arms. They fell back into the sparsely stuffed couch, clinging together like magnets. Pietro didn't even care that his ribs hurt. He wanted her closer still. The feel of being in each other's arms was heady, intoxicating, comforting and safe. He kissed her hungrily to make sure he could actually taste her. You couldn't taste in a dream, could you?

Shock and confusion returned all too soon. He gently took her face in his hands and pulled her back so he could look at her.

"What? How, Iris?"

Her smile was enigmatic.

A sudden jab felt as if a blunt blade had been twisted through his skin and deep into his side. The pain pushed the breath out of him.

Her face twisted in concern. "What's wrong? Please tell me The Hole didn't harm you!"

"No, no, my love. All good. Nothing hurts when love for you

is in my heart. What happen, Iris? How is this possible?" Pietro gestured around her own living room.

All she did was hum.

He was more confused than ever. "Tell all. All," he begged.

Deep admiration fused with tender love washed over him as she told him the details of her tea with the colonel.

She ended lavishly with: " 'Let Me Call You Sweetheart' made this happen, Pietro."

He kissed her, their tears of laughter and relief mingled. Apart only to catch their breath, he held her face and butterfly-kissed her freckles. His hands moved to her hair.

There was something different about her.

His senses and his brain had been on overdrive. Now that he understood the miracle of this night had happened through Iris's courage and it wasn't a dream, he was back in the moment. He ran hands over her head of short, soft, red curls and felt a great shock. He pulled back and looked at her. Her red hair was a halo of curls. Gone were her luscious locks.

Her eyes were misty. "It was the only way I could make some money toward my fare. It seems human hair wigs are in high demand. Especially red ones."

His mind whirled as he thought of Iris's mother's words. *Going to America.* His heart dropped to his newly shined boots.

"America?" He croaked out the word, wishing he didn't have to say it at all.

And then he watched her mouth saying the words: "You are more important than America. I realized after I fell in love with you that Italy was my only destination. Though I have to pay back my fare for the America trip I'm not going on first, then it's Italy, here I come! And into your arms, whenever that may be."

He was so relieved, tears filled his eyes. She'd cut off her luscious, long hair for him. She, a fashion beacon, who used her long hair for a million different looks. It was one of the things he loved about her. A sexy, modern, interesting woman who used fashion to express her individuality. A halo of short curls was definitely not fashionable. He was awestruck, for the second time in the last half-hour, by the incredible woman she was and deeply humbled by her courage and conviction. And her sacrifice for him.

Her eyes dropped, and he realized she was embarrassed by her new look. "It will grow," she promised him, refusing to meet his gaze.

"*Mia Cara.* You have never looked more beautiful to me, and nothing will please me more if your hair has no time to grow before I see you again." And he meant it with all his heart. He ran his fingers through her curls and pulled her head toward his. He showed her tenderly, then passionately, how much he meant it.

A loud knock on the door made them guiltily jump apart and straighten clothes.

"Coming," Iris promised. She walked backward so they would not lose a second looking at each other.

She opened the door, and Buffer bounded in. The dog went straight to Pietro, his tail wagging. Mrs. Fuller and the colonel stood in the doorway as Pietro roughed the big dog's ears.

"Heavens!" said Mrs. Fuller. "That dog doesn't like anyone who likes Iris. It's almost as if he knows you."

Colonel saved the moment. "Dogs usually know who the good guys are."

Iris had disappeared down the passage.

Mrs. Fuller must have taken pity on him, because she smiled and said, "You know, Pietro, strange things happen. My mother was an Afrikaans school teacher; my father, an English cavalry soldier during the Boer War. He was her knight on a white horse who literally swept her off her feet." Pietro saw Iris's mother's eyes mist over. "They were a real-life Romeo and Juliet. You never know, Pietro, you just never know."

Iris dashed into the hall, holding a red chiffon scarf.

"Well, ladies, we have to get back. Lots to do before the guys leave us on Tuesday."

"Tuesday?" Iris gasped. "That's two days away."

"Yes. Indeed. That's why I thought you two should finally have a chance to chat before Pietro leaves us," Colonel said without emotion.

Mrs. Fuller looked at the colonel with blatant admiration. "You are such a humanitarian, Peter. I am not nearly as kind. Just don't expect me to *ever* forgive those bloody Jerries!"

"I would never have brought one of those home," chortled the colonel.

"Nice that Iris got to chat to a talented, may I say, handsome young man, even if he *is* Italian," Iris's mother said, smiling at Pietro, who was being herded to the front door by the colonel.

Iris put out her hand to Pietro in a formal, almost masculine show of courtesy. "So very nice to spend time with you, at last, Pietro, that is without your exuberant friends buying supplies and the guards, of course."

He took Iris's hand and shook it. "My pleasure. Thank you for your *ospitalità* ... hospital, Iris. Mrs. Fuller." He picked up Iris's mother's hand and bowed ever so slightly as he held it.

The colonel jostled Pietro out of the door and down the steps. As soon as the elder went around to his side of the jeep, Pietro turned around so he could see Iris.

She bounded three steps at a time to reach him and flew into his arms, sobbing. He held her while watching her mother over her shoulder. The elder's mouth was agog.

Far in the distance, Pietro heard Mrs. Fuller say, "Well, that was fast."

To which he vaguely heard the colonel shoot over his shoulder, with a laugh in his voice: "Just like her mother."

He didn't see or hear what happened around them next. He closed his eyes and blocked his ears to only the sound of Iris's touch and her sobs against his cheeks. God, how he loved her.

"Enough now!" Pietro felt a foreign appendage come between them and realized it was the colonel's hand.

Iris hissed at him, "A moment, Colonel. A moment." And the big man backed off. Pietro filed that away to think about later when he could concentrate all his admiration on the fire in his remarkable woman.

Still clutching Pietro, she bunched the red scarf in her hand, and he felt her push it into the waistband of his trousers as she whispered: "I will be at the dock. Use this to wave so I can see you on deck. I will have Buffer and a red hat. When you wave the scarf, it will mean that you are sending your love, and I will wave my hat to show you the same."

First smoke, then the colonel's angry face came between them. They were both alarmed, so far removed from the real world they were. "Now!" He said between gritted teeth.

He grabbed Iris's hand and literally dragged her back to her mother. She refused to tear her eyes away from Pietro as she was led backward.

Colonel shouted down to Rogers: "You go. I will get a taxi back to camp."

Rogers herded Pietro into the back of the jeep. Pietro continued facing Iris so his eyes could remain locked with hers. As the jeep accelerated, he waved the red scarf with one hand while holding on for dear life with the other.

The jeep rounded a corner, and the darkness swallowed her up.

He felt tears sting his cheeks in the wind. Gone. *Dio mio.* She was gone. His emptiness was abysmal. He felt hollow and desperately sad. An empty vessel.

And then he found his resolve. His dogged determination rose like fire from within his belly and surged upward. If she could do what she did for him, he would make sure he did not get on that ship for her. For them.

On the front porch, Colonel stood between mother and daughter. Iris turned her wet face toward the colonel's ear and whispered, "Thank you." Louder, she said, "Mom, you have one pretty special man here. I think he will be perfect for our family." She kissed his cheek affectionately before she turned to go inside where her Buffer was waiting.

GOING, GOING, GONE

Fifty huge canopy-covered trucks were lined up on "their" service road. How cruel that he was to begin the journey to leave her so close to where they'd explored their love.

The sharp, constant pain had started in earnest the day before. It was so bad, his body heaved like a dog with a bone stuck in its throat, because there was nothing left in his stomach to vomit up. Between spasms, he'd escaped to a privacy stall in the ablution block so as not to put a damper on his friends' great excitement.

But there was no fooling them. Antonio was first to check on him, his jolly face blatantly fearful. Though the radio had reawakened the pragmatic, mechanical part of his brain, he remained childlike. Pietro made a concerted effort to calm his dear friend by telling him he was sick with having to leave Iris. Antonio understood and left him alone after much back-patting, Antonio's answer to all ills.

Enzo, who arrived a couple of hours later, was not nearly as gullible. "You look like shit. You need the doctor *now*. You look like you're going to die."

"You've been exposed to theater too long. You've become dramatic," Pietro managed.

"I will find Doc and bring him here. I won't let you die for anything. Not even Iris."

Pietro put a firm, sweaty hand on Enzo's wiry arm. "You will ruin my life if you get the doctor, Enzo. He could delay the ship. Then everyone is affected because of me. I have a plan."

"What kind of ridiculous plan leaves you dead?"

"I love you, my friend. Without you, these years would have been debilitating. I would have died in a fetal position with no shoes. Or I would have died mentally; that would've been far worse. You lifted me up from my intense despair. You and Iris made me whole again. Go back to Italy knowing you saved my life. No matter what."

"You sound like you *plan* to die."

"It's not my plan, but one can't always successfully play God."

"What *is* your plan?"

"All I know is that I will die if I can't stay with Iris, so I am trying to live."

"You are delirious, you horny young fool. Italy. Fame. It will keep you occupied until you can reunite with her."

"Fame? I don't need that anymore." Bile rose quickly, and he pushed Enzo away.

"What can I do?" Enzo's voice was helpless.

"You can bring me honey and a cloth for a poultice. Then you can fuck off and not draw attention to me. Pretend this is psychosomatic and I am deeply lovesick. Heartbroken. Now go, friend. Please. I don't intend to die. That would really foul things up."

The older man moved reluctantly toward the door.

"Then I will begin Plan B," Enzo said, and disappeared.

Pietro leaned against the wall and slowly sank to the floor.

He fished in his pocket and took out a pill. He'd known that he had to give them up and face the pain in order to time his full-blown appendix attack just right. But their ever-changing departure date made it difficult to know what to do. Tonight was too soon for the thing in his belly to misbehave.

He pushed the pill far down his throat so he wouldn't vomit it back up. Seriously, if he somehow jeopardized the others' triumphant return to Italy, that wouldn't be fair, but if he had misjudged it and it was too late, he would be on that fucking boat that would take him away from Iris. Perhaps forever. Then he might as well stop the pills altogether and die, because what were the chances of them seeing each other ever again? So slim. So very, very slim in spite of the high price of her beautiful hair she'd paid in advance. Bless her. A thousand times. Bless her. Who the hell knew when passengers would once again sail the high seas for pleasure? The world was too broken to rely on such a plan.

He swallowed hard, willing himself not to puke as he lay flat to let the pill safely go through his system and keep him in check until later. He took a trickle of honey every few hours and laid the poultice on his side.

In the wee hours, prior to roll call for all the tents to be taken down before they loaded the trucks, Pietro was able to make it back to their tent. It was a sign that all would be well, he felt sure.

Antonio's smile of welcome was humongous. A just reward for his effort.

Enzo was excited. "I know you, you stubborn horny fool mule! So, an ingenious plan has been conceived by yours truly, The Pussy Thief. If you insist, you can add 'Mastermind' to my title. The guys are all on board. We will fool them into thinking you are on the truck, then on the ship. Our forgers have your face on another's documents, and he will board the ship twice.

It's complicated, but trust me. Once we have sailed far enough out of port for it not to make sense to turn back, Rogers will open the envelope I gave him with strict instructions as to when and where to find you."

Pietro would likely never know the full story, but of this he was certain, his fellow prisoners were an enterprising, creative lot, and they'd walk through fire before they would let Pietro down.

***

This was his only chance. His last chance to stay.

The doctor's voice came back to him. "Absolutely no physical exercise. Especially no stomach strain. It could burst that appendix just like that." Doc had snapped his fingers.

"I am counting on that, Doc," he thought during the dismantling, folding and packing of their tent—their home for the last couple of years.

Using his core and not his back, he hoisted his friends, one by one, up and over the high back of the last truck in the long line, facing the direction they were headed.

"How will you get in? Nobody to hoist you up. It's too high, and you're no acrobat!" Antonio was the last and the heaviest to use Pietro as a staircase to get into the truck.

Pietro stepped up on to the mudguard. "I am not coming, my friend. I must stay with Iris. Go safely without me. When you are feeling alone, just close your eyes and you'll hear me in your ear: '*O Sole mio* ... ' " Tears sprung to Antonio's eyes, and as they sang, Pietro felt his wet cheeks blow icy cold in the winter air.

He and his boys had deliberately chosen the last truck in the convoy. Burbero peered from the driver's seat into the side-view mirror to make sure no one was left on the ground. "OK, you bloody merrymakers, we leave for the port! See you in Durbs!

Gotta say, I'm going to miss the hell out of you guys!" Pietro could hear he was grinning. His heart softened as he thought of Stef.

His friends knew the drill. They would distract Burbero so he wouldn't check his rear or side view mirrors again until they were well around the bend and out of sight.

He felt the big piece of solid machinery start to move. He shouted over the din, *"Andare con Dio i miei amici,"* and he pulled the red scarf out of his back pocket and jumped off the back of the truck.

Pietro felt a moment of suspended animation, and his last image was that of his beloved friends waving and Antonio's voice, loudest of all, during their collective, off-key "O Sole Mio."

In this moment of suspension, he felt all things: gratitude, joy, sadness, excitement, fear. But most of all, he felt love. In mid-air he positioned himself so that he'd land on the side of his appendix. And with Iris on his mind, Pietro willingly braced himself for his imminent crash.

A DOG'S TAIL/TALE

Buffer was on a leash. He was not happy about that, nor was he impressed by the embarrassing red bow around his furry neck. That his freedom was being held in check was disgraceful enough, but the bow? Lucky he loved her. Just lucky!

She looked beautiful in the hugest red hat he'd ever seen. At least they matched, he and his mistress. Color aside, they always had.

He could feel her wound-up tension. She didn't take her eyes off the big gray, unsteady building in the big water bowl. There seemed to be thousands of little brown ants milling about on the top of it. Ha! And he had heard humans say that dogs were color-blind. His eyes had dimmed over the years, and he couldn't quite make out what the brown things were, and they were too far away to smell, but they sure looked excited.

Humans! What else would emit periodic noise at different decibels? Holy bones! Thank goodness they didn't know how to howl. It would have been an insult to his ears.

His mistress was in no mood for the happy noises, he could tell.

She never took any notice of him, and that was annoying,

even when he licked her hand. She was so busy with the big red hat, waving it like a tail, as if she was happy to see somebody, but then he felt her disappointment, and the hat drooped along with her spirits.

There went the hat thing again like the back end of a rabid dog. Personally, he preferred the conservative approach. Wag only when you know you will be patted by someone you want to pat you. The hat-wagging brought mighty roars of approval from the gray, floating building. But that didn't seem to please her either. Boy! Was she in a mood!

She shouted every now and then, "Pietro? Pietro?" Of course the ants couldn't hear her, and her hand dropped down, still holding the hat, looking less and less chic, if he had to be honest. Her face lost its eagerness, her smile went away, and water poured from her eyes.

He paced in front of her, back to her side and in front of her again, looking at her intently. Nothing. He licked her hand with the roughest edge of his tongue. Now that should get her attention. Nothing. She didn't even know he was alive.

Oh, being a dog was a bitch! Ha! He fancied himself a comic sometimes but figured this wasn't the time to work on his material.

A kind of walkway attached to the floating building was taken away, there were lots of tug-of-war ropes that were flapped about, then the building drifted off into the big water bowl.

You'd think it was a full moon, the way she was howling! What was a dog to do? They were standing right at the rail, but she kept tugging at him like they should be going farther. There was that salty water in front of them, and he absolutely refused to go in that stuff. He would do anything for her, but there were lines he had to draw.

Oh, fleas! His mistress's wail got louder and louder as the brown-covered ant-people became small moving dots, and the floating building went farther and farther away. That big hat of hers was being waved so frantically, he felt the wind it created, and it smelled like those flowers the mom was always cutting and the prickly things that stuck into his feet and ...

He must be getting old. He so quickly slipped into a reverie of late. Where was he?

Ticks! How could he let this happen? She was in a heap on the pavement in a most unladylike position. Oh, the mom would be horrified. Mistress's legs were splayed and torn. Oh, fetching sticks! What was a dog to do?

She was wailing now, like he'd never heard her in all his years. A lost, hungry, confused, frightened puppy.

He nudged her chin to show her he was there. Nothing. He licked her face, and she just pushed him away. Not unkindly, mind. But he'd never been pushed away by her before, and frankly, he was hurt.

He really wanted to ignore her, to punish her for treating him—well, like a dog.

Her wailing was getting worse, and he was beside himself. Even when the man of the house, who had found him, never came home, he could comfort her. She'd never been like this. Never.

Her body seemed to fold in on itself, and he felt so sad, he wanted to howl, but sophisticated house-dogs simply didn't do the wild thing.

He nuzzled her, and though she seemed entirely unaware, he hoped she'd know she wasn't alone.

People were staring, but his mistress didn't notice. He wanted to bark them away and leave her to her grief, but he didn't want to scare her. Unlikely she would hear him anyway.

She'd turned her body on the concrete so she could watch the floating thing, which was just a spec on the horizon now, and she threw her red hat into the big, salt water bowl, but it blew back and into her hand. My! She was playing fetch without moving. Impressive.

Her heaving sobs had quieted only because she needed to breathe. Her eyes were unblinking, her body shaking as she watched the big water bowl. Something was making her hurt more than a thorn in the paw. He nudged her again. Nothing. He had no option but to get a little rough with her and used his snout to push her head up so she would acknowledge him.

At last it worked! Her eyes—they were nothing but water-slits now—looked at him for the first time in forever.

"My Buffer."

He was so relieved. He licked her mucus-glazed face, and her words tumbled out.

"Could I be so blind, Buffer? Could he have cared for me not at all? Why? Why would he not have been bothered to wave to me? I believed in him with all my heart. He made no effort to even lift his red scarf. I believed every word he told me and then, even before his ship left South African waters, he had forgotten me in his eagerness to get back to Italy. How could this be, my Buffer?"

Then another torrent of wails. Smelly bones!

He knew he had to do something to help her get up, but he couldn't leave her to find a person. So he did what he never imagined he'd stoop so low to do.

He howled.

Actually, once he got the hang of it, he wondered why he had never done it before. It was quite exhilarating. Liberating. He felt wild and wanton. But just for a second or two before he reminded himself of his mission.

Sweet lamb shanks! It worked! He found a person.

An elderly man bent down and patted his head. He ducked. He chose who could pat him, thank you very much.

"What is it, boy?"

Well? Can't you see? My mistress is desperately upset, and I need to get her into a moving thing and home.

The man looked at the mistress, and Buffer saw his face change.

Happy beef ribs! I found a good one. The man bent down and touched her shoulder.

"Are you all right, young lady?"

She didn't turn away from the water. He had to get her attention before the kind man went away. He squeezed his way past her shoulder, wedging himself uncomfortably between her and the bars that stopped her falling into the salty water bowl. He nudged her head up with his snout. He felt huge relief as her eyes focused for a minute and looked up.

"A taxi back to Maritzburg. Please?"

The nice person understood, because his head was going up and down. A good sign. The man went to lift her up, but Buffer couldn't let him touch her without him knowing he was watching. He nudged the man in warning.

"All right, old boy. Just helping her."

Old boy? Humph! A nice human perhaps, but rather rude!

A BLESSING AND A CURSE

Iris and Buffer were in the back seat of the taxi. She was only vaguely aware of how she got here. At least Buffer was by her side. An older man who was vaguely familiar waved at her through the window. She still had her red hat. She was sure she'd tossed it into the ocean.

There was an ear-piercing shriek as an army jeep blocked the path of the taxi, and a man leaped out and ran toward them.

Buffer bristled, then settled as his mistress recognized the man who'd yanked open the back door.

"Sergeant Rogers?" In Durban? Forty miles from camp? Iris was so confused.

"He's in hospital." Rogers was panting, like he'd run all the way from Maritzburg.

"What? Who? How?" asked Iris, shaking her head.

"Your Pietro. He jumped off the truck. His appendix burst."

"Jumped off the truck ... appendix?" *What the hell*? She scrunched her eyes as if that would clear her head and help her make sense of this confusion.

"Doc said he'd had a very tender appendix for the last four

months or so. Must have been using Doc's pills to quiet the appendix and then stopped them suddenly, to let the little bugger inside there do what the pills were preventing. Bloody thing burst!"

"Oh, God. Is he all right?" Iris's throat closed in fear. She wondered if he heard her.

"He's fighting for his life. They had to sail without him because of the complications. No telling how long it will be before he recovers, *if* he recovers."

"So he isn't on that ship?" It was all she could think about.

"No."

She was out of the cab with her arms around Rogers's neck before he finished.

He gently ducked his head and removed her still-clenched hands. "But you'd better come with me. Truth is, we don't know if he'll make it."

"What? No. No. No." Wait! Was he exaggerating? "Sergeant, an appendix won't kill you, will it?"

"A burst appendix may well, but worse than that, he is allergic to antibiotics, so his own body has to generate the antibodies to kill the infection. He's terribly weak."

"Oh, God, Sergeant! Let's go! Why are we still here? I'll make him strong."

"Better get your Samson suit on, Delilah! You'll need it. Come. Quickly! You and your dog, in with me. And pray, Miss ... Iris, like you've never prayed in your whole bloody life."

For seven days, Iris sat at his bedside in the main hospital, because the camp had been dismantled and the army building was bare. She barely ate or drank. She read him *The Prophet* a hundred times. She told him she loved him in every way she knew how. At night, when the hospital staff was mostly other-wise engaged, and his fever had subsided, she lay down next to his inert form and melded her body into his. She was comforted by his warmth and tried to transfer her health to him. She knew she would forever want to take away his pain, even at her own expense.

When he sweated and lashed out demonically, muttering in Italian and begging his mother to love him or asking if Stef could see him, she wept. But when his face took on its beautiful tenderness and he called her name, smiling, she felt her heart would break. She sat next to him and mopped his forehead with vinegar and water to bring down his temperature, whispered sweet nothings to him, studied his beautiful face and kissed him softly a thousand times a day.

She sang to him and laughed when, in his foggy state, he frowned. She knew her off-key warble would be like a siren during a harp solo to his operatic perfection, and she kissed his mouth because she loved him so.

No amount of Iris's begging, rage at the injustice, or more begging could convince the hospital administrator that Lena, Sofie and Fourfeet should be exempt from the "Whites Only" rules for visitors and patients.

Iris tried a different angle with the administrator, asking for her dog to join her in her vigil. She was turned down again and began to doubt her well-oiled persuasive skills.

She cried a lot, thinking of her world without him. She thanked God every hour on the hour for her gift, which lay in this bed. Then she asked him every half an hour if he would please spare her Pietro and make him well.

Sergeant Rogers visited often. He brought in a radio he'd found hidden in the chicken coop, along with an exquisitely carved mahogany bust that strongly resembled Iris.

On the sixth day, the colonel barged into the hospital room.

Though he was still angry with her, that was clear, his feathers were a little less ruffled, and Iris could see his admiration for Pietro when he looked at him. It touched her, and she was so happy she'd baked the worst-tasting cake in all of Maritzburg.

She'd been worried sick that Pietro would be jailed when he got well (she was convinced he would recover; her God wouldn't let him die after all this, surely!). She garnered every ounce of her Ibhubesi courage and asked: "Colonel, when my Pietro is better, then what? What will become of him?"

"I'm glad you asked. I was waiting for him to wake up, but the bloke seems intent on keeping us guessing."

"Please, Colonel!" Damn it. He was learning how to torture her.

"Well, this is certainly an unprecedented happenstance," he said, infuriating Iris with his peculiar way with words.

"What, Colonel? What for God's sake, will happen to him?"

"Well, there are no guidelines for a POW who misses his deportation ship due to illness. And the cost of housing only him in a humongous camp until a vessel can take him back to Italy is ridiculous. So I talked to the dean of the Cape Town University, and he is open to starting an opera curriculum. I told him I have just the man."

Iris thought she was hearing things.

"And legally?" she asked, afraid of the answer.

"Well, the law says if you have a job in this country, you can stay. The world is in such a mess, a single POW is the least of its problems, but I would caution you severely, *never, ever* to disclose what you two did behind my back. The consequences will be dire for many, many years to come."

Iris saluted. "I promise." And she meant it. Then she hugged him. He let her.

On the seventh day, her mother came in. The two women

looked at each other for a long moment. Her mother said "Jinx," and Iris ran to her, held her tight, and both cried their eyes out.

On the eighth day, he opened his eyes, smiled at her and whispered, "My Iris. My love. I let Italy go. You will always be my home."

EPILOGUE, PART II

Inside the Shoebox

4 November 1960
  Durban, South Africa

The box was open.

The girl heard the sound of her own gasp as she gazed at the myriad of colors, inhaled the exotic aromas and let her fingers touch the different textures of the overlapping treasures.

Now *this* was a birthday surprise.

She began taking out each item carefully, smelling it, touching it and using her vivid imagination to conjure up her own reality.

———

—A brown and white photograph of a beautiful girl. She was old, sixteen or so, with long wavy hair, smiling into the camera.

She liked the girl instantly. On either side of the girl in the photograph were two black women, one large and one skinny. The three had their arms around one another and wore wide grins that seemed to blur into one big one, with a few teeth missing on one end. The girl had never seen such closeness between black and white people. She should have thought it odd, but it was strangely comforting. When she turned over the picture, in fancy cursive writing it read: "Lena, me and Sofie. My favorite mothers. 1937."

—A pencil sketch of two beautiful people standing really close together. Kissing. He wore a dull sort of uniform, and the girl had on a flouncy dress above the knee. Wait! It was the girl from the photograph she'd just seen, a woman now. On the back of the sketch in the cursive hand it said: "Our first date. Escape successfully executed. Three exquisite hours. 1944 outside POW camp on 'our' road. Only Pietro would have the guts to break out and break back in again—and all for me."

—A small box double the size of a matchbox filled with notes covered in different colors. She picked up one of the notes, and blue ink smudged her fingers. The ink would get her into real trouble. She said, "Sorry, Granny," as she wiped her hand on the crocheted blanket. She closed the little box reluctantly for inspection another time, and as she turned it over and down, she saw the writing on the back: "Some of our notes exchanged between 1944-1945. Thank you, Sergeant Rogers, Solomon and Fourfeet."

—A letter. She loved letters. She opened it up reverently. The pencil scrawl was hard to decipher, and she had to skip a couple of sentences because they were—wait! She thought they were words her mom used sometimes. "Mia Cara Rossa. You are me only amore. You save me Iris, not one but two occurrences. You gave me mine voice so I can find you outside the prison. You worthy all risk to escape. You be mine light. Mine sunshine. Mine first. Mine only love. Mine heart he cannot take your angry. Come back to me. Your for ever love. Pietro." The cursive said, "My P left this for me when we thought Gregg was lost to us forever. Escape 1944."

Aha! Thought the girl. *The moral of the story is you don't need good grammar and excellent handwriting skills to find your perfect somebody.* Her mom read *Aesop's Fables* to her every now and then at bedtime, which made her search for morals everywhere.

—A huge, dry flower that she'd unwrapped from delicate paper: Dull, wafer-thin, pointed, fingernail-shaped petals surrounded the still-rich, chocolate-brown, fuzzy inside. She knew sunflowers, dead or alive, and imagined those "lady's fingernails" once as yellow as the sun. She picked up the flower by its brittle stem, and the delicate petals detached and floated back into the box. She jumped, and her hand flew to her lips as she squealed. Now she was in trouble. But then her older, more sensible, nine-year-old self assured her that since it was she who had broken the seal, nobody knew the sunflower was whole when she took it out of the box.

Then she saw the inside of the wrapping. "Oh, good," she squealed, thrilled to see the pair again in a pencil sketch. This time the pretty girl wore a pair of trousers and a fancy blouse. Boy! This one knew fashion! The two gazed at each other with pure love. "In the midst of the war, we made love next to the sunflower field. I knew he was my everything. Successful Escape

II 1944. P.S. It was really escape III, but we won't count the second one because we didn't touch." The girl felt a little giddy and terribly guilty. She knew trespassing was frowned upon. The Lord's prayer said so. But she couldn't stop now.

—Another beautifully drawn picture that looked similar to the last, but the pretty girl wore a dress. The girl bent her leg up at the knee. They were kissing again. Boy! These two! On the back it said, "Our last rendezvous, late 1944, before Tap Tap arrived. He hurt me, and Pietro hurt him. Colonel Cairns was 'talked into' Pietro's leniency by yours truly and the rest is ... well, history!"

—A squashed red thing she pulled and pushed until it unfolded and it turned into a lady's fancy hat: Boy! You didn't wear this if you were trying to be a wallflower. She smiled. Her mom had just told her what a wallflower was, and it amused her no end. What a perfect way to describe a pretty, shy person. The wearer of this large-brimmed crimson hat with flowing ribbons was the opposite of a wallflower. A ceiling thorn? Her dad would know. She popped it on her head, held the brim and turned her head this way and that, like a model. Her mom was a model when she first came to South Africa. She wanted to be a smithword. Word-smith? Like her dad.

—A strange-looking thing in a jar: It looked like a big, fat, white worm in murky, green-tinged water. Yuck. She couldn't help herself. She swirled the jar and felt her face pull in a disgusted grimace as the thing twirled around in slow motion, as if the greenish liquid was keeping it alive. There was a whole essay written on the lid of the jar. She looked at it askance, reluctant to read the saga lest it proved to be the magic formula that would prompt the white worm to explode out of the jar and ... Curiosity prevailed, and she read: "This clever little imp kept us in the same country! P.S. The real one exploded. This is a substitute of unknown origin, courtesy of Pietermaritzburg Hospital. 1945." Well! That was a mystery unto itself!

—A sheet of complicated music notes: The title of the song was "Next Thursday. Same Time." Music by Pietro Saltamachio. Lyrics by Iris Fuller. It was all so mysterious. She read the words neatly penned under lines of squiggled notes: "Time is short, my love, and see you I must. You'll be gone, my love, oh how my heart aches. Until I die, it's our love I will trust. Let's meet next Thursday, same time, my love, for both our sakes. Next Thursday, same time, my love. Next Thursday, same time. Written in hospital September 1945 while my Pietro recovered from near-death to stay with me."

What a romantic song. She sighed and smiled at the same time. This Pietro and Iris loved each other as much as the two from her favorite book, *Beauty and the Beast*. At nine, it was *easy* to recognize real love. It was all kissy-kissy. She knew. Her mom and dad did it all the time!

—A newspaper cutting from *The Sunday Times:* Brittle and yellowed. The bold title read "Demoted colonel allegedly killed by inmate in county jail." *Why is this horrible thing in this happy box?*

She really didn't want to read any more, but she couldn't help herself. "Once head of the POW camp ... " She wondered briefly if a POW camp was like a field trip. She loved field trips.

Oh, dear, she wasn't concentrating on her birthday gift because this was kind of scary. But she read on: "Julian Keiser was serving time for various charges. He died today, allegedly stabbed by a fellow inmate. He was initially jailed for battery and attempted rape charges brought by a woman whose name was not released to the press at the end of the war on 13 May 1945 and convicted a few months later of war crimes and neglect per the Geneva Convention. Dr. De Kleyn said: 'A menace to society has been eliminated.'" There was one word written in the same cursive, "Bastard."

She shivered. She wanted only to glance at the gritty, yellowed photo of the unsmiling man in the grainy newspaper picture, but the man's eyes held hers for longer than she intended. A cold shiver shook her small body, and she quickly folded the yellowed cutting and buried it at the very bottom of the box so she wouldn't take it out again by accident.

—A black and white photograph: A man who looked like a young version of her dad, standing between a handsome man and the pretty lady. Hey, it was them again! Pietro and Iris. But oddly, she had a short crop of curls, and if she hadn't been so pretty, she could have looked like a boy. What was she thinking with that mop of hair? Had she *no* fashion sense? She laughed out loud. She loved fashions.

The three in the photograph shared the kind of smile only best friends do when they share a massive secret. She read the same beautiful cursive ink writing in the small yellow border around the photograph. "Happy days! Gregg wasn't MIA after all!" An ink arrow pointed to the man in the middle. Hey! That was her Dad. She wondered what "mia" could be? She hoped it wasn't a disease.

—Another grainy picture: Her young dad and Pietro (she loved calling them by their names now), with their shirts off, pointing with two index fingers apiece to what looked like different scars on the other's chest. Wait! She knew that scar on his right shoulder! It happened just before her dad met her mom. She laughed at them. How silly they were.

—A colored photo of an older lady gazing up at a tall man in a uniform: Her granny. She hadn't seen her in a long while, but as she studied the picture, she smelled roses. Her heart warmed. Then she saw a bunch of roses in her granny's hands. Like a bride. "Oh! Look!" she called to no one at all. "That's Grandpa Pete!" He looked particularly pleased with himself, and no wonder. Her granny's hand was tucked, like it belonged, in the crook of his arm. She had never seen so many medals, ribbons and bars together at one time, and they all lined up on the left side of Grandpa Pete's chest on his fancy uniform. The cursive writing she'd come to trust as her guide through her delicious gift box read: "Mom and Colonel's wedding. Catholic church no less. Thank God for annulments." Now, that one was way beyond her. One day she'd ask her dad about that too.

—Another photo of her grandparents' wedding: This time bride and groom weren't the focal point of the picture. In the foreground was what looked just like the steel bars going down to their own pool in the backyard, except there was no pool in the picture, just the shape of bars covered in flowers. On the back was written: "At last, roses covered the steel bars. Was it Mom's patience or Dad from on high, giving his approval?"

—A color picture of Iris: It was what her mom called a "close-up." Her hair was long again and red, like a sunset. The girl loved sunsets. Iris sat at a sewing machine, her hand on the small wheel. The girl had seen one like it in the museum on a field trip. It was as if Iris had been startled while she was really busy and she'd just lifted up her eyes, but the camera caught her cheeky grin anyway. The cursive on the back read, "Who needs Hollywood? I have Cape Town Opera, the runway, my boys and my Whirr Whirr! Not necessarily in that order!"

—Wow! Another picture. She loved pictures. They told a story. Here was Pietro, this time wearing a stage costume. She knew costumes. She wore one in the school play last year. It was hot and un-comfy. His costume had big, what were they called? Leg of sheep sleeves? Silly! Leg of mutton sleeves! His mouth was open, and his arm was out. She thought he might be singing to the lady high up on a rickety balcony. She squinted at the beautiful cursive in the bottom right corner: "Pietro, my handsome prince, wearing one of my masterpieces."

—A picture of Pietro holding what she presumed was a baby: She was getting good at this. She was glad Pietro had new clothes since the sketches. Perhaps Iris had taught him how to dress. At last! Back to what she presumed was a baby because of the expression of adoration Pietro and Iris wore as they gazed at the small bundle: There was a dog next to Iris, looking up at the swaddle of blankets. She had never seen a man, a lady and a dog look so happy. The cursive said simply: "My boys. 1948."

The last item in the box. She was so disappointed her birthday was nearly over. Perhaps she'd start again, there was so much to ...

She felt suddenly guilty. She looked up and saw him.

She swore her bottom lifted a foot off the floor, such was her great fright. She quickly looked at the green yucky jar and thanked all the saints that came to mind that she hadn't knocked it over in her shock, but her relief was short-lived as her father's stern face loomed inches from her own.

"Daddy? You were at work!"

"And was just passing by the house. So I came by to say hello to my birthday girl."

"Mom's at Aunty Wendy's." She couldn't look at him.

"Hmmm. No doubt." His right eyebrow was arched. *Here comes trouble.*

She felt bad. Like she had let him down.

"Why did you open the box when you knew you shouldn't?"

"Because it's been calling to me for nearly a whole year, and you said I should make my own decisions, and this is my first big decision, and it was my present to myself, and I ... "

He held up his hand. She closed her mouth, and tears sprang to her eyes. It was the first time in her life she had disappointed him. Deep shame burned her cheeks.

The box's contents were strewn all around her. Even if she lay down over them, her body wouldn't cover all the treasures she'd unearthed. And besides, she'd squash them. And she knew these things were very, very precious to somebody.

She realized neither she nor her dad had moved.

"What did you find out during your first big decision?" His eyebrow was still arched.

Her face flushed hot again. "That I am not old enough to make them yet?"

"And? Why is that?"

"Because by opening the box, it just made me more curious."

"Is curious a good thing?"

"It killed the cat, but I suppose for people it's good. It makes you think. Like *MAD Magazine*." It was her dad's treat for her when she was sick.

"And so I want you to think about what you have found in this box, then put it to rest in your mind. When your mom says you may, take this box to your aunty and uncle. One day, when you're sure it's safe, tell their remarkable story."

"I can keep a secret. Why can't you tell me now?"

"Because there could still be consequences. It's too soon. Your mother will know when the time is right. Listen to her."

"Why is it too soon?"

"Because the war is still not over in some people's minds, and they are on a witch hunt to see who they can blame, who they can arrest for misdeeds."

"A witch hunt?" Holy smokes, scary stuff! No wonder the box was sealed so tight.

"That's right. Now do you understand the importance?" His voice was stern.

"And what if, once 'the time is right,' nobody's left to answer my questions?"

"Then follow your heart, because your heart is always your most accurate guide."

"But I want to ask you *and* follow my heart!"

He smiled sadly and lowered his eyes.

"Too soon, my little sunshine. Too soon."

She didn't want to lose this momentum. "Where are the people in love and the black ladies and the dog and the baby now?"

"Aunty Iris and Uncle Pietro live in Cape Town. Your uncle is very famous; your aunt too, in her own clever way." She was mesmerized by the pride in her father's voice. "Your cousin,

Stefano, is five yours older than you. You'll meet him one day. Sadly, the rest are all gone, in one way or another."

Her dad's face had changed from immense pride to sadness, which made her feel bad, because she realized this box made him sad in ways she'd never understand. She felt her face crumple knowing she was responsible for her dad's sorrow. Remorse for her ill deed poured down her cheeks, but she knew it was now or never.

"But Daddy, why can't we go and see Aunty Iris and Uncle Pietro and Stefano?"

"They live more than a thousand miles away." Her dad laughed. "That's a long way for our old car to travel. And it would take us so many days to get there. We'd have to turn around and come right back before my holiday leave ended."

"Can they come here?"

"Their lives are very busy, but they write a lot. And one day if it gets cheaper to phone, we'll do that so you can talk to them. How's that?"

"Wonderful, Daddy."

"But never a word about the box, okay?" He looked at her sternly.

"Never! But why do we have the box, and why didn't they keep it?"

"It's so secret, that box, that it's best kept far from them, so as not to incriminate them, even by accident—as is evident that these things can happen." He looked at her sternly.

"What's 'incrimimate'?" She was still confused.

"If these very secrets"—his arm encompassed all the scattered treasures—"are found out, your aunt and uncle will get into terrible trouble. You see, they came from different sides of the great war."

"Oh." She tried, but it still made no sense.

"But you and Mommy—you are South African and she is Italian. Weren't you on opposite sides, too?"

"Yes, when she saved my life we were. But by the time I went back to Italy to find your Mom, much had changed, and the war had been over for three years, so nobody minded. I just picked her up and carried her home with me. And then we had you, sunshine, to seal our love."

The girl giggled, and her father's face lit up.

"Why do you call Mom 'Lorelei' when her name is 'Vivia'? the girl asked.

"Because she lured me in like the sorceress Lorelei with her song. I will read you the old German folk tale one day," her dad promised.

"You fell in love with Mom when you first saw her in Italy, didn't you?"

"Who wouldn't?" he asked her, and they both smiled. Knowing it was so.

"You look so much like your aunty, my love." His voice was so tender, it made the girl's heart swell. "She was my first sunshine, and you were born on her birthday."

"That makes us both special to you, Daddy, Aunty Iris and me?"

"Always and forever, my little sunshine." His voice was unusually gruff.

He squatted down on his haunches, opened his arms and invited her into his safe, forgiving haven. She sniffed loudly and felt her shame begin to evaporate.

After a beautiful long minute, her dad pushed her gently away. "Now, go and get the sealing wax in the top drawer next to the stove. The matches too. And the string. Brown paper. It won't be just the same, but your mom is unlikely to study the seal in the near future, and blobs are hard to remember in detail. Besides which, she will forget about the box, because you are going to hide it so far back in the garage, an army of carpenter ants of biblical proportion couldn't discover it. Is that not so, my little sunshine?"

"Not even a Bible full of carpenters, my Dad."

And they bent their heads together earnestly resealing the mysterious shoebox.

When they were jointly huffing and puffing and blowing the blood-red blobs dry, the girl felt unusually sad, because in her young heart she knew, with uncanny certainty, that it would be a long, long time till she had the box in her hands again, to unravel its many mysteries.

---

4 November 2000

As life is wont to do, it twisted and turned and changed in unexpected ways, and she never got that chance to get to know her uncle and her aunt. The time she saw them she would rather forget. It was her father's funeral.

But later on a Cape Town layover, when she was an airhostess, she visited them for a couple of hours. Her aunt and uncle were everything she'd imagined them to be in the garage when she was nine. She watched them carefully, imagining what they'd shared, and believed she would never again in her lifetime witness the rapture, the reverence, the sheer adoration with which Iris looked at Pietro and he at her.

Pietro became known as the Father of Opera in South Africa, and Iris? Iris was the designer of the most exciting, elaborate costumes South Africa had ever seen and enjoyed on Pietro's operatic stage. She was famous for her haute couture fashions in the up-and-coming South African fashion scene.

When her mom said it was okay, she took the box with her when next she visited Cape Town. It was still sealed just as her father and she had left it. When she produced it from her suitcase, the two, in their seventies, went white, and her aunt grabbed it from her and disappeared, likely to hide the thing. Later, as they enjoyed a glass of wine on their balcony overlooking the bay of their gorgeous city, the young woman said: "Before he died, Dad said I should tell your amazing story one day." They'd smiled at her and at each other, and her aunt said, "I think it's one we'll take to our graves" and changed the subject.

But she had to know, so later she asked: "If that box made you so anxious, why didn't you ask my folks to destroy it for you years ago?"

Aunty Iris smiled sadly. "Because I never believed life could be as kind as to keep us together. I always thought someone officious would come knocking and take my love away. I had to keep that box, just in case it was all I had left."

The two women wept softly. Uncle Pietro smiled, labored up on his stick, hugged Iris and whispered, "Mia Cara Rossa, be still. I am here. Forever."

She cried when her Aunty Iris and Uncle Pietro died in their mid-eighties. And within a week of each other. They simply couldn't bear to be apart for long.

Years passed and, now a seasoned woman, she felt compelled to tell Pietro and Iris's love story because there was no one left to get hurt. She was eager for details, but the box was gone, and her mother's head was oft befuddled by dementia, so she had no accurate guide other than what she remembered from decades before.

Her dad was long gone. Though it had been thirty-three years since he'd left her, left them, left this world forever, the void was hollow and deep. Not a day passed when she didn't ache for his wisdom, his love of words and his unconditional love for her.

And so it was that she told her own version of Pietro and Iris's love story.

The biggest of the many gifts her dad had given her, one she'd clung to for decades, was the conversation they shared as together they poured the last of the sealing wax on to the brown-paper-covered shoebox on her ninth birthday.

Her dad became solemn and said, "Don't ever settle for a love that's any less than the *right* love, my little sunshine."

In her innocence, the girl had asked, "How will I know when it is *the right love*, Daddy?"

And he answered: "Every once in a great while, you make eye contact with someone you have never seen before, and it's as if you see into the other's soul. The connection between you is so deep and so strong, you blindly accept with all that is true, although it's beyond all logic and reason, that the person before you is as necessary to your existence as the very air you breathe."

THE END

AFTERWORD

War Serenade truly began as a fairy tale for me. It was my favorite story, and the fact that I knew the characters, who were dear friends of my parents, made it even more delicious. The love story of a handsome Italian opera singer who became a POW in a South African camp was in itself fairly exotic. But that he fell in love with a local beauty, who was literally sitting in the third row of the audience during his performance outside the prison walls, became delectable fodder for my young imagination.

I remember visiting these friends of my parents and gazing at them with true reverence. They were everything and more than my mother's fairy tale promised. He was handsome, charming, heavily accented, and she was a delicate beauty with spice and spunk that shone through her very polite, cultured demeanor.

I'd always been driven to tell their story because it was so wonderfully romantic, but I quickly found out that telling a happy story is not all that scintillating. It's the dark that makes light more interesting. So it is with story. So once I changed their names, I was liberated as a writer, since I no longer owed them a truth. I could make him a little more of a cad and her a little more of a wild child and their ultimate union a whole lot tougher.

War Serenade was twice optioned as a screenplay but never made into a movie. Writing this book took three years of loving labor before it came out into the world. I hope with all my heart that it will stir you in some small way or, dare I hope, as much as their story did me.

And what's next? A novella called *Rebel Bride,* originally a short story written by my dad for my mom. Though I lost my dad when I was 20, we will write this one together. It's about a Zulu "Romeo and Juliet" who defied the laws of their land to become husband and wife. One of the characters who appeared in *War Serenade* may just be related to these lovers ...

Subscribe to **jillwallace.com** for vignettes and news of upcoming books. Watch for exciting competitions, too!

ACKNOWLEDGMENTS

Where does one start?

At the beginning, I suppose.

Thank you, Mommy, for making this true story about your friends my afternoon nap-time staple. It was a hell of a ride for a four-year-old who would never again be satisfied with a fairy tale. Thank you, Daddy, for making me want to write it down, and still being here, rooting for me.

Thank you to the first person to believe in the best in me. My heart, my wolfsister, my Lanie—Alana McIntosh. Thank you for still believing 47 years later. You've always given me the guts I never knew I had. There will never be a time when I will not need your wind beneath my wings. I would be desperately lonely without you.

Kitty Low—thank you, my Kits, my wolfsister, for your 47 years of loving support. You have always been my loyal champion, my believer and my darling friend.

A huge "Thank You" to my beloved husband, who is always there to inject gentle logic into my flightiness. Athol Roy Wallace, you allow me to follow my dreams, no matter how whimsical. I am so grateful.

My brother, Peter Olivier, helped me understand the facts of this (once) true story. Thank you, Brother Pete.

Thank you, my sister, Vivienne Snyman, who read and re-read scripts and novel a thousand times; thank you, Fifi.

Son-of-my-heart, Terry Wallace, always enthusiastic about my writing endeavors and a better writer than I'll ever be—I have one word for you, my T: "Write!"

Daughter-of-my-heart, Lesley Wallace, thank you for giving me Abby and Anny, who I learn from all the time!

Thank you, MaryAnn Amato, the first literary professional to give me the fuel to start this 17-year-long fire.

My sincere thanks to my dear friend Betsy Galbraith, who was there for my first Screenwriters Pitchfest and who's stayed with me for the long ride, and the rest of my cherished VA girls: Beth Barg, Debby Clark and Brenda Morcom, who all read endless copies of my scripts and offered their astute advice, much of which I followed in this book, especially Bism's TM expertise.

Thanks, Jim Mercurio and Glenn Bennest. You expertly taught me craft, plot, character, dialogue, and I hung on to every word.

Thanks to esteemed author and my dear friend, Martha Powers, who nagged me to write this book and made me join STAR.

Thanks to the amazingly accomplished authors of the SpacecoasT Authors of Romance, who are my constant inspiration.

To my wonderful readers along the way, a huge thank you: Brenda Zukowski, Lorena Spensley, Roberta Spensley, Kathy Rheaume, Jennifer Petche, Darlene Hughes, Joni O'Connor, Lisa Hotaling, and to Joanne Baines, who tried her best to get the movie made.

Thanks to Renee Davis, who used her jazz platform to promote *War Serenade,* and my Jazz girls, who believed.

Thank you, Sara Maraj and Ivette Griffith, for your pillars of strength.

To my Beach Breasties: Tammy Jones and Suzanne von Achen, I have this to say–our ceremonies reap rewards!

Debbie Shannon, for being a cheerleader all the way and my final reader—thank you, you clever scribe, you!

So many people have been my divine influence during this process, and if I haven't mentioned you by name, please know that over the dozen and a half years during which this book has evolved, this old mind has faded some, but know that I appreciate you and know without doubt, you had an influence on *War Serenade* in one way or another.

Thank you to my dedicated assistant, Lindsay Kate Davis.

Thank you to Maryellen Covais, who read with enthusiasm and gratefully became my final editor.

Thank you, Chris Kridler—absolutely awesome cover designer, editor, and incredible publisher. You guided, you pushed gently, you created, you inspired and you published. Your sublime kindness, amazing knowledge and unlimited patience are beyond measure.

ABOUT THE AUTHOR

Jill Wallace was born and bred in South Africa but has lived half of her life in America and often feels like a Baobab Tree with roots that look like branches: same but different. She began her writing journey as a screenwriter, and *War Serenade* was a twice-optioned script before it transformed into a novel. She lives on Florida's Space Coast with her husband and two over-pampered Aussie Shepherds who rule the roost.

Get vignettes, excerpts, news on her next book and more by signing up for her newsletter at JillWallace.com.

facebook.com/jwallaceauthor
twitter.com/jwallaceauthor
instagram.com/jwallaceauthor